KILN
PEOPLE

KILN
PEOPLE

David Brin

TOR®

A Tom Doherty Associates Book

New York

KILN PEOPLE

Copyright © 2002 by David Brin

This book is printed on acid-free paper.

Edited by Beth Meacham

Design by Michael Mendelsohn

A Tor Book
Published by Tom Doherty Associates, LLC
175 Fifth Avenue
New York, NY 10010

www.tor.com

Tor® is a registered trademark of Tom Doherty Associates, LLC.

ISBN 0-765-30355-8

First Edition: January 2002

Printed in the United States of America

0 9 8 7 6 5 4 3 2 1

For Poul Anderson, who explored for all of us, making the future fun . . .

. . . and Greg Bear, who takes on every shadow, with edge . . .

. . . and Gregory Benford, who delves stark beauty in the dark ocean of night . . .

. . . all of them shamans by the campfire.

Indispensable.

KILN
PEOPLE

PART I

Adieu! for once again the fierce dispute
    Betwixt damnation and impassion'd clay
    Must I burn through . . .

But when I am consumed in the Fire,
    Give me new Phoenix wings to fly at my desire.

      —John Keats,
        "On Sitting Down to Read *King Lear* Once Again"

■

1

A Good Head for Wine

*. . . or how Monday's green ditto brings home fond
memories of the river . . .*

It's hard to stay cordial while fighting for your life, even when your life
doesn't amount to much.

Even when you're just a lump of clay.

■   ■   ■

Some kind of missile—a stone I guess—smacked the brick wall
inches away, splattering my face with stinging grit. There wasn't any
shelter to cower behind, except an overstuffed trash can. I grabbed the
lid and swung it around.

Just in time. Another slug walloped the lid, denting plastic instead of
my chest.

Someone had me nailed.

Moments ago, the alley had seemed a good place to hide and catch
my breath. But now its chill darkness betrayed me instead. Even a ditto
gives off some body heat. Beta and his gang don't carry guns into this
part of town—they wouldn't dare—but their slingshots come equipped
with infrared sights.

I had to flee the betraying darkness. So while the shooter reloaded, I
raised my makeshift shield and dashed for the bright lights of Odeon
District.

It was a risky move. The place swarmed with archies, dining at cafés
or milling about near classy theaters. Couples strolled arm-in-arm along
the quay, enjoying a riverside breeze. Only a few coloreds like me could
be seen—mostly waiters serving their bland-skinned betters at canopied
tables.

I wasn't going to be welcome in this zone, where owners throng to
enjoy their long, sensuous lives. But if I stayed on back streets I'd get
hacked into fish food by my own kind. So I took a chance.

Damn. It's crowded, I thought, while picking a path across the plaza,
hoping to avoid brushing against any of the sauntering archies. Though
my expression was earnest—as if I had a legit reason to be there—I must
have stood out like a duck among swans, and not just because of skin

color. My torn paper clothes drew notice. Anyway, it's kind of hard to move delicately while brandishing a battered trash lid between your vitals and the alley behind you.

A sharp blow struck the plastic again. Glancing back, I saw a yellow-hued figure lower his slingshot to load another round. Furtive shapes peered from the shadows, debating how to reach me.

I plunged into the crowd. Would they keep shooting and risk hitting a real person?

Ancient instinct—seared into my clay body by the one who made me—clamored to *run*. But I faced other dangers now—from the archetype human beings surrounding me. So I tried to perform all the standard courtesies, bowing and stepping aside for couples who wouldn't veer or slow down for a mere ditto.

I had a minute or two of false hopes. Women chiefly looked past me, like I didn't exist. Most of the men were more puzzled than hostile. One surprised chap even made way for me, as if I were real. I smiled back. *I'll do the same for your ditto someday, chum.*

But the next fellow wasn't satisfied when I gave him right of way. His elbow planted a sharp jab, *en passant*, and pale eyes glittered, daring me to complain.

Bowing, I forced an ingratiatingly apologetic smile, stepping aside for the archie while I tried to focus on a pleasant memory. Think about *breakfast*, Albert. The fine odors of coffee and fresh-baked muffins. Simple pleasures that I might have again, if I made it through the night.

"I" will definitely have them again, said an inner voice. *Even if this body doesn't make it.*

Yes, came a reply. *But that won't be me. Not exactly.*

I shook off the old existential quandary. Anyway, a cheap utility rox like me can't smell. At the moment, I could barely grasp the concept.

The blue-eyed fellow shrugged and turned away. But the next second, something struck pavement near my left foot, ricocheting across the plaza.

Beta had to be desperate, shooting stones at me amid a throng of real citizens! People glanced around. Some eyes narrowed toward me.

And to think, this morning started so well.

I tried to hurry, making a few more meters farther across the plaza before I was stopped by a trio of young men—well-dressed young archies—intentionally blocking my path.

"Will you look at this mule?" the tall one said. Another, with fashionably translucent skin and reddish eyes, jabbed a finger at me. "Hey, ditto! What's the rush? You can't still be hoping for an afterlife! Who's gonna want you back, all torn up like that?"

I knew how I must look. Beta's gang had pummeled me good before I managed to escape. Anyway, I was only an hour or two short of expiration and my cracking pseudoflesh showed clear signs of enzyme decay. The albino guffawed at the trash can lid I was wielding as a shield. He sniffed loudly, wrinkling his nose.

"It smells bad, too. Like garbage. Spoilin' my appetite. Hey! Maybe we have cause for a civil complaint, you reckon?"

"Yeah. How about it, golem?" the tall one leered. "Give us your owner's code. Cough up a refund on our dinner!"

I raised a placating hand. "Come on, fellas. I'm on an urgent errand for my original. I really do have to get home. I'm sure you hate it when *your* dittos are kept from you."

Beyond the trio, I glimpsed the bustle and noise of Upas Street. If only I could make it to the taxi stand, or even the police kiosk on Defense Avenue. For a small fee they'd provide refrigerated sanctuary, till my owner came for me.

"Urgent, eh?" the tall one said. "If your rig still wants you, even in this condition, I'll bet he'd pay to get you back, eh?"

The final teen, a stocky fellow with deep brown skin and hair done in a wire cut, appeared more sympathetic.

"Aw, leave the poor greenie alone. You can see how badly it wants to get home and spill. If we stop it, the owner may fine *us*."

A compelling threat. Even the albino wavered, as if about to back off.

Then Beta's shooter in the alley fired again, hitting my thigh below the shielding trash can lid.

Anyone who has duped and inloaded knows that pseudoflesh can feel pain. Fiery agony sent me recoiling into one of the youths, who pushed me away, shouting.

"Get off, you stinky thing! Did you see that? It touched me!"

"Now you'll pay, you piece of clay," added the tall one. "Let's see your tag."

Still shuddering, I managed to hobble around so he stood between me and the alley. My pursuers wouldn't dare shoot now, and risk hitting an archie.

"Fool," I said. "Can't you see I've been shot?"

"So?" The albino's nostrils flared. "My dits get mangled in org-wars all the time. You don't see me griping about it. Or bringing a fight to the Odeon, of all places! Now let's see that tag."

He held out a hand and I reflexively reached for the spot under my forehead where the ID implant lay. A golem-duplicate has to show his tag to a realperson, on demand. This incident was going to cost me . . . that is, it would cost my maker. The semantic difference would depend on whether I made it home in the next hour.

"Fine. Call a cop or arbiter," I said, fumbling at the flap of pseudo-skin. "We'll see who pays a fine, punk. I'm not playing simbat games. You're impeding the double of a licensed investigator. Those shooting at me are real criminals . . ."

I glimpsed figures emerging from the alley. Yellow-skinned members of Beta's gang, straightening paper garments and trying to look innocuous amid the crowd of strolling archies, bowing and giving way like respectful errand boys, not worth noticing. But hurrying.

Damn. I never saw Beta this desperate before.

". . . and my brain holds evidence that may be crucial in solving an important case. Do you want to be responsible for preventing that?"

Two of the teens drew back, looking unsure. I added pressure. "If you don't let me get about my owner's business, he'll post a charge for restraint of legal commerce!"

We were attracting a crowd. That could slow Beta's bunch, but time wasn't on my side.

Alas, the third punk—with the artificially translucent skin—wasn't daunted. He tapped his wrist screen.

"Giga. I got enough juice in the bank to cover a blood fine. If we're gonna pay this dit's owner, let's have the joy of shutting it down hard."

He seized my arm, clenching with the strength of well-toned muscles—*real* muscles, not my anemic imitations. The grip hurt, but worse was knowing I'd overplayed my hand. If I'd kept my mouth shut, they might have let me go. Now the data in this brain would be lost and Beta would win after all.

The young man cocked his fist dramatically, playing for the crowd. He meant to snap my neck with a blow.

Someone muttered, "Let the poor thing go!" But a noisier contingent egged him on.

Just then a crash reverberated across the courtyard. Voices cursed harshly. Onlookers turned toward a nearby restaurant, where diners at an outdoor table hopped away from a mess of spilled liquid and shattered glassware. A green-skinned busboy dropped his tray and murmured apologies, using a rag to wipe glittering shards off the upset customers. Then he slipped, taking one of the infuriated patrons along with him in a spectacular pratfall. Laughter surged from the crowd as the restaurant's maître-dit rushed out, berating the greenie and seeking to appease the wet clients.

For an instant no one was looking at me except the albino, who seemed miffed over losing his audience.

The waiter hammed it up, continuing to dab at upset archies with a sodden cloth. But for a moment the green head briefly glanced my way. His quick nod had meaning.

Take your chance and get out of here.

I didn't need urging. Slipping my free hand into a pocket, I pulled out a slim card—apparently a standard credit disk. But squeezing it *thus* made silvery light erupt along one edge, emitting a fierce hum.

The albino's pinkish eyes widened. Dittos aren't supposed to carry weapons, especially illegal ones. But the sight didn't scare him off. His grin hardened and I knew I was in the clutches of a sportsman, a gambler, willing even to risk realflesh if it offered something new. An experience.

The grip on my arm intensified. *I dare you,* his ratty glare said.

So I obliged him, slashing down hard. The sizzling blade cut through fleshy resistance.

For an instant, pain and outrage seemed to fill all the space between us. His pain or mine? *His* outrage and surprise, for sure—and yet there was a split second when I felt united with the tough young bravo by a crest of empathy. An overwhelming connection to his teenage angst. To the wounded, self-important pride. The agony of being one isolated soul among lonely billions.

It could have been a costly hesitation, if it lasted more than a heartbeat. But while his mouth opened to cry out, I swiveled and made my getaway, ducking through the roiling crowd, followed by enraged curses as the youth brandished a gory stump.

My gory stump. My dismembered hand clenched spasmodically at his face till he recoiled and flung the twitching thing away in disgust.

With that same backward glance I also spotted two of Beta's yellows, dodging among disturbed archies, impertinently shoving several aside while they slipped stones into their wrist catapults, preparing to fire at me. In all this confusion they were unworried about witnesses, or mere fines for civil ditsobedience. They had to stop me from delivering what I knew.

To prevent me from spilling the contents of my decomposing brain.

I must have been quite a spectacle, running lopsidedly in a shredded tunic with one amputated arm dripping, hollering like mad for startled archies to get out of the way. I wasn't sure at that moment what I could accomplish. Expiration senility might have already begun setting in, made worse by pseudoshock and organ fatigue.

Alerted by the commotion, a cop rushed into the square from Fourth Street, clomping in ungainly body armor while his blue-skinned dittos fanned out, agile and unprotected, needing no orders because each one knew the proto's wishes more perfectly than a well-drilled infantry squad. Their sole weapon—needle-tipped fingers coated with knockout oil—would stop any golem or human cold.

I veered away from them, weighing options.

Physically, my ditto hadn't hurt anyone. Still, things were getting dicey. Real people had been inconvenienced, even perturbed. Suppose I got away from Beta's yellow thugs, and made it into a police freezer. My original could wind up getting socked with enough low-grade civil judgments to wipe out the reward for tracking Beta down in the first place. The cops might even get careless about icing me in time. They've been doing that a lot lately.

Several private and public cameras had me in view, I bet. But well enough to make a strong ID? This greenie's face was too bland—and blurred even more by the fists of Beta's gang—for easy recognition. That left one choice. Take my tagged carcass where nobody could recover or ID it. Let 'em guess who started this riot.

I staggered toward the river, shouting and waving people off.

Nearing the quayside embankment, I heard a stern, amplified voice cry, *"Halt!"* Cop-golems carry loudspeakers where most of us have synthetic sex organs . . . a creepy substitution that gets your attention.

From the left, I heard several sharp *twangs*. A stone struck my decaying flesh while another bounced off pavement, caroming toward the real policeman. Maybe now the blues would focus on Beta's yellows. Cool.

Then I had no more time to think as my feet ran out of surface. They kept pumping through empty space, out of habit, I guess . . . till I hit the murky water with a splash.

■   ■   ■

I suppose there's one big problem with my telling this story in first person—the listener knows I made it home in one piece. Or at least to some point where I could pass on the tale. So where's the suspense?

All right, so it didn't end quite there, with my crashing in the river, though maybe it should have. Some golems are designed for combat, like the kind hobbyists send onto gladiatorial battlefields . . . or secret models they're rumored to have in Special Forces. Other dittos, meant for hedonism, sacrifice some *élan vital* for hyperactive pleasure cells and high-fi memory inloading. You can pay more for a model with extra limbs or ultra senses . . . or one that can swim.

I'm too cheap to spring for fancy options. But a feature I always include is hyperoxygenization—my dittos can hold their breath a long time. It's handy in a line of work where you never know if someone's going to gas you, or throw you in the sealed trunk of a car, or bury you alive. I've sorbed memories of all those things. Memories I wouldn't have today if the ditto's brain died too soon.

Lucky me.

The river, cold as lunar ice, swirled past me like a wasted life. A small voice spoke up as I sank deeper in the turbid water—a voice I've heard on other occasions.

Give up now. Rest. This isn't death. The real you will continue. He'll carry on with your dreams.

The few you had left.

True enough. Philosophically speaking, my original *was* me. Our memories differed by just one awful day. A day that he spent barefoot, in boxer shorts, doing officework at home while I went rooting through the city's proxy underworld, where life is cheaper than in a Dumas novel. My present continuity mattered very little on the grand scale of things.

I answered the small voice in my usual way.

Screw existentialism.

Every time I step into the copier, my new ditto absorbs survival instincts a billion years old.

I want my afterlife.

By the time my feet touched the slimy river bottom, I was determined to give it a shot. I had almost no chance, of course, but maybe fortune was ready to deal from a fresh deck. Also, another motive drove me on.

Don't let the bad guys win. Never let them get away with it.

Maybe I didn't have to breathe, but movement was still tricky as I fought to get my feet planted, getting headway through the mud, with everything both slippery and viscous at the same time. It would have been hard to get traction with a whole body, but this one's clock was ticking out.

Visibility? Almost nil, so I maneuvered by memory and sense of touch. I considered trying to fight my way upriver to the ferry docks, but then recalled that Clara's houseboat lay moored just a kilometer or so downstream from Odeon Square. So I stopped fighting the heavy current and worked with it instead, putting most of my effort into staying near the riverbank.

It might have helped if I'd been made with variable-setting pain sensors. Lacking that optional feature—and cursing my own cheapness—I grimaced in agony while pulling one foot after another through the sucking muck. The hard slog left me time to ponder the phenomenological angst faced by creatures of my kind.

I'm me. As little life as I have left, it still feels precious. Yet I gave up what remains, jumping in the river to save some other guy a few credits.

Some guy who'll make love to my girlfriend and relish my accomplishments.

Some guy who shares every memory I had, till the moment he (or I) lay on the copier, last night. Only he got to stay home in the original body, while I went to do his dirty work.

Some guy who'll never know what a rotten day I had.

It's a coin flip, each time you use a copier-and-kiln. When it's done, will you be the rig . . . the original person? Or the rox, golem, mule, ditto-for-a-day?

Often it hardly matters, if you re-sorb memories like you're supposed to, before the copy expires. Then it's just like two parts of you, merging back together again. But what if the ditto suffered or had a rough time, like I had?

I found it hard to keep my thoughts together. After all, this green body wasn't built for intellect. So I concentrated on the task at hand, dragging one foot after another, trudging through the mud.

There are locales you pass by every day, yet hardly think about because you never expect to go there. Like this place. Everyone knows the Gorta is filled with all sorts of trash. I kept stumbling over stuff that had been missed by the cleaner-trawls . . . a rusted bike, a broken air conditioner, several old computer monitors staring back at me like zombie eyes. When I was a kid, they used to pull out whole automobiles, sometimes with passengers still inside. Real people who had no spare copies in those days, to carry on with their smashed lives.

Those times had some advantages. Back in Grandpa's day, the Gorta *stank* from pollution. Eco laws brought the stream back to life. Now folks catch fish from the quay. And fish converge whenever the city drops in something edible.

Like me.

Real flesh is supple. It doesn't start flaking after just twenty-four hours. Protoplasm is so tenacious and durable that even a drowned corpse resists decay for days.

But my skin was already sloughing, even before I fell in. Expiration can be held off by willpower for a while. But now the timed organic chains in my ersatz body were expiring and unraveling with disconcerting speed. The scent swirled, attracting opportunists who came darting in from all sides for a feed, grabbing whatever chunks seemed close to falling off. At first I tried batting at them with my remaining hand, but that only slowed me down without inconveniencing the scavengers much. So I just forged ahead, wincing each time a pain receptor got snipped off by a greedy fish.

I drew a line when they started going for the eyes. I was going to need vision for a while yet.

At one point warm water shoved suddenly from the left, a strong current pushing me off course. The flow did drive off the scavengers for a minute, giving me a chance to concentrate. . . .

Must be the Hahn Street Canal.

Let's see. Clara's boat is moored along Little Venice. That should be the second opening after this one. . . . Or is it next?

I had to fight my way past the canal without being pushed down into deep water, somehow finally managing to reach the stone embankment on the other side. Unfortunately, persecuting swarms reconverged at that point—fish from above and crabs from below—drawn by my oozing wounds, nipping and supping on my fast-decaying hide.

What followed was a blur—a continual, shambling, underwater slog through mud, debris, and clouds of biting tormentors.

It's said that at least one character trait always stays true, whenever a ditto is copied from its archetype. No matter what else varies, something from your basic nature endures from one facsimile to the next. A person who is honest or pessimistic or talkative in real flesh will make a golem with similar qualities.

Clara says my most persistent attribute is pigheaded obstinacy.

Damn anyone who says I can't do this.

That phrase rolled over and over through my diteriorating brain, repeating a thousand times. A million. Screaming every time I took a painful step, or a fish took another bite. The phrase evolved beyond mere words. It became my incantation. Focus. A mantra of distilled stubbornness that kept me slogging onward, dragging ahead, one throbbing footstep at a time . . . till the moment I found myself blocked by a narrow obstacle.

I stared at it a while. A moss-covered chain that stretched, taut and almost vertical, from a buried anchor up to a flat object made of wooden planks.

A floating dock.

And moored alongside lay a vessel, its broad bottom coated with jagged barnacles. I had no idea whose boat it was, only that my time was about up. The river would finish me if I stayed any longer.

Using my one remaining mangled hand, I gripped the chain and strained to free both feet of the sucking mud, then continued creeping upward in fits and jerks, rising relentlessly toward a glittering light.

The fish must have sensed their last chance. They converged, thrashing all around, grabbing whatever flaps and floating folds they could, even after my head broke surface. I threw my arm over the dock, then had to dredge memory for what to do next.

Breathe. That's it. You need air.

Breathe!

My shuddering inhalation didn't resemble a human gasp. More like the squelch that a slab of meat makes when you throw it onto a cutting board and then slice it, letting an air pocket escape. Still, some oxygen rushed into replace the water spilling from my lipless mouth. It offered just enough renewed strength to haul one leg aboard the planking.

I heaved with all my might, at last rolling completely out of the river, thwarting the scavengers, who splashed in disappointment.

Tremors rocked my golembody from stem to stern. Something— some part of me—shook loose and fell off, toppling back into the water with a splash. The fish rejoiced, swirling around whatever it was, feeding noisily.

All my senses grew murkier, moment by moment. Distantly, I noted that one eye was completely gone . . . and the other hung nearly out of its socket. I pushed it back in, then tried getting up.

Everything felt lopsided, unbalanced. Most of the signals I sent, demanding movement from muscles and limbs, went unanswered. Still, my tormented carcass somehow managed to rise up, teetering first to the knees . . . and then onto stumps that might loosely be called legs.

Sliding along a wooden bannister, I flopped unevenly up a short flight of steps leading to the houseboat that lay moored alongside. Lights brightened and a thumping vibration grew discernable.

Garbled music played somewhere nearby.

As my head crested the rail, I caught a blurry image—flickering flames atop slim white pillars. Tapered candles . . . their soft light glinting off silverware and crystal goblets. And farther on, sleek figures moving by the starboard rail.

Real people. Elegantly dressed for a dinner party. Gazing at the river beyond.

I opened my mouth, intending to voice a polite apology for interrupting . . . and would someone please call my owner to come get me before this brain turned to mush?

What came out was a slobbery groan.

A woman turned around, caught sight of me lurching toward her from the dark, and let out a yelp—as if I were some horrible undead creature, risen from the deep. Fair enough.

I reached out, moaning.

"Oh sweet mother Gaia," her voice swung quickly to realization. "Jameson! Will you please phone up Clara Gonzalez, over on the *Catalina Baby*? Tell her that her goddam boyfriend has misplaced another of his dittos . . . and he better come pick it up right now!"

I tried to smile and thank her, but scheduled expiration could no longer be delayed. My pseudoligaments chose that very moment to dissolve, all at once.

Time to fall apart.

I don't remember anything after that, but I'm told that my head rolled to a stop just short of the ice chest where champagne was chilling. Some dinner guest was good enough to toss it inside, next to a very nice bottle of Dom Pérignon '38.

2

Ditto Masters

. . . or how realAlbert copes with a rough day . . .

All right, so that greenie didn't make it home *in one piece*. By the time I came to fetch it, only the chilled cranium was left . . . plus a slurry of evaporating pseudoflesh staining the deck of Madame Frenkel's houseboat.

(Note to self: buy Madame a nice gift, or Clara will make me pay for this.)

Of course I got the brain in time—or I wouldn't have the dubious pleasure of reliving a vividly miserable day that "I" spent skulking through the dittotown underworld, worming through sewers to penetrate Beta's lair, getting caught and beaten by his yellowdit enforcers, then escaping through town in a frenzied dash, culminating in that hideous trudge through underwater perdition.

I knew, even before hooking that soggy skull into the perceptron, that I wasn't going to savor the coming meal of acrid memories.

For what we are about to receive, make us truly thankful.

Most people refuse to inload if they suspect their ditto had unpleasant experiences. A rig can choose not to know or remember what the rox went through. Just one more convenient aspect of modern duplication technology—like making a bad day simply go away.

But I figure if you make a creature, you're responsible for it. That ditto wanted to matter. He fought like hell to continue. And now he's part of me, like several hundred others that made it home for inloading, ever since the first time I used a kiln, at sixteen.

Anyway, I needed the knowledge in that brain, or I'd be back with nothing to show my client—a customer not known for patience.

I could even find a blessing in misfortune. Beta saw my green-skinned copy fall into the river and never come up. Anyone would assume it drowned, or got swept to sea, or dissolved into fish food. If Beta felt sure, he might not move his hideout. It could be a chance to catch his pirates with their guard down.

I got up off the padded table, fighting waves of sensory confusion. My real legs felt odd—fleshy and substantial, yet a bit distant—since it seemed like just moments ago that I was staggering about on moldering stumps. The image of a sturdy, dark-haired fellow in the nearby mirror looked odd. Too healthy to be real.

Monday's ditto's fair of face, I thought, inspecting the creases that sink so gradually around your real eyes. Even an uneventful inloading leaves you feeling disoriented while a whole day's worth of fresh memories churn and slosh for position among ninety billion neurons, making themselves at home in a few minutes.

By comparison, *outloading* feels tame. The copier gently sifts your organic brain to engrave the Standing Wave onto a fresh template made of special clay, ripening in the kiln. Soon a new ditto departs into the world to perform errands while you have breakfast. No need even to tell it what to do.

It already knows.

It's you.

Too bad there wasn't time to make one right now. Urgent matters came first.

"Phone!" I said, pressing fingers against my temples, pushing aside disagreeable memories of that river bottom trek. I tried to concentrate on what my ditective had learned about Beta's lair.

"*Name or number,*" a soft alto voice replied from the nearest wall.

"Get me Inspector Blane of the LSA. Scramble and route to his real locale. If he's blocked, cut in with an *urgent.*"

Nell, my house computer, didn't like this.

"*It's three o'clock in the morning,*" she commented. "*Inspector Blane is off duty and he has no ditto facsimiles on active status. Shall I replay the last time you woke him with an urgent? He slapped us with a civil privacy lien of five hundred—*"

"Which he later dropped, after cooling off. Just put it through, will you? I've got a splitting headache."

Anticipating my need, the medicine cabinet was already gurgling with organosynthesis, dispensing a glassful of fizzy concoction that I gulped while Nell made the call. In muted tones I overheard her arguing priorities with Blane's reluctant house comp. Naturally, that machine wanted to take a message instead of waking its boss.

I was already changing clothes, slipping into a bulky set of Bullet-guard overalls, by the time the Labor Subcontractors Association inspector answered in person, groggy and pissed off. I told Blane to shut up and join me near the old Teller Building in twenty minutes. That is, if he wanted a chance to finally close the Wammaker Case.

"And you better have a first-class seizure team meet us there," I added. "A big one, if you don't want another messy standoff. Remember how many commuters filed nuisance suits last time?"

He cursed again, colorfully and extensively, but I had his attention. A distinctive whine could be heard in the background—his industrial-strength kiln warming up to imprint three brute-class dittos at a time. Blane was a guttermouth, but he moved quickly when he had to.

So did I. My front door parted obligingly and Blane's voice switched to my belt portable, then to the unit in my car. By the time he calmed down enough to sign off, I was already driving through a predawn mist, heading downtown.

I closed the collar of my trench coat, making sure the matching fedora fit low and snug. Clara had stitched my private eye outfit for me by hand, using high-tech fabrics she swiped from her Army Reserve unit. Great stuff. Yet the protective layers felt barely reassuring. Plenty of modern weapons can slice through textile armor. The sensible thing, as always, would be to send a copy. But my place is too far from the Teller Building. My little home kiln couldn't thaw and imprint quickly enough to make Blane's rendezvous.

It always makes me feel creepy and vulnerable to go perform a rescue or arrest in person. Risk isn't what realflesh is for. But this time, what choice was there?

■ ■ ■

Real people still occupy some of the tallest buildings, where prestigious views are best appreciated by organic eyes. But the rest of Old Town has become a land of ghosts and golems, commuting to work each morning fresh from their owners' kilns. It's an austere realm, both tattered and colorful as zeroxed laborers file off jitneys, camionetas, and buses, their brightly colored bodies wrapped in equally bright and equally disposable paper clothes.

We had to finish our raid before that daily influx of clay people arrived, so Blane hurriedly organized his rented troops in predawn twilight, two blocks from the Teller Building. While he formed squads and passed out disguises, his ebony lawyer-golem dickered with a heavily armored cop—her visor raised as she negotiated a private enforcement permit.

I had nothing to do except chew a ragged fingernail, watching daybreak amid a drifting haze. Already, dim giants could be seen shuffling through the metropolitan canyons—nightmarish shapes that would have terrified our urban ancestors. One sinuous form passed beyond a distant streetlight, casting serpentine shadows several stories high. A low moan echoed toward us and triassic tremors stroked my feet.

We should finish our business before that behemoth arrived.

I spied a candy wrapper littering the sidewalk—a strange thing to find here. I put it in my pocket. Dittotown streets are usually spotless, since most golems never eat or spit. Though you do see a lot more cadavers, smoldering in the gutter, than when I was a kid.

The cop's chief concern—to ensure none of today's bodies was real. Blane's jet black copy argued futilely for a complete waiver, then shrugged and accepted the city's terms. Our forces were ready. Two dozen purple enforcers, lithe and sexless, some of them in disguise, moved out according to plan.

I glanced again down Alameda Boulevard. The giant silhouette was gone. But there would be others. We'd better hurry, or risk getting caught in rush hour.

■　■　■

To his unwatered joy, Blane's rented mercenaries caught the pirates off-guard.

Our troops slinked past their outer detectors in commercial vans, disguised as maintenance dits and courier-golems making dawn deliveries, making it nearly up the front steps before their hidden weapons set off alarms.

A dozen of Beta's yellows spilled out, blazing away. A full-scale melee commenced as clay humanoids hammered at each other, losing limbs to slugfire or exploding garishly across the pavement when sprays of incendiary needles struck pseudoflesh, igniting the hydrogen-catalysis cells in spectacular mini-fireballs.

As soon as shooting started, the armored city cop advanced with her blue-skinned duplicates, inflating quick-barricades and noting infractions committed by either side—anything that might result in a juicy fine. Otherwise, both sides ignored the police. This was a commercial matter and none of the state's business, so long as no organic people were hurt.

I hoped to keep it that way, sheltering behind a parked car with realBlane while his brute-duplicates ran back and forth, urging the purples on. Quick and crude, his rapid-rise dittos were no mental giants, but they shared his sense of urgency. We had just minutes to get inside and rescue the stolen template before Beta could destroy all evidence of his piracy.

"What about the sewers?" I asked, recalling how my recent greendit wormed its way inside yesterday . . . an excursion as unpleasant to remember as that later trek along the river bottom.

Blane's broad face contorted behind a semi-transparent visor that flashed with symbols and map overlays. (He's too old-fashioned to get retinal implants. Or maybe he just likes the garish effect.) "I've got a robot in there," he grunted.

"Robots can be hacked."

"Only if they're smart enough to heed new input. This one is a cable-laying drone from the Sanitation Department. Zingleminded and dumb as a stone. It's trying to bring a wide-baud fiber through sewer pipes into the basement, heading stubbornly for Beta's toilet. Nobody's getting past the thing, I promise."

I grunted skeptically. Anyway, our biggest problem wasn't *escape,* but getting to the hideout before our proof melted.

Any further comment was cut off by a novel sight. The policewoman sent one of her blue copies strolling right in the middle of the battle! Ignoring whizzing bullets, it poked away at fallen combatants, making sure they were out of commission, then severed their heads to drop into a preserva sac for possible interrogation.

Not much chance of that. Beta was notoriously careful with his dits, using fake ID pellets and programming their brains to self-destruct if captured. It would take fantastic luck to uncover his real name today. Me? I'd be happy to pull off a complete rescue and put this particular enterprise of his out of business.

Noisy explosions rocked Alameda as smoke enveloped every entrance of the Teller Building, spreading down to the car where Blane and I took shelter. Something blew off my fedora, giving my neck a sharp yank. I crouched lower, breathing hard, before reaching into a pocket for my fiberscope—a much safer way to look around. It snaked over the hood of the car at the end of a nearly invisible stalk, swiveling automatically to aim a tiny gel-lens at the fight, transmitting jerky images to the implant in my left eye.

(Note to self: this implant is five years old. Obsolete. Time to upgrade? Or are you still squeamish after last time?)

The blue copdit was still out there, checking bodies and tallying damage—even as our purple enforcers stepped up their assault, charging through every convenient opening with the reckless abandon of fanatic shock troops. As I watched, several stray slugs impacted the police-golem, spinning it around, blowing doughy chunks against a nearby wall. It staggered and doubled over, quivering. You could tell the pain links functioned. Purple mercenaries may operate without touch cells, ignoring wounds while blasting away with pistolas in both hands. But a blue's job is to augment the senses of a real cop. It feels.

Ouch, I thought. *That's got to hurt.*

Anyone watching the mutilated thing suffer would expect it to auto-dissolve. But the golem straightened instead, shivered, and went limping back to work. A century ago, that might have seemed pretty heroic. But we all know what personality types get recruited for the constabulary nowadays. The real cop would probably inload this ditto's memories . . . and enjoy it.

My phone rang, a hi-pri rhythm, so Nell wanted me to take it. Three taps on my upper-right canine signaled *yes.*

A face ballooned to fill my left eye-view. A woman whose pale brown features and golden hair were recognizable across a continent.

"Mr. Morris, I'm sifting reports of a raid in dittotown . . . and I see the LSA has registered an enforcement permit. Is this your work? Have you found my stolen property?"

Reports?

I glanced up to see several floatcams hovering over the battle zone, bearing the logos of eager sniff-nets. It sure didn't take the vultures long.

I choked back a caustic comment. You have to answer a client, even when she's interfering. "Um . . . not yet, Maestra. We may have taken them by surprise but . . ."

Blane grabbed my arm. I listened.

No more explosions. The remaining gunfire was muffled, having shifted deep into the building.

I raised my head, still tense. The city cop stomped past us in heavy armor, accompanied by her naked blue duplicates.

"Mr. Morris? You were saying something?" The beautiful face frowned peevishly inside my left eye, where blinking offered no respite. *"I expect to be kept informed—"*

A squadron of cleaners came next, green and pink–candy-striped models, wielding brooms and liquivacs to scour the area before rush hour brought this morning's commuters. Expendable or not, cleaner-dits wouldn't enter a place where fighting raged.

"Mr. Morris!"

"Sorry, Maestra," I replied. "Can't talk now. I'll call when I know more." Before she could object, I bit a molar, ending the call. My left eye cleared.

"Well?" I asked Blane.

His visor exploded with colors that I might have interpreted if I were in cyberdit form. As a mere organic, I waited.

"We're in."

"And the template?"

Blane grinned.

"Got it! They're bringing her up now."

My hopes lifted for the first time. Still, I scuttled low across the pavement to reclaim the fedora, planting its elastic armor back over my head. Anyway, Clara wouldn't appreciate it if I lost it.

We hurried past the cleaners and up twenty steps to the main entrance. Broken bodies and bits of pseudoflesh melted into a multicolored haze, lending the battleground an eerie sense of unreality. Soon, the dead would be gone, leaving just a few bullet-spalled walls and some rapidly healing windows. And splinters from a huge door the purples blew to bits when they forced their way inside.

Newsbots swooped down, gattling us with questions. Publicity can be helpful in my line of work, but only if there's good news to report. So I kept mum till a pair of Blane's LSA brutes emerged from the basement, supporting a much smaller figure between them.

Slimy preserving fluid dripped from naked flesh that shone like glittering snow, completely white except where livid bruises marred her shaved head. And yet, though bald, abraded, and ditto-hued, the face and figure were unmistakable. I had just been speaking to the original. The Ice Princess. The maestra of Studio Neo—Gineen Wammaker.

Blane told his purples to rush the template to a preserva tank, so it wouldn't expire before testifying. But the pale figure spotted me and planted her heels. The voice, though dry and tired, was still that famously sultry contralto.

"M-mister Morris . . . I see you've been spendthrift with your expense account." She glanced at the windows, many of them shredded beyond self-repair, and the splintered front door. "Am I expected to pay for this mess?"

I learned several things from the ivory's remark. First, it must have been snatched *after* Gineen Wammaker hired me, or the ditto wouldn't know who I was.

Also, despite several days stored torturously in WD-90 solution, no amount of physical abuse could suppress the arrogant sensuality that Gineen imbued into every replica she made. Wigless, battered and dripping, this golem held herself like a goddess. And even deliverance from torment at Beta's hands hadn't taught her gratitude.

Well, what do you expect? I thought. *Wammaker's customers are sickies. No wonder so many of them buy Beta's cheap bootleg copies.*

Blane responded to the Wammaker replica as if she were real. Her presence was that overpowering.

"Naturally, the Labor Subcontractors Association will expect some reimbursement. We put up considerable resources to underwrite this rescue—"

"Not a rescue," the ivory model corrected. "I have no continuity. Surely you don't think my original is going to inload me after this experience? You've recovered her stolen property, that is all."

"Beta was ditnapping your dittos off the street, using them as templates to make pirate facsimiles—"

"Violating my copyright. And you've put a stop to it. Fine. That's what I pay my LSA dues for. Catching license violators. As for you, Mr. Morris—you'll be well compensated. Just don't pretend it's anything heroic."

A tremor shook the slim body. Her skin showed a skein of hairline cracks, deepening by the second. She looked up at the purples. "Well? Are you going to dip me now? Or shall we wait around till I melt?"

I had to marvel. The ditto knew it wasn't going to be inloaded back into Gineen's lovely head. Its life—such as it was—would end painfully while her pseudobrain was sifted for evidence. Yet she carried on with typical dignity. Typical arrogance.

Blane sent the purps on their way, hurrying their small burden past the striped cleaners, the blue-skinned cops, and remnant evaporating shreds of bodies that had been locked in furious combat only minutes before. The way his eyes tracked Wammaker's ivory, I wondered—was Blane one of her fans? Maybe a closet renter?

But no. He snarled in disgust.

"It's not worth it. All this expense and risk, because a prima donna won't bother to safeguard her dits. We wouldn't have to do any of this if they carried simple autodestructs."

I didn't argue. Blane is one of those people who can be completely matter-of-fact about kiln tech. He treats his own dittos like useful tools, no more. But *I* understood why Gineen Wammaker won't implant her copies with remote-controlled bombs.

When I'm a ditto, I like to pretend I'm immortal. It helps me get through a drab day.

■ ■ ■

The police barriers came down just in time for rush hour as great lumbering dinobuses and spindly flywheel trollies began spilling their cargoes—gray office-golems, cheaper green and orange factory workers, swarms of candy-striped expendables, plus a sprinkling of other types. Those entering Teller Plaza gawked at the damaged walls. Grays called up their news services for summary replays of the fight. Several of them pointed at Blane and me, storing up some unusual memories to bring home to their archies, at day's end.

The armored policewoman approached Blane with a preliminary estimate of costs and fines. Wammaker was right about dues and responsibilities. LSA would have to foot most of the bill . . . at least till the day we finally catch Beta and force a reckoning. When that happens, Blane can only hope that deep pockets lay somewhere along Beta's obligation trail. Deep enough for LSA to come out ahead on punitive damages.

Blane invited me to join him in the basement, inspecting the pirate copying facility. But I'd seen the place. Just a few hours ago "I" was down there getting my ceramic hide pounded by some of Beta's terracotta soldiers. Anyway, the LSA had a dozen or so ebony crime-scene analysts under contract who were much better equipped to handle the fine-toothed-comb stuff, using specialized senses to sift every nook and particle for clues, hoping to discover Beta's real name and whereabouts.

As if it ever does any good, I thought, stepping outside for some fresh air. *Beta is a wily son of a ditch. I've been hunting him for years and he always slips away.*

The police weren't much help, of course. Ditnapping and copyright violation have been civil torts ever since the Big Deregulation. It would stay a purely commercial matter, so long as Beta carefully avoided harming any real people. Which made his behavior last night puzzling. To chase my greenie into Odeon Square, firing stones from slingshots and barely missing several strolling archies—it showed something like desperation.

Outside, I waded through a hubbub of folks coming and going. All were dittos, so an archie like me had right-of-way. Anyway, with golem-bodies still smoldering unpleasant fumes nearby, I moved away quickly, frowning in thought.

Beta seemed upset last night. He's captured me before, without ever interrogating so fiercely!

In fact, he usually just kills me, with no malice or hard feelings. At least to the best of my knowledge. Those times that I recovered memories.

The same distress that drove Beta's yellows to torture my green last night also made them careless. Shortly after pummeling me, they all departed, leaving me tied up in that basement factory between two autokilns that were busily cranking out cheap Wammaker copies, imprinting their kinky-specialist personalities from that little ivory they had ditnapped. Carelessly, the yellows never even bothered to check what tools I might have tucked away under pseudoflesh! Escaping turned out to be much easier than breaking in—(too easy?)—though Beta soon recovered and gave chase.

Now I was back and victorious, right? Shutting down this operation must be a real blow to Beta's piracy enterprise. So why did I feel a sense of incompletion?

Strolling away from the traffic noise—a braying cacophony of jitney horns and bellowing dinos—I found myself confronting an alley marked by ribbons of flickertape, specially tuned to irritate any natural human eye.

"Stay Out!" the fluttering tape yammered. *"Structural Danger! Stay Out!"*

Such warnings—visible only to realfolk—are growing commonplace as buildings in this part of town suffer neglect. Why bother with maintenance when the sole inhabitants are expendable clay people, cheaply replenished each day? Oh, it's a remarkable slum, all right. Cleanliness combined with decay. Just another of the deregulated ironies that give dittoburgs their charm.

Averting my gaze, I strolled past the glittery warning. No one tells me where I can't go! Anyway, the fedora should protect against falling debris.

Giant recycling bins lined the alley, fed by slanting accordion tubes, accepting pseudoflesh waste from buildings on both sides. Not all dittos go home for memory inloading at the end of a twenty-hour work day. Those made for boring, repetitive labor just toil on, fine-tuned for contentment, till they feel that special call—beckoning them to final rest in one of these slurry bins.

What I felt beckoning, right then, was my bed. After a long day and a half—that felt much longer—it would be good to make today's copies and then drop into sweet slumber.

Let's see, I pondered. *What bodies shall I wear? Beyond this Beta affair, there are half a dozen smaller cases pending. Most call for just some fancy web research. I'll handle those from home, as an ebony. A bit expensive, but efficient.*

There has to be a green, of course. I've been putting off chores. Groceries, laundry. A toilet keeps backing up. The lawn needs to be mowed.

The rest of the gardening—some pruning and replanting—fell under the category of pleasure/hobby time. I'd save that to do in person, maybe tomorrow.

So, will two dittos suffice? I shouldn't need any grays, unless something comes up.

Beyond the recycling bins lay another gap between buildings—a back alley veering south, with ramps leading to an old parking garage. Overhead, the narrow lane was spanned by hand-strung utility wires and clotheslines where cheap garments flapped in the morning breeze. Shouting voices and raucous music floated down rickety fire escapes.

Nowadays, everybody needs a hobby. For some people, it's a second life—sending a ditto a day down here to golemtown, joining others in pretend families, engaging in mock businesses, dramas, even feuds with the neighbors. *"Clay operas,"* I think they're called. Whole derelict blocks have been taken over to feign Renaissance Italy or London during the Blitz. Standing in that alley, under the flapping clotheslines and raucous-scratchy music, I had only to squint and imagine myself in a tenement ghetto of more than a century ago.

The romantic attraction of this particular scenario escaped me. Real-folk don't live like this anymore. On the other hand, what's it to me how people spend their spare time? Being a golem is always a matter of choice.

Well, almost always.

That's why I kept working on the Beta Case, despite endless irritations and pummelings—and the me's that vanish, never to be seen again. Beta's style of industrial thievery had much in common with oldtime slavery. A disturbing psychopathology underlay his profitmaking criminal enterprise. The guy needed help.

All right, so dittotown has all sorts of eccentric corners and eddies—from Dickensian factories to fairyland amusement centers to open war zones. Were any of this alley's curious features relevant to my case? The area had been scanned by some LSA floater-eyes before this morning's raid. But human vision can notice things cameras don't. Like bullet scars on some of the bricks. Recent ones. Spalled mortar felt fresh between my fingertips.

So? Nothing strange about that in dittotown. I don't like coincidences, but my top priority at the moment was to settle with Blane and go home.

Turning back, I reentered the lane between those big recycling tanks, only to halt when a hissing sound dropped from somewhere overhead.

It sounded vaguely like my name.

I stepped aside quickly, reaching under my vest while peering upward.

A second faint hiss focused my attention on one of the accordion shafts slanting from upper floors of the Teller Building to a slurry bin. Squinting, I saw a silhouetted figure writhe inside the flexi-translucent tube, pawing at a small tear in its fabric. The humanoid shape had wedged itself, splaying both legs to prevent falling a final two meters into the tank.

The effort was futile, of course. Acrid vapors would devour whatever scanty pseudolifespan the poor fellow had left. Anyway, the next ditto to jump in that tube would land with enough force to dislodge this fellow's decaying limbs, carrying them both into the soup!

Still, it happens now and then—especially to teens who haven't grown accustomed to life's new secondary cycle of nonchalant death and trivial rebirth. They sometimes panic at the recycling stage. It's natural. When you imprint memories and copy your *soul* into a clay doll, you take along a lot more than a To Do list of the day's errands. You also bring survival talents inherited from the long era when folks knew just one kind of death. The kind to be feared.

It all comes down to personality. They tell you in school—don't make disposable dittos unless you can let go.

I raised my gun.

"Say, fella, would you like me to put you out of your—"

That's when I heard it again. A single whispered word.

"Mo-o-r-r-r-isssss!"

Blinking several times, I felt that old frisson down the spine. A feeling you can only experience fully in your real body and your original soul—with the same nervous system that reacted to shadows in the dark when you were six.

"Um . . . do I know you?" I asked.

"Not as well . . . as I know you . . ."

I put my weapon away and took a running leap, grabbing the upper edge of the recycling tank, then hauled myself on top. No sweat. One of your chief tasks each day, when you find that you're the real one, is to keep the old body in shape.

Standing on the lid brought me a lot closer to the fumes—an aroma that you find somewhat attractive when you're a golem in its last hour. In organic form, I found it rank. But now I could see the visage peering through torn plastic, already slumping from peptide exhaustion and diurnal decay, the cheeks and molded brow ridges sagging, its former bright banana color fading to a sickly jaundice. Still, I recognized one of Beta's favorite, bland disguises.

"It seems you're stuck," I commented, peering closer. Was it one of the yellows that tormented me last night, when I was a captive green? Did this one shoot pellets at me, across Odeon Square? He must have escaped this morning's raid by fleeing upstairs ahead of Blane's purple enforcers, then jumping into the accordion tube through some mislaid hope of getting away.

Still vivid in memory was one yellow Beta, leering as he expertly stimulated the pain receptors that even my greens find realistic. (There are drawbacks to being a first-rate copier.) I recall wondering at the time, *why?* What did he hope to accomplish with torture? Half of the questions he asked didn't even make sense!

Anyway, a deep assurance helped me ignore the pain. *It doesn't matter,* I told myself over and over, during last night's captivity. And it didn't. Not very much.

So why should I feel pity for this golem's suffering?

"Been here a long time," it told me. *"Came to learn why there's been no contact from this operation . . ."*

"A long time?" I checked my watch. Less than an hour had passed since Blane's purples attacked.

". . . and found it was taken over, like the others! They chased me . . . I climbed in this tube . . . sealed the top . . . I figured—"

"Hold it! 'Taken over,' you say? You mean just now, right? Our raid—"

The face was slumping rapidly. Sounds escaping from its mouth grew steadily harder to understand. Less like words than gurgling rattles.

"I thought at first . . . you might be responsible. After hounding me for years . . . But now I can tell . . . you're clueless . . . as usual . . . Morrissss."

I wasn't standing there, breathing nasty fumes, in order to be insulted. "Well, clueless or not, I've put this operation of yours out of business. And I'll shut down others—"

"Too late!" The yellow fell into hacking coughs of bitter laughter. *"They've already been taken over . . . by—"*

I stepped closer, nearly gagging on decay reeks that spilled from cracks in the golem's skin. It must be *hours* past deadline, holding together by willpower alone.

"Taken over, you say? By whom? Another copyright racketeer? Give me a name!"

Grinning caused the face to split, separating flaps of yellow pseudoskin, exposing the crumbling ceramic skull.

"Go to Alpha . . . Tell Betzalel to protect the emet!"

"What? Go to who?"

"The source! Tell Ri—"

Before he could say more, something snapped. One of Beta's legs, I guess. The smug expression vanished, replaced on that skeletal face by a look of sudden dread. For the span of an instant, I imagined I could *see* the Soul Standing Wave through Beta's filmy clay eyes.

Moaning, the ditto dropped from sight . . .

. . . followed by a splash. As fumes gusted, I offered a feeble benediction . . .

" 'Bye."

. . . and jumped back down to the alley. One thing I didn't need right
then was to let another of Beta's perverse little paranoia games into my
head! Anyway, the brief encounter was recorded by the implant in my
eye. My oh-so-analytical ebony golem could ponder the words later.

A job like mine requires focus. And ability to judge what's relevant.
So I dismissed the incident from mind.

Until next time, I thought.

■ ■ ■

Back on Alameda, I decided not to wait for Blane to finish in the
basement. Let him d-mail me a report. This job was done. My end of it,
at least.

I was walking back to my car when a feminine voice spoke up from
behind me.

"Mr. Morris?"

For a brief instant I envisioned Gineen Wammaker, the real one,
having rushed downtown to congratulate me. Yeah, I know. Fat chance.

I turned to see a brunette. Taller than the maestra, less voluptuous,
with a narrower face and somewhat higher voice. Still very much worth
looking at. Her skin was one of the ten thousand shades of authentic
human-brown.

"Yes, that's me," I said.

She flashed a card covered with splotchy fractals that automatically
engaged the optics in my left eye, but the patterns were too complex or
newfangled for my obsolete image system to deconvolute. Irritated, I bit
an incisor to frame-store the image. Nell could solve the puzzle later.

"And what can I do for you, Miss?" Maybe she was a news sniffer,
or a thrill perv.

"First, let me congratulate you on this morning's success. You have
a sheen of celebrity, Mr. Morris."

"My fifteen seconds," I answered automatically.

"Oh, more than that, I think. Your skills had already come to our
attention, before this coup. Might I prevail on you to spare a moment?
Someone wants to meet you."

She gestured down the street a short distance, where a fat limousine
was parked. An expensive-looking Yugo.

I considered. The maestra expected me to call with final assurance that third-hand Wammaker toys would stop flooding the market. But hell, I'm human. Inside, I felt as if I had already reported to *one* Gineen—the white ditto. Why should anyone have to go through that twice? Illogical, I know. But Miss Fractal gave me an excuse to put off the delectably unpleasant duty.

I shrugged. "Why not?"

She smiled and took my arm, in the old thirties style, while I wondered what she wanted. Some press flacks love to sniff detectives after a showy bust—though reporters seldom drive Yugos.

The limo's door hissed open and the sill lowered, so I barely had to duck my head entering. It was dim inside. And lavish. Bioluminescent cressets and real wood moldings. Pseudoflesh cushions beckoned, wriggling voluptuously, like welcoming laps. Crystal decanters and goblets glittered in the bar. Fancy. Schmancy.

And there, sitting cross-legged on the backseat like he owned the place, was a pale gray golem.

It's a bit odd to see a rox riding in style with an attractive rig assistant, but how better to show off your wealth? In fact, my host looked as if he'd been *born* gray. Silver hair and skin like metal, all angles and high cheekbones . . . *not* gray, I realized, but a kind of platinum.

He looks familiar. I tried sending a snap-image to Nell, but the limo was shielded. The platinum golem smiled, as if he knew exactly what had happened. I took small comfort from the fact that this creature had no legal rights.

So what? It could still buy and sell you in a second, I told myself, taking the opposite seat while Miss Fractal alighted primly onto a living cushion between us. Opening the limo's cooler, she took out a bottle of Tuborg and poured me a glass. Basic hospitality. My daytime brew is a matter of public profile. No points for research.

"Mr. Morris, let me present Vic Aeneas Kaolin."

I managed to quash any outward surprise. No wonder he looked familiar! As one of the founders of *Universal Kilns,* Kaolin was one of the richest men along the entire Pacific coast. Strictly speaking, the "Vic" honorific—like Mister—should only be used with the real person, the original who can vote. But I sure wasn't about to stand on protocol if this fellow wants his elegant drone to be called Vic . . . or Lord Poobah, for that matter.

"A pleasure to meet you, Vic Kaolin. Is there a service I can offer?"

The metal-shiny ditto returned a thin smile, nodding through a window at the contract cleaners, still sweeping up battle remnants.

"Congratulations on your success cornering a wily foe, Mr. Morris. Though I'm not sure about the endgame. All this violence seems unsubtle. Extravagant."

Did Kaolin own the blemished Teller Building? Wouldn't a trillionaire have more important chores for his duplicates than hand-delivering a damage lien to a private eye?

"I just performed the investigation," I said. "Enforcement was up to the Labor Subcontractors Association."

The young woman commented. "LSA wants to be seen acting decisively about the problem of ditnapping and copyright piracy—"

She stopped when the Kaolin copy raised a hand with skin texture nearly as supple as realflesh, including simulated veins and tendons. "Enforcement isn't an issue. I believe the matter we want to discuss is an investigation," he said quietly.

I wondered—surely Kaolin had employees and retainers to handle security matters. Hiring an outsider suggested something out of the ordinary. "Then you didn't simply rush down here on impulse, because of all this." I motioned at the untidy scene outside.

"Of course not," said the young assistant. "We've been discussing you for some time."

"We have?" Kaolin's ditto blinked, then shook its silvery head. "No matter. Are you interested, Mr. Morris?"

"Naturally."

"Good. Then you'll accompany us now." He raised a hand again, brooking no argument. "Since you're here in person, I'll pay your top consulting rate until you decide to accept or refuse the case. Under a confidentiality seal, agreed?"

"Agreed."

Both his belt phone and mine recognized the key words "confidentiality seal." They would grab the last few minutes of conversation from latent memory, covering them under a date/time stamp to serve as a contract, for the time being.

Kaolin's limo started up.

"My car—" I began.

The young woman made a complex gesture, tapping fingers rapidly together. An instant later, there flashed in my left eye a brief text message from my Volvo, asking permission to slave its autodrive to the big Yugo. It would follow close behind, if I said okay.

I did so with a tap of incisors. Kaolin's assistant was very good. Perhaps even worth lavishly hiring in the flesh. I wished I caught her name.

A forward glance caught the shadow of a driver beyond the smoky panel. Was that servant real, too? Well, the rich are different than you and me.

▪ ▪ ▪

It was still morning rush hour and the limo had to weave slowly around huge dinobuses, discharging golem passengers from racks slung along sinuous flanks. The buses shuffled and grunted, undulating their long necks gracefully, swinging humanlike heads to gossip with each other as traffic lurched along. From their imposing height, the imprinted pilots had a fine view of the wounded Teller Building. They could even peer into high windows and around corners.

Every kid dreams of becoming a bus driver when he grows up.

Soon we departed Old Town with its blend of shabbiness and gaudy color—its derelict buildings taken over by a new race of disposable beings, built either for hard work or hard play. Crossing the river, we made good time even with my car following behind, tethered by invisible control beams. The architecture grew brighter and more modern, even as the people became bland-looking, equipped only with nature's dull pigmentation, ranging from pale almost-white to chocolate brown. Trollies and dinobuses gave way to bikes and joggers, making me feel lazy and neglectful by comparison. They tell you in school—take care of your organic body. One rig is all you get.

Aeneas Kaolin's duplicate resumed speaking.

"I've been backtracing your impressive set of narrow escapes yesterday. You appear to be resourceful, Mr. Morris."

"Part of the job." I shrugged. "Can you tell me what this is about now?"

Again, the thin smile. "Let Ritu explain." He motioned to his living assistant.

Ritu, I noted the name.

"There has been a kidnapping, Mr. Morris," the dark-haired young woman said in a low, tense voice.

"Hm. I see. Well, recovering snatched property is one of my specialties. Tell me, did the ditto have a locator pellet? Even if they cut it out, we can possibly nail down where—"

She shook her head.

"You misunderstand, sir. This was no mere theft. Not a *dittograb,* as they say on the street. The victim is a real person. In fact, it is my father."

I blinked a couple of times.

"But . . ."

"He's more than just a *person,*" inserted Kaolin. "Dr. Yosil Maharal is a brilliant researcher. A co-founder of *Universal Kilns* and a major patent holder in the realm of corporeal duplication. And my close friend, I should add."

For the first time, I noticed that the platinum's hand trembled. From emotion? Hard to tell.

"But why not go to the police?" I asked. "They handle crimes against real people. Did the kidnappers threaten to kill Maharal if you tell? I'm sure you've heard there are ways to notify special authorities without—"

"We've already discussed the matter with state and national gendarmeries. Those officials have been unhelpful."

I took this in for several seconds.

"Well . . . I'm at a loss how I could do better. In a situation like this, cops can sift memory files from every public and private camera in the city. For a capital crime, they can even unleash DNA sniffers."

"Only with a major warrant, Mr. Morris. No warrant was issued."

"Why not?"

"Lack of sufficient cause," Ritu replied. "The police say they won't file an application without clear evidence that a crime was committed."

I shook my head, trying to adjust my perceptions. The young woman opposite me wasn't just Aeneas Kaolin's efficient assistant. She must be a rather rich person in her own right, perhaps a high official in the company that her eminent father helped establish—a company that transformed the way modern people go about their lives.

"Forgive me," I asked, shaking my head. "I'm confused. The police say there's no evidence of crime . . . but you say your father was kidnapped?"

"That's our theory. But there are no witnesses or ransom notes. A motivationist from the Human Protection Division thinks that Dad simply snuck away, on his own volition. As a free adult, he has the right."

"A right to *try.* Not many have the skill to pull off a clean escape, deliberately dropping out of the World Village. Even if you exclude all the private lenses and myob-eyes, that leaves an awful lot of publicams to avoid."

"And we sifted thousands without tracking down my father, I assure you, Mr. Morris."

"Albert," I corrected.

She blinked, hesitantly. Her expression was complex, dour one moment, then briefly beautiful when she smiled. "Albert," she corrected with a graceful, slanted nod.

I wondered if Clara would call her attractive.

The limo was driving past Odeon Square. Memories of last night made my toes itch . . . recalling sensations of having them gnawed off by crabs during that hellish underwater trek. I glimpsed the restaurant where a waiter-dit saved me by distracting the crowd. Naturally, it was closed this early. I vowed to drop by and see if the fellow still had a labor contract there. I owed him one.

"Well, we can check out the possibility that your father played hookey. If he arranged to drop out of sight, there should be signs of preparation in his home, or the most recent place he was spotted. If the locales haven't been disturbed. How long since you saw your father, Ritu?"

"Almost a month."

I had to choke back a cough. *A month!* The trail wouldn't just be cold by now but sedimentary. It was all I could do to keep a blank face and not insult the clients.

"That's . . . a long time."

"As you might guess, I tried first to utilize my own contractors and employees," Kaolin's ditto explained. "Only later did it dawn on us that the situation calls for a genuine expert."

I accepted the compliment with a nod, yet worried why he would want or need to butter me up. Some people are naturally gracious, but I had a feeling this fellow did little without calculation. Flattery from the rich can be a danger signal.

"I'll need to scan Dr. Maharal's house and workplace. And permission to interview his associates. If clues lead to his work, I'll have to know all about that, too."

Kaolin's expensively realistic face didn't look happy. "There are . . . sensitive matters involved, Mr. Morris. Cutting edge technologies and potentially crucial breakthroughs."

"I can post a strong confidentiality bond, if you like. Would half a year's income do?"

He chewed on it for a few seconds. Duplicates are often empowered to speak for their originals—and the most expensive grays can think as well as their archetype, at some metabolic cost. Still, I expected this one to defer any final decision till I spoke to the real Vic.

"An ideal solution," it suggested, "would be if you came aboard as a Kaolin household retainer."

Not ideal to me, I thought. Fealty oaths are a big fad among aristos, who like the feudal image of lords and faithful vassals. But I wasn't about to let go of my individuality. "An even better solution would be for you to take the word of a professional who lives by his reputation. It's a better guarantee than any oath."

I was only making a counterproposal—part of a negotiation that would finish with Kaolin's original. But the gray ditto surprised me with a firm nod.

"Then that is all we'll require, Mr. Morris. Anyway, we appear to have arrived."

I turned to see the limo approach a tall fence made of blue metal that shimmered with an ionization aura. Beyond the guarded gate, campus grounds extended to three huge bubbledomes, gleaming mirrorlike under the sun. The centermost reared over twenty stories high. No logos or company emblems were needed. Everybody knew this landmark—world headquarters of Universal Kilns.

Another giveaway was the crowd of demonstrators, shouting and waving banners at vehicles streaming through the main entrance—a protest that had waxed and waned for over thirty years. In addition to standard placards, a few aimed holo projectors, splatting car windows (and a few unwary faces) with colorfully irate 3-D comments. Naturally, Kaolin's limousine filtered out such intrusions. But I mused over a few painted posters:

There Is Only
One Creator!

Brown Is Beautiful

Man-made "Life" Mocks
Heaven and Nature!

And, of course—

One Person:
Just One Soul

Naturally, these protestors were all archies, continuing a struggle that had been lost in both the courts and the marketplace before many of them were born. Yet they persisted, denouncing what they saw as technological arrogation of God's prerogatives—condemning the daily creation of manufactured beings. Millions of disposable people.

At first, looking out the right side, I saw only True Lifers clamoring and carrying on. Then I realized, several of them were shouting epithets at *another* crowd—a younger, hipper-looking throng on the left side of the entryway, equipped with more holo throwers and fewer placards. The second group had a different message:

End the Slavery of Clay People!

"Synthetic" Is a Social Slur

UK Serves the "Real" Ruling Class!

Rights for Roxes!

All Thinking Beings Have Souls

"Mancies," said Kaolin in a low voice, glancing at this second crowd, which included lots of bright-skinned dittos. Unlike the True Lifers, who were a familiar sight, this Emancipation movement had burgeoned much more recently—a crusade that still had many people scratching their heads.

The two protest groups despised each other. But they agreed on hatred of Universal Kilns. I wondered, would they put aside their animus and join forces if they knew the company chairman, Vic Aeneas Kaolin himself, was passing nearby?

Well, not "himself." But close enough.

As if he knew my thoughts, he chuckled. "If these were my only enemies, I wouldn't have a care in the world. Moralists make a lot of noise . . . and sometimes mail a pathetic bomb or two . . . but they are generally predictable and easy to sidetrack. I get a lot more aggravation from *practical* men."

Which particular opponents did he mean? Kiln technology disrupted so many fundamentals of the old way of life, I still puzzle why it wasn't throttled in the crib. Beyond ravaging every labor union and throwing millions out of work, roxing almost triggered a dozen wars that only quelled after intense diplomacy by some first-rate world leaders.

And some people say there's no such thing as progress? Oh, there's progress, all right. If you can handle it.

Security scanners cleared the limo and we left the demonstrators behind, passing a main entrance where buses delivered ditto workers, discharging them from leathery racks. But most arriving employees were organic humans who would make their copies onsite. Quite a few archies approached on bicycles, glowing from the sweaty workout, looking forward to a steam and massage before getting to work. Companies like UK take good care of their people. There are benefits to giving a fealty oath.

We cruised beyond the main portal, then on past sheltered loading docks, shipping machinery like freezers, imprinting units, and kilns. Most of the ditto blanks that people buy are made elsewhere, but I did glimpse some specialty items as we swept by—rigid figures dimly visible inside translucent packing crates, some of them uncannily tall, or gangly, or shaped like animals out of some legend. Not everyone can handle being imprinted into a non-standard human shape, but I hear it's a growing fashion among trendsetters.

The limo approached a formal entrance, clearly meant for VIP arrivals. Liveried servitors with emerald skin, the same color as their uniforms, rushed up to open our doors and we emerged under a canopy of artificial trees. Flowers dropped fragrant petals in rainbow profusion, like soft rain, dissolving into sweet, pigmented vapor before touching ground.

Looking around, I saw no sign of my Volvo. It must have peeled off to a more plebeian parking place. The dented fenders wouldn't suit this ambiance.

"So, where to now?" I asked the gray Kaolin replica. "I'll need to meet your original and finalize—"

His blank expression stopped me.

Ritu explained. "I thought you knew. Vic Kaolin doesn't see visitors in person anymore. He conducts all business by facsimile."

I *had* heard. He wasn't the only rich hermit to retreat into a sanitized sanctum, dealing with the world via electronic or pseudoflesh deputies. But in most cases it was affectation, a pose—a way to limit access—with exceptions made for important matters. The disappearance of a renowned scientist might qualify.

I started to say this, then saw that Ritu no longer paid attention. Her pale eyes shifted to stare past my right shoulder, both irises flaring while her chin quivered in shock. At almost the same moment, Kaolin's copy let out a reflex gasp.

Ritu vented a single word as I swiveled.

"Daddit!"

A clay person approached us from behind the floral arbor—with skin a much darker shade of gray than Kaolin's elegant platinum-colored unit. This ditto was embossed to resemble a slender man about sixty, walking with a faint limp that seemed more habit than a current affliction. The face, narrow and angular, bore some resemblance to Ritu, especially when it shaped a wan smile.

The paper garments were taped in several places, but a gleaming *Universal Kilns* ID badge said YOSIL MAHARAL.

"I've been waiting for you," he said.

Ritu didn't leap into its arms. Her use of the paternal-mimetic greeting meant the Maharal household must have kept real and simulated distinct, even in private. Still, her voice quavered as she grabbed a dark gray hand.

"We were so worried. I'm glad you're all right!"

At least we can guess he was all right some time in the last twenty-four hours, I observed quietly, noting the torn garments and cracked pseudoskin. Expiration wasn't many hours away. Flakes of some outer covering, perhaps remnants of a disguise, peeled off corners of dit-Maharal's face. The ditto's voice conveyed both tenderness and fatigue.

"I'm sorry to fret you, Pup," it said to Ritu, then turned to Kaolin. "And you, old friend. I never meant to upset you both."

"What's going on, Yosil? Where *are* you?"

"I just had to get away for a while and work things out. Project Zoroaster and its implications . . ." ditMaharal shook its head. "Anyway, I'm feeling better. I should have a good handle on things in a few days."

Kaolin took an eager step.

"You mean the solution to—"

Ritu interrupted. "Why didn't you get in touch? Or let us know—?"

"I wanted to, but I was wallowing in a pit of suspicion, not trusting the phones or webs." ditMaharal gave a rueful chuckle. "I guess some of the paranoia is still clinging to me. That's why I sent this copy, instead of calling. But I just wanted to reassure you both that things do feel much better."

I faded back a few steps, not wanting to intrude while Ritu and Kaolin murmured, evidently glad and relieved. Naturally, I felt a twinge over losing a lucrative case. But happy endings are never a bad thing.

Except that I somehow felt uneasy—unsure that anything "happy" was going on here. Despite the prospect of going home with a fat check for half a morning's consultation, I had that hollow feeling. The one that always haunts me when a job feels unfinished.

3

Something in the Fridge

. . . or how realAI decides that he needs
some help . . .

I parked by the Little Venice Canal and keyed myself aboard Clara's houseboat, hoping to find her at home.

It suited Clara to live on the water. At a time when most people—even the poor—seem feverishly intent on building up their homes, maximizing both ornate space and possessions, she preferred spartan compactness. The river's briny tide, its unsteady rocking, reminded her of the world's instability—which she found somehow reassuring.

Like those bullet holes in the north bulkhead, streaming rays of summer illumination into the boat's tiny salon. "My new skylights," Clara called them, soon after we both managed to wrestle the gun out of Pal's hands, that time when he broke down right there in front of us, the one and only time I ever saw our friend sob over his bad luck. The very day he got released from the hospital—the half of him that remained—in his shiny new life-support chair.

Later, as we were about to drive Pal home, Clara brushed aside his apologies. And from that moment she vowed to keep the perforations unpatched, treasuring them as valued "improvements."

You can see why I would always come by the boat, too, whenever I feel punctured or let down.

Only this time, Clara wasn't home.

Instead, I found a note for me on the kitchen counter.

GONE TO WAR, it said.
DON'T WAIT UP!

I muttered sourly. Was this payback for the way my zombie-self ditsrupted Madame F's dinner party last night? Neighborly relations mattered to Clara.

Then I recalled, *Oh yes, a war.* She did mention something a while back, about her reserve unit being called up for combat duty. For a battle against India, I thought. Or was it Indiana?

Damn, that sort of thing could last a whole week. Sometimes more.

I really wanted to talk to her, not spend the time worrying about where she was and what she might be doing, out there in the desert.

The note went on:

PLEASE LEAVE MY WORKER ALONE.
I HAVE A PROJECT DUE TOMORROW!

Glancing toward her little sim-study, I saw light rimming the door. So, before departing, Clara must have made a duplicate, programmed to finish some homework assignment. No doubt I'd find a gray or ebony version of my girlfriend inside, swathed in the robes of a virtuality cha-dor, laboring to fulfill some academic requirement in her latest major—maybe Bantu Linguistics or Chinese Military History—I couldn't follow the way her interests kept swerving, like a hundred million other per-manent students on this continent alone.

Me, I was one of a vanishing breed—the employed. My philosophy: why stay in school when you have a marketable skill? You never know when it'll become obsolete.

The magnetic latch released silently when I touched it, easing open the door of the study. True, her note asked me stay out, but I feel insecure sometimes. Maybe I was just checking to be sure that my biometrics still had full trust access, throughout the boat.

They did. And yes, there was her gray, studying at a tiny desk clut-tered with papers and data-plaques. Only the legs showed—pasty-clay in texture but realistically shapely. Everything above the waist lay shrouded under holo-interactive fabric that kept bulging and shifting as the ditto waved, pointed, and typed with wriggling hands. Word mumbles escaped the muffling layers.

"... No, no! I don't want some commercial hobby simulation of the Fizzle War. I need information on the real event! Not history books but raw debriefing transcripts having specifically to do with bio-crimes like TARP. ... Yes, that's right. Real harm done to real people back when war was ...

"I know the trial records are forty years old! So? Then adapt to the old data protocols and ... Oh, you dim-witted excuse for a ... and they call this artificial intelligence?"

I had to smile. Mere duplicate or not, it was Clara right down to the soul—cool in a crisis yet capable of great affection. And all too prickly toward the incompetence of strangers, especially machines. It did no good to lecture her that software avatars couldn't be browbeaten like infantry recruits.

I found it curious—and maybe a bit creepy—how Clara could assign a duplicate to do classwork, yet never bother to inload the golem's memories. How does that help you learn anything? All right, I'm old-fashioned. (One of my "endearing" qualities, she says.) Or maybe it's hard to imagine what keeps a golem motivated, with no promise of rejoining its original at the end of the day.

Well, you do it too, sometimes, I thought. *Didn't you lend Clara an ebony last week, to help her with a term paper? Never came back, as I recall. Not that I mind.*

I hope we had some good, scholarly fun.

■ ■ ■

Though tempted, I decided against bothering the homework-ditto. Clara liked specialists. This one would be all drive and intellect, toiling till its ephemeral brain expired. Again, it comes down to personality. Zingleminded focus on each task at hand, that's my Clara.

The houseboat reflected this. In an era when people spend copious spare time lavishly furnishing their homes or building hobby-hoards, her place was severely efficient, as if she expected to shove off at a moment's notice, heading toward some distant shore, or perhaps a different era.

Tools were evident, many showing handmade touches, like an all-weather navigation system worked into the grain of a carved mahogany walking stick or a set of formidable, self-targeting fighting bolas wrought from meteoritic nickel-iron. Or the his and hers armored chadors that hung from a nearby coatrack. Decorative outer layers of burnished titanium chain mail covered the real apparatus—a floppy cowl of plush emitters that could transport you anywhere you want to go in VR space. Assuming you had a good reason to visit that sterile digital realm.

Our matched set of chadors stayed here on the boat—the closest thing to a firm expression of commitment I had from her so far. That and a pair of solido-dolls of us hiking together on Denali—her straight brown hair cropped close, almost helmetlike, around a face that Clara always dismissed as too elongated to be pretty, though I had no complaints. To me she looked grown-up, a real woman, while my own too-youthful features seem forever pinched in a dark moodiness of adolescence. Maybe it's why I overcompensate, working hard to keep a serious job, while Clara feels more free to explore.

Otherwise? No clutter of collectibles. No trophies from a hundred battlefields where her combatant dittoselves crawled through shellfire, charging laser positions in her team's more famous matches.

At one level, I was involved with a college student. At another level, a warrior and international celebrity. So? Who hasn't grown accustomed to living several lives in parallel? If humanity has one majestic talent, it's an almost infinite capacity to get used to the Next Big Thing . . . then take it for granted.

I looked back at the note Clara left for me. Her thumbprint, bio-sculpted to resemble a familiar winking leer, marked the end, pointing to a second scrap of paper underneath:

I LEFT A ME IN THE FREEZER
IN CASE YOU GET LONELY.

Her duplication machine—a sleek model from Fabrique Gabon—took up a quarter of the boat's petite salon. The storage compartment, translucent with frost, revealed a humanoid figure—Clara's shape and size—presumably imprinted and ready for baking in the kiln.

Pondering the well-proportioned silhouette, I felt like a husband whose absent wife left a ready-to-heat supper in the fridge. A strange thought, given Clara's attitude toward marriage. And yes, Clara likes to make specialists. This ivory wouldn't be big on intellect or conversation.

Well, I'll take what I can get.

∎ ∎ ∎

But not now. Between one emergency and another, I'd been up for forty hours and needed sleep more than surrogate sex. Anyway, a vague sense of unease gnawed as I drove back to my own place.

"Did you check on the waiter at La Tour Vanadium?" I asked Nell, parking the Volvo in its little garage. My house computer answered in a customary mezzo-soprano.

"I did. The restaurant reports that one of their waiters lost his service contract last night, for upsetting clients. They are hiring skilled dittos from another source, starting tonight."

"Damn." This meant I owed the guy. Manual labor contracts aren't easy to come by, especially at classy eateries, where owners demand uniform perfection from the staff. Identical waiters are more predictable, and employees who are cast from the same mold don't squabble over tips.

"Did they give his name?

"There is a privacy block. But I'll work on it. Meanwhile, you have ongoing cases. Shall we go over them while imprinting today's duplicates?"

Nell's tone was chiding. Our normal routine had gone completely off-kilter. Usually, by this hour I'd have already turned out copies to run errands and make inquiries while the rig went back to sleep, napping to conserve precious brain cells for the creative side of business.

Instead of collapsing into bed, I headed for my kiln unit and lay down while Nell thawed several blanks for imprinting. I looked away as they slid into warming trays, doughlike flesh puffing and coloring as millions of tiny achilles catalysis cells began their brief, vigorous pseudolives. Today's kids may take this all for granted, but most people my age still find it a little unnerving, like seeing a corpse waken.

"Go ahead," I told Nell, while neural probes waved around my head for the critical phase of imprinting.

"First, I've been fending off Gineen Wammaker all morning. She's anxious to talk to you."

I winced as tickling sensations began dancing across my scalp, comparing my ongoing Soul Standing Wave to the basic ground state stored in memory.

"The Wammaker job is done. I completed the contract. If she's gonna quibble over expenses—"

"The maestra has already paid our bill in full. There are no quibbles."

Blinking in surprise, I almost sat up.

"That's not like her."

"Perhaps Ms. Wammaker noticed that you were abrupt with her this morning, and subsequently refused her calls. That could have put you in a position of strength, psychologically speaking. She may worry that she provoked you once too often, perhaps losing your services for good."

Nell's speculation had some merit. I felt no desperate need to keep working for the maestra. Relaxing again, I felt the tetragramatron's sweep intensify, copying my sympathetic and parasympathetic profiles for imprinting.

"What services? I said the job is done."

"Apparently she has another in mind. Her offer is our top-standard fee, plus ten percent for a confidential consultation early this afternoon."

I pondered it . . . though you really aren't supposed to make crucial decisions while imprinting. Too many random currents surging in your brain.

"Well, if playing hard-to-get works, make a counter offer. Top-standard rate plus thirty. Take it or leave it. We'll send a gray if she accepts."

"The gray is thawing as we speak. Shall I also continue preparing an ebony?"

"Hm. A bit expensive, if I'm making a gray anyway. Maybe he can finish with Wammaker early and get home in time to help."

"That should suffice for casework. But we still need a green—"

Nell paused abruptly.

"I'm receiving a call. An urgent. From someone named Ritu Liza-betha Maharal. Do you know this woman?"

Again, I barely refrained from sitting up, ruining the transfer.

"I met her this morning."

"You could have told me."

"Just pipe it in please, Nell."

A wall screen lit up, showing the slim face of Vic Kaolin's young assistant. Her real skin flushed taut with emotion, not at all like the relieved expression I last saw an hour ago.

"Mr. Morris . . . I mean Albert . . ."

She blinked, realizing that I lay supine in the kiln. Many folks consider imprinting private, like getting dressed in the morning.

"Forgive me for not getting up, Miss Maharal. I can interrupt if it's urgent, or call you back in a few—"

"No. I'm sorry to disturb you while you're . . . It's just that I—I have terrible news."

Anyone could tell as much from her expression—bleak and grieving. I hazarded a guess.

"Is it your father?"

She nodded, tears welling.

"They found his body in . . ." She stopped, unable to proceed.

"His *rig*?" I asked, shaken. "Not the gray ditto I met, but the *real* . . . your father's dead?"

Ritu nodded.

"C-could you please send a you over here, right away? Send it to the Kaolin estate. They're calling this an accident. But I'm sure Dad was murdered!"

4

Gray Matters

. . . or how Tuesday's first ditto suffers
a setback . . .

Running subvocal commentary.

Notes-as-we-go.

If this body of mine were real, a passerby might see my lips move, or hear a low whisper as I tape this. But talking into a microphone is irritating and inconvenient. Folks can listen. So I order all my gray ditto blanks with silent-record feature and a compulsion to recite.

Now I *am* one of them.

Damn.

■   ■   ■

Oh, never mind. I'm always just a bit grumpy getting up off the warming tray, grabbing paper garments from a rack and slipping them over limbs that still glow with ignition enzymes, knowing I'm the copy-for-a-day.

Of course I remember doing this thousands of times. Part of modern living, that's all. Still, it feels like when my parents used to hand me a long list of chores, saying that today will be all work and no play . . . with the added touch that Albert Morris's golems have a high chance of getting snuffed while taking risks he'd never put his realbod through.

A lesser death. Barely noticed. Unmourned.

Ugh. What got me in this mood?

Maybe Ritu's news. A reminder that *true* death still lurks for us all.

Well, shrug it off! No sense brooding. Life's fundamentally the same. Sometimes you're the grasshopper. Some the ant. The difference now is that now you can be both, the very same day.

While I donned a scratchy gray jumpsuit, real-me got up from the padded scan-table and cast a glance my way. Our eyes met.

If *this* me makes it back here to inload tonight, I'll remember that brief moment of contact from both sides, worse than staring deeply in a mirror, or bad déjà vu, which is one reason why we do it seldom. Some folks get it so bad, they try never to meet themselves at all, using screens to shut themselves off from the golems they make. Others couldn't care less—in fact, they find their own company charming! People are various. Humanity's great strength, I hear.

Fresh from imprint, I knew exactly what my organic archetype was thinking at that moment of eye contact. A rare bit of envy. Wishing *he* could go see the beautiful Ritu Maharal in person. Maybe offer some help or comfort.

Well, tough, Albert. That's what I'm for. She did ask for a ditto, after all. A high-quality gray.

Don't worry, boss. All you gotta do is inload me later. I'll get continuity and you'll remember every detail. Fair exchange. Trading one day's experience for an afterlife.

▪   ▪   ▪

Transport is always troublesome on busy days. We have just one car, and archie holds onto it, in case he has to go out. Got to keep the rig body safe from rain and hard objects. Like traffic hazards. Or bullets.

Too bad, since he usually stays home in bathrobe and fuzzy slippers, "investigating" cases by roaming the Net, paying for research scans with a flick-ident of our retina. So the Volvo mostly sits in the garage. We dittos get around by bus or scooter.

There are just two scooters left, and we made three golems today. So I have to share the little Vespa with a cheap little green who's heading downtown on errands.

I drive, of course. The greenie rides behind, silent as a wart, as we *putt-putt* all the way to the rendezvous where Ritu's sending a car to meet me. There's a small park, just off Chavez Avenue. Shady enough for a ditto to wait without melting in the sun.

I stop the scooter, leaving the motor running. Greenie slides forward to grab the handlebars as I dismount. Smooth maneuver. Done it lots of times.

He takes off without looking back. Tomorrow I'll remember what Greenie's thinking right now. If he makes it home. Which seems doubtful as I watch him weave through traffic, slipstreaming a delivery van. Ack, you can lose a perfectly good scooter that way! I really should drive more carefully.

Standing here, waiting for the car from Universal Kilns, I close my eyes and feel summer's warm languor. My grays need good senses, so right now I can smell the nearby pepper tree as kids in long pants clamber the rough branches, shredding musty bark and shouting at each other with the sober intensity that children bring to play. And roses and gardenias—I inhale complex fragrances through sponge-sensor membranes, feeling almost alive.

Not far off, more than a dozen hobbyists can be seen, crouching in broad sun hats, indulging a passion for gardening—yet another way to pass time in a world without enough jobs. It's one reason I chose this place for pickup. The local horticulture club is superb. Unlike my neighborhood, where nobody gives a damn.

I glance around to make sure I'm not in anybody's way. Parks are mostly for archies. The kids are all real, of course. Most folks only copy a child in order to teach rote lessons—or to send an occasional me-gram to Grannie. Some parents are reluctant to do even that, fearing subtle damage to growing brains. Such conservatism may fade as we take the technology for granted, like any other routine miracle.

(I hear that some divorced couples are pioneering new styles of visitation. Mom lets Dad take Junior's ditto to the Zoo, then refuses to inload the kid's happy memory, out of spite. Yeesh.)

Most of the adult caregivers in the park are rigs, too. Why not? You can fire up a clay copy and send it to the office, but when it comes to hugs and tickles, flesh has no substitute. Anyway, it makes you look bad, sending your child out tended by a purple or green. That is, unless you hire a poppins from one of the Master Nannies—a status symbol few can afford at this end of town.

. . . wait a sec . . . The phone just rang. I pick up my portable to listen in as Nell answers. She passes the call to my real self.

It's Pal. I can see him in the tiny display, propped in a big wheelchair, his half-paralyzed face surrounded by wish sensors. He wants me to come by. Something's up. Too sensitive to explain over public netwaves.

My rig answers in a grumpy voice. Been awake two days. (Poor guy.) Can't come in person and too tired for another imprinting.

"I've got three dits out on errands," I hear me tell Pal. *"One of them will drop by your place, if time allows."*

Huh. Pal lives downtown. Just a few blocks from the Teller Building. He couldn't have mentioned this sooner?

Three dits? The green won't be up to handling Pal, and I can't picture Gineen Wammaker letting the other gray escape early, so it's probably up to me. I've got to go console and consult poor Ritu Maharal—while cops glare and mutter about "meddling private eyes"—then take a stinking crosstown bus to hear Pal rant his latest conspiracy theory till I'm ready to expire. Great.

Ah. Here's the car from UK. It's no Yugolimo, but nice. Driver's a stolid-looking purple—all focus and reflexes. Good for delivering you safely. Not someone you'd go to for sage advice about personal relationships.

I get in.

He drives.

City streets roll by.

Pulling out a cheap slate, I dial up something to read. The *Journal of Antisocial Proclivities.* There are always new developments to keep up on, if you want to stay employable in your field. My real brain always dozes when I try to read this kind of stuff. Good at concepts, but the Standing Wave drifts. So I pay extra for gray blanks with good attention foci.

I never would have made it through college without those dittos I sent to the library.

■   ■   ■

Wait a minute.

I lift my gaze from the article when the triple domes of Universal Kilns pass by on the right, then fall behind. We must be heading somewhere else. But I thought—

Ah, yes. Ritu never actually mentioned UK. She said "the Kaolin estate."

So, I've been invited to the great one's sanctum, after all. Well, la-de-da.

Let's go back to reading about the use of pseudo-incarceration in Sumatra, where it seems they're using multi-dittoing to simulate a twenty-year prison sentence in just two. Saves money and chastens the wicked, or so they say. Yuck.

The next time I look up, we're driving through an exclusive neighborhood. Big houses beyond tall hedges. Mansions perched at the end of long drives, each one bigger, more impressive, and better protected than the one before it. My left-eye sensors trace guardian fields lining the tops of walls. Decorative spearheads mask sleep-gas jets. Mock ferrets squat in trees, watchful against interlopers. Of course, none of it would keep out a real pro.

The Kaolin Manor entrance looks unassuming. No garish protections. The best are unseen.

We flow straight through, then up a curving drive.

It's a big stone chateau, surrounded by meadows and old trees. A few modest outbuildings, gardens, and hedge-sheltered guest cottages can be seen, off to one side. The gardens are disappointing. Nothing special. Few of the rare specimens I'd plant, if I were rich. Then I spot an architectural anomaly—a mirrorlike dome covering the roof of one entire wing. The sanctuary that a famous recluse retired to, years ago, leaving the rest of the mansion for servants, guests, and golems. Apparently, Aeneas Kaolin takes his hermitage seriously.

There's just a white hospital van parked in front of the main house. I expected official vehicles. Police inspectors. Portable forensic labs. Normal procedure when murder is afoot.

Clearly, Ritu's notion of foul play isn't shared by the authorities. Well, that's why she called me.

A butler sends his copper-colored duplicate to open my door. Another escorts me inside. Nice treatment, seeing as how I'm not real.

I'm inside now, under a vaulting atrium. Fine wood paneling. Nice decorative touches—lots of wall-mounted helmets, shields, and pointy weapons from other ages. Clara would love this stuff, so I freeze a few picts to show her later.

Conversation wafts my way as I'm led to a book-lined library, now serving a more somber function. The splendid oak table bears a cherry-wood casket with an open lid. Somebody's dear departed, lying in state. A dozen or so human figures are in view, though just two are real—the corpse and a grieving daughter.

I should move toward Ritu, since she summoned me. But it's a platinum Kaolin-ditto who dominates the scene. Is it the same one I met earlier this morning? Must be, since it gives a nod of recognition before returning attention to a vid call—consulting with underlings and advisers, I reckon. All the onscreen images look worried. Yosil Maharal was a vital member of their organization. Some major project may be in big trouble.

Damn. I half-hoped Kaolin himself would show up for this tragic scene, taking a short ride down from that silvery dome. Maybe he's a genuine recluse, after all.

A jet black technical specialist finishes waving his wand of instruments over the casket, subjecting the cadaver to cascades of glittering light. The expert turns to Ritu Maharal.

"I have repeated all scans, Miss. Again, there is nothing to indicate your father's accident had anything to do with foul play. No toxins or debilitating drugs. No needlemarks or infusion bruises. No trace of organic interference. His body chemistry does show signs of extreme fatigue, consistent with falling asleep at the wheel before driving inadvertently over the highway viaduct where he was found. This matches the conclusion of police investigators, who went over the wrecked vehicle and found no signs of tampering. And no indication of other persons, either in or near the car. I'm sorry if this news displeases you. But accidental death appears to be the correct diagnosis."

Ritu's face seems carved from stone, her coloration almost ditto white. She keeps silent, even as a tall gray moves close to put an arm around her. It's a duplicate of her father—the one I met just a couple of hours ago—with a face resembling the corpse. Of course no man-made process can imitate the texture of real skin, durable enough to last decades, yet so worn and haggard-looking after more than half a century of cares.

ditto Maharal stares down at his real self, knowing that a second, lesser death will come soon. Duplicates can only inload memories back to the original who made them. The Template Effect. So now he's orphaned with no home base, no real brain to return to. Only a ticking expiration clock and pseudocells fast running out of *élan vital*.

In a sense, Yosil Maharal lingers on, able to contemplate his own passing. But his gray ghost will vanish in at most a few more hours.

As if sensing this, Ritu throws both arms around her daddit, squeezing tightly . . . but briefly. After a few seconds, she drops her arms and lets a matronly green lead her away. Perhaps an old nanny or family friend. Departing, Ritu averts her gaze, avoiding both fathers—the dead and the dying.

She doesn't see me.

What shall I do? Follow?

"Give her a while," a voice says.

I turn and find ditMaharal, standing close.

"Don't be concerned, Mr. Morris. My daughter is resilient. She'll be much better in half an hour or so. I know Ritu wants to talk to you."

I nod. Fine. I'm paid by the minute. Still, curiosity is my driver, whether I'm riding around in flesh or clay.

"She thinks you were murdered, Doc. Were you?"

The gray shrugs, looking rueful. "I must have sounded odd this morning, when we first met. Maybe a bit paranoid."

"You downplayed it. But I felt—"

"—that there must be something? Where there's smoke, there must be fire?" ditMaharal nodded, spreading his hands. "I was already recovering from my panic when I made this copy. Still, it felt—and feels—like emerging from a spell."

"A spell?"

"A fantasy of technology gone mad, Mr. Morris. The same fear, perhaps, that Fermi and Oppenheimer experienced when they watched the first mushroom cloud at Trinity Site. Or something like the curse of Frankenstein, long delayed, but now coming true with a vengeance."

Those words would give my original a case of the shivers. Even as a gray, I experience some visceral dread.

"You no longer feel that way?"

Maharal smiles. "Didn't I just call it a fantasy? Humanity managed to evade destruction by atom bombs and designer germs. Maybe it's best to trust that people will take on future challenges with common sense."

He's playing it coy, I think.

"Then could you please explain why you went into hiding, in the first place? Did you feel someone was after you? Why change your mind? Maybe your rig had a relapse after making you. The accident suggests sleepless anxiety, maybe panic."

Maharal's ghost-ditto ponders this for a moment, meeting my gaze— one gray to another. But before he can answer, Vic Aeneas Kaolin comes striding over, a stern look on his platinum face.

"Old friend," he tells ditMaharal. "I know this is a hard time for you. But we must think about salvaging what we can. Your final hours should be put to good use."

"What do you mean?"

"A debriefing, of course. To salvage your work for posterity."

"Ah. I see. Pressure-injecting my brain with a million meshtrodes, zapping me with gamma rays to make an ultratomograph, then sifting every pseudoneuron through a molecular strainer. It doesn't sound like a pleasant way to spend my last moments." Maharal mulls it over, working his jaw with realistic expressions of tension. And I can sympathize. "But I suppose you're right. If something can be preserved."

ditMaharal's reluctance is understandable. I sure would hate to go through stuff like that. But how else can anything be retrieved? Only the original human template can inload a duplicate's full memory. No other person or computer can substitute. If the template's missing or dead, all you can do is physically sift the copy's brain for crude sepia images— the only data that's machine-readable from golemflesh.

The rest—your consciousness Standing Wave, the core sense of self that some call the soul—is little more than useless static.

There used to be an old riddle. *Are the colors you see the same as the ones I see? When you smell a rose, are you experiencing the same heady sensations that I do, when I sniff the same flower?*

Nowadays we know the answer.

It's *No.*

We may use similar terms to describe a sunset. Our subjective worlds often correspond, correlate, and map onto each other. That makes cooperation and relationships possible, even complex civilization. Yet a person's actual sensations and feelings remain forever unique. Because a brain isn't a computer and neurons aren't transistors.

It's why telepathy can't happen. We are, each of us, singular and forever alien.

"I'll have a car take you to the lab," ditKaolin tells ditMaharal, patting the arm of his friend, as if the two were real.

"I want to be present during the debriefing," I inject, stepping in.

Kaolin isn't happy about this. Again, I spot a trembling of his elegantly sculpted hand as he frowns.

"We'll be covering sensitive company matters—"

"And some of the recovered images may shed light on what happened to that poor man." I gesture toward realMaharal, lying cold in his coffin. Left unsaid is the fact that I've been hired by the body's sole legal heir. Ritu could sue me for malpractice if I don't attend the sifting. Legally, she might prevent anyone from dissecting her father's ghost.

Kaolin considers, then nods.

"Very well. Yosil, would you go on ahead to the lab? Mr. Morris and I will come along once you've been prepped."

ditMaharal doesn't answer at first. His expression seems far away, gazing at the door where Ritu departed, minutes before.

"Um, yes? Oh, all right. For the sake of the project. And the members of our team."

He clasps Kaolin's elegant hand briefly and gives me a curt nod. When next we meet, his head will be under glass and under pressure.

Now Maharal's ghost departs toward the big atrium and the front door.

I turn back to Kaolin.

"Dr. M. mentioned having been fearful, on the run, as if someone might be hunting him."

"He *also* said the fear was unjustified," Kaolin replies. "Yosil was recovering from that paranoia when he made the ditto."

"Unless he later had a relapse . . . which could help explain the fatal accident if Maharal felt compelled to flee something, or someone." I thought for a moment. "In fact, the ditto never actually *denied* that anyone was after him. He only said the danger felt less frightening when he was made. Can you think of a reason—"

"Why anyone might want to hurt Yosil? Well, in our business there are always dangers. Fanatics who think Universal Kilns is a front for the devil. Every now and then, some nut tries to unleash holy vengeance." He snorts disdainfully. "Fortunately, there is a famous inverse relation between fanaticism and competence."

"That correlation is statistical," I point out. Antisocial behavior is my field, after all. "There are exceptions. In a large, educated population, you'll have at least a few genuine Puerters, McVeighs, and Kaufmanns—both diabolical and brainy—who prove competent enough to wreak . . ."

My voice trails off, suddenly distracted. Kaolin answers, but my attention veers.

Something's wrong.

I glance left, toward the grand hallway, following a trace—something troubling that teased the corner of one eye.

What is it?

The broad, arched corridor looks unchanged, still lined with ancient arms and trophies from historical conflicts. Yet something's amiss.

Think.

I had been dividing my attention, the way I always do, real or rox. Maharal's ditto just departed in that direction, heading for the atrium . . . where a right turn would take him out the front door for that final trip to Universal Kilns.

Only he *didn't* turn right. I think he turned left instead. It was only a glimpse, but I feel sure of it.

Is he trying to see Ritu, one last time?

No. She quit the library in the opposite direction, with her green companion. So where's the ditto heading?

On one level, it's none of my business.

The hell it isn't.

The magnate is explaining why he doesn't worry about fanatics. It sounds like a canned speech. I interrupt.

"Excuse me, Vic Kaolin. I have to check on something. I'll be back in time to ride with you to the lab."

He looks surprised, perhaps miffed, as I turn to go. The marble floor squeaks under my cheap shoes as I hurry down the hall, sparing a moment to grab one more good look at the oldtime weapons and banners. Clara will kill me if I don't memorize enough for a decent image tour.

At the atrium, I glance right. The butler and his three copies look up, interrupting their conversation. (What could the duplicates possibly have to talk about? My selves almost never have anything to say to each other.)

"Did you see ditMaharal come by here?"

"Yessir. Just a moment ago."

"Which way did he go?"

The butler points behind me, toward the rear of the mansion. "Is there anything I can do for—"

I hurry in the direction indicated. It may be a dumb impulse to give chase like this, instead of quizzing Vic Kaolin while I have the chance. If Maharal were real, his detour wouldn't bug me. I'd assume he went to the toilet. Take a pee before going on your last ride. Nothing more natural.

But he *isn't* natural. He's a thing, with no bladder and with no rights, who's been asked to walk into a room where agonizing interrogation and death await. Anyone might veer from that path. I know I have, on at least three occasions.

Striding past the grand staircase, I duck into a minor hallway lined with cloakrooms and closets. Beyond a pair of double doors, dishes clatter amid a murmur of cooks. The gray *might* have dodged through there. But sensors in my left eye discern no vibration. The big swinging doors haven't been touched for at least several minutes.

Hurrying past the kitchen, I pick up a faint scent that most normal humans barely notice or else avoid. A sweat-sweet tang of ultimate redemption.

The Recyclery.

Most of us just put our expired dittos (or leftover parts) in a sealed bin on the street for weekly pickup. But businesses that deal in high volumes need their own rendering plants to compress and filter the remains. Down a short, windowless passage stood a door few dittos pass through twice. Did Maharal go that way, preferring a quick end in the vats over the agony of brain-sifting? He didn't seem the kind to suicide over mere pain. Still, there are other possible reasons . . . like dying to keep a secret.

Seeking alternatives, I turn left to look down a broader hallway. Ahead lies a glass-covered veranda, furnished in wicker, overlooking a lawn and private woods.

A screen door is still hissing gradually shut, closing against a pneumatic damper. Deciding quickly, I hurry and push through, stepping onto a parquet balcony. To the left stands a big screened aviary filled with greenery and cooing sounds. Kaolin's famed avocation is bird-raising, especially genetically enhanced racing doves.

Not that way. To the right, steps lead down gardened slopes. Hurrying after my hunch, I'm rewarded soon by a soft noise. Footfalls, somewhere ahead.

I can sympathize if Maharal's ghost doesn't want to go through the torment of image-sifting. If he'd rather stroll under a blue sky for his last hour or two. But I work for his heir and legal owner. Anyway, if villainy murdered his original, the culprits should be held accountable. I want whatever clues lie hidden in his ceramic skull.

A flagstone path plunges past a wide meadow toward a grove of old trees. Sycamores and purple prunus, mostly. Nature's nice, when you can afford it.

There! I glimpse a moving figure. ditMaharal, all right. He leans forward, shoulders hunched, hurrying. It was just intuition before. Now I'm sure, the golem's up to something.

Only what? This trail swings by the brow of a low hill to overlook a row of small houses on the other side, lined up along a compact street, complete with sidewalks and front lawns—a quaint old suburban neighborhood, transplanted to Vic Aeneas Kaolin's east forty acres. This must be where his domestic employees live. The richer you are, the more benefits you have to provide in order to keep real servants.

Man, he sure is rich.

No sign of Maharal. My immediate concern, did he plunge into the tract? He may vanish among the houses.

I turn, scanning.

There! Half-crouched behind a hedge, he's trying to open a backyard gate.

Better not spook him. Instead of charging ahead, I creep just inside the pocket forest, staying shadowed as I work my way closer.

Only a few people are about, this time of day. An orange gardener mows someone's lawn with a noisy machine. A woman hangs laundry from a clothesline, something I never used to see in the days before kilning, when time was so precious you never had enough. Now the air's better and some folks find sun-drying worth a ditto's hour.

The woman's skin is sunburned pink—a human shade. Huh. Well, maybe she enjoys the tactile feel of pinning up wet clothes in a breeze. Sends her dittos to do other things.

■　■　■

Soft retro music flows from an open window at one end of the small neighborhood, clashing with two loud voices that rise in shrill argument from a house in the middle. The same one where Maharal's hands fumble over the back gate and finally seize the latch. Hinges squeak as he slips through—and I'm running, skidding down the forested slope, dodging trees and coming in so fast that I barely stop in time to avoid hitting the fence. Enzyme speedup warms my limbs, expending stored energy at four times rate. All right, so I'll expire a bit earlier. Thems breaks.

Maharal shut the gate after himself, so I must reach over like he did, feeling for the latch. Not the ideal way to perform a modern break-in. Normally I'd test for alarms and such. But this little neighborhood sits within Kaolin's ultra-security cordon, so why bother? Besides, I'm in a hurry.

The wood is frayed and pungent, the latch just a rusty hook. I slip into the backyard, observing crabgrass speckled with dog droppings . . . a worn baseball and glove . . . a few half-melted toy soldiers lying in the sun. Everything is homey and old-fashioned, down to the man and woman screaming in the stucco house.

"I'm finished letting people walk all over me. You'll pay, sadistic bastard!"

"For what? I have the same deadline every week, ask anybody."

"Any excuse to leave here, going crazy with screaming kids—"

"Talk about crazy—"

That ill-advised riposte brings a shriek. Through a window I glimpse a matronly figure with orange hair and pale skin, hurling crockery at a cringing man. They look real; people seldom assign a domestic spat to dittos, saving that full passion for flesh that knows it will endure ten thousand bitter tomorrows, long enough to serve up vengeance for each hurt, real or imagined.

I spot Maharal's ghost, skulking past three small boys, aged maybe four to nine, who sit in the muggy shade of a dilapidated porch, as the screen door amplifies each miserable clatter and yell. I'm surprised some roving lawyerbot hasn't been attracted by now, zeroing in to offer the kids a brochure on parental malpractice.

ditMaharal puts a sly finger to his lips, and the eldest boy nods. He must know Maharal, or else the cloud of misery is too dense for speech as the gray hurries by, heading toward the little street. It's the only way out, so I follow seconds later, imitating Maharal's gestured plea for silence.

The boys look more surprised, this time. The middle one starts to speak . . . then the eldest grabs his arm, using both hands to twist in opposite directions, raising cries of pain. Instantly, all three are embroiled in flying punches, emulating the violence indoors.

My grays imprint Albert's conscience, so I hesitate, wondering if I should intervene . . . Then I spot something both weird and reassuring about the two who are closest. *They're dittos!* Despite a caucasian-beige coloration, the skin texture's artificial. But why put kid-duplicates through a cruelly simulated summer afternoon? Surely the memories won't be inloaded.

Sounds perverted. Make a mental note to look into this later. But it gives me an excuse to leave, jogging down a narrow drive past someone's cherished restoration of an old Pontiac. Why would a scientist's ghost spend his last hours skulking through a servants' enclave, rife with midget soap operas? My concentration is broken by gratitude for my own childhood as I hasten around the corner of a tall hedge, only to find—

Maharal!

The gray stands in front of me . . . smiling . . . aiming a weapon with a flared nozzle.

No time to think. Suck a deep breath! Put your head down and charge!

A roar fills my universe.

What happens next depends on what he just shot me with—

5

Clay Station

. . . or how Tuesday's second gray begins a rough day . . .

Damn.

I'm always grumpy getting up off the warming tray . . . grabbing paper garments from a rack and slipping them over limbs still glowing with ignition enzymes, knowing I'm copy-for-a-day.

Of course I remember doing this a thousand times. Still, it always feels like getting a long list of nasty chores, taking risks you'd never put your protobody through. I start this pseudolife filled with premonitions of a lesser death, dark and unmourned.

Ugh. What put me in this mood? Could it be Ritu's news? A reminder that *real* death still lurks for us all?

Well, shrug it off! Life's still the same as it was in the old days.

Sometimes you're the grasshopper.

Sometimes an ant.

■ ■ ■

I watched gray number one head off to meet Miss Maharal. He took the Vespa, with today's greenie riding on the saddle behind him.

That left one scooter for me to use alone. Seems fair. Number one gets to see Ritu and snoop around the affairs of a gazillionaire. Meanwhile, I must go visit the great witch of Studio Neo. At least I get to have my own transport.

realAlbert turns away, shuffling out of the kiln room with nary a backward glance. Well, he needs to lie down. Rest the body. Keep it fit so we dupes can inload sometime tonight. I don't feel snubbed. Much. If you've gotta be clay, it's good to be gray. At least there are realistic pleasures to enjoy—

—like swerving through traffic, surprising stolid yellow-striped truckers as I cut in front of them, always alert for the telltale buzz of my cop-detector and making sure not to inconvenience any real people. Aggravating dits can be sport, just so long as each violation stays below the five-point threshold programmed into the publicams lining every street. (The threshold where they drop privacy constraints and form a grand posse.) I once racked up eleven four-pointers in a day, without triggering a single fine!

This little Turkmeni scooter doesn't have as much power as the Vespa, but it's agile and durable. Cheap, too. I make a note to order three more. Anyway, it's risky having only two scoots on hand. What if I suddenly need to make an army, like happened last May? How will I rush a dozen red or purple copies of myself where they're needed? By dinobus?

Nell obediently jots down my note, but she won't put through a buy order till realAlbert wakes. Neurons okay all big purchases. Clay can only suggest.

Well, I'll *be* Albert tomorrow. If I inload. If I make it home. Which shouldn't be too problematic, I guess. Meetings with the maestra are wearing, but seldom fatal.

Slowing down for a light now. Stopping. Taking a moment to glance west, toward Odeon Square. Fresh memories of last night's desperate flight and narrow escape still perturb my Standing Wave, even if it was only a green who suffered so.

I wonder who the waiter was. The one who helped me get away.

Light's changed. Go! Maestra hates it when you're late.

■   ■   ■

Studio Neo, just ahead. Charming place. It fills what used to be a huge windowless urban mall. Nowadays shopping is either a chore—you ask House to arrange deliveries—or else you do it for pleasure, strolling in person along tree-lined avenues like Realpeople Lane, where balmy venturi breezes flow all year round. Either way, it's hard to picture why our parents did it in sunless grottos. A fluorescent-lit catacomb is no proper world for human beings.

So now malls are set aside for the new servant class. Us clayfolk.

Jitneys and scooters zip around the vast parking structure, conveying fresh dittos to clients all over town. And not just any dittos. Most bear specialized colors. Snow white for sensuality. Ebony for undiluted intellect. A particular scarlet that's oblivious to pain . . . and another that experiences everything with fierce intensity. Few of these creatures return to their point of origin when the *élan* cells run down. Their rigs don't expect them back for memory inloading.

Most Neo customers *do* return the scooters, however. To reclaim the deposit.

I park the Turkomen in a coded space set aside for folks like me—ditto intermediaries traveling on business, conveying important information between real people. Grays get priority, so the more luridly colored step aside as I enter the main arcade. Most do it reflexively, holding doors for me, almost as if I were human. But a few whites give way grudgingly, casting impertinent glares.

Well, what do you expect from whites? Pleasure is partly a matter of ego. Their kind needs self-importance in order to function.

Studio Neo occupies all four layers of the old mall, filling the grand atrium with a myriad holographic glows—an emporium of creative effort, illuminated by the garish logos of more than a hundred pushy production companies, each of them aspiring for pinnacle position in this anthill—a place up at the top the pyramid, where I'm heading right now.

The hungriest and most ambitious producers station dittowares right next to the escalators, offering free samples.

"Try me now and take home a special memory . . ." croons a pale

form in a diaphanous gown, her figure enhanced in ways that real tissue couldn't possibly support. *"Then let us home-deliver. Your rig could enjoy me in person tomorrow!"*

Tomorrow, *she* will be sludge in a tank. But I don't say it. Manners, inherited from simpler days of youth, make me say, *"No, thanks"*— wasting breath on a creature who couldn't care less.

"Had a rough day?" another one chants, this one exaggeratedly male, rippling in places where no natural man ever rippled—that is, outside the pages of a comic book. *"Maybe your rig will inload you anyway, if you bribe him with something unique to remember. Try me and find out how good it gets!"*

Or how weird it gets. No way to tell, of course, what kind of flesh this creature's soul-imprint came from, whether a courtesan or a gigolo. The most aggressive or compliant of each kind tend to be crossovers, overcompensating for their upbringings, with relish.

This time I manage to pass without comment, riding the escalator to better precincts.

Some of the second-story firms offer specialized golem blanks. Put your mind into a toothy reptile, or a dolphinlike form to go deep-diving. Or go partying in a body with made-to-order parts. Some have hands like Swiss Army knives. I sometimes buy accessories from a discreet technical boutique, choosing enhancements for dittos sent on dangerous assignments. Pal shops here too, experimenting with ever more outré golems. He'd prefer that *all* his memories come that way, and none from his ravaged fragment of a natural body.

The next tout to approach isn't selling sex. A gray like me, she's dressed in conservative linen paper, fashioned like a TV doctor's costume, all the way down to the endoscope hanging from her trim neck.

"Pardon the intrusion, sir. May I ask if you've been practicing *prudent imprinting?*"

I have to blink; it sounds familiar. "Oh, right. You mean protecting my real self from diseases that a ditto—"

"—might bring home and transmit through inloading. Yes, sir. Have you given any thought to how dangerous it can be to reclaim a golem that's been who-knows-where in the course of a day? Exposed to everything from viruses to memic toxins?"

She offers a slim pamphlet and suddenly I remember a story in the news recently, played up mostly for humor, about people who evidently think we're living in the bad old plague days of the Fizzle War.

"I try to stay clean. If there's any question, I inload without touching my rig."

"Memic toxins don't require physical contact," the imitation doctor insists. "They can spread via inloaded *memories*."

I shake my head. "We'd be told if any such thing were—"

"There have been outbreaks in more than a dozen cities, around the globe." Her professional demeanor slips, pushing the pamphlet. "They're hiding the truth!"

They? A conspiracy fan, then. Talk about memic toxins! Could all of the agencies responsible for public safety—and all of their employees—collude to prevent the public from learning of a new plague? Even that wouldn't suffice today, with so many clever amateurs around. Then there are the Henchman prizes, made alluring to draw confessions out of the most trusted lieutenant.

"An interesting hypothesis," I murmur, backing away. "But then why haven't the free-nets—"

"The toxin designers are clever. Varying symptoms from town to town! The free-nets correlate incidents, rumors, anecdotes. Nevertheless—"

Continuing to back up, I gratefully let the up escalator catch my heel, yanking me aboard the moving steps while feigning an apologetic-polite smile. The "doctor" stares after me for a moment, then swivels to approach another passerby.

Maybe later I'll ask Nell to do a sift search on the topic of "memic plagues." Till then, call it another aberrant entertainment served up by Studio Neo.

Now I'm passing the really classy establishments. "Scenarios Unlimited" will send you an expert interviewer—an ebony, zinglemindedly dedicated to create a script to match your budget and favorite fantasy. Then he'll return with props and a complete cast of characters to play out any scene, from high literature to your darker dreams.

"Proxy Adventures" will take your imprinted-but-unbaked copy to some far corner of the world where they'll kiln-activate it, put it through a day of frenetic escapades, then return the flash-frozen cranium in perfect condition, so you recall everything. A twenty-four-hour adventure, ready to serve.

Then there are specialists offering services no one imagined before golemtech. Almost anything that's illegal to do to another human in flesh can be done to a ditto—though often with with fees and a perversion tax.

No wonder Inspector Blane hates this place. It's one thing to contract out your duplicates for honest labor. Unions fought it and lost, and now millions earn a living in several places at once, doing whatever they happen to be good at, from janitorial service to nuclear reactor mainte-nance. A fair market offers top expertise to all, at affordable prices.

But expertise in *entertainment*? Brought down from the silver screen, liberated from the boob tube, leaping off the pages of pulpy romance novels, made tactile and personal . . . They say that when the Web started, the heaviest single use was for porn. Same here. Only now it walks and talks back to you. It can do whatever you want.

■ ■ ■

Wait a sec.

It's the phone. I pick up in time to hear Nell pass the call to my real self.

Pal's half-paralyzed face fills the little display, surrounded by wish sensors to command his magic wheelchair. He wants me to come over.

My rig sounds grumpy and tired. He won't do another imprint.

"I've got three dits running around on errands," he tells Pal. *"One will drop by, if time allows."*

Three? The green won't be up to handling Pal. And gray number one has to see Ritu Maharal about her murdered dad. There's a chance he may even meet and question the real Vic Kaolin—something worth tell-ing Clara about, when she gets back from her war.

So it's up to me. If Wammaker lets me escape early, I'll go listen to Pal's latest wild-eyed theory or scheme. Crum. I can already feel my short "life" getting used up.

■ ■ ■

Top floor, where rooftop heliports give quick access to rich clients. Where illustrious producers serve fine coffee and fancy hors d'oeuvres, even to visiting grays! Here, elegant shops let you hire first-rate actors to play convincing roles in bodies molded to resemble anyone across time. There's a penalty when a ditto doesn't resemble its rig, but it's small when no fraud is involved. Not that producers refuse a little fraud, now and then.

Wealthy clients also come here to arrange extravaganzas. Once, some-one hired Clara's reserve infantry platoon, off-duty, to be extras in a bloody rendition of Caligula's final orgy-slaughter. She snuck me in to watch the performance from behind a purple curtain. The reenactment was vivid, lurid, and maybe even educational in its attention to historical detail. The swordfights were superb. Clara's golem died especially well.

Still, I didn't care for the show.

"I'm glad you feel that way," she agreed. In fact, not one member of her outfit inloaded memories from that evening's brutal carnage. It kind of makes you proud of our boys and girls in khaki.

■　■　■

I'm still more than twenty meters from the elegant portico of Wammaker's when a cowled figure catches my eye, gesturing from the shadows.

"Mr. Morris. Good of you to come."

Taking a step closer, I recognize the ditto under the hood. Maestra's executive assistant, her face a conservative gray tone, perfectly matching her attire.

"Will you come with me, please?"

She beckons and I follow . . . away from Wammaker's. "Our meeting concerns sensitive topics, better discussed elsewhere," she explains, handing me a cowled robe like her own. "Please put this on."

If I were real, I might worry. Could the maestra be planning some ornate revenge for my breezy behavior toward her earlier? But then, so what? I'm just a ditto.

I put the robe on and follow.

A small service elevator takes us down, back to the low-rent floors of the old mall. Doors open and my guide heads straight for a nondescript storefront with opaque windows, bearing the name RENEWAL ASSOCIATES. I follow her into a realm of hanging fabrics that shimmer with piezoluminescence, wafting in tailored breezes. Some effort's even gone to growing indoor plants that provide a welcoming atmosphere. Mostly simple ferns and ficus. But your eye is meant to be drawn elsewhere, to holo posters of Gineen and her best affiliates—women and men whose copies offer sybaritic pleasures to those weary of mere sex.

Off the waiting room stand shaded booths where clients may consult privately with special advisers. Still, it's not as elegant as Wammaker's. The maestra must be branching out.

"Please wait," the assistant says, pointing to a straightback wooden chair . . . no doubt a precious antique, and uncomfortable as well. I stand again as soon as she departs. My golem blanks have relax-a-stilt joints. Sitting is redundant.

Of course I'll be kept waiting, so I pull out a cheap reading plaque and dial up the *Journal of Antisocial Proclivities.* Since Ritu Maharal proclaimed that her father was murdered, I thought about looking up homicide. (I wonder how gray number one is doing right now. Have I reached any conclusions yet?) But after passing through Studio Neo, my thoughts wander toward another problem. Decadence.

Are the new puritans right? Is golemtech hardening our hearts?

Clara calls this place a "soul-callus."

"Today we can wallow in depravity without paying for it in disease or hangovers," she said only last week. "The oldest profession's been updated for a new age, without prisons, prudity, or any need for empathy. What a deal."

Me, I'm usually less cynical. Life is better in lots of ways. Wealthier. More tolerant. No one cares what shade of brown your real skin is.

But my grays do vary a bit from one another and this one feels a dour suspicion that Clara may be right.

Blinking, I notice that the reading plaque already glows with a selected journal article. It must've done an iris-dilation interest scan while I pondered gloomy thoughts. (Who *says* dittos don't have a subconscious?)

Sublimation of the Immortality Impulse: A Return to Necromancy?

Ouch. What a title for a scientific paper! Not my usual cuppa tea. Still it's intriguing. I wonder . . .

"Mr. Morris?"

It's the assistant. I expected to be snubbed longer than that. Maybe Wammaker really is worried about something this time.

Looking up, I notice the assistant's gray dittobody has blue eyes.

"The maestra will see you now."

6

It's Not Easy Being Green

. . . or how Tuesday's third ditto discovers
sibling rivalry . . .

I hate getting off the warming tray, throwing paper garments over limbs that still glow with ignition enzymes.

Not only am I a copy today, I'm the greenie.

Damn.

After a thousand times, it still feels like I'm being punished. Given a long list of nasty chores. Sent to take all sorts of risks you'd never put Lord Protobody through.

I start this pseudolife filled with dark feelings.

Ugh. What a mood. Archie must *really* be tired to start me off with a Standing Wave as gloomy as this. Any worse and I might've been a frankie . . .

Well, shrug it off! Today you're an ant.

And green, at that. Leave philosophy to your betters.

■   ■   ■

Well, last night *another* green took on Beta's henchdits, and won. A hero-duplicate, who slogged through hell to bring back vital news. So a green can matter! Even if today's job is to fetch groceries, clean toilets, mow the lawn, and other horrors.

Grays get fancy realtime recorders. But I gotta do quick dumps into an old microtape ring. Post hoc. Don't know why I bother. If Archie wants to know what I did today, he can inload and find out.

■   ■   ■

I rode into town behind gray number one, keeping both eyes tight shut while he swerved like a maniac, risking both of our carcasses, and nearly wrecked our last Vespa. Schmuck.

Left him in a park, waiting to meet the UK limo they're sending over. He'll see the beautiful Ritu soon, and talk to Vic Kaolin, and maybe investigate a murder.

And later, maybe tonight, realAlbert will get lonesome. He'll go thaw the sybarite Clara left for us in her freezer. I felt a wave of irrational jealousy about that. A temptation to drive over to her houseboat and use it myself!

Of course I didn't. Her dit would take one look at me and refuse to waste itself on the coarse senses of a green. Anyway, what's the point? If I inload, I'll rejoin Albert and share it all in realflesh. And when Clara returns from the front, I'll share that reunion, too.

So I went about my chores. Visited the market, adding some fresh items to the normal delivery—fruits and deli stuff, plus a gourmet dish or two. Should arrive by the time Archie wakes from his nap. I hope I'll like the herring. It's Danish.

Dropped by the bank and updated my level three passcodes. Everyone does a monthly update in person, with biometric and chemical scans to verify you're you. But for weeklies a ditto will do. No one can fake a personal Standing Wave. Anyway, it's been years since the Big Heist. Some analysts think cyber crime is already passé.

That may be. But villainy still worries citizens. It comes up as a top priority every election. There must be nearly a hundred real cops in this city alone. If Yosil Maharal was murdered, that makes twelve homicides in the state so far this year. And summer's barely half over.

I don't fear being unemployed soon.

■   ■   ■

Oh, the phone rang while I was shopping. It was Pallie, needing some attention again.

Albert grumbled. *"I've got three dits running around on errands. One will drop by, if time allows."*

Three dits?

Gray number one is busy with Ritu Maharal and Vic Kaolin—a big case, maybe a real moneymaker. Gineen Wammaker may tie up gray number two all day.

Care to bet *I'll* be sent to hear Pal's latest conspiracy theory?

Crum. What's a greenie for?

■   ■   ■

Had to pick up the lawn mower from fix-it shop. Repairs cost eight-fifty, plus abatement fees for the old gas engine. Tied it securely to the back of the Vespa, but that messed the scooter's balance. Nearly cracked up in a fast curve on the way home. Got a five-point violation, too. Crap.

At least the mower started right up. (Mitch, the repair guy, knows his stuff. He was there in person, this time.) Soon I had the lawn edged better than that orange-striped "gardener" everyone else in the neighborhood hires. Things grow on my tiny patch of earth. Roses. Fresh carrots and berries. I like growing things, same as Clara needs to hear water lapping on the hull of her houseboat.

Next, tackle the pile of dishes in the sink, then toilets. Might as well clean the whole damn house while I'm at it. Except vacuuming. Lord Archie's gotta nap.

Ho-hum.

Some days I weigh existential matters. Simple ones a green can grasp. Like, should I volunteer NOT to inload tonight? I mean, why remember this banality? Albert's already experienced nearly a hundred subjective years, counting golem recollections. Some techies put a theoretical max at five centuries. So why not conserve?

I've debated this with myself lots of times, and recall always deciding to inload. Well, duh! Only those dittos who chose continuity became part of continuing memory. But Nell says more than a hundred and eighty of my copies chose oblivion instead. Dispirited deputy-selves who endured dreary days that I'm better off forgetting.

Heck, there are days I had *in person* that I'd erase, if I could. An ancient problem, I guess. At least nowadays you get a little choice in the matter.

Pausing at Archie's work screen, I looked over our ongoing cases— about a dozen routine investigations, tracked by priority and progress charts. Most can be pursued by Net—making remote enquiries, sifting data from public sources, or persuading the owners of private streetcams to share their posse archives without a court order. Sometimes I send out my own spy-wasps to follow suspects around town. I couldn't afford to stay in business if everything had to be done in person, or even by golem-duplicate.

Half of the cases involve my specialty—snaring copyright violators. Pros like Beta offer endless aggravation, but fortunately most rip-offs are done by amateurs. The same goes for face thieves, who send out dittos with illegally forged features, pretending they were roxed from other people. Troublemaking kids, mostly. Catch 'em. Fine 'em. Teach 'em to behave.

Then there are jealous spouses—a private eye's standby, since the days of ragtime.

Some modern marriages are complex, admitting new partners by joint consent. Most folks prefer old-fashioned monogamy. But what does that mean nowadays? If a husband sends a ditto to fool around while he's busy at work, does that constitute fantasy, flirtation, or outright infidelity? If a wife rents a little whitey to get through a lonely afternoon, is that prostitution, or a bit of harmless diddling with an appliance?

Most people think flesh-on-flesh still feels best. But clay can't get pregnant or pass disease. It lets you rationalize, too. Some partners draw the line at inloading memories after a dittosex affair. If it isn't remembered, it didn't happen. No recall, no foul.

But if you can't remember it, what was the point?

All the complications can get confusing for creatures with jealous whims that formed in the Stone Age. Anyway, hurt feelings aren't my concern, just facts. The crux is that civilization fails without accountability. What people do with it is their own concern.

Scanning the screen, I see I'll need four dits tomorrow. Two just for stakeouts and tails. The freezer is well stocked with blanks, but our scooter situation is dire.

Onscreen I see that gray number two just requested more Turkomens. I prefer Vespas, but who listens to a green?

Looking around the house, I see more cleaning to do. Pencils to sharpen and notes to file. More grotty chores, so the real me can spend precious fleshtime being creative.

I'd let out a long sigh . . . if this body were equipped for it.

To hell with all this. I'm going to the beach!

7

Price of Perfection

. . . gray number two gets an offer he can't refuse . . .

The maestra has guests.

Four are females, identical, with frizzy pink hair and earthen-red skin so dark it's almost umber. They look nervous, agitated. One stares constantly at a vid-screen, nodding and grunting. A sluglike string of flesh seems to ooze out the side of her head, clamping a pseudopod onto an electronic sensor pad.

She's *jacked in,* of all things! Sending and receiving straight from her clay brain into the Net—direct linkage, digital to neuroanalog—a nasty, unwholesome process that can fry you silly.

The remaining guest is male, modeled on an archetype who must be painfully slender in person. Following a fashion trend, this ditto avoids the stodgy old standard colors that were prescribed during the first generation of kilning.

His skin is *plaid.*

Ouch. I can barely make out his face amid the visual noise. Instead of paper garments, he wears lavish cloth. And the woven pattern of his shirt and pants actually matches the skin dye job. Expensive styling for a ditto!

Gineen Wammaker steps forward in delectable person, her real flesh nearly as pale as one of her pleasure roxies. Only flashing green eyes give away her inner nature as a fierce businesswoman who demolishes competitors without mercy. She takes my facsimile hand in her real ones.

"How good of you to send a gray so quickly, Mr. Morris. I know how busy you are, and how focused your profession requires you to be."

In other words, she forgives me, even though I really should have come in person. Still, Wammaker's sarcasm is milder than usual. Something's fishy, all right.

"I hope the bonus I sent shows adequately my gratitude for your part in shutting down the pirate copying facility."

I haven't seen any bonus. Maybe she wired it while I waited outside. Typical. Anything to keep you off-balance.

"It's a joy to be of service, Maestra." I bow and she inclines her head slightly, letting golden locks spill over bare shoulders. We don't fool each other a bit. Ironically, that's a basis for respect.

"But I grow inattentive. Let me introduce my associates. Vic Manuel Collins and Queen Irene."

The male is closer. We shake hands and I can tell his gaudy decorations mask the texture of a standard gray ditto. As for his title; "Vic" used to mean something. But the term has grown swank and overused among the idle rich, most of whom were never venture capitalists, or anything useful at all.

Just one of the umber-colored females steps forward, acknowledging my presence but offering no smile, nor a hand to shake. "Queen" is another modern ambiguity. I'll wait and see if my suspicions are verified.

Gineen offers seats, plush and body-conforming. A candy-striped servdit—one-half scale—offers refreshments. Being gray, I can taste-sample a powdery Zairian truffle that explodes into aromatic dust at the back of my throat. A gift for Albert to remember when I inload. Still, Wammaker is showing off, being lavish with visiting dupies. Part of her appeal, I suppose.

Sitting now, I can see past the shoulder of the umber rox who is jacked in, fixing her attention on a pict-screen. It shows a large room where still more red dittos come and go rapidly—all of them copies of the same basic person-image, though some are scaled way down to one-third size or less. At least a dozen hover around a single figure in the middle, hard to make out amid the throng. There's a lot of machinery—kiln apparatus and life-support gear.

"I asked you here, Mr. Morris, to discuss a little matter of technology and industrial espionage."

I turn back to Wammaker.

"Maestra? I specialize in tracking people—both clay and flesh—mostly to uncover copyright violations and—"

My host lifts a hand. "We suspect certain technological innovations have been hoarded. *Significant* breakthroughs, that could threaten to make copyright meaningless, are being monopolized clandestinely."

"I see. That sounds illegal."

"It most certainly would be. Technologies are most perilous when exploited in secret."

My thoughts churn. It may be illegal, but why tell *me*? I'm no cop or tech-sleuth.

"Who do you suspect of hoarding?"

"Universal Kilns Incorporated."

Blinking, I hardly know where to begin.

"But . . . they pioneered the field of soulistics."

"I do know that, Mr. Morris." Her smile is indulgent.

"They also benefit most from an open and orderly market."

"Naturally. In fact, UK continues to engage in normal commercial research, coming up with gradual improvements in the copiers they sell. Technical details about these improvements *can* be kept confidential temporarily, till patents are filed. Even so, they have a legal duty to warn people if some major innovation threatens to fundamentally alter our culture, or economy, or world."

"Fundamentally alter"? Creepy words that make me curious as hell. And yet, one fact is paramount—I shouldn't be holding this conversation.

"That may be, Maestra. But right now I have to tell you—"

The plaid-skinned male interrupts with a voice that's rather deep for such a wiry frame.

"We've been tracking leaked information from inside those shiny domes at UK. They're up to something, possibly a big change in the way people make and operate golems."

Curiosity gets the better of me. "What sort of change?"

Vic Collins takes a wry expression on his garishly cross-shatched face. "Can you guess, Mr. Morris? What do *you* figure might transform the way folks use this modern convenience?"

"I . . . can think of several possibilities, but—"

"Please. Stretch yourself. Give us an example or two."

Our eyes meet and I wonder, *What's he up to?*

Some people are known for imprinting imaginative grays, capable of creative thinking. Is that what all this is about? A test of rapid reasoning, outside my organic brain? If so, I'm game.

"Well . . . suppose people could somehow absorb *each other's* memories. Instead of just imprinting and inloading between different versions of yourself, you'd be able to swap days, weeks, or even a lifetime of knowledge and experience with someone else. I guess it could wind up being like telepathy, allowing greater mutual understanding . . . the gift of seeing ourselves as others see us. It is an old dream that's—"

"—also quite impossible," the dark red womandit cuts in. "Each human's cerebral Standing Wave is unique, its hyperfractal complexity beyond all digital modeling. Only the same neural template that created a particular duplicate wave can later reabsorb that copy. A rox can only go home to its own rig."

Of course that's common knowledge. Still, I'm disappointed. The dream of perfect human understanding is hard to give up.

"Go on, please," Gineen Wammaker urges in a soft voice. "Try again, Albert."

"Um. Well, for years folks have wished for a way to imprint *at long range.* To sit at home and copy your Standing Wave into a ditto blank that's far away. Today, both bodies have to lie right next to each other, linked with giant cryo-cables. Something about noise-to-bandwidth ratios . . ."

"Yes, that's a common complaint," Gineen muses. "Say you have urgent, hands-on business to do in Australia. Your quickest bet is to make a fresh ditto, pack it into an express mail rocket, and hope it splashes gently on target. Even the quickest round trip, returning the ditto's skull packed in ice, can take all day. How much better if you could just transmit your standing wave over a photonic cable, imprint a blank that's already on the scene, look around a bit, then zip the altered wave right back again!"

"It sounds like teleportation. You could go anywhere—even the Moon—almost instantly . . . assuming you shipped some blanks there in advance. But is this really needed? We already have robotic telepresence over the Net—"

Queen Irene laughs.

"Telepresence! Using goggles to peer through a faraway set of tin-eyes? Manipulating a clanking machine to walk around for you? Even with full retinal and tactile feedback, that hardly qualifies as *hands-on*. And speed-of-light delays are frightful."

This "queen" and her sarcasm are starting to bug me.

"Is that it? Has Universal Kilns achieved long-range imprinting? The airlines will hate it. And what's left of the unions."

Hell, I can see aspects that *I'd* loathe, too. Maybe you could teleport anywhere in minutes. But cities would lose their individual charm. Instead of local experts and artisans holding sway, each town would wind up having the same waiters, janitors, hairdressers, and so on. The best of every skill and profession, duplicated a gazillion-fold and spread all over the world. No one else would have a job!

(Envision some New York super private eye opening a branch office here, stocking it daily with flawless gray duplicates, raking in fat fees while he sits in a penthouse overlooking Central Park. I'd have to go on the purple wage. Get some time-killing hobby. Or go back to school. Ack.)

Obviously, the maestra doesn't fear competition.

"If only that were the breakthrough at hand," she comments wistfully. "Tele-dittoing would open up major business opportunities for me, globally. Alas, that's not the innovation we're talking about. Or not the most worrisome one. Do try again."

Damn, what a bitch. Riddles are just the sort of delicious torment Gineen Wammaker specializes in. Even knowing this, I'm tempted to keep showing off.

But first there's a matter of professional ethics to settle.

"Look, I really think I ought to inform you that—"

"Lifespan," says Vic Collins.

"I beg your pardon?"

"What if a ditto body"—he gestures at his own—"could be made to last more than a day? Possibly *much* more."

Pause. Ponder it. This possibility hadn't occurred to me.

I choose words carefully. "The . . . whole basis of kilning—the reason it's practical—is that a golembody carries all of its own energy, right from the start."

"Stored as super molecules in a clay-colloidal substrate. Yes, go on."

"So there's no need to imitate the *complexity* of real life. Ingestion, digestion, circulation, metabolism, waste removal, and all that. Science is centuries away from duplicating what evolution took a billion years to create—the subtle repair systems, the redundancy and durability of genuine organic . . ."

"Nothing like that is required for longer duration," answers Collins. "Just a way to *recharge* the supermolecules in each pseudocell, restoring enough energy for another day . . . then another, and so on."

Reluctantly, I nod. Clara said that military dittos come packed with fuel implants, letting a few versions last several days. But that's still living off storage. *Recharging* would be quite another matter. A breakthrough, all right.

"How many times . . . how long can a ditto . . . ?"

"Be renewed? Well, it depends on wear and tear. As you say, even high-priced blanks have little self-repair capability. Entropy grinds down the unwary. But the chief short-term problem—how to keep a roxbody going one more day at a time—may be solved."

"A dubious solution," mutters the umber-colored Queen Irene. "Long-lasting dittos could diverge from their human prototype, making it harder to inload memories. Goals may wander. They might even start caring more about their own survival than how to serve the continuity being that created them."

I blink, confused by her terminology. *Continuity being?*

Glancing left, I see her identical sisdit, who remains jacked into a remote terminal, staring at a flatvid screen. Portrayed there, I glimpse over a dozen interchangeable workers, all the same unique crimson shade, swarming around a huge, pale figure, like worker bees jostling around—

Ah. I get it. *Queen* Irene. Pallie told me about this, taking dittoing to its next logical stage. Still, witnessing it makes me shudder.

"There could be other repercussions," Vic Collins adds. "The whole social contract may be upended, if our suspicions are correct."

"That's what we want *you* to investigate, Mr. Morris," Gineen Wammaker concludes.

"Are you proposing industrial espionage?" I ask warily.

"No." She shakes her head. "We don't seek to steal any technologies, only to verify their existence. That much is perfectly legal. With confirmation, we can then sue Universal Kilns under one of the transparency laws. For hoarding, if nothing else."

I stare at her. This is preposterous, on about a dozen levels.

"You honor me with your trust, Maestra. But as I told you, tech-sleuthing is just a sideline for me. There are real experts."

"Whom we find less suitable than you."

I'll bet. What you're asking skirts a razor's edge away from illegal. An expert would know how to keep on the safe side of that border. I might make one mistake and wind up in hock to UK, paying off a criminal-tort lien till the next ice age.

Fortunately, there's an easy way out of this.

"I am flattered, Maestra. But the biggest reason I can't take this assignment is a possible conflict of interest. You see, even as we speak, another gray of mine is at Universal Kilns, consulting about another matter."

Expecting disappointment or anger, I see only amusement in Wammaker's eyes. "We're already aware of this. There were newscams and other spy-eyes all over the Teller Building this morning, remember? I saw Ritu Maharal pick you up in a UK limo. Putting that together with public reports of her father's untimely death, I find it simple to imagine what your other gray is discussing, right now at Kaolin Mansion."

At Kaolin Mansion? I thought gray number one was going to UK headquarters. These people know more about my business than I do!

"ditto Morris, there's a way to insulate you and your rig from legal jeopardy for conflict of interest. Nowadays, it's possible for the left hand *not* to know what the right hand is doing, if you get what I mean."

Unfortunately, I think I do.

There goes my hope of an afterlife.

"It's really quite simple," says Vic Collins. "All we have to do is—"

He stops, interrupted as a phone rings.

It's *my* phone, chattering an urgent rhythm.

The maestra looks miffed, and rightly so. Nell knows I'm in a meeting. If my house computer thinks the call is so damn important, she ought to wake Archie.

I grunt an apology, flipping the wrist plate over one ear.

"Yes?"

"Albert? It's Ritu Maharal. I—I can't see you. Don't you have vid?"

Pause a sec. But none of my other selves will answer, so I must.

"This phone is a cheap strap-on. I'm just a gray, Ritu. Anyway, don't you already have one of me—"

"Where are *you?"* she demands. Something in her voice makes me sit up. It sounds like grief, giving way to rising panic.

"Aeneas is waiting in the car, getting impatient. He expected you and my . . . father's ditto to join him. But you both vanished!"

"What do you mean, vanished? How could they . . ."

Now I realize—she thinks I'm *that* gray! The confusion could be cleared up with a few words, but I don't want to cue in Gineen, or her weird friends. So what *can* I say?

Just in time, another voice cuts in, a bit groggy. It's Archie, roused from his nap again.

"Ritu? It's me, Albert Morris. Are you saying that my gray is missing? And your father's too?"

I flip-shut the phone. My first priority must go to the clients here in front of me—even if I won't be working for them in a minute or two.

Silence reigns. Finally, Wammaker leans forward, her golden hair spilling past pale shoulders to her famed decolletage.

"Well, Mr. Morris? About our offer. We need to know what you're thinking."

I take a deep breath, knowing it will hasten the metabolism of my fast-draining pseudocells, bringing slightly closer an extinction that can only be forestalled by making it home tonight. Home, to rejoin my original with what I learn today. And yet, I already know Wammaker's plan— a way that I might legally spy for her without conflict of interest. It requires that I—this gray doppelganger—sacrifice all hope of survival, for the good of more important beings.

No, it's even worse than that. What if I refuse? Can she let me leave, knowing that I *might* report this meeting to Vic Kaolin? Sure, I post a PI confidentiality bond for all customers. I'd never break a patron's confidence. But the paranoid maestra could decide not to risk it, since UK can buy my bond for pocket change.

To be safe, she'll destroy this body of mine, content to pay Albert triple damages.

And he'll take the cash, too. Who bothers to avenge a dit?

Wammaker and her guests watch me, awaiting an answer.

Looking past them, I seek visual comfort in something green and growing—indoor plants that the maestra of Studio Neo has scattered casually about her meeting chamber, to give it a homey feel.

"I think . . ."

"Yes?"

Her famous indecent smile pulls at something dark inside you. Inside even clay.

Take another deep breath.

"I think your ficus looks a bit dry. Have you tried giving it more water?"

8

Feats of Clay
. . . Tuesday's greenie finds his faith . . .

Moonlight Beach is one of my favorite spots. I go there with Clara whenever the crowds let up, especially if we have tourism coupons that are about to expire.

Of course, it's set aside for archies. All the best beaches are. I've never been here as a green before . . . unless some of my missing dittos vanished the same way I did today. By throwing away all hope and playing hookey.

Parking the scooter in a public rack, I hiked to the bluff edge for a look, hoping to find the place half-empty. That's when rules relax, archies feel less territorial, and coloreds like me can safely visit.

Tuesday's a weekday. That used to make a difference, when I was a kid.

But no such luck. People swarmed across every open area with blankets, umbrellas, and beach toys. I spied a few bright orange lifeguards, padding about with webbed arms and feet, puffing their massive air sacs while patrolling for danger. Everyone else was some shade of human-brown, from dark chocolate to pale as sand.

If I set foot down there, I'd stand out like a sore thumb.

Peering south past a distant fluttering marker, I saw the rocky spit that's set aside for my own kind. A brightly tinted mob, crammed together at the point where rip tides and jagged outcrops make things dicey for real flesh. No lifeguards ventured down there, just a few yellow-striped cleaners, equipped with hooks to dispose of the unlucky. Anyway, who wants to waste beach time on an imitation? It's hard enough getting a reservation to come in person.

Suddenly, I felt resentful of all the rules . . . the waiting lists and tourism allotments . . . just to spend a little time at the shore. A century ago, you could do what you wished and go where you liked.

That is, if you were rich and white, a small inner voice reminded me. *The whitish-brown of a ruling elite.*

The mere idea of racism seems bizarre today. Yet each generation has problems. As a kid, I endured food rationing. Wars were fought over fresh water. Now we suffer afflictions of plenty. Underemployment, the purple wage, state-subsidized hobby-frenzy, and suicidal ennui. There are no more quaint villages or impoverished natives. But that means having to share all of Earth's fine places with nine billion fellow sightseers—and another ten to twenty billion golems.

"Go ahead, brother. Make a statement."

The voice broke my gloomy reverie. I turned to see another greenie, standing off to one side of the trail. Archies and their families ignored him as they passed, though he brandished a placard flowing with bright letters:

Compassion is color-blind.
Look at me. I exist. I feel.

The ditto grinned, meeting my gaze and gesturing toward Moonlight Beach.

"Go on down there," he urged. "I can tell, you want to make them see you. Seize the day!"

I've noticed more of these creatures lately. Agitators for a cause that leaves most people mystified—at once both echoing past righteous struggles and trivializing them. I'm torn between disgust and a wish to pillory him with questions. Like why does he *make* dittos, if he hates being discriminated against when he *is* one?

Would he give equal rights to entities that last no longer than mayflies? Shall we give the vote to copies that can be mass-produced at whim—especially by the rich?

And why doesn't *he* go down to the beach, right now? Jostling among real humans, trying to jog their conscience, till one of them gets irritated enough to demand his ID pellet, posting a fine against his owner for some minor insult. Or till one of them decides to *pay* a fine, for the pleasure of cutting him to tiny pieces.

Of course that's why he stands on this bluff, holding up a sign but otherwise staying out of the way. This fellow is probably a brotherdit to some of the protestors I saw this morning, outside Universal Kilns. Somebody whose fervor is to send out proxies that demonstrate all day. An expensive avocation . . . and an effective way to protest.

That is, if his cause weren't absurd! More proof that most people have way too much free time nowadays.

Suddenly, I wondered what the hell I was doing there. I began today having fantasies about taking Clara's pleasure-ditto for myself, wallowed in philosophical issues beyond reach of a mere green, then abandoned the chores I had been made for, running off to waste beach time in a body that can't enjoy the sand's texture or the sea's tart taste.

What's wrong with me today?

Then it hit me. A weirdly thrilling perception.

I must be a frankie!

A borderline case, for sure. No staggering around with arms out-stretched, going *unh-uhhhhnh* like Boris Karloff. Still, they warn you that dog-tired neurons are a recipe for trouble when you imprint, and poor Albert must have been running on fumes when he made me.

I'm a false copy. A Frankenstein!

Realizing this, a strange acceptance settled over me. The beach lost its allure and the agitator's rhetoric palled. I retrieved my scooter, aiming it downtown. If this frankied rox lacks enough patience for house chores, maybe I'll take it over to Pal's and listen to him for a while.

If anyone can relate to my condition, it'll be Pal.

■　■　■

Update. Post-recorded about an hour later.

I just had some bad luck. Bad and weird.

On my way to Pallie's, I suddenly found myself trapped between some hunters and their prey.

Maybe I was preoccupied, careless, and driving much too fast. Anyway, I missed the warning signs. Maser flashes from the helmets worn by a pack of urban idiots, baying and yelling as they chased their quarry through the steel and masonry canyons of Old Town.

Other dittos veered aside. Lumbering dinobuses squatted down and hunched their scaly flanks. But I saw thinning traffic as an opportunity and zoomed straight toward the opening. Soon, maser beams were all over me, piercing clothes and tingling pseudoflesh. They resonate when they touch real skin, warning hunters not to shoot. But there aren't many archies downtown anymore, so it makes a great recreational battleground . . . for jerks.

They came dashing round the next corner, sweeping the intersection with hi-tech sensors and weapons. A hunter shouted, raising his bulbous, cannonlike thing in my direction!

Why me? I sniveled. *What'd I ever do to you?*

The shooter fired and fierce heat passed behind my left ear. A poor shot, if he was aiming at me.

Swerving my scooter to speed the other way, I braked barely in time to avoid hitting a gangly, naked humanoid! Bright yellow but stained with red concentric target-circles on his chest and back, he teetered in front of the Vespa staring past me, wild-eyed, then spun about to flee.

The pursuers screamed jubilation—sludgeheads grabbing an afternoon's adrenaline rush. Their guns sizzled, shooting past me again, cheerfully risking a dit-bystander fine if they fried *my* corpus in the bargain. And maybe I should've gone for the trade! Met the guns with outstretched arms. Albert would get double damages for a mere frankie. Good trade.

Instead, I hunched on the handlebars, slamming the throttle. The Vespa answered with a reedy wail, rearing like a bucking pony. At its high point, something hit the front tire. There were other impacts, on the machine and my body, as my scooter dug in and fled.

The quarrydit was fast—puffing, running and dodging like mad. Still he spared me a brief glance as I passed, and I realized two things.

One: he has the same face as one of the hunters.

Two: I could swear he's having a good time!

Well, the world is filled with all kinds of kinkiness and folks with too much free time. But I was busy controlling the wounded Vespa. By the time I turned a corner, beyond the line of fire, it was coughing, smoking, then died.

■   ■   ■

I stood next to my poor scooter, mourning its fatal wounds, when the phone rang, emitting an urgent rhythm.

By reflex, I tapped my left ear, with its cheap implant, in time to hear one of Albert's other selves answer.

"Yes?"

"Albert? It's Ritu Maharal. I—I can't see you. Don't you have vid?"

Words buzzed while I examined the scooter. Some kind of gummy substance splattered over the hybrid engine, shorting it out. I didn't dare touch the stuff, clearly devised to incapacitate dittos.

"... I'm just a gray, Ritu," a voice answered. *"Anyway, don't you already have one of me—"*

"Where are *you? Aeneas is waiting in the car, getting impatient. He expected you and my . . . father's ditto to join him. But you both vanished!"*

I found more of the same gunk on the right leg of my paper garment. Hurriedly, I tore and kicked away the shredded pants, then searched for more.

"What do you mean, vanished? How could they . . ."

"Ritu? It's me, Albert Morris. Are you saying that my gray is missing? And your father's too?"

Dull pain sensations drew my attention to a place in my back where something truly bothersome was going on. Turning to look at my spine in the Vespa's mirror, I spotted a *hole,* half the size of my fist, in the lower left . . . and it was growing! If I were human, I'd already be crippled or dead. As things stood, I couldn't have much time left.

I spotted the intersection of Fourth and Main . . . still too far from Pal's to reach him by foot. There were camionetas and jitneys on Main Street. Or I could stick out my talented green thumb and try to hitch. But where?

Then I remembered. The Church of the Ephemerals lay on Upas Street, just two blocks away!

I turned and started running east, while my archetype kept on talking to the alluring Ritu Maharal.

"So my gray was last seen following your father's—"

"Out the back door of the mansion. After that, no one's seen or heard either of the dittos. . . . Oh, no. Aeneas just walked in. He looks angry. He's ordering a complete search of the grounds."

"Do you want me to come over and help?"

"I—just don't know. Are you sure the gray hasn't checked in?"

The pain in my back got worse as I stumbled down Fourth. Something was chewing me up from within! I still had enough sense to step aside for anybody who looked real. Everyone else got out of my way as I grunted and shouted, running toward the one place that might offer help.

An edifice of dark stone loomed ahead. The place used to be a Presbyterian church, but all the real parishioners left this part of town long ago, letting it refill each day with a new servant class. One supposedly without souls to save.

That's when the Ephemerals took over.

Underneath a multicolored rosette symbol, the glass-faced announcement board foretold a coming sermon. *Culture can be continuity*, said a cryptic message in uneven letters. *There's more to immortality than inloading.*

Staggering up the front steps, I passed an assortment of dittos—all shades and colors—who were lounging about, smoking and chatting as if none of them had chores to do. Many were damaged or disfigured, even missing arms or legs. I hurried past, plunging into the dim coolness of the vestibule.

It wasn't hard to spot the lady in charge—dark brown and real—sitting on a stool next to a table piled high with papers and supplies. She wrapped the arm of a greenie whose whole left side looked badly burned. Overhead, another of the rosette symbols gradually turned, like a circular mandala or a flower whose petals all flared to wide tips.

"Open your mouth and inhale this," the volunteer told her patient, pushing a pop-breather at the poor roxie's face. Snapped, it billowed a compact cloud of heavy fumes the green sucked gratefully.

"It'll numb your pain centers. You must be careful then. Any bump or minor injury might—"

I interrupted.

"Excuse me. I've never been here before, but—"

She jerked her thumb to the left. "Please get in line and take your turn."

I saw a rather long queue of injured dittos, patiently waiting. Whatever mishap brought each one to this place, their owners clearly wouldn't inload such memories. Nor were these golems quite ready for recycling. Not with ancient instincts still screaming at them to fight on. The Standing Wave's oldest imperative is *endure*. So they came here. Like me.

But I couldn't afford to be patient. Turning around, I insisted.

"Please, ma'am. If you'd just look at this."

She raised her eyes, tired and perhaps cranky after long hours in this makeshift clinic. The volunteer nurse started to utter a curt dismissal, only it died on her lips. She blinked, then shot to her feet.

"Somebody help me here, stat! We've got an eater!"

■   ■   ■

What followed was weird, in a crazed-panicky-resigned kind of way. Like a scene from some old wartime hospital drama, updated with the hasty banter of a pit crew at an auto race. I lay prone on a filthy tabletop, listening through a haze while others dug into my back with makeshift, unsanitized tools.

"It's a clayvore! Damn, look at the bastard move."

"Watch out, it's big one. Grab those needle-nose pliers."

"Try to catch it whole. Eaters are illegal in this state. We may get a month's rent from the bastard who used this!"

"Just grab the little devil before it gobbles something vital. Hey, it's trying for the central ganglia—"

"Shit. Oh wait, I think . . . Got it!"

"Oh man, look at the nasty mother. What if they ever gave these things a taste for real flesh?"

"How do you know they haven't, in some secret lab?"

"Don't be paranoid. The Henchman Law ensures—"

"Shut up and put that awful thing in a jar, will you? Now someone get me a cup of plaster. The ganglia's intact. I think we can get by with a patch."

"I don't know. The wound's pretty deep and this green's young. Maybe we should give the motivators a quick test."

I listened from quite some distance away. The pop-breather stopped pain, all right—a merciful aspect of ditto design, required by law. It also explains why there are few free clinics. This was the first time I ever used one . . . to the best of my knowledge, that is. What a futile idea, after all—spending effort to save creatures who will vanish in a few hours anyway. Like ditto emancipation, most folks don't see the point.

Yet there I was, fighting to survive, and grateful for the help.

As I said before, a ditto's personality is almost always based on its archetype. *Almost* always. Maybe I came here for help today because I'm a frankie. Because I no longer share Albert's wry stoicism. At least not completely.

Anyway, the operation was far shorter than any visit to a realperson hospital. No worry about recovery or infections or malpractice suits. I had to admire the volunteer staff, making do with makeshift equipment and stale, off-market parts.

Ten minutes later I was sitting among other brightly hued patients and derelicts in the old church's wooden pews, sipping Moxie Nectar while antidotes countered the pain drug. Underneath a hand-carved sign that read *Helping the Kneady* a crippled purple stood at the old preacher's rostrum, reciting to us from a sheet of paper that she held in her good hand.

"It is not for Man to set boundaries, or to define the limits of soul.

"Once, human beings were as children, needing simple tales and naive visions of pure truth. But in recent generations the Great Creator has been letting us pick up His tools and unroll blueprints, like apprentices preparing to work on our own. For some reason, He's permitted us to learn the fundamental rules of nature and start tinkering with His craft. That's a fact as potent as any revelation.

"Oh, it is a heady thing, this apprenticeship and the powers that go with it. Perhaps, in the long run, it will turn out to be a good thing.

"But that doesn't make us all-knowing. Not yet.

"Most religions hold that some immortal essence stays inside a real human being—the original body—when copies are made. The golem-duplicate is just a machine, like some kind of robot. Its thoughts are projections—daydreams—sent in a temporary shell to perform errands. To help make your ambitions come true.

"For a rox, afterlife comes only by reuniting with its rig . . . just as the rig achieves it someday by reuniting with God. That's how older religions dismiss the ambiguity, the moral quandary, the troublesome morality of making new intelligent beings from clay.

"But doesn't some bit of immortal tincture transfer, each time we copy? Don't we still feel passion and pain, while wearing these brief forms? Does heaven have a place for us, as well?

"If it doesn't, well, maybe it ought to."

The sermon droned on while I regathered my thoughts. Again, I saw the rosette pattern overhead—this time in a stained glass window that looked half-finished. Several crippled dittos worked in a corner, fashioning another flared bit for the flower. Only this petal looked more like a fish of some kind.

I always figured the people who ran this place—the Ephemerals Temple—were related to the self-righteous kooks who picket Universal Kilns, like that greenie at the beach. So-called mancies who want citizenship for dittos. Or maybe the religious aspect meant they were kin to those *other* demonstrators . . . conservatives who see roxing as an affront to God.

But neither seems to be true. They aren't asking for equal rights, only compassion. And to save a little soul-stuff, here and there.

All right, so maybe they're *sincere* kooks. I'll ask Nell to send the Ephemerals a donation. If realAlbert doesn't veto it.

Still, I got out of there as soon as I could stand, seeking a quiet place to make this recording. Maybe Al and Clara will listen to it together and ponder a few new notions.

That's enough immortality for me. For a frankenstein mutant.

Meanwhile, it's time to get busy. I may not be a faithful duplicate of my original, but we still share some interests. Things I'd like to know before vanishing away.

9

The Sleeper Wakes

. . . or how realAlbert learns he can only count on himself . . .

Even in the old days it was normal to wonder, now and then, if you were real. At least it was normal for zen masters and college sophomores.

Now, the thought can strike you in the middle of a busy day. Running errands and doing business, you actually lose track of which table you got up from that morning. You can't help checking, lifting a hand to glance at the color, or giving flesh a quiet pinch.

The worst part is dreaming.

Dittos hardly ever sleep. So the mere fact *that* you're dreaming ought to reassure.

It ought to. But nightmares have their own logic. You can thrash in bed, worrying that you aren't really you . . . but someone else just like you.

■ ■ ■

My brain still felt loggy when Ritu Maharal's second call got me up for good. Clara would say it serves me right. "Only old-fashioned cyberfarts think they can ignore the sun."

Easy advice, from someone in her profession. Wars are mostly scheduled, nine-to-five affairs nowadays. But in my line of work it's easy to slip off-track. Well, four hours of rest—plus a bottle of ginger-fizzy Liquid Sleep—would have to do. Anyway, Ritu's news had me worried.

Shambling into my office, I checked the ditto roster to see how my copies were faring. If gray number one had gone missing, some clue might be evident on the board. Or maybe another of my selves could be diverted to Kaolin Manor.

I blinked at the glowing emblems, unable to believe my eyes. *All three* status lights flashed amber for inaccessible/incommunicado!

"Nell, can you explain this?"

"Not completely. Gray number one vanished less than an hour ago, at the estate of Vic Aeneas Kaolin."

"I know that already."

"Then do you also know they just found that gray's ID pellet lying on the ground in an off-limits area, restricted to Kaolin's intimate servants? The Vic's attorney wants to know what your ditto was doing there."

"How the hell should I know?" And to think, this day began so well. "Put that aside for now. What's going on with gray number two?"

"A coded message just came in. That gray has gone over to no-return, autonomous mode."

I blinked in surprise.

"He did? Without consulting me?"

"It's always been your policy to give grays this leeway."

"Yes, but why—"

"The copy was offered a quick, profitable job with a consortium led by Gineen Wammaker. In order to avoid conflict of interest with your other cases, the investigation must take place under conditions of sequestered cognizance."

"Under conditions of what?" I shook my head. "Oh, you mean no self-telling. I can't inload the dit, or even find out what it does."

This wasn't the first time a copy of mine took a sealed assignment, heading off on its own in order to make a quick profit for the real me. I've been well paid for investigations that I'll never remember, even if the customer was satisfied.

What goes through my mind, when I decide to accept such a case? Sitting here in my real body, I can't picture making the sacrifice. But I guess something in my character makes it possible—even likely—under the right circumstances.

Just hearing about it leaves me feeling rather creepy. "That gray had better be careful," I said in a low voice. "I don't trust the maestra."

"The ditto knows Wammaker can be devious. Do you want me to play back its message? Voice profiles ranged from cautious to paranoid."

Should I find that reassuring? My grays are exceptionally good. In fact, some years ago I was invited to join a research study of people who imprint especially high-fidelity golems. Anyway, what could I do but shrug and accept the situation? If you can't trust your own gray, who *can* you trust?

"All right, then tell me what happened to the *green*. This place is a mess. Dishes piled in the sink, trash bins full. Where's it gone?"

In response, Nell threw a phone image on the wall. A bland version of my own face abruptly glistened like a plaster cast, stained a color reminiscent of dying chlorophyll.

"Hi me," the visage waved jauntily against a shabby background, evidently somewhere in dittotown. *"I just dictated a full report, which I'll send in a minute. But here's the short version.*

"You blew it, Albert! Shouldn't imprint when you're wipe-out tired like you were this morning. You've always been lucky, but this time you finally made a frankie."

The green face paused to let the news sink in, grinning with ironic resignation that looked at once familiar and yet odd, somehow. I can't say for sure that *I* ever smiled quite that way.

"What's it like being a mutant copy? I know you're curious, so let me tell you. It feels downright weird. Like I'm me . . . and not me . . . at the same time. Know what I mean?

"Of course you don't. Anyway, the crux of it is that I won't be doing your dishes or vacuuming your house today. But not to worry! You don't have to call the cops or a disposal service. I'm no public hazard . . . no crazy stuff. I just have a few interests of my own, that's all.

"If I get a chance, I'll send one last report before I expire. I owe my creator that much, I suppose.

"Thanks for making me. Guess I'll see you around."

■　■　■

The green ditto winked and signed off. I stared at the blank wall until Nell broke in.

"To the best of my knowledge, this is your very first Frankenstein duplicate. Shall I make an appointment for you to get a routine medical scan? Life Upkeep is having a sale on checkups this week."

I shook my head.

"You heard him. I was tired, that's all."

"Then shall I put out a notice, renouncing the green's pellet?"

"And let every sicko hunt-fetishist go gunning for it? The poor thing seems harmless. I wonder, though . . ."

Could the same effect have touched the *grays* I imprinted this morning? They were made from more expensive blanks, and the scan times were longer. Anyway, with both of them incommunicado, what could I do but hope for the best?

There was little more to be learned from the green's dictated report, only some colorful incidents at Moonlight Beach and that dittotown church where they repair golems—interesting and dramatic, but no new light shed.

Nell broke in. *"Now that we've updated ditto status, there is work to do. Several ongoing cases need attention. And Ritu Maharal expects you to call back with conjectures about her father's fatal accident."*

I nodded. There are always too many things going on to handle all by myself.

"Break out a specialist," I ordered. "An ebony. Top of the line. I'd better imprint right away."

"An ebony has already been prepped."

The storage unit hissed, emitting oily fog as a fresh golem blank slid onto the warming tray, wearing a mirrorlike, glossy black sheen. More expensive than a quality gray, it came pre-tuned for intense focus, amplifying high levels of professional concentration for a full twenty-four hours—assuming that your original already has those qualities. Which may explain why you don't see ebonies as often as sybaritic whites. A full day of intense pleasure may be as wearing to inload as a day of hard work, but a lot more people have an aptitude for pleasure.

The kiln was ready. The soul-sifter's writhing tendrils awaited my head. But first I needed a moment to seek calm. Losing contact with two grays was bad enough, but for one of my greens to turn *frankie?* The unprecedented occurrence had me worried. Was I rested enough to keep it from happening again?

Turning away from the copier, I pushed open the back door of my small house and stepped into the garden. Warm sunshine on my face helped a lot. So did the smell of growing things. Moving over to my very own zen lemon tree, I plucked a small fruit and used a penknife to slice open one end, rubbing some juice onto my wrists. The scent filled my sinuses and I closed my eyes, clearing my thoughts.

Soon confidence returned. Back to work.

Laying my head between the soul-pickups, I gave the mental signal to begin. This would be a long, careful scan, taking maybe ten minutes, so I tried to stay relaxed and immobile as delicate fingers began riffling through me—mostly the brain but also heart, liver, and spinal cord—copying from the template of my Standing Wave, pressing its image into the nearby clay figure. It all felt familiar, like hundreds of other times. Yet on this occasion I felt self-consciously aware of the *undercurrent*—ripples of emotion and semi-random memories that imprinting evokes at a level below clear consciousness. Vague, oceanic feelings of connectedness washed over me, sensations that William James called "the religious experience," before mankind got around to transforming the spiritual realm into just another area of technological expertise.

It was only natural for my drifting thoughts to contemplate the greenie . . . especially the time it reported spending at the Ephemerals Temple. Apparently there was more to the place than a bunch of kooks, wasting their altruistic impulses on wounded mayflies. It made me wonder.

What happens to the soul of a ditto who loses his salvation—who never gets to inload back into the "real" self who made him? It always seemed a metaphysical and rather futile question—except three of me faced that situation today.

For that matter, what happens when your *original* dies? Some religions think there's a final transfer, loading your entire lifestream into God, in much the same way that your golems pour their memories back into you at the end of each day. But despite fervent yearnings—and well-funded private research—no one's ever found proof of such transfer to some higher-level archetype-being.

Unsettling thoughts. I tried to let go and just drift, letting the unit do its work. But moments later, Nell interrupted with another high-priority call.

"It is from Vic Aeneas Kaolin," my house computer said. *"You have no operational self-copies to take it. Shall I answer with an avatar?"*

Use a crude software emulation to greet a trillionaire? I quivered at the notion. Might as well insult him with a recorded voice saying, *I'm not in right now, leave a message.*

"Put him through to me here," I ordered. This was going to be one of those days.

The image that erupted in front of me showed the tycoon's familiar visage—slender and heavy-browed—sitting in a tidy office with an ornate fountain-sculpture bubbling in the background. I almost sat up in surprise when I saw that he was brown! One of the pale, North European shades. It would be worthwhile interrupting the scan in order to show respect for his rig.

Then I spied a glint . . . a brief, specular reflection off his cheek. A non-specialist might be fooled by the guise, but I could tell this was another golem, baked in human shades. It wasn't even illegal, since you can wear any color you like in the privacy of your own home, as long as no fraud is involved.

I remained supine, letting the tetragramatron unit continue sifting and imprinting a duplicate of my soul.

"Mr. Morris."

"ditKaolin," I replied, indicating that I saw through the amateurish guise. He paused, then inclined his head ever so slightly. After all, I was the real person in this conversation.

"I see you are imprinting, sir. Shall I call back in an hour?"

As before, I found his way of speaking a bit old-fashioned. But you can afford affectations when you're rich.

"It's a deep scan, but I'll hardly need a whole hour." I smiled, while keeping my head quite still between the tendrils. "I can call you back in ten—"

"This will only take a minute," the ditto interrupted. *"I want you to come work for me. Right away. At double your normal rate."* He appeared happily confident that I would leap up and accept without hesitation. Strange. Was this the same fellow whose lawyers sent threatening notes a little while ago, because they found the pellet of my missing gray in a restricted area? The same Kaolin who wouldn't let me send a copy of my own to investigate the disappearance?

"If this has to do with Dr. Maharal's tragic death, you know that I've already been retained by his daughter, Ritu. Accepting your offer right now could risk conflict of interest, unless special arrangements are made."

"Special arrangements" could mean spinning off *more* grays who never come home. That thought, mixed with the turbid sensations of imprinting, left me feeling a bit queasy.

Kaolin's ditto blinked, then glanced offscreen. Perhaps he was receiving instructions from his archetype—the real mogul-hermit. Curiosity flamed within me. There were all sorts of rumors about the tycoon. Some of the more garish stories described him as hideously deformed by a rare, genetically engineered plague developed in his own laboratories. I made sure this conversation was being recorded at high fidelity. Clara would want details, when she came home from her war.

The brown golem brushed away my objection. *"That's a mere technicality. You will perform the same investigation, but I can pay for your exclusive services, sparing poor Ritu the expense during her time of grief."*

That "exclusive services" part sounded like this morning's Fealty Oath ploy, repackaged a bit. True, I could always use money. But the world is more than money.

"Have you cleared this idea with Ritu?"

The flesh-colored ditto paused, again checking some information source offscreen. Barring a recent memory transfer, this one would have no personal knowledge of me, only what he had been told.

"No, but I'm sure she'll find my offer—"

"Anyway, she's already paid for today, in advance. Why not wait and see what I come up with? We can all compare notes tomorrow. Put everything on the table. Does that sound fair enough?"

Kaolin was clearly unused to being put off.

"Mr. Morris, there are . . . complications that Ritu doesn't know about."

"Hm. You mean complications relevant to her father's death? Or the abduction of my gray?"

Grimacing, the platinum ditto realized his mistake. He was on the verge of giving me probable cause to subpoena him, if I chose.

"Until tomorrow, then," he said, with a curt nod. The image vanished and I chuckled briefly, then closed my eyes with a sigh. Perhaps now I could finish imprinting in peace.

Alas, no longer distracted by the phone call, I felt once again immersed in the turbulence of soul-sifting. Emotion flurries and flashes of memory, most of them too brief to recognize, kept surging out of dark, unconscious storage. Some of them felt like anticipating the past, others like remembering the future. It grew stifling, especially when the perceptron tendrils entered both nostrils for the final and deepest phase of imprinting—the phase called "breath of life."

Nell broke in.

"I have another incoming call, from Malachai Montmorillin."

This was the utter last straw. Almost gagging on the tendrils, I grunted—

"Can't listen to Pal raving right now."

"He appears to be quite insist—"

"I said no! Use that buzzoff avatar on him. Anything. Just keep him away till I finish work tonight!"

Maybe I shouldn't have been so vehement. The same intense feeling would carry over into the ebony. Anyway, poor Pal couldn't help being the way he was.

But I didn't have time for his crazy games right then. Sometimes you just have to focus on the job at hand.

10

Golem Home

. . . or how gray number two gets to have more fun than he really wants . . .

The Rainbow Lounge has a retro name and revo clientele. Once you step past a flickersign that says No REALFOLK ALLOWED, it feels like you've entered some nightmarish TwenCen sci-fi movie, filled with cavorting mutants and leering androids.

Of course, a lot more than just a warning keeps archies away. True-flesh can't endure the bone-jarring rhythms hammered by a vibrating dance floor. Staccato-strobes hurl juttering lightning arcs that would send organic neurons into conniptions. The atmosphere, clotted with soot from a hundred smoldering ash pipes, could lace your native lungs with lively tumors. The stench—mildly intoxicating to dittos—must be filtered before venting to outside air.

Back in one-body days, Saturday night mattered. Now, places like the Rainbow hop around the clock, even on a Tuesday afternoon—whenever fresh dittos can arrive, baked for harsh pleasure in their owners' kilns, decorated in everything from paisley spirals to moiré patters that turn skin into blurry art. Some come molded as gaudy sex caricatures or sport scary accessories, like razor talons or acid-dripping jaws.

"Would you like a head-check?" The red attendant behind a counter offers me a glowing tag. Next to coatracks stand refrigerated cubbyholes. A tag for cranial storage can help ensure that violent memories will be savored later.

"No thanks," I tell her. And yes, I admit that I used to frequent spots like this. Hey, who gets past their teen years nowadays without sampling depths of hedonism that would shame Nero? Why not, if the only thing you keep are memories? And even that's optional. Nothing that happens to your ditto can harm the real you, right?

That is, if you ignore certain rumors . . .

For many, the intensity fix is addictive—inloading experiences too raucous for mere protoplasm. Especially the unemployed, spending their purple wage to beat back the ennui of modern life.

■ ■ ■

"Please wait over there, ditMorris. I'll come for you shortly."

Jarred from doorway contemplation, I glance at my guide, another red-hued femdit. Her speech carries through the racket with remarkable clarity. Sonic interference dampers, embedded in the walls, shape a channel for her words to reach my ears. A tech-marvel you can take for granted, when you happen to own the place.

"Pardon? *Where* should I wait?"

Queen Irene's red golem points again, past the dance floor and beyond the Grudge Pit. This time I see an empty table with a winking RESERVED light.

"Will this take long? I haven't got all day."

That expression has special meaning for a creature like me, self-sentenced to oblivion for the good of my maker. But my guide only shrugs, then heads off through the crowd to inform her sisters that the hired spy has arrived.

Why should I spend my last eighteen hours working for people I don't like, doing a job I don't understand? Why not escape! The street is just meters away.

But if I did escape, where could I go? realAlbert would force me to spend all of my remaining span in quick-court, fighting the maestra's breach-of-contract suit. Anyway, I'm probably being watched right now, targeted by a sighting beam. I can see more copies of the same umber-colored female hurrying about, serving drinks, mopping spills and sweeping bits of broken customers. Several of the reds glance my way. They'll know if I make a break for it.

I head for the table, wading through a maelstrom of noise. *Living* noise that grabs your body like a cloying lover, hampering every move. I don't like this "music," but the garish dancers do, throwing themselves into frenetic collisions that few could mimic in flesh. Bits of clay fly, as if from a potter's wheel.

Staunch partiers have a saying—if your ditto makes it home in one piece, you didn't have a good time.

■   ■   ■

Seating booths line the walls. Others lounge at open tables that project garish holo images—whirling abstractions, vertigeffigies, or gyrating strippers. Some draw the eye against your will.

Sidling around the mob, I pass through a fringe minimum, where the sonic dampers overlap, canceling everything to a hush, like inside a padded coffin. Stray bits of dialogue converge from all over the club.

"... so there's this clamber-amble, creeping up my leg? I look down an' see it's wearing Josie's face, grinning at the tip! So I got maybe three secs to decide, did she send it as a poison pet or an apology? Get the pixel?"

"... the committee finally accepted my thesis, only they slapped a perversion tax, on account of 'sadistic themes'! The nerve. I bet none of those old turds ever read the gospels of deSade!"

"... uh ... taste this ... d'you think they're watering the benzene?"

Another step, and I'm beyond the quiet fringe minimum, abruptly staggering under a double-reinforced roar. Screams bellow from the Grudge Pit, where swaggering bravos carve each other while other clients tender themselves as prizes to the winners. The latest victor stands over his steaming victim, crossing both wrists with raised weapons that whirl like spinning scythes, throwing enzyme-soaked gore onto cheering by-standers. Bets are paid with glimmering eye-picts, or wads of stained purple bills. Under their garish skin decorations, you can spot which dismembered dittos were bought at a public kiln for twenty welfare dollars.

The winner's triumphant turn brings us eye-to-eye. We lock a gaze briefly and his grin freezes—in recognition? I don't recall ever seeing his particular pseudoface. The connection lasts but an instant, then he turns back to admiring cheers.

A similar victory might have won him a chiefdom in some olden tribe. Now, well, at least he gets a moment to pretend. Of course, a real pro like my Clara could eat punks like this for breakfast. But she has better things to do right now, two hundred klicks away at the front lines, defending her country.

The RESERVED light goes dark when I sit where I'm expected, wondering how Clara's war is going. Part of me feels sick that I'll never see her again. Though of course *I* will, as soon as one army or the other wins ... or else when combat breaks up for the traditional weekend truce. realAlbert had better be good to her, or I'll come back from wherever golems go, and haunt the lucky bastard!

"What'll it be?" a waitress asks. A special model, resembling the other Irene-copies, but voluptuous, with big hands for carrying trays.

"Just a Pepsoid. With ice." My grays are self-sufficient, but it's hot in here and an electrolyte boost won't hurt. On Wammaker's expense account.

Turns out that I'm near another sonic fringe. If I lean to one side, I can slip my head into a zone of relative silence, damping out the thudding music and shrieking battle cries, leaving only dribbles of chatter from the booths.

"... What're you smoking? Izzat buckyball-black? Can I sniff?"

"... Did you hear they closed the Pithy Pendulum? Health spectors found a zhimmer virus in the filters. Your infected ditto brings it home and WHAM! Next thing, your rig's drooling in a psycho ward..."

"... I love that bug-eye look! Are they functional?"

Wordless sounds of ersatz passion also carry. Through haze, I glimpse couples and trios writhing in alcoves. And if your body plan won't fit your partner's, the management rents adapters.

"Hush," I tell the table, which erects a curtain of white noise, quashing the surrounding din. "Give me news from the war front."

"Which war?" a voice buzzes, silicon-based, not clay. Specifics are needed. "Five major matches and ninety-seven minor league events are currently in progress around the globe."

Ah. So who is Clara fighting, this week? I should pay closer attention to the standings. If this were a sports bar, the contest would be on a big screen, twenty-four hours.

"Um, try the combat range nearest town."

"The Jesse Helms International Combat Range lies two hundred and fifty-four kilometers south by southeast. This week, the Helms Range is proud to host a return match between the Pacific Ecological Zone of the United States of America and the Indonesian Reforestation Consortium. At stake are iceberg harvesting rights in the Antarctic—"

"That's it. How's the PEZ team doing?"

A holo image spreads across the table, zooming toward sunburned mountainy terrain demarcated by sharp boundaries. Outside, beyond a palm-treed resort oasis, lies a protected landscape of desert mesas. Inside: a pocked and tormented patch of Mother Gaia that's been sacrificed for the sake of the rest. A vast cousin of the Rainbow Lounge, where human drives are channeled, with far more at stake.

"Pacifican forces made significant territorial advances during Monday's initial action. Casualties were low. But IRC tribunes assessed a number of penalties that may cancel out these gains..."

Sparkles flash before me as the POV drops closer to Earth. Sparkles that seem rather gay-looking, till you recognize rocket-artillery barrages and fierce laser strikes. Clara works in a realm of awful killing machines that could wreak horror if they ever spilled beyond the world's combat ranges. I'm torn between zooming toward the front lines or swerving to that tree-lined oasis, at the border. Only—

—someone barges suddenly through the wispy privacy screen, blocking half the holo image.

"So, it is you." A figure stands before me, tall and snake-skinned. *"How convenient."*

It's the gladiator I saw just minutes ago in the Grudge Pit, exulting over a steaming victim. He looms closer, purple hands still swathed in wet clay grue, like some brutal potter.

"How'd you get out of the river?" he demands.

All at once, I realize it's the rowdy who blocked my way last night, on Odeon Square! Only that had been his archie back when I was green, trying desperately to escape Beta's yellowdits.

"River?" Let's play innocent. "What makes you think I went swimming? Or that I'd remember you?"

His fighter-ditto isn't made for subtle expressions. The face goes rigid as he realizes what he just gave away. Then he shrugs, deciding not to care what his words reveal.

"You remember me, all right," he growls. "I saw you jump in. And I *know* you made it back home to dump."

Know? How could he know? Never mind. Modern wisdom says never to be surprised if hidden knowledge leaks. Over the long term, no secret endures.

Let's see if he appreciates sarcasm.

"A golem walking the length of a river! Well, goodness. Anyone who accomplished something like that should be the talk of the town! Maybe you should try jumping in yourself sometime."

The suggestion doesn't sit well.

"I kept your damn arm. Baked it hard. Want it back?"

I can't help smiling as I recall his stunned expression when I left him standing in the plaza gripping my severed wrist. A rare happy memory from a lousy ditto-day.

"Keep it. Make a nice urn."

He scowls. "Stand up."

Instead, I yawn and stretch, both posturing and buying time. Courage is conditional. If this body of mine were made for partying, I just might try to slab and spin this guy, for the hell of it. realAlbert, with plenty to live for, would flee such a mad fool without shame. *My* options are murkier. I'm gray and an orphan, with no chance of continuity but some puzzles I'd like to solve in my remaining hours. All told, I'd rather management came to shoo him off. Alas, not a single red Irene is in sight.

"I said, get up!" Bully-boy growls, preparing to strike.

"Do I get choice of weapons?" I ask abruptly.

Hesitation. He can't just cut me to bits when I've made it a matter of honor. Duels have rules, y'know. And people are watching.

"Sure. After you." He gestures toward the Grudge Pit, insisting that I lead the way.

I need an out before we get there. There are a few tools in my pocket—a small cutter and a cyberscope—but he won't make the same mistake as last night, letting me strike up close, by surprise.

Where the hell are my hosts? If I had any idea they were so lax, I'd have made that break earlier! Hit the street. Maybe head for Pal's. Advise Albert to avoid the maestra in future, like a plague.

We weave past tables, most of them aglow with shimmering bolos, lighting garish faces. No one looks familiar in the young crowd. Anyway, this character is probably part of the in-group. Flexing my knees a bit lower with each step, I think-prep an enzyme rush while slowing the pace, as if suddenly reluctant.

As I hoped, my nemesis plants a beefy hand in my back. Gives a push.

"Go on! The armory's just ahea—"

I won't chance it against his hyped-up reflexes. Instead of whirling at him from a fake stumble, I leap sideways and *up,* landing on a nearby table, kicking aside glasses to slip between the projected holos of two female dancers, rubbing their hips in erotic rhythm.

I think he yells, but there's so much noise from upset clients—they reach for me, so I jump again!

Like a pip, shot from between the gyrating dancers, I fly from that table to another, landing this time amid a swirling maelstrom of jagged virtual scythes, spinning round and round like Death's personal tornado. It's so realistic that I cringe, half expecting to be puréed. But my body passes through the illusion, even as more customers scream outrage and glass crunches underfoot. Hands grab an ankle, so I spin-kick, knocking them off.

Of course the light storm blinds me, too. I can barely glimpse my next target, a table where a gently spinning Earthglobe beckons. I flex—

—but a sudden force knocks the rickety platform, spoiling my launch. I strike the next table edge-on, rolling in pain amid chairs, kicking feet and broken bottles.

Blows buffet my left side, driving a groan. My tormentor, or an irritated customer? Rather than look, I scuttle like a crab while groping in a pants pocket for my cutter—too short-range to serve as much of a weapon.

Uh-oh. Boots ahead. Many. He's called friends. They're bending and peering under tables. In moments—

My hand falls on the base of this table, held to the floor by three heavy bolts.

Cut them? Why not? Here goes—

The table wobbles . . . tips . . .

Grab it. Now surge *upward*!

They jump back in alarm. It's not much of a weapon, but with the holo still shining I appear to be brandishing more than a bitty cocktail table! Writhing images extend another two meters, like shining snakes. A flail made of burning light.

Just light, yet they cringe. Imprinted with barely altered caveman souls, they can't help seeing a flaming torch. Soon I'm circled by a zone of respect, empty out to the holo's reach. And now, some spectator voices cheer for *me*.

I spot the punk, with pals, all wearing studded black as if they invented the look. Pathetic.

They clench and snarl. In bare moments, rational evaluation will win out, overcoming cave reflexes. They'll charge through the cool light. But hemmed by onlookers, what can I . . .

All at once the tenor of sound shifts. The thundering dance music vanishes. Angry shouts are damped. Past the sucking whistle of my hyper-breathing, an amplified voice penetrates.

"ditMorris, if you please . . ."

Swerving again, I feint at the bravos. They retreat, perhaps for the last time as their eyes narrow angrily.

Then, abruptly, they give way—pushed aside by a band of newcomers, small but forceful, using sound-wands to clear a path. Red females, restoring order to their club.

It's about time.

Backing toward the Grudge Pit, the chief punk gives me a final look, surprisingly passionless, even amused or gratified. The pounding "music" returns. Soon, the Rainbow is back to normal.

One of the Irenes, unapologetic, shakes her ruddy finger.

"ditMorris, kindly put that table down!"

It's hard to comply for a moment. Instinct, you know.

"Please, no more distractions. You're expected. The hive awaits."

The holo display sputters out and I drop my makeshift weapon. That's it? No apology for leaving me at the mercy of idiots?

Oh, stifle the complaint, Albert. It's not like your life was in danger, or anything important.

Jerking her crimson head, my guide beckons me to follow her toward the back of the club, then through a plush curtain. Blessed silence reigns suddenly, as the heavy drape falls behind us. Silence so welcome that I sway. It takes several beats before I can think. Then—

Wait . . . I've seen this room before.

During the meeting at Studio Neo, one red-clay Irene had been jacked into a screen showing throngs of umber duplicates, fussing around a single pale figure, supine on a fancy life-maintenance couch. Now, up close, I see the real woman lying amid the bustle, staring blankly while tended by one-third scale duplicates. Fluid drips into her mouth. Mechanical arms massage her limbs. The face, though flaccid and distant, is clearly the template for every red I've seen running about this place. Her shaved head bears a medusa of writhing cables, leading to industrial strength freezers and kilns.

A fresh-baked copy emerges, still glowing from the oven. It stretches for a languorous moment before accepting paper overalls, then stepping away, targeted to do some chore without direction or instruction. Meanwhile, another reenters from the outside world, clearly tottering on depleted cells. Without ceremony, two sisters neatly sever the day-old head, dropping it into a memory transfer coil.

The archie's pale face winces for an instant during inload. The discarded body rolls off for recycling.

Some foresee this as our future, I muse. *When you can spin off countless copies to perform any task, your durable organic body will serve one function, as a place to deposit memories and pass them on, a sacred prisoner like the ant queen, while bustling workers carry out life's real activity and savor.*

I find the prospect repulsive. But my grandparents thought the same of basic imprinting. The words "golem" and "ditto" were epithets, till we got used to them. Who am I to judge what future generations will think normal?

"ditMorris, welcome."

I turn. The Irene facing me has the skin texture of a high-quality gray, tinted with her trademark umber glaze. Standing near is the other rox I met at Studio Neo, "Vic" Manuel Collins, with the eye-hurting plaid dye job.

"You call *this* welcome? I'd like to know why you left me out there, to be—"

Collins lifts a hand. "Questions later. First, let us see to your repairs."

Repairs?

Looking down, I see bad news. Deep gashes in my left side! One leg cut more than halfway through along its length and oozing badly. Hopped-up on action enzymes, I felt little.

Ack, I'm ruined.

"You can repair *this*?" My chief emotion is numb curiosity.

"Come along," says the nearest Irene. "We'll fix you up in no time."

No time? I ponder in a daze, following. To a ditto, "no time" is a very demanding phrase.

11

Ghosts in the Wind

. . . as realAlbert does some modern footwork . . .

There didn't seem to be much I could do about my missing duplicates. Gray number two was on autonomous mode; he couldn't legally contact me, and the maestra might prevent it even if he wanted to. The greenie had sent a weird declaration of independence, before going off on his own. And there was no sign at all of gray number one, who vanished at Kaolin Manor along with a ghost of Yosil Maharal. The Universal Kilns security staff had taken charge of that mystery, sifting the estate for any sign of both missing dittos. So far to no avail.

I didn't expect them to achieve much. It's easy to smuggle a rox in a box. Millions, cushioned mummylike in CeramWrap, get shunted all over the city each day by truck, courier, or pneumatic tube. And it's even easier getting rid of a dead one—just flush the remains into a recycler. Without a pellet, one batch of golem slurry is no different than any other.

Anyway, I had investigations to take care of, including one for a client who was willing to pay top rates. Ritu Maharal wanted me to look into the mysterious death of her father. As legal heir, she could now access his records, from credit purchases to calls from his wrist phone. Maharal's movements during time spent working for UK were another matter. But when Ritu asked Vic Aeneas Kaolin for those chronicles, the tycoon assented, grudgingly, to keep her from going public with "wild stories" about her father being murdered.

The permissions came through soon after I finished making an ebony specialist, tuned for total focus on professional skill. That duplicate went right to work, waving its arms and chattering rapidly under the muffled folds of a virtual reality chador, immersed in a world of rapidfire data-globes and zooming images. All logic and focus, the ebony could handle the rest of my caseload for the time being, letting me concentrate on one task—discovering where Yosil Maharal spent the last few weeks.

∎ ∎ ∎

Never mind what cyber marketeers say about their fancy autonomous search programs. Data-sifting is an art. We may live in a "transparent" society, but the window glass is frosted and foggy in countless places. Peering through those patches can take skill.

I started by setting up a digital avatar—a simple software represen-tation of myself—and launching it through the publicam network. Though less intelligent or flexible than a creature with a Standing Wave, it carried some of my expertise combined with a relentless drive to hunt down any images that Yosil may have left while traveling on city streets. Ritu gave me about sixty solid sightings to start with—places he was confirmed to have been at exact times. The avatar zoomed in on those space-and-time coordinates, then tried to follow the scientist as he moved from one re-corded scene to the next. Gradually, a map began to fill in, detailing his movements during the months before he died.

Often, that kind of search is enough, all by itself. Few people have a knack for evading the publicam mesh.

Alas, Maharal must have been one of them. Indeed, he proved wily at escaping from view, almost at will. My avatar's search left a chart with many gaping holes, some lasting a week or more!

Ritu's pockets were deep and she wanted answers fast. So I put out bids for sightings by *privately* owned lenses, which are far more numer-ous than public cameras. Restaurant security scanners, window-ledge lurkers, newsbugs, amateur sociologists, even nature lovers and urban sporting clubs—anyone whose sensors might have spotted Yosil when he was out of publicam range. Since Ritu owned her father's copyright now, there wasn't even a voyeur tax. Low bids poured in. I let the avatar haggle and choose enough pix to fill in Yosil's trail.

Meanwhile, *I* focused on the scene of his death.

∎ ∎ ∎

Outside the city, it's like another world. A primitive realm of immense areas where vision is blurry, even nonexistent . . . unless you happen to be there in person, using your own eyes.

Adult: If a tree falls in the forest with no one around to hear it, does it make a sound?

A modern child: It depends. Let me check if any of the local cams had sonic or vibrational pickups.

Cute. But in fact, most places on Earth still aren't covered by any close-in cams at all! It's a lot easier to disappear in the countryside, beyond any sign of habitation.

Unfortunately, that's where Maharal spent his last hours, and possibly days.

I started with police images of the crash site, offering stunning holographic detail out to a diameter of two hundred meters surrounding Maharal's wrecked vehicle—a big Chevford Huntsman with an extravagant methane engine. It lay crumpled and half-burned at the bottom of a ravine. The river was dry this time of year, but giant granite boulders testified to the smoothing effects of a torrent that scoured the streambed during some winters.

The desert, I thought, glumly. *Why did it have to be the damn desert?*

Overhead, spanning the gully, stood the highway viaduct where Maharal's vehicle began its fatal plummet, the guardrail a twisted snake of shredded metal. I spent some time nosing around the scene, shifting and interpolating from one hovering copcam to the next. While emergency vehicles came and went, muscular dittos heaved at the wreck—sometimes with fancy tools, but then dropping them to use raw strength—striving to free the dead scientist's corpse.

The road made a sharp turn just before reaching this lonely site. Skid marks intersected the maimed guardrail . . . as if the driver had realized his peril suddenly, though too late. This, combined with results from Maharal's autopsy, convinced authorities that he must have simply dozed off at the wheel.

The tragedy never would have happened if he used the car's auto-navigation system. Why would someone drive at night, in an unlit desert, with all safety features cut out?

Well, I answered my own question, *robot-piloting leaves a trace. You don't use autonav when you're worried about being followed.* Maharal's gray ditto had admitted that the good doctor spent his last days oscillating in and out of paranoia. This supported the story.

Reversing the flow of time, I watched emergency vehicles converge backward and then disperse again, one by one, till just a solitary camview was available . . . a speckly image from the first sheriff's cruiser to arrive on the scene. When I tried ratcheting still earlier, the fatal patch of desert not only went dark, it vanished from memory, like a blind spot you couldn't even look at. It appeared only on maps. An abstraction. For all anyone knew for sure, it did not even exist during the time in question.

Farm country would've been better. Agriculturalists use a lot of cameras to monitor crops. Anything irregular, like a stranger, might show up. But the hectare in question featured just a simple EPA toxicity detector, vigilant against illegal dumping. The nearest real lens was more than five klicks away—a habitat scanner programmed to count migrating desert tortoises and such.

Still, I didn't give up. There are ten thousand commercial and private spy-sats orbiting this planet, and even more robot aircraft cruising the high stratosphere, serving as phone relays and newscams. One of them *might* have been focused on this obscure place when the accident happened, recording a handy image of Maharal's headlights, swerving and then spinning as the car plunged to its doom.

I checked . . . and there was no such luck. All the high-resolution lenses were busy elsewhere that night, zooming onto busier sites. Tech-pundits keep promising we'll have WorldOmniscient viewing in a few years, with close-ups of the whole Earth available to everyone, all the time. But right now, that's just sci-fi stuff.

My best bet was to try a little trick of my own, using the coarse data from a micro-climate orbiter. Not a true camera, the weathersat is assigned to track wind gusts across the southwest, using Doppler radar.

Traffic stirs the air, especially in open countryside. Long ago I figured out that you can trace the passage of a single vehicle, if conditions are right. And if you're lucky.

Using special processing software, I massaged the weathersat's recorded scan of the area near the viaduct, moments before the crash. Looking for very small patterns, I prodded and palped the Doppler elements till they were grainy, fluctuating at the edge of chaos.

At first, it looked like nothing more than a storm of multicolored noise. Then I began picking out patterns.

There!

It looked like a trail of mini-cyclones, spinning along both sides of the desert road—a ghostly wake, barely perceptible against a background of noise-washed pixels. Pushing the clock slowly backward from the time of the crash, I followed that spectral trace as it writhed southward along the road, vanishing and then reappearing like a phantom snake, moving at the pace of a speeding car.

This might work, I thought, *so long as Maharal didn't pass any other traffic . . . and assuming the air stayed quiet all that lonely night.*

Almost any outside disturbance could erase the wraithlike spoor.

Comparing distance and time scales, I could tell one thing about Maharal's condition that night as he sped toward his tryst with death— the Universal Kilns scientist sure must have had a bee up his shorts! He topped over a hundred and twenty klicks along most of that curvy road. The guy was just asking for trouble.

Could someone have been following him? Chasing? The trail of cyclonic disturbance was too ragged and smeared to tell if it was made by one vehicle or two.

I asked Nell to keep following the faint pattern as far back in time as she could.

"Acknowledged," my house computer answered, almost sounding human. *"If you aren't too busy, there are some other matters that have come up while you were immersed in work. Your colleague Malachai Montmorillin called several more times. I put him off, per your instructions."*

I felt a little guilty. Poor Pal. "I'll make it up to him tonight. Orders stand."

"Very well. I have also received a pneumatic shipment from Universal Kilns. Five new ditto blanks."

"Put them away. And please stop bothering me with trivia."

Nell went silent. I could see on one monitor that she was concentrating on following Maharal's desert track. So I turned away to check on the cyber-avatar that I had unleashed in the city cam-web.

The results looked gratifying!

Purchased images and camera-posse reports were pouring in, providing a picture of where Yosil Maharal had spent much of the last few months, at least when he was in town. I skim-sampled the resulting movie at high speed, tailing the late researcher as he moved from one eyeview to the next . . . shopping in a fashionable arcade, for instance, or visiting his hygienist for a routine oral-symbiont upgrade. The mesh of spottings still amounted to only a couple of hours a day, on average. But after all, Maharal spent most of his time working in the lab at Universal Kilns, or at home.

Except for those mysterious trips to the countryside, that is. It was essential to forge a link between his city trail and those cryptic sojourns out of town.

Still, I felt content with progress so far. If the city mesh kept filling in at this rate, I should have something worthwhile to report to Ritu.

A sharp twinge brought my hand to my right temple. One byproduct of all this work was a growing headache. Real neurons can only take so much holovideo input. Anyway, it was time I got up to relieve my bladder.

Stopping at the chemsynth unit on my way back, I ordered a tension potion—something to ease the knot in my neck, but without any thought-dulling endorphins. I took the frothy concoction back to the study . . . only to find someone in my place! Somebody built like me, but with longer fingers and a disdainful expression that I seldom wear. At least I hope I don't.

The glossy, emulated skin was the color of deep space. Agile hands danced over my controller-array.

"What are you doing?" I demanded. The ditto had its *own* cubbyhole.

"Tidying up this mess while waiting for you to come out of the john. Your search avatar thinks that it's tracked down most of Maharal's missing in-town movements."

I glanced at the screen. "Yeah? Eighty-seven percent coverage ain't bad . . . for the time Maharal wasn't at home or the lab. What are you getting at?"

Again, a sardonic smile.

"Oh, nothing, maybe. Except that some of these so-called sightings may not be Dr. Yosil Maharal at all."

I gave the ditto a hollow look, which only invited more disdain.

"Care to make a wager, Boss-me? I'll bet my inload that Maharal's got you fooled. In fact, he's been tricking *everybody* for a very long time."

12

Leggo My Echo

. . . or how a green frankie
seeks enlightenment . . .

Out of politeness, I waited till the crippled purple preacher finished her sermon before I stood up to leave the Ephemerals. Unfortunately, the sweetly inspirational tone was marred by an altercation that broke out in the vestibule as I made my way outside. A man whose skin tone verged egregiously between golem-beige and human-brown shouted while waving a placard covered with in flowing, cursive script:

You all miss the point.
There's a next step a'coming . . .

Angry congregants milled, trying to nudge the interloper through an exit without shoving—on the offchance that he might be real. The uncertainty fostered by his ambiguous coloration was augmented by sunglasses, along with flaming red hair and a beard that could either be fake or genuine. The fellow was committing half a dozen misdemeanors just by looking this way—like some kind of ditto-human crossbreed—an effect he must have been aiming for.

"You're all a bunch of daisies!" he cried, as a dozen or so Ephemerals crowded him toward a side door. "Colored on the outside, but dull as flesh within! Don't you know it takes *blood* to pull off a revolution? The protoplasm elite will never give way to the New Race without violence. They'll cling to domination till they're wiped off the face of the Earth! Only then can we progress to the next level!"

I had to admit, standing there, that sometimes you just gotta admire the passion of the truly insane—a passion that bulls right past all sense or reason. I mean, was he really suggesting that dittos can exist, somehow, *independently* of organic originals who were woman-born? How was that even remotely logical? The variety of inventive ideas—and ideologies—that people can come up with never ceases to amaze me, especially when they're stoked by the ultimate drug, self-righteousness.

Turning and departing by the front door, I descended wide stone steps to the street with the fanatic's words still ringing in my ears.

"Get ready!" the crackpot yelled in a fervid voice that seemed to cling, even as I walked away.

"A new age is coming for the ditsenfranchised . . . if you prepare!"

■ ■ ■

Nobody wanted to talk about the waiter who caused a brief uproar last night, at La Tour Vanadium.

When I arrived, most of the restaurant staff—contract specialdits from busboys to maître d'—were darting about wordlessly, clearing away lunch and setting tables for the early dinner crowd. A few customers lingered while twin chartreuse waiters hovered nearby. Gym bags lay at the archies' feet. A nice chardonnay can be just the thing after exercise, soaking warm neurons with a happy glow.

Optimists predict that someday a real body may last as many decades as a ditto has hours. Well, far be it from me to begrudge this.

Wearing cheap paper overalls from a vending machine, and still feeling throbs in my back from that hasty patch-up at the Ephemerals, I knew I wouldn't impress the manager. One copper-colored eye narrowed behind a monocle-spex, scanning to verify my blurry copy of Albert Morris's investigator license. He'd know in seconds if my maker had disowned me.

Would Albert do that, just because I refused to clean his toilets? Could I already be on the hit list of some pervo hunt club? Worse, he might declare me a *danger to society.* A police exterminator could be swooping down, right now, like an avenging hawk . . .

I was betting my life on Albert's softheartedness, unable to renounce his first frankie.

The manager flipped up his monocle, handing back the smudged ID. "As I told your house computer, there is nothing to investigate. You can't seriously be interested in yesterday's little accident! Since when is it a felony to spill some drinks and break a little glass? We obtained waivers from every customer, offering free meals in recompense."

"Generous, but—"

"Is someone reneging? Is that why you're here? We can call an online jury to watch recordings. Any reasonable panel—"

"Please. I'm not here to plant a grudge lien. I just want the waiter."

"There's nothing to extort. He was covered by our insurance, until we terminated his contract."

"So he *was* fired. Did he work here long?"

"Two years. This morning he had the nerve to claim that last night's incident wasn't his fault. His ditto never made it home, so it must have been hijacked and replaced by an imposter!" The manager sniffed disdain. But if I had hackles, they'd have risen.

"Give me contact info and I won't bother you again."

He glared. It would be simple to snub a utility green. But what if Albert himself followed up?

"Oh . . . all right." His monocular flipped down as he signaled commands. Then, with a dismissive grunt, he turned away.

Damn. Instead of speaking or writing the name, he sent an info-blip to Nell! I could phone her for it, but then maybe I'd have to talk to Albert, like a teen crawling back to Dad. Double-damn. Heading for the exit, I wondered about this obsession to solve one minor riddle before I expire. The matter seemed unimportant. Why worry about it?

I stopped in the doorway, my cheap green senses adjusting to daylight, when something caught my eye. *Literally.* Like a gnat darting nearby, it came buzzing near my face. I swatted, deterring the pesky thing briefly. Then it came back.

Premature ditto decay can attract scavengers, and there was plenty of damaged pseudoflesh hanging off my back. I swiped at it again. It tumbled—then streaked right at me, diving with uncanny speed!

I fell back against a wall, clutching my eye. Worse than the pain were the explosions of color! Skyrocket flashes converged, forming shapes. Forming letters:

No time
Take a cab to Fairfax Park
Pal

13

Doing Their Ditto Work

. . . or how Tuesday's second gray starts
getting paranoid . . .

Unconsciousness can be disturbing to a realperson.

For a ditto, it's like death. And wakening is akin to being born again.

■   ■   ■

Where am I?

A sideways glance tells me I'm still in Irene's hive. Across a wide chamber, I glimpse the huge pale figure of her archetype body—the queen—tended by more than a dozen reddish mini-copies. Full-sized versions come and go swiftly on errands. Not one says a word. No one has to.

In bleary contemplation, I envision an atom's core and its surrounding fog of virtual particles. Irene-duplicates keep emanating from the maroon-colored mass to perform missions for the hive. Others—aged and experienced—spiral in bearing the modern nectar: *knowledge* to accumulate and share with more copies. And at the center, a realperson whose role it is to absorb and redistribute that knowledge, using imitation bodies to do everything else.

I've got to admit, Irene is impressive. Her self is very large.

Come on, Albert, focus.

How long was I out? Feels like moments. They were going to repair me . . . fix the awful damage inflicted by those angry gladiators in the Rainbow Lounge.

Did it work? There's no pain, but that means nothing.

Arms and hands all seem to work. Clasping my side now . . . my leg.

In place of gaping wounds, I feel lumpy ridges, like hard scar tissue. Beneath, large areas feel numb, senseless. But all limbs flex and stretch satisfactorily. Splendid work, for a quick splice and patch job.

But then, if anyone would have advanced repair technology, you'd expect it to be Queen Irene.

Sitting up, I find I'm clothed in generous gray cloth.

"How do you feel?"

It's the high-quality Irene—dyed from a gray blank—standing along-side her associate, the male golem with plaid skin. Vic Collins.

"Surprisingly good. What time is it?"

"Almost two-thirty."

"Huh. That didn't take long."

"We've automated the repair process considerably. Without much help from Universal Kilns, I might add."

"So you suspect them of suppressing this technology, too?"

"As you can imagine, the company prefers that people buy lots of new blanks. Of course, fixing damaged dittos would be economical, ecological, merciful—"

"Does this relate to your other concern? A breakthrough in extending ditto lifespans."

Vic Collins nods. "They are linked. You can hardly expect UK to be eager about sharing technologies that undercut their market. But the law says they must patent and publish advances or else lose them."

Hence the eagerness of this small consortium to do a little quasi-legal espionage. If they can get the goods on a suppressed or hoarded technology, the Whistle-blower Prize could be substantial. Up to thirty percent of the resulting patents. In this case, it could make them tycoons. I'm tempted to pursue the topic, but time can press when your remaining span on Earth is measured in hours. Unlike Irene, I have no rig to return home to. Not if I keep the deal we've made.

"Speaking of UK," I prompt.

"Yes, we should be going, if you feel ready."

I hop off the table. Except for the unpleasant feeling of numbness under my scars, things appear to be okay. "Did you get the stuff?"

"We gathered the supplies and information you require in order to penetrate Universal Kilns."

"Not *penetrate*. I agreed to scout for you, in a strictly legal manner."

"Forgive my poor choice of words. Please come this way."

There's no pain. Still, I limp a bit while following Irene and Collins out the rear of the Rainbow Building. A silent ocher driver waits in the sheltered alley, holding the door of a van with opaque windows. I pause, wanting to get a few matters clear before entering.

"You still haven't explained exactly what I'll be looking for."

"We'll brief you along the way. There are important matters we hope you'll uncover with your renowned investigative prowess."

"I'll do my best"—then I reiterate for the spool recorder inside me—"within the law."

"Naturally, ditMorris. We would not ask you to do anything illegal."

Right, I think, trying to penetrate his gaze. But it's futile. Eyes made of clay aren't windows to the soul. It's still a matter of debate whether there's any "soul" inside of creatures like us at all.

Entering the van, I find the fourth member of our party, smiling with a celebrated mixture of distance and seductiveness, crossing snow white legs that glisten with their own luster beneath sheer, extravagant silk.

"Greetings, Mr. Morris," murmurs the voluptuous pleasure-ditto.

"Maestra," I reply, wondering.

Why would Gineen Wammaker dispatch a top-of-the-line pearl model to accompany us? A simple gray should suffice, to hear my report. Or why send a rox at all? Any useful information can be sent by Web.

My grays carry a good semblance of normal male reaction sets. So her art affects me—both attracting and repelling at once, beckoning some of the more sick-hostile corners of sexuality. Her famed, perversely alluring specialty.

Like any decent adult, I can quash such reactions. (Especially by thinking about honest, self-respecting Clara.) Surely Wammaker knows this, so the aim can't be to influence me.

So why is she here? Especially as a pearl . . . a creature of profuse sensuality . . . unless this mission represents another chance for her to enjoy some depraved bliss?

My worries, already verging on paranoia, bloom anew.

"Let's go," she tells the driver. Gineen clearly doesn't mind that I stare. Perhaps she even knows what I'm thinking.

I'm wishing that I had a better class of clientele.

14

Under False Colors

. . . or how realAlbert gets duped again . . .

What are you saying?" I asked the jetto. "That my web sightings may *not* be Maharal?"

With finger flicks and winked signals, my ebony duplicate fetched data and put moving pictures onscreen. I watched a collage of recordings made weeks ago as Yosil Maharal strolled down an avenue filled with pedestrians and gyrocyclists. One of those fashionable display arcades where you can sample a myriad products, select features you like, and have made-to-order items delivered by courier-ditto before you get home.

From a distance, Maharal appeared to enjoy a window-shopping stroll, sauntering through one boutique after another. A district like this one has more cameras than a typical street, letting Nell's software avatar sew an almost gap-free retrospective mosaic as our target moved from one lens view to another, with time stamps glowing in a low corner.

"Did you notice anything happen, just now?" the ebony asked.

"What's to notice?" I twitched, feeling awkward under that unblinking gaze, knowing what contempt I tend to feel toward my real self, whenever I'm black.

He clicked his tongue. The onscreen image froze and raster-scanned. Enhancing cells zoomed toward where Maharal had joined a small crowd, watching a street performer weave sculptures out of smoke-gel. The fragile artifacts grew and blossomed like delicate apparitions, lifted and shaped by the puffs of air exhaled from the virtuoso's pursed lips. When a child clapped her hands, reverberations made the creation shudder and bow toward her, before rising again as the artist breathed new layers.

Working with similar skill, my golem specialist swiftly crafted a composite image from three cameras, scattered around the plaza. Maharal's picture grew more grainy as we zoomed in on his face. The UK scientist was smiling. All seemed normal, till I felt a creepy suspicion.

"Zoom closer," I said, with misgivings. "The skin texture . . . by God, it's not real!"

"I see it now," Nell commented. "Note the subject's forehead. The pellet dimple has been concealed under makeup."

I slumped. We were looking at a ditto.

"Hm," the ebony commented. "It appears that our good doctor committed a nine-point misdemeanor. Those flesh tones are human-brown. Shade ninety-four X, to be exact. Definitely illegal for duplicates to wear in public."

This was unlike Kaolin's weak ploy, when he phoned me earlier. His archetype guise had been amateurish and quasi-legal since he was at home at the time. But Maharal, in his developing paranoia, must have felt it worth risking a stiff fine in order to drop out of the city-village without a trace.

I glanced at the time stamp. Twelve minutes since the last time Maharal passed near a hi-res publicam, allowing a good reality check. He must have made the switch during that interval. But exactly when? The collage was awfully tight. "Please backtrack, Nell. Show the most biggest coverage gap since fourteen-thirty-six."

From the plaza, Maharal's ghost image began scurrying in reverse till he vanished into a shop offering fine utility coats for men. My avatar did a quick negotiation with the store's internal security system . . . which refused to share any images because of a quaint privacy policy. Nothing would budge the stubborn program, not even Maharal's death certificate and Ritu's permission slip. I might have to go talk to the manager in person.

"How long was he in there?" I asked.

"A little over two minutes."

More than enough time for Maharal to trade places with a waiting ditto. But it was a risky move. Despite the lens-detecting scanners they sell nowadays, you can never absolutely guarantee you're not being watched. Even inside a buried oil drum. (I know, from personal experience.) Still, Maharal must have felt pretty confident.

Now I must assign a new software avatar to do a careful backscan and find out when the *ditto* entered the store. It must have come in disguise, then spent hours in there, crouched behind coatracks or something. After the switch, realMaharal would have waited a while, changing carefully into another disguise before reemerging, positive that his decoy had derailed any normal search routines.

I've pulled the same ruse myself, many times.

"He may have the shopowner's complicity," my ebony specialist pointed out. "The ditto could arrive in a shipping crate and realMaharal might depart the same way."

I sighed over the drudgery ahead, inspecting and analyzing countless images.

"Don't sweat it. I'll handle the sift from my cubicle," the specialist assured me. "I've already got our other cases under control. Besides, I think you'll want to look at what your other search uncovered at the crash site."

He got up and moved toward the little niche where I recall spending many happy hours—a cramped cubbyhole that I find comfortably cozy whenever I'm ebony, tuned to want nothing more than the pure joy of professional skill. Watching my copy go, I felt a little envious . . . and grateful to both Maharal and Kaolin for helping invent dittotech.

It's a terrific boon, if you have a marketable skill.

■   ■   ■

The ebony was right. Investigation of the crash site had reached a new plateau.

Onscreen, my display depicted a vast swathe of desert southeast of town—a strange realm where trustworthy realtime images were as sparse as drinkable water and where it took sophisticated trickery to sift the trail of a moving car. Following my instructions, Nell had traced a ghostly spoor of whirling cyclones back through the night, moving earlier and ever farther from Maharal's death rendezvous. The overlay showed a dotted line weaving toward a range of low mountains near the Mexican border, not far from the International Combat Arena. Once inside those hills, I knew the trail of mini-tornados must vanish amid a whirl of canyon turbulence.

But I'd seen enough to feel an eerie chill. I knew this country.

"Urraca Mesa," I whispered.

Nell spoke up.

"What did you say?"

I shook my head.

"Dial up Ritu Maharal," I ordered. "We need to talk."

15

Copycats

. . . in which a Frankenstein monster learns why he shouldn't exist . . .

Fortunately, my greenie expense allowance was still active—Albert hadn't disowned me yet—so I was able to hire a micro-cab from Odeon Square, weaving across Realtown on a single gyro-wheel with two cramped seats. Swift it may have been, but the trip was also excruciating as the driver kept going on and on about the *war*.

Apparently, the battle in the desert had begun going sour for our side. The cabbie blamed this on bad leadership, illustrating his point by calling up recent action highlights in a viewbubble that enveloped me, trapped on the rear saddle, amid scenes of violent carnage by bomb and shell, by cutter beam and hand-to-hand dismemberment, all lovingly collated by this avid aficionado.

Albert had learned plenty from Clara over the years, enough to know this armchair general's opinions weren't worth spit. The guy had a taxi franchise with *eleven* yellow and black–checkered duplicates driving hacks, presumably all yapping at cornered customers. How did he keep a high enough satisfaction index to merit so many cabs?

Speed was the answer. I had to give him that. Arrival offered me the day's greatest surge of pleasure. I paid the cabbie and escaped into the cement maze of Fairfax Park.

▪ ▪ ▪

Big Al doesn't like the place. No greenery. Too much space was given over to concrete ramps, spirals, and jutting slabs, back when real kids might spend every spare moment of lifespan careening on stunt bikes, skateboards, and flare skooters, risking broken necks for sheer excitement. That is, till new pastimes lured them away, leaving behind a maze of metal-reinforced walls and towers like forsaken battlements, some of them three stories high, too costly to demolish.

Pallie loves the place. All that buried rebar acts like a partial Faraday Cage, blocking radio transmissions, thwarting spy-gnats and eavesbugs, while the hot concrete surface blinds visual and IR sensors. Nor is he above bouts of nostalgia, shooting the old slopes in his latest, souped-up wheelchair, popping rims and sliders, hollering and teetering while catheters and IV tubes whip around him like war pennants. Some kicks have to be experienced in flesh, I guess. Even flesh as harshly wounded as his.

Albert kind of puts up with Pal—partly out of guilt. Feels he might have tried harder to dissuade the guy from going out that night when ambushers jumped him, roasting half his body and leaving the rest for dead. But honestly, how do you "dissuade" a thrill-addict mercenary who'd stroll into a blatant trap, just asking to get his balls shot off? Hell, I'm more cautious in clay than Pal is in person.

I found him waiting under the shadow of "Mom's Fright," the biggest skooter ramp—with a swoop chute so sheer it makes you sick just looking at it. He had company. Two men. Real men, who eyed each other warily, separated by Pal's biotronic wheelchair.

It felt awk being the sole ditto, and the feeling got worse when one of them—a brawny blond—gave me the *look,* staring through me like I wasn't there.

The other one smiled, friendly. Tall and a bit skinny, he struck me as somehow familiar.

"Hey, green, where's your soul?" Pal jibed, raising a burly fist.

I punched it. "Same place as your feet. Still, we both get around."

"We do. How'd you like that message wasp I sent? Cool, eh?"

"Kind of cyber-retro, don't you think? Lot of effort for a simple come-hither. Hurt like hell when it pierced my eye."

"Omelettes," he said, apologizing backhandedly. "So, I hear you cut yourself loose!"

"Shrug. How much good to Albert is an Albert who's not Al?"

"Cute. I didn't figure Sober Morris *could* make a frankie. Anyway, some of my best friends are mutants, real and otherwise."

"Sign of a true pervert. Do you know if Al's planning to disown me?"

"Nah. Too soft. He did post a credit limit, though. You can charge two hundred, no more."

"That much? I didn't clean a single toilet. Is he angry?"

"Can't tell. He cut me off. Got other probs. Seems he lost *both* of this morning's grays."

"Ouch. I heard about the first, but . . . damn. Number two had the Turkomen. That was a good scooter." I pondered this a second. No wonder my AWOL raised so little dust. "Two grays gone. Huh. Coincidence? Happenstance?"

Pallie scratched a scar, running from his shaggy black hair to a stubbled chin.

"Thinking no. Reason I sent the wasp."

The big blond grunted. "Will you cut this useless chatter? Just ask the vile thing if it remembers us."

Vile thing? I tried to meet the fellow's eye. He refused contact.

Pal chuckled. "This is Mr. James Gadarene. He thinks you might recognize him. Do?"

I looked the man up and down. "No recollection . . . sir." Adding some formality might be a good idea.

Both strangers grunted, as if half-expecting this. I hurried on.

"Of course that's no guarantee. Albert himself forgets faces. Even some guys he knew in college. Depends how long ago we met. Anyway, I'm a frank—"

"This memory would be less than *twenty hours* old," Gadarene interrupted without actually looking at me. "Late last night, one of your grays rang my doorbell, flashed some private eye credentials and demanded an urgent meeting. The ruckus even woke some of my colleagues in our compound next door. I agreed—reluctantly—to meet the gray, alone. But in private the damned thing only paced around, blathering nonsense that I couldn't even begin to comprehend. Finally, my assistant came in from the next room with news. The gray wore a static generator. It was deliberately jamming my interview recorder!"

"So you have no chronicle of the meeting?"

"Nothing useful. That's when I got fed up and tossed the cursed thing out."

"I . . . don't recall anything remotely like that. Which means the real Albert Morris doesn't either. Or he didn't, as of ten this morn. Before that, all of our dittos have been accounted for, stretching back at least a month. Every one brought home a complete inload . . . though some were pretty banged up." I winced, recalling last night's awful trek under the river. "Heck, I don't even know what 'offices' you're talking about."

"Mr. Gadarene heads an organization called Defenders of Life," Pallie explained.

At once I grasped the fellow's hostility. His group fiercely opposes dittotech on purely moral grounds—a stance requiring great tenacity now-adays, when realfolks live surrounded and outnumbered by countless creatures of servile clay. If one of Albert's copies *had* behaved in the manner just described, it would be an act of towering rudeness and deliberate provocation.

From Gadarene's bitter expression, I guessed a special ire toward me. As a frankie I had declared independence, professing to be a free, self-motivated life form . . . though a *pseudobeing* with few rights and fewer prospects. At least other dittos could be viewed as extensions or appendages of some real person. But I'd seem the worst kind of insult toward heavenly authority. A soul-less construct who dares to say *I am.*

At a best guess, I'd wager his people never donate to the Temple of the Ephemerals.

"Same thing happened to us, early this morning," the other fellow said—the tall man who looked vaguely familiar.

"I think I do recognize you," I mused. "Yes . . . the greenie I ran into, picketing at Moonlight Beach. Its face copied yours."

From his wry smile, I could tell the man already knew about my encounter with his cheap demonstrator-ditto. The green may have already inloaded. Or perhaps it phoned home to report my resemblance to their wee-hours visitor.

"Mr. Farshid Lum," said Pal, finishing introductions.

"Friends of the Unreal?" I guessed. The biggest organization of man-cies I'd heard of.

"Tolerance Unlimited," he corrected with a frown. "The FOTU manifesto doesn't go far enough in demanding emancipation for synthetic beings. We think short-lived people are just as real as anyone else who thinks and feels."

That drew a snort from the blond. And yet, despite a philosophical chasm that gaped between them, I sensed common purpose. For now.

"You say a Morris copy also barged into *your* place—"

"—ranted for a while and then left, yeah," Pallie inserted. "Only this time we got some clear images through the static. It was one of your brodits, or sure looked like one."

He handed me a flat pix. Though blurry, it resembled Albert, as close as any gray takes after its rig.

"Appearances can be faked. So can credentials. The static indicates that someone didn't want too close an inspection—"

"I agree," interrupted Gadarene. "Moreover, when we phoned Mr. Morris this morning for an explanation, his house computer—"

"—Nell—"

"—dismissed the whole event as impossible, since you didn't have any duplicates active at the time we were being harassed. The house refused even to wake Albert Morris for comment."

"Curious," I comment.

"In fact, your rig has both of our groups listed as crank organizations," said Lum, with a wry expression, as if he wore the moniker with pride. "Since the house filtered and refused my queries, I went to the public Albert Morris net profile, looking for one of his friends. Someone who *would* talk to us."

"Me," Pal said. "I'm not bothered by cranks. I like 'em!"

"Likes attract," I muttered, winning brief but angry eye contact from Gadarene.

"Yeah, well, my cup ranneth over when I got *two* queries, from groups that normally despise each other. Smelling a rat, I tried calling Al, but he brushed me off. Too busy for an old Pal, today. So I went snooping for someone else who might shed light on the matter . . . and found you."

"Me? I already said, these stories don't fit anything I remember."

"And I believe you. But do you have any ideas? What comes to mind?"

"Why ask me? I'm just a green, not exactly equipped for analytical thought."

"Oh, but you won't let that stop you!" Pallie laughed.

I frowned at him, knowing he was right. I couldn't refuse to poke away at this, even if I'm made of the cheap stuff.

I turned to Gadarene and Lum.

"Looking at it from your point of view, several possibilities arise."

I held up one finger. "First, I might be standing here *lying*. Al could have some valid reason for wanting to poke two irate public advocacy groups in the eye, stir them up, then claim it wasn't him that done it."

"Please," Pallie shook his head. "It's the sort of thing *I* might try. But Albert's about as much fun as a judge."

For some reason, the insult made me smile. Yeah, poor Sober Albert.

"Well, then, maybe someone's trying to set him up."

Once upon a time, crime and prosecution revolved around establishing or demolishing alibis. If you could prove that you were somewhere else at the time of a crime, it meant you didn't do it. Simple as that.

The alibi excuse started vanishing back in the cyber age, a time when countless big and little heists redistributed cash by the billions while perpetrators hunched over remote computer screens slurping caffeine, dispatching electronic minions to rob in supposed anonymity. For a while, it looked as if society would bleed a death of a myriad cuts . . . till accountability was restored and most of the surviving cyberfarts either went to jail or grew up.

Today, the whereabouts of your protoplasmic self hardly matters. Culpability is a matter of opportunity and will. Effective alibis are hard to come by.

"Interesting you should come up with that idea," Pallie commented. "The same thing occurred to me as I watched this morning's raid on Beta's hideout—that was good work, by the way. I saw Albert meet Ritu Maharal . . . and later heard about her father's death. But what really got me going is the maestra."

"Gineen Wammaker? What about her?"

"Well, for one thing, I know that Al's second gray dropped out to do a closed-cognito job for her."

I hesitated. It wouldn't be kosher for me to confirm that such a contract existed. I owed Albert some loyalty, since he hadn't made me an outlaw. The sap.

"All right, both women asked Al to send a gray over. And both grays vanished. So? It's probably a coincidence. Anyway, those grays were baked and imprinted hours *after* mystery dittos barged in to bother you two gentlemen. What's the connection?"

"That puzzled me, too. So I called Wammaker."

"How I envy you. And what did the Ice Princess say?"

"That she never asked for a Morris-ditto! At least, not since the Beta job was finished. In fact, she told me that Detective Morris is far too rude to be a suitable retainer in future, and furthermore that—"

"Can we get on with this?"

James Gadarene evidently didn't like discussing the maestra of Studio Neo, whose perverse specialties went out of their way to tweak oldtime morality. The blond shifted his bulk irritably, and a bit ominously. He struck me as the sort who sometimes dismembers dittos—willingly paying fines—for the sheer pleasure of punishing evil with his bare hands.

"All right," Pal continued cheerfully. "So I figured I'd find out what I could about your second gray. See if Wammaker's lying. It meant accessing the camera-web and doing some path tracing."

"You?" I chuckled at the idea of Pallie carefully assigning search-avatars and sifting a gazillion intermeshed images. "You never had the patience."

He shook his head ruefully.

"Naw, I'm just an old-fashioned action figure. Still, I know a few graying digital mavens who owe me favors. All they had to do was track a series of sub-myob traffic infractions when the gray drove from your house to the mall. Once inside, the ditto was in view by publicams, much of the time. It parked its scooter and took the escalator . . . but never actually reached Wammaker's."

"No?"

"Instead, it got waylaid by the maestra's assistant—at least that's who it looked like, barely visible under a skulkhood. Together they went two floors down to a rented storefront . . . and disappeared."

"So? Maybe Gineen wanted to meet some distance from her regular clients. Especially if the matter's sensitive."

"Could be. Or . . . what if someone *else* wants to use Albert's gray, while making everyone think Gineen hired it?"

I tried to wrap my head around the idea.

"You mean someone faked Gineen's initial call to Albert this morning, then arranged it so lots of cams would see the gray approach Wammaker's . . . But then"—I shook my head—"it'd take lots of skilled fakery. A false Gineen to make the call. Then a fake assistant."

"And fake Alberts, sent earlier to bother these good citizens." Pallie nodded toward both Gadarene and Lum.

The bigger man groaned. "None of this made any sense when you explained it to me an hour ago, and it sure hasn't gotten any better. Some of us have just one life, you know. You'd better put all this together soon."

"I've been trying," Pal answered, a bit miffed. "Actually, this kind of deductive stuff is more Albert's kind of thing. What d'you think, Greenie?"

I scratched my head. Purely out of habit, since there are no follicles or parasites on my porcelain pate.

"All right. Let's say all these charades were meant for different audiences. Take those dittos who invaded your premises last night . . . they didn't talk about anything significant, you say?"

"Just blather, as far as I could tell."

"But they took pains to keep the blather from being recorded. So you can't *prove* it was nonsense, can you?"

"What d'you mean? What else could it have been?"

"It might *look* as if you were conspiring together."

"Con . . . conspiring?"

"Look at it from an outsider's point of view, Mr. Gadarene. They see a gray enter your establishment, then leave—hastily and furtively—an hour or so later. One might conclude that you discussed matters of substance. This could all have been arranged in order to establish a *plausible link* between your group and Albert Morris."

"Then the same thing happens at my place," said Lum.

"And at Studio Neo. Only this time the *gray* is real but the *visit* is faked," Pal prompted. "Was that also for public consumption?"

"Partly," I nodded. "But I'll bet chief audience for *that* bit of theater was the gray itself. Recall that it went on detached mode right after the meeting, yes? It must be convinced, even now, that it's working for the real maestra. She's not the most likable person—"

Gadarene snorted loudly.

"—but she's a businesswoman of substance, with high credibility at fulfilling contracts and staying in the letter of the law. The gray might despise and distrust her. But he'd take an interesting case for a good fee."

"Let me get this straight," offered Farshid Lum. "You think someone *pretended* to be Wammaker in order to sign your gray up for a task—"

"A task that might be a cover for something Al would never agree to," Pal suggested.

"—and that bit of theater earlier, at Tolerance Unlimited—"

"—and the Defenders," Gadarene cut in, "was designed to make it seem *we* are involved in whatever diabolical . . . ." He groaned. "I'm still confused. We're not getting any closer!"

"Oh yes we are." Pal looked at me. "You have an idea, don't you, my green friend?"

Unfortunately, I did.

"Look, I'm not designed for this. I'm not a brainy ebony or a high-class gray. Anything I offer will just be conjecture."

Lum waved away my demurral. "I've looked up your profile, Mr. Morris. Your reputation for creating fine analytic selves can't be matched. Please, continue."

I might have complained right then that I'm *not* one of Albert's "selves." But it would be moot.

"Look, we still don't have much data," I began. "But if this chain of wild deductions can stand, I'll guess a few things.

"One: the person or group behind it all has sophisticated dittoing abilities, especially the art of giving a golem a face it's not supposed to have. Since that's illegal, we're already in dangerous territory.

"Two: there's apparently some need to enlist willing participation by one of Albert's grays. Appearances won't do. The gray must be convinced to give genuine effort—providing some skill that Al's known to be good at. The mission has to *appear* legal . . . or at least worthwhile and not too heinous . . . for the gray to cooperate."

"Yes, go on," Pal prompted.

"Three: there's a multipronged effort to assign blame for whatever's going to happen. Guilt-by-association. Fake calls from the maestra. An apparent meeting at Studio Neo . . ."

"And us," Lum commented, abruptly serious. "The charade of waking me at night was meant to look like a sneaky conference of conspirators. But why me? And why pull the same stunt on Mr. Gadarene's group of misguided spirits?"

Pal chuckled loud enough to drown out the blond's growl. "But that's the beauty of it! On the surface, it seems your two groups could never get together. You seem at opposite poles. Ironically, that makes a conspiracy seem almost workable."

When they stared at him, Pal spread his burly hands wide, making the wheelchair roll.

"Think! Is there somebody you *both* hate? Some person, group, or organization that both groups despise. So deeply, you might plausibly join forces?"

I watched both men struggle with the concept. Accustomed to demonizing each other, they clearly found it hard to conceive that they shared any common interest.

I knew the answer already, and felt chilled down to my clay substrate. But I didn't prompt them.

They'd get it in a minute or two.

16

Send In the Clones

. . . as Tuesday's gray number two employs his art . . .

Continuing realtime recitation. Time to enter the Funnel. It's one of my favorite parts of this job. Getting a chance to prove that I can fool a world that's filled with eyes.

"We arranged for the items you requested."

The red-hued Irene-golem hands me a plain satchel. I inspect the contents. Everything's there.

"You sent a lens sniffer ahead, along the route I described?"

"We did, per your instructions. The sniffer verified surveillance gaps in the places you predicted. Current details are noted." She hands me a data-plaque.

"Current? As of when?"

"About an hour ago, while you were being repaired."

"Hm."

An hour can be eternity. But I'm optimistic while scanning the map with its glowing icons and overlapping cones of vision. Yes, the city swarms with eyes, the way a jungle fills with insects. Coverage gaps are precious in my line of work. Today's most difficult hurdle will be to cover my tracks long before I reach Universal Kilns. I'll need several changing sites along the way—shadow gaps that are just big enough to allow a quick shift in appearance without being noticed—preferably near locales with lots of dittos coming and going.

Irene might have faith in her sniffers—programmed to spot the tell-tale reflective glint of a glass camera lens—but even the best military scanners can't detect every pinhole spex that may lurk in some crevice or tree trunk. Any number of pin-spies might have been installed since I last used this Funnel route. Fortunately, most of those have low resolution. They'll miss a truly artful transformation.

I have mixed feelings about revealing this path—one of Albert's recent favorites—to Gineen and her cohorts. True, nearly every Funnel has limited useful lifespan, as countless amateurs keep finding and rendering them useless. And my pay for this job makes the sacrifice worthwhile.

Still, I'd be happier if I had days to prepare, with multiple dittos working in tandem. Everything would be more secure.

Don't sweat it. I offered no guarantees on such a rush job, and Albert gets fifty percent for just trying. Worst case, they are the ones risking exposure.

And yet, my mind spins with potential failure modes. One is coming up ahead.

We slow beneath a highway overpass, coming to rest behind an identical van that quickly accelerates away, resuming our former course and speed, leaving us parked in its place. The driver—briefly glimpsed—is another inherently loyal Irene-golem. The old car-switcheroo, first used more than a hundred years ago, but lately modified with reconfigurable chassis and chameleon stretchyskin so this van will look quite different when Gineen and her gang depart again.

Scanning the concrete walls that support the overpass, I spy just one trafficam, its lens recently covered with bird droppings. The real stuff, in case there's later analysis.

So far, so good. Still, I'm unhappy, feeling slovenly and unprofessional. These measures may fool publicams and voyeurs—possibly even private snoops hired by Universal Kilns. But it takes more than a few tricks to dupe real cops. This will work only if our little adventure stays shy of outright illegality.

"You'll get out here, wait exactly eight minutes, then proceed to that grove," Vic Collins explains, pointing one of his plaid-dyed fingers toward a copse of geniformed licorice-drop trees. "We control, or have taken out, all of the cameras between here and there."

"You sure about that?" Lack of preparation time requires a brute force approach that I'd rather have supervised myself.

He nods.

"Unless any sky-eyes are retargeted in the next few minutes. Within the grove, you'll make your first change, ditch the bag, along with the clothes you're wearing, and emerge as a utility orange-dit. We'll send a dog in later, to pick up the satchel."

"Be sure that you do. If I'm traced back to the grove, a savvy examiner will guess this car-switching dodge."

"Then you mustn't let anyone trace you back to the grove," Vic Collins concludes. "We are counting on your skill."

Oh, brother.

"The bus station is key. I'll do a dodge and weave there, through the ditto crowds. Are more supplies waiting in the locker I specified?"

"You'll find another bag containing a change of clothes and skin dye." Collins holds up a hand, guessing my next question. "And yes, the dye is a gray variant—perfectly legal. We can say myob to the cops."

"Myob is as myob does," I retort. "If I so much as suspect I'm involved in anything higher than a Class Six misdemeanor, I'll drop out. No matter how big a liability bond you posted."

"Relax, ditMorris," Irene soothes. "We have no fear of the law. Our sole aim in this subterfuge is to keep UK from linking us—"

"—or suspecting today's little reconnaissance, yes. They could make things unpleasant, even if we're legal."

"These precautions are for your rig's protection as much as ours, ditMorris. With what you learn today, we can narrow down our suspicions and follow up by slapping specific datapoenas on Universal Kilns, under the tech-disclosure laws. The beauty of it is that they'll never have a reason to ever link you to our lawsuit."

It makes sense. That is, assuming I don't choose to tell Aeneas Kaolin all about this, just as soon as I pass inside Universal Kilns!

Sure, I'd forfeit my bond and lose most of Albert's hard-won credibility points, but there'd be compensations. Maybe he would make me a subject of his ditto life-extension experiments. I could have more than another twelve hours, maybe lots more!

Huh. Now where did *that* thought come from? It was almost . . . well, *frankie* . . . confusing the more important "I" with the trivial *i* that's thinking these thoughts.

How bizarre!

Anyway, why daydream about doing things that I'll never do. Or cheap posterities that I'll never win?

"And after the bus station?" Vic Collins prompts.

"I'll catch the 330 dino to Riverside Drive and UK headquarters. Head straight for the employee entrance, wave my ID, and hope their security AI is as lax as you expect. Again, if you're wrong about that, if they ask *any* inconvenient questions, I'll just turn around and leave."

"We understand," the red ditto says with a nod. "But we're confident they'll let you in."

Irene and company somehow know that Ritu Maharal hired one of Albert's grays. One that went missing a few hours ago. Still, the guards at UK *may* just wave me through, assuming I'm on business for a major stockholder. The trick may work at the outer portal, where hundreds of realfolks and dittos pass each hour. Hell, gaggles of tourists line up there for excursion passes, forming guided groups to view the factory where their disposable bodies are made.

But Wammaker and her pals expect me to breeze through several *more* checkpoints, each more secure than the last, blithely peering about as I plunge deeper, on the lookout for tech-hints without ever once actually committing fraud or telling a clearcut lie!

(Did Vic Collins also arrange for a security lapse in advance? Some inside bribery to lubricate things? He seems the kind who might know how, with his furtive-yet-superior manner. It's a good thing I have all our conversations taped, on the recorder I'm subvocalizing into right now.)

And they *did* pay in advance. Crypto-cash, encoded to one of Albert's accounts. All I need do is try. Put in a modest effort. A seventy-five percent fee just for getting inside.

Still, I wish they'd just let me drive my scooter to Universal, instead of going through this rigmarole. *Amateurs.* The rest of my "life" was devoted to them. Doing my professional best to make this ditzy, half-ass spy job work.

But what if their suspicions are right, and I help prove it?

If Universal Kilns is deliberately suppressing major improvements in dittotech, the news could be big. Albert's reputation might skyrocket.

And I'll have made him a new enemy. One of Earth's biggest corporations.

17

Graying Gracefully

. . . realAl decides on an expedition, a companion, and a disguise . . .

Ritu Maharal appeared reluctant to accompany me on a last-minute trip to the desert. But how could she refuse? Hardly any of the reasons that her mother might have used—from modesty to a hectic schedule—have any bearing nowadays.

"It's quite a distance along twisty roads," she said, clearly looking for an out. "There could be delays. If we're gone more than a day, how will we get home?"

I had a ready answer.

"If it looks like we're about to expire, we can stop at a ditimart and get our heads frozen."

"Have you ever shipped your head from a ditimart?" Onscreen, her oval face gave a pursed frown. "The ditsicle can take *days* to arrive, and it's never as fresh as the ads claim."

"We won't have to ship. I'll copy another gray and stash it in the car, to thaw if time runs short. That way I can finish scouting around some more, and still bring the heads back in a cooler."

At least, that's what I told Ritu. In fact, I had other plans. Plans she didn't have to know about.

NOHB. None of her business.

"You're sure this is important?" she asked, shaking her gleaming black locks a bit petulantly. I wondered; was this major UK stockholder quibbling over the cost of a golem?

"You tell me whether it is, Ritu. You say you want your father's death solved, yet you never bothered to tell me that your family owned a cabin by the border, just a hundred clicks from the crash site."

She winced. "I *should* have mentioned it. But honestly, I thought Dad got rid of the place ages ago, before I was sixteen. Do you think it might relate to his . . . accident?"

"In my experience, nothing can be dismissed early in an investigation. So please, gather any data you can find regarding that property. And before you imprint, do spend a little time thinking about your childhood trips to the cabin, so your gray won't have trouble remembering."

I often do that—ask the client to think hard about a subject before they send a golem to be questioned. For some reason, most people fail to imprint their Standing Wave completely. The sloppy-copy effect—a kind of swiss cheese amnesia when the ditto tries to access older memories. It never happens to me. My grays even recall some things that I can't in real form. I wonder why.

Hesitating another moment, Ritu finally agreed with a jerky nod.

"Very well. If you think it's important."

"I'm hopeful it may help break the case."

She drummed elegant, long fingertips on the desk in front of her screen. "I'm at Universal Kilns right now. Going through some paperwork to keep busy . . . though Aeneas has given me an indefinite leave of absence."

None of that was relevant to my current needs, not on any practical level. Yet I realized, suddenly, that I'd been insensitive. After all, this was about the recent death of her father.

"Yeah, well, I know it's a hard time for you. Tell me, did they ever find—" I paused, but there were no better words. "Did they find Dr. Maharal's ghost?"

"No." Ritu stared past the monitor, looking stricken and a bit confused. Her full lips quivered. "There's been no sign of the ditto. Aeneas is quite upset about it. He thinks your missing gray might have something to do with the disappearance."

More likely the other way around, I thought, recalling the lengths Yosil Maharal took, back when he was alive, trying to drop out of sight. Top theory at the moment? My gray must have caught Maharal's ghost sneaking off. Pursuing, I must have carelessly fallen for a trap.

I do that sometimes—underestimate the quarry. Nobody's perfect . . . and you *can* get lazy when such mistakes are never permlethal. It kind of makes you marvel at those detectives of olden times, who confronted and confounded remorseless evil while equipped with just one life. Now those guys really had it.

So gray number one may be a puddle of dissolved slurry right now, sinking into the grass somewhere on Aeneas Kaolin's mansion grounds. And by now Maharal's ghost could be . . . what? Whiling away its last hour or so in seclusion somewhere? Maybe spending it with a hired Wammaker copy, for all I knew.

Or else, more likely, executing some final chore for its enigmatic maker. Something deep, complex, and possibly nefarious. I couldn't shake a creepy feeling about that.

"I'm willing to send another gray to the estate, and help in the search," I offered.

"That may not be a good idea right now," Ritu answered, dubious. "Aeneas wants his own people handling that end. But you and I can still investigate other matters. In fact, this desert trip may be useful, after all. When do we start?"

Wondering at her change in tone, I nodded.

"Well, you could make a copy there at UK—"

"I'd rather do it at home . . . and pack a few things. Also, there may be some pictures of the cabin in my scrapbook."

"That could help."

Ritu worked her mouth. "Are you sure this can't wait till morning?"

In fact, waiting might be wise. And yet, I felt a growing sense of urgency. A need to get on with the part of my plan that Ritu Maharal didn't have any reason to know about.

"I'll swing by and pick you up by six. That way, we can cross the desert at night and reach mesa country around dawn."

Ritu shrugged, appearing resigned.

"Okay. Here's my address—"

"No." I shook my head. "We'll meet at your father's place instead. I've been meaning to give it a look-over. We can do that before heading out."

■　■　■

I had to pack quickly. The Volvo has an expandable compartment in back, custom-designed to haul up to three imprinted golem blanks in a vac-pac, or just one with a ready-bake kilnette. There's even room leftover to haul some forensic supplies. I had already prepared a gray ditsicle for the trunk. That left enough time for a makeover.

I stripped down, stepped into the shower, and asked Nell to gray me.

"First protect your eyes," she reminded.

"Oh, yeah." I grabbed a container off the shelf and popped out a fresh pair of dark, full-orb contact lenses. I hadn't done this for a while, so they stung a bit going in.

"Ready."

A tingling sensation began creeping upward, starting with my toes.

"Spread your legs and lift your arms," Nell said.

I complied, feeling a bit creepy as she played a resonance laser over my skin, burning off hairs and dead skin cells in a zillion microscopic protein explosions, closer than a razor could shave. Air jets blew away ash and dross, followed by ion-focused droplets of a special solution, to both seal and nurture my pores during the hours they'll spend cut off from air.

Next came the paint job, quick-staining with my own secret formula. In minutes—lacking only some touch-ups with ditspackle—I could pass for a high-class golem. Except under very close inspection. I held off inserting the mouthpiece for a while yet. It can be a bit uncomfortable.

The procedure's not exactly illegal—not like disguising a *golem* to look real in public. But it's highly discouraged. Someone could shoot me dead when I'm like this, and get off with a mere fine. Small wonder it's not done very much. Ironically, that's why a gifted amateur like Yosil Maharal nearly pulled off an inverted version of the same ruse a few weeks ago. Studying those recorded images, my ebony specialist had been lucky to spot certain telltale discrepancies in skin texture. Discrepancies I carefully eliminated there in my dressing room.

Of course I could mention another difference between me and Ritu's late father.

When *he* tried this subterfuge, it was aimed at concealing some dark secret. But my reasons were simpler.

I was doing it for love.

■　■　■

Well, it felt that way at the time. Ebony-me even complained about the impulsiveness of my decision to go on this trip in person.

"You're acting on emotion. Clara left an ivory in her fridge. That should slake your animal drives till the weekend when she returns."

"An ivory's not the same. Anyway, Maharal's cabin happens to be near the battlefield! I can't pass up this opportunity to drop by and surprise her."

"Then send your *own* ivory. There's no need to go in person."

I didn't answer. The ebony was just being snippy. He knew that Clara and I can take or leave casual dittosex, even with occasional outsiders, because it doesn't matter. No more than a passing fantasy.

Because it's no real substitute for the real thing. Not to us.

"This isn't a productive use of time," said my hyperlogical doppelganger, trying a different tack while I tossed some clothes in a bag.

"That's what I have you for," I retorted. "Be productive! Can I assume our other cases are in hand?"

"They are." The glossy black version of me nodded. "But what happens when I expire, less than eighteen hours from now?"

"Stick your head in the icer, of course. I imprinted another jet, along with a gray and a green, in case you need 'em to take over."

Ebony-me sighed, as usual regarding my real self as childish and irresponsible.

"None of the new dittos will have my recent memories. Continuity will be broken."

"Then thaw your replacement an hour early and update him."

"With *words*? You know how inefficient—"

"Nell will help. Anyway, I should be back before Wednesday's ebony fades. Then I'll inload his memories, and yours, from the freezer."

"So you say now. But you've been distracted before and let brains spoil in the fridge. Anyway, suppose you get *killed* wearing that foolish disguise?"

Long fingers, the color of space, reached out to pinch my faux-gray skin.

"I'll take every precaution not to let that happen," I promised, pulling away and avoiding those dark eyes. It's tough lying to yourself, especially when you're standing right in front of you.

"Be sure and do that," ebony muttered. "I'll make a lousy ghost."

■ ■ ■

Heading to Maharal's place, I shut off the Volvo's hypercautious autopilot and drove manually. Weaving through traffic helped ease my nerves . . . though some green peditstrians yelled obscenely when I swerved past. All right, I could drive better. Blame my disguise for influencing me subconsciously. Or it could have been the war news.

"... recent battlefield reversals and heavy casualties have pushed retreating PEZ-USA forces into a pocket, with their backs against the Cordillera del Muerte Mountains. Although the position seems strong for defensive tactics, oddsmakers have already begun offering early buyouts of final outcome wagers, assuming the battle to be lost.

"If so, and if the disputed icebergs go to Indonesia, this debacle will cast doubt on President Bickson's plan for staying off the SouthWestern Eco-Toxic Aquifer Plume.

"Faced with SWETAP-related backlash from voters, congressional leaders have already started gathering e-signatures for a demarchy petition, demanding that Bickson offer terms and cut PEZ losses before their armed force is completely annihilated.

"But a Glasshouse spokesgolem ruled out that option, insisting that hope remains for victory on the battlefield. 'It's all or nothing,' the Bicksondit said. 'When it comes to fighting SWETAP, half a berg is the same as none at all.' "

Cursing, I told the radio to shut up. Instead, I asked Nell for a reminder-summary of Yosil Maharal's personal background.

Despite having twelve whole hours to research, she hadn't been able to dig up much about his childhood before arriving as a refugee from one of those nasty little ethnic wars they used to have over in South Asia, after the turn of the century.

Adopted by distant relatives, the shy boy thrived on schoolwork, showing little interest in social affairs. Later, as a budding scientist, Yosil ignored the fashionable but doomed cyber and nanotech fads, zeroing instead on the virgin field of neuro-ceramics. After Jefty Annonas cracked the mysterious floating wonder of the Soul Standing Wave—more intricate than any genome—Maharal joined a start-up company led by the greatest Vic of our time, Aeneas Kaolin.

He never married. Maharal's gene-merging and nurturing agreement with Ritu's mother originally featured some twisty responsibility diagrams, at one point including a gay couple, an estate management bank, and an heirless cousin. But all of those adjunct- and demi-parents cashed out several years before Mom died in a copter crash, when Ritu was twelve.

Yikes. And now Daddy's punched his clock, too. Life ain't fair. Poor kid.

I felt a little guilty, pushing her to take this trip. But I had a hunch about this "cabin" of her father's, and Ritu's help may be vital. Anyway, if her gray found the journey traumatic, realRitu could just toss away the head without inloading. No memory, no foul.

Our ancestors, who suffered far more than we do, never had that option.

■　■　■

A black, all-terrain limousine stood out front of the address Ritu gave me. I sent a scan of the plates to Nell, who replied that it belonged to Universal Kilns.

So. Good of Kaolin to lend her a limo, I thought. *But then, it's not every day you lose a close friend and your assistant loses a father.*

I parked my battered car behind the gleaming Yugo and headed for the house—a larger-than-average veridian home, without much yard but covered by slanting solarium panes to trap each ray of sunlight, dark plates for photovoltaic energy and green for drip-treating household waste. There were enough of the gleaming sewage cells to serve an active family, but just a few had active algae cultures. In fact, most looked completely unused.

A bachelor pad, then. And the bachelor spent long periods away from home.

I mounted fourteen steps, passing between decorative loquots that deserved better care. Pausing next to the poor things, I felt tempted to pull out my cutter and prune some crossing branches. After all, I was early.

Then I noticed the front door stood ajar.

Well, I was expected. Still, there was some ambiguity. As a licensed private detective and a quasi-agent of the civil posse, I couldn't just walk in. By law, I had to announce myself.

"Ritu? It's me, Albert." I left out the grammatically correct ditto modifier, though I came disguised as a golem. Most people are sloppy about it, anyway.

The atrium floor was speckled from an active-element mosaic skylight, shifting random colors and playing bright-dark tricks on the eye. Ahead, stairs climbed around two landings before reaching the upper story. Glancing left, I saw an open-plan sitting room, furnished in a rather fogeyish cyberpunk style.

A faint clatter—more like a hurried rustle—came from my right, beyond a set of double doors, carved wood with frosted panels. No lights shone within that room, but a *shadow* could be made out, moving furtively on the other side.

A murmur . . . a few words that I couldn't hear at all well, sounded like *". . . now where would Betty have hidden . . ."*

Creepiness prickled my spine. I touched one of the doors. The glass was both rough and cool—perfect sensations that reminded me of the chief thing that I must not forget:

You're real. So be careful.

As if I needed prompting! Fey suspicions thrummed my Standing Wave, coursing back and forth between the only organic heart and brain I'll ever have. As a ditto, I might go barging into the next room, just to see what's what. But as an organic heir of paranoid cavemen, I settled for giving one door a shove, then staying well back from the threshold as it swung open.

I spoke louder. "Hello, Ritu?"

Inside lay Yosil Maharal's home office, featuring a desk and bookshelf covered with old-fashioned papertomes and lasersheet folios. One shelf of a display case held awards and honors. Others displayed strange trophies—like an array of mounted *hands,* ranging widely in size and coloration. Some were sliced open to show metal parts, relics of a time when dittoclay had to be slathered over robot frames, when clanking duplicates were techno-playthings for the rich, at once both crude and awe-inspiring, enabling just an elite to divide their lives and be in two places at the same time.

An era when dittos were called "deputies," and those who could afford them seemed ordained to have much bigger lives than the rest of humankind. Before Aeneas Kaolin gave self-copying to the masses.

It was quite a display. But right then my chief concern lay in the part of the room I couldn't see, far from the window, steeped in shadows.

"Lights on," I tried from the doorway. But the house computer was voice-keyed, barring unknown guests from even courtesy control. Yosil was some host.

I *could* try transmitting the command through Nell, asserting my investigation contract with Maharal's daughter and heir. But the chain of handshakes and probate haggles could take minutes, distracting me the whole time.

No doubt a conventional light switch lay just yonder, within easy reach . . . and reach of some lurker-in-the-dark, armed with any weapon my eager imagination could provide.

Was I being paranoid? Fine.

"Ritu, if that's you, just tell me to come in . . . or to wait outside."

I heard a soft sound, within. Not breathing, but another rustle. I felt tension beyond the door. Something like coiled energy.

"Is that you, ditAlbert?"

The voice came from upstairs, behind me. Ritu, calling down, without a hint of guile.

"Yeah! It's me," I answered without turning. "Did you . . . do you have other company?"

Through the frosted glass, I spied another shudder. This time a straightening, perhaps signaling resignation. I backed away several steps across the atrium, giving leeway to whatever might emerge.

I also eyed escape paths, just in case.

"What did you say?" Ritu shouted again from above. *"I didn't expect you for an hour. Can you wait?"*

A silhouette crossed the closed half of the glazed double door. Tall, angular . . . and gray—it drew closer.

For an instant, I thought I had it! A furtive gray, in this house? Who else could it be but the ghost? *Maharal's ghost!* The one that didn't want to spend its last moments in a lab, being dissected for trace memories. It would be a shambling wraith by now, persisting by sheer will power, burning its final reserve of *élan vital* before melting away.

I readied to pounce, demanding answers. Like what happened to my own ditto! The one I sent to the mansion this morn—

—then blinked in surprise. The figure that emerged *wasn't* Maharal's ghost. Not even gray, strictly speaking.

A gleaming platinum stepped under the speckled light. The golem-sigil on its brow shone like a jewel.

"Vic Kaolin," I said.

"Yes," the ditto nodded, covering its agitation with pugnacity. "And who might *you* be? What business do you have in this house?"

Surprised, I raised a spackled eyebrow.

"Why, the job you hired me to do, sir."

That wasn't strictly true. I wanted to probe this ditto's level of ig-norance. His glossy expression froze, transforming rapidly from pugna-cious to guarded.

"Ah . . . yes. *Albert*. It's good to see you again."

Despite its lame effort at a recovery, this was clearly a different dit-Kaolin than the one I met early this morning, as dawn broke over the shattered windows of the Teller Building. Nor did it share any recent memories with the one who phoned me at home around noon, hectoring me while I imprinted the ebony. This one didn't remember me at all.

Well, in itself, that meant little. It could have been imprinted hours before all that. But then, why *pretend* to know me? Why not just admit ignorance? He could send a query to his rig. Get an update from the real Kaolin.

Here's a life lesson—don't embarrass the mighty. Let 'em save face. Always give them an out.

I pointed into the home office of Yosil Maharal. "Did you find any-thing useful?"

The guarded expression deepened. "What do you mean?"

"I mean you're here for the same reason I am, right? Looking for clues. Something to explain why your friend kept skipping town, evading the all-seeing World Eye for weeks at a stretch. And especially what he was doing last night, racing across the desert, careening over highway viaducts."

Before he could answer, Ritu called down again.

"Albert? Who are you talking to?"

ditKaolin's dark eyes met mine. Following my adage, I gave him that out.

"I met a shiny new Aeneas, coming up the walk!" I shouted up the stairs. "We entered together."

The platinum ditto nodded. Acknowledging a debt. He would have preferred going unnoticed, but my cover story would do.

"Oh Aeneas, I wish you wouldn't hover so! I'm all right, really." She sounded exasperated. *"But as long as you're here, would you show Albert around?"*

"Of course, dear," ditKaolin answered, gazing briefly upstairs. "Take your time."

When he faced me again, there was no trace of agitation, or pugnacity. Only serene calm.

"What were we discussing?" he asked.

Crum! I thought. *You'd think a rich bastard could order up ditto blanks that concentrate better.*

Aloud, I prompted, "Clues, sir."

"Ah, yes. Clues. I looked for some, but—" The platinum head shook, left and right. "Maybe a professional like you can do better."

Despite everything, Kaolin is only guessing that I'm a ditective, I thought. *Why doesn't he just ask?*

"After you." I gestured politely, insisting he reenter the office ahead of me.

He turned, spoke a command, and light filled the room. So Maharal must have given voice authorization to his boss. Or else—

I felt another vague suspicion simmer in the part of my skull where I chain that crazy but creative beast, paranoia. Keeping the ditto in sight, never turning completely away from him, I looked over a display case while tapping cipher-code with my teeth.

Nell. Verify Kaolin sent this dit. Confirm it's legit.

She acknowledged the work order, flashing in my left eye. But even with my priority as the real guy, this query could take time, leaving me wondering about a possibility.

Dr. Maharal had been an expert in duplication tech, and a gifted hobbyist at the arcane art of disguise. He also seemed blithe about mere inconveniences like the law. With his Universal Kilns access, he could borrow all sorts of templates . . . including possibly that of Aeneas Kaolin.

So, could this platinum be another Maharal ghost, masquerading as the Vic?

But that didn't make sense. realMaharal's corpse had been cold for nearly a day, but the platinum looked much newer. No way this could be Ritu's daddit, in disguise.

Well, organic imagination doesn't have to make sense, I recalled. *Nor must paranoia be reasonable. It's a beast who barks at nothing . . . till the day it's right.*

There was a simple way to verify the platinum's identity. As a real person, I could turn and demand its pellet . . . at the cost of revealing my own costume ruse. I chose against it. Nell should answer soon, anyway. So I fixed my attention on Maharal's home.

The office showed signs of recent amateur tampering. Table legs were shoved out of old carpet impressions. The contents of book and display cases had all shifted, disturbing dust layers as someone groped all over, perhaps looking for hidden panels.

I learned a lot just by glancing at the lasersheet folios. They were barely touched, so Kaolin must not have been looking for purloined data or software.

Then what?

And why was he trying to search all by himself? He has security people. He can hire forensic experts or even rent a downtime police unit.

At first I thought the problem might be Ritu, standing up to her boss and barring Kaolin access to her father's home. That could explain today's furtive entry—trying to search the place without alerting her—which implied some need to keep her in the dark.

Except that Ritu's easygoing attitude just moments ago, giving us both leave to look around, didn't fit the image of a rift between Kaolin and Maharal's daughter. At least not an obvious one.

Glancing at the Vic, I saw he had regained his famed, sphinxlike composure. Dark eyes tracked me, perhaps still annoyed that I had found him here. Yet he appeared willing to make the best of things. Supervising an expert hireling at work, that was more his style.

There were pictures on the walls, both inside the office and in the hall beyond. A fraction showed Yosil posing with people I didn't recognize—I used my archaic but serviceable eye-implant to take iris-snaps of some, for Nell to identify. But most of the framed images showed a younger Ritu at various events like graduation, a swimming competition, riding a horse, and so on.

Maybe I should have given the place a major workover—a chemsift for substances on the International Danger List would take just minutes with a good scanner. But whatever Maharal was up to, I suspected that it wouldn't show in obvious ways.

An inertial transect might be more revealing. Strolling from room to room, I opened closets and cupboards, peering into each one long enough to freeze a complete perspective-set, transmitting each one to Nell, and then moving to the next. She wouldn't need color, just multiple angles and position stamps, down to half a centimeter, using surveying principles George Washington would have understood. Any secret chambers or compartments should appear in the resulting geodesic.

Kaolin expressed approval. But again, if he wanted this kind of work done, why not hire a whole survey team and do a thorough job?

Perhaps the matter was so sensitive, he could only trust his own duplicates.

If so, my presence must be cause for mixed feelings. I had stopped working for Kaolin when Yosil Maharal's body was found crumpled in his car—when the case switched from suspected kidnapping of a valued employee to a daughter's vague misgivings about murder.

I made a mental note to ask Ritu about her father's relationship with the UK chief. If it *was* murder, I could imagine scenarios putting the Vic on a shortlist of suspects.

Take what happened to Maharal's ghost—and my gray—a few hours ago. Might Kaolin have arranged for them both to vanish on his estate? Maybe the gray sniffed too close to some dire truth. Maybe the ghost had good reason to flee.

Soon the first-floor transect was complete. Nell's preliminary analysis showed no secret chambers. At least nothing bigger than a breadslice. But she did cite one anomaly.

Two photographs were missing. They had been hanging near the bottom of the staircase when I first arrived. Now, my home computer reported they were gone! Their shadows still showed up by infrared, a bit cooler than the surrounding wall.

I turned in search of Vic Kaolin . . . and spotted him emerging from the lavatory. Plumbing sounds gurgled in the background. *He just disposed of something by flushing it away!* The platinum ditto looked back at me, a portrait of innocence, and I cursed under my breath.

If I had come as an ebony specialist, tuned and equipped for close forensic site analysis, I might have watched him with one eye literally in the back of my head. Now, there seemed little I could do about it. Quizzing Kaolin would only alienate him without explaining the photos.

Better to wait, I decided. Let him think I didn't notice. Maybe ask Ritu about the pictures later.

I went out to my Volvo, opened the trunk, and fetched a thumper with seismic pickups. Lugging the equipment back up the steps, I planted detectors all around the house. In moments I would know if there were secret chambers underground. Unlikely, but worth checking out.

While waiting for the data to come in, I poked around the recycling unit out back, with its separate slots for metals, plastics, mulchable organics, and electronics. And clay. The bins should all have been empty, since Yosil Maharal spent the last few weeks away from home. But the telltales showed some mass in the golem-disposal unit. Enough for one full-size humanoid form.

I opened the access panel—only to witness a dim gray figure sag before the sudden onslaught of air, rapidly finishing its collapse to slurry.

Smell can be a powerful sense. From vapors wafting off the slumping mass, I could tell much. *It died well before expiration . . . and no more than an hour ago.* Acting quickly, I reached inside to grope through where the skull had been, feeling through dissolving fibrous matter till I snagged a small, hard object. The ID pellet. Later, in private, I might give it a quick scan and find out if this meant anything . . . or if a neighbor had simply deposited an excess ditto in the Maharal Dumpster to avoid recycling fees.

Wiping my hand on a towelette, I sauntered back to verify the seismic readings. Sure enough, they showed no hidden chambers. I don't know why I bother. Maybe the romantic spirit in me keeps hoping for the catacombs of Treasure Island, something beyond the normal run of city-cam traces, chasing down copyright violators and dallying spouses. At least that was Clara's diagnosis. Somewhere deep under Albert Morris lay the soul of Tom Sawyer.

My heart beat faster when I thought of her, and the direction I'd be driving in just a little while. Maybe, after a hard day's work in the desert, after Ritu's ditto expired, I might swing by the battle range and surprise—

That was when I sensed a change. Something missing. A presence, like a shadow, now gone.

The silent, lurking presence of ditAeneas Kaolin.

I looked for the limo and saw only blank space at the curb. The limo was gone.

Perhaps the golem left in order to avoid Ritu's gray, who could be heard now puttering around downstairs. But that didn't make any sense, did it?

Nothing did.

In moments, Ritu's gray emerged from the house, carrying a small valise, and locked the door behind her. "I'm ready," she announced in a somewhat aloof tone, though short of outright unfriendly. In her case, if any character trait clearly bridged the gap from original to copy, it was the sense of *tension* I had picked up earlier. An edgy guardedness that kept one at a distance while somehow augmenting her severe beauty.

I hurried to collect my thumpers and other hardware, throwing them into the trunk atop the portakiln. Soon we were heading southeast through a shrouding twilight. Toward the desert, where mysteries still prowl and nature can rip away all civilized masks, revealing the stark struggle life has always been.

18

Orange You Glad?

. . . as Frankie is red his rites . . .

It's not that Pallie can't make dittos. He's actually quite gifted, with a flexible self-image that can propel almost any golem-shape, from quadruped to ornithrope to centipede. That rare ability to imprint non-human forms might have let him be an astronaut, ocean prospector, even a bus driver. But Pal's dittos can't deal with inaction, amplifying his core restlessness. A ditective should stay patient and focused—say during a long stakeout—but his copies can't. With great intelligence and imagination, they'll rationalize any excuse to transform inertia into motion.

It's why he went in person that night, three years ago, to a rendezvous with treacherous men. Pal's way of being cautious, I suppose.

So we had to lug his real self along with us in Lum's van. Pal's wheelchair slid in back as the mancie leader hopped into the pilot seat. Then, with a devilish grin, Lum offered *me* shotgun position—a blatant dig at Gadarene, who rumbled ominously. Wanting no trouble between the two reluctant allies, I stepped aside for the big conservative, adding a respectful bow. Anyway, I'd rather ride with Pal, wedged in back between the van's hull and a battered portakiln.

The oven felt warm when I sat on it. Someone was cooking. Lacking a sense of smell, I couldn't tell whom.

We set off, merging with traffic. The optically active cerametal hull sensed the direction of my gaze from millisecond to millisecond, automatically transforming a narrow patch from opaque to transparent wherever I happened to be looking, slewing this micro-window about to match my wandering cone of attention. Anyone standing outside the van might see four small dim circles jiggering about, like tiny manic spotlights, one for each occupant, revealing little to outsiders. But to each of us inside, the van appeared made of glass.

Lum caught a nav beam, which sensed four passengers—three of them real—and granted carpool priority, speeding us along. *North,* toward the hi-tech district, following my hunch about where to find trouble. Funny how Lum and Gadarene were ready to trust a frankie's instincts. As if I knew what I was talking about.

Fluids dripped through IV tubing and diagnostic lights winked as I checked Pallie's medconsole. The unit was pissed off at him for using stimulants, back when he showed off for us at the abandoned scooter park.

"Just like old times, eh?" he said, giving me a wink. "You, Clara, and me, tackling the forces of evil together. Brains, beauty, and physique."

"Well, that describes Clara. What about you and me?"

He chuckled, flexing a sinewy forearm. "Oh, I wasn't bad at muscle stuff. But mostly I provided *color*. Sadly lacking in the modern world."

"Hey, aren't I green?"

"Aye, and a lovely faux-viridian shade you are, Gumby. But that's not what I mean."

I knew exactly what he meant: the *color* our grandparents supposedly had, back in the zesty twentieth and early twenty-first, when people took risks every day that few moderns would think of facing with their precious trueflesh. It's strange how much more priceless life can feel, when you have more of it to grasp.

Me? I had sixteen or so hours left. Not much time for ambition or long-range plans. Might as well spend it all.

I turned to Gadarene, whose attention focused toward a World Eye portal on his lap. "Any luck tracing the gray?"

The big man scowled. "My people have put out a hue and cry. We're offering top bids for a pix-trace, but the trail's blank. Nothing since the gray was last seen, at Studio Neo."

"There won't be," I said. "Albert knows how to vanish when he wants to."

Gadarene flushed. "Then contact your rig. Have him recall the ditto!"

The organo-chauvinist leader appeared frantic. I didn't want to provoke him. "Sir, we've gone over this. That gray is on autonomous mode. It won't communicate with realAlbert, because that could constitute violation of contract. If the gray is being deceived by experts, they'll take measures to ensure it *stays* deceived."

"I bet the first thing they did to the gray was disable the recall feature in its pellet," Pallie said, and I added, "They'll put e-sniffers on Al's house. Nell will catch on eventually, but it can work for a span. So we can't contact Morris directly. If the conspirators notice, they may spook or change plans."

Gadarene muttered, "I still can't figure it out. *What* plans?"

"To make us look bad," said Lum, dropping his normally sunny mien. "Both your group and mine. We're being set up as patsies.

"I'll bet Universal Kilns is behind this," Lum continued. "If they can convince the world we're terrorists, they may get a demarchy writ to eliminate the pickets and demonstrations. No more disclosure lawsuits and net harassment from groups opposing their immoral policies."

"You mean they'd sabotage themselves, to blame us?"

"Why not? If the stunt generates public sympathy, all the better! It might even throw off those anti-monopoly bills that keep coming up, trying to reverse the Big Deregulation."

Pal chuckled again.

"What's so funny?" Gadarene snapped.

"Oh, I was just thinking about how innocent you both sound, right now. Are you practicing for the cameras?"

"What do you mean?" Lum asked.

"I mean that you non-violent protestors have been up to your own skulduggery, I bet. Some flashy way to demonstrate your disapproval of Universal Kilns. Moralists can always justify going outside the law when it suits their sense of righteous timing."

Gadarene frowned sullenly at Pal. Lum said, "That's different."

"Is it? Never mind. I'm not interested in canned rationalizations. Just tell me how far along your preparations have come."

"I don't see why—"

"Because you're playing out of your league, gentlemen!" I cut in, a bit too loud for a respectful green. But I had caught Pal's drift and it made sense. "Professionals are at work today, hatching a scheme that's been long arranging. Right now it doesn't matter if the secret mastermind is Universal Kilns, or some enemy of theirs. Whatever they're planning to do in the next few hours, they've set you fellows up to take the blame."

"But maybe we can help, if you come clean," Pallie offered. "Don't tell me you haven't dreamed and schemed about striking a blow against UK. Tell us, right now, if you've done *more* than dream! Have you been up to something that could be used against you? Something that could pin you to a crime?"

Both men glared at Pal and me—and sideways at each other. I could almost taste their mutual distrust. Their internal struggle for a way out.

Gadarene spoke first; perhaps he was more accustomed to bitter confession.

"We've . . . been digging a tunnel."

Lum stared at his longtime adversary. "You have? Well, imagine that."

He blinked a few times, then shrugged with a wry chuckle. "We've got one, too."

▪ ▪ ▪

The triple domes of Universal Kilns HQ shimmered, set afire on their western flanks by a late afternoon sun. I couldn't help thinking of three giant pearls, planted atop a busy anthill, since those grassy slopes sheltered an even larger industrial plant underground. But with its coat of greenery, the factory looked more like a college campus, placid and unthreatening, rimmed by a deceptively innocent-looking hedge.

To modern citizens, the site was legendary, even Promethean. A cornucopia spilling forth treasures—hardly a cause of ire. But not everyone felt that way. Outside the main gate, beyond a screen of trees, lay a camping ground that was staked out years ago under the Open Dissent Act, when Aeneas Kaolin first moved his corporate headquarters here. Each maverick or radical group with a grievance had its own patch—a cluster of canopies and expando-vans—to marshal demonstrations.

Why keep agitating over a cause that's long-lost? Because cheap dittos make it *easy* . . . an irony that most radicals were much too sober to notice.

ARTIFICIAL PEOPLE *ARE* PEOPLE

So proclaimed the largest banner, identifying Lum's community of tolerance zealots, though smaller signs marked passionate subsects, each with an agenda weirder than the next. I mean, sure, I'd rather not have to bow to Gadarene, just because I'm green. But I'm a frankie. For anyone else, isn't it just a matter of taking turns? Sometimes grasshopper, sometimes ant. Even after my time at the Ephemerals, I still found it hard to grasp what kind of society these people had in mind.

Still, they came from a tradition that had saved the world. The tolerance-and-inclusion reflex was strong for good reasons—because it took centuries of pain to acquire. Confused or not, these folk stood on high moral ground.

Not far away, another sign broadcast shining holo letters, expressing a more clearcut demand:

SHARE THE PATENTS!

The "open source" movement wanted all of UK's technologies and trade secrets released to the public, so every garage hobbyist might experiment with new dittoing techniques and wild golem variants, promising a burst of total creativity. Some envision an age when you'll imprint your Soul Standing Wave into everything around you—your car, your toaster, the walls of your house. Hey, why not each other? To enthusiasts out there—eager, overeducated, and bored—every boundary of self and other was spurious. A small step from being several places at once to being *everywhere,* all of the time.

Those techno-transcendentalists stayed away from yet another encampment where the denizens had a different complaint altogether—that the world already has too many people in it, without doubling or tripling Earth's population each day with fresh swarms of temporary consumers. Wearing green robes of the Church of Gaia, they wanted humanity pared way down, not exponentiated. Dittos may not eat or excrete, but they use resources in other ways.

Grunting with delight, Pal nudged my arm and pointed.

A single figure could be seen pacing just outside the big encampment, picketing the picketers!

SELF-RIGHTEOUSNESS IS AN ADDICTIVE DISEASE, GET A LIFE! chided the placard carried by a creature with extremely long, shaggy arms and a head like a jackal's. Perhaps the ditto's appearance was some kind of arty, satirical statement. If so, I didn't get it.

Some people—most people—have way too much time on their hands, I thought.

Once, years ago, this site swarmed with a more pragmatic and far angrier breed of protester. Labor unions, upset over a convulsed job market, stirred up Luddite movements across the globe. Riots surged. Factories burned. Golem-workers were lynched. Governments teetered . . .

. . . till overnight, passions ebbed. How do you suppress a technology that lets people do all the things they want to do, all at the same time?

As our van passed into the compound, I glimpsed a final placard, carried by a bearded man who beamed happily as he paced, even though everyone else seemed to avoid him, even with their eyes. His message— in a fine, flowing cursive calligraphy—was one I saw just an hour or two earlier:

You all miss the point.
There's a next step a'coming . . .

Gadarene's bunch bivouacked to one side, separated from the other groups by a gulf of mutual hostility. Instead of sending cheap dittos to this site each day, his followers were real people. Every one of them.

As we pulled up, a dozen or so men and women emerged from big trailers, accompanied by gaggles of youngsters. Their clothing had that look—colorful but inexpensive—evidently purchased on the purple welfare wage.

I've met abstainers before, but never in such numbers. So I couldn't help staring. Here were people who refused to copy themselves. Ever. It felt like gazing at creatures of another age, when fate cruelly forced all men to live cramped lives. Only these folks lived that way deliberately!

On seeing Lum step from the van, members of the flock grumbled threateningly. But Gadarene silenced them with a curt headshake. Instead, he bid two strong youths to hoist Pal from the back. Others hauled the portakiln as we followed him into the biggest trailer.

"I am still not sure I should show you this," he groused. "It is the work of years."

Pal stifled a yawn. "Take your time. We've got days and days to decide."

Sarcasm can be effective. Still, I often wondered how my friend managed to live this long.

"How do we know it isn't already too late?" Lum asked.

"Best guess, the enemy won't act till nightfall," I replied. "If it's a bomb, they'll want to maximize the flashy visual effects, while minimizing real human casualties."

"Why?"

"Killing archies tends to really piss folks off," Pal said. "Property crimes are different. Deregulated. Anyway, conspiracies tend to unravel when you get down to mass murder. Henchmen turn whistle-blower. No, they'll wait till second shift, with only dittos at work, to produce lots of gaudy dismemberments without criminal culpability.

"Which means there may still be time to act," Pal concluded, "if you quit stalling and show us what you've got."

Gadarene still squirmed. "Why not ask Lum first? He's got a tunnel, too."

"I'll be using that one." Pal nodded. "But Mr. Lum's passage is too small for Albert here . . . I mean Frankie. *Your* tunnel has to be bigger, eh, Gadarene? Human size."

The big conservative shrugged, giving in at last.

"We dug by hand. It took years."

"How did you evade seismic detection?" I asked.

"With an active lining. Any sonic or ground wave that hits one side of the sheath is re-radiated on the other. We used a quadrupole grinder at the digging surface, canceling noise beyond a few meters."

"Clever," I said. "And how close are you to breaking through?"

Gadarene looked away, avoiding my eyes. He mumbled in a voice almost too low to hear, "We made it . . . a couple of years ago."

Pallie guffawed. "Well, that takes it! Such passion, digging like moles to reach the hated enemy. Then nothing! What happened? Lost your nerve?"

If looks could kill . . . But Pal had already survived worse.

"We couldn't agree on which action would be . . . suitable."

I found myself kind of sympathizing. It's one thing to labor with a vague/distant goal of punishing the wicked. It's another to actually *do* it in ways that edify the world, attract public support, while keeping your precious realhide out of prison. The Gaia Liberation folks learned this the hard way, during their long war against the gene-techs.

"Was that your problem, too?" I asked Lum.

The mancie leader shook his head. "Our shaft took a twisty route, so we just broke through. Anyway, our aims are different. We aim to liberate slaves, not to sabotage their birthplace."

Pal shrugged. "Well, that explains why it's happening right now. You both have leaks or spies. Or your digging was detected after all. Either way, *someone knows*. They'll use your tunnel shafts to deflect blame for what's about to happen. Last night's charade—sending fake Morrisdits to visit you—was just frosting on the cake you're being cooked in."

I didn't add that Albert, my maker, appeared targeted for the worst baking of all.

Unhappy silence reigned, till Lum spoke up.

"I'm confused. Don't you two hope to *use* our tunnels, to get inside and look for the missing gray?"

"We do."

"But if the enemy already knows about the tunnels, won't there be traps waiting for you?"

Pal's sanguine grin is the most infectious I know. He can really convince you that he knows what he's doing. "Trust me," he said, turning both palms up. "You're in good hands."

■ ■ ■

His ditto radiated the same air of confident aplomb ten minutes later, as I stared down a narrow hole in the ground, contemplating how quickly my short existence could end in such a place.

"Don't sweat it, Frank," the mini-golem said in a piping voice, perfectly imitating Pal's blithe speech rhythms. "I'll take point-position. Just follow my glossy butt."

The creature looked like an oversized ferret, with a stretched, semi-human head. But the strangest part was its fur, all glistening, with tiny bulges that moved all over the place, like it was infested with parasites or something.

"What if there *is* a trap in there?"

"Oh, I give odds there will be," Little Pallie answered. "Let me worry about that. I'm ready for anything!"

This, from someone whose dittos almost never made it home in one piece. I wished realPal were still present, so I could chew him out one last time. But he went over to the Emancipators' camp with his portakiln, preparing to dispatch yet more hisselves down their twisty, specialized tunnel—one cleverly designed to resemble a network of harmless animal holes worming semi-randomly toward the giant industrial complex. Providence is kind to the half-mad, I guess. Pallie could happily dispatch a dozen or more kamikaze dittos, each of them thrilled to take part in a suicide mission. It was all good fun to him-and-them.

If my body had been built for any decent pleasure, I would have turned around and sought it out, right then and there, leaving that place behind. Or maybe not.

"Come on, Gumby," the pseudoferret told me with a toothy grin. "Don't go into a funk on me. Anyway, you're committed now. Where else can you go in *that* color?"

I glanced down at my arms, now dyed—like the rest of me—in a hue widely known as UK Orange. An in-house shade, trademarked by Aeneas Kaolin long ago. If this caper didn't work, copyright violation would be the least of my worries.

Well, at least I'm not green anymore.

"Tally-ho!" squalled Pal's diminutive ditto. "Nobody lives forever!"

With that cheery motto, the Paldit squirmed around and dived into the hole.

No, I thought in reply. *Not forever. But a few more hours would be nice.*

I cross-checked the friction rollers on my wrists, elbows, hips, knees, and toes. Then I knelt to slip inside. Without looking back, I sensed the hulking, nervous figure of James Gadarene, hovering nearby, watching.

Then something happened that actually moved me, in a strange way. I was already a couple of meters into the awful passage when I heard the big zealot utter some kind of benediction.

Maybe I wasn't supposed to hear it. Still, unless I'm mistaken, Gadarene actually asked his God to go with me.

In all the time I've walked this Earth, it's one of the nicest things I've heard anybody say.

19

Fakery's Bakery

. . . in which gray number two gets a second wind . . .

Tuesday afternoon fades and a vast industrial complex prepares to change shifts. The entry/exit portal throngs with moving bipeds, all of them human in one fashion or another.

In olden times, the whole population of a factory—thousands of workers—would swing into motion at the blowing of a whistle, half of them heading home, tired from eight or ten—or even twelve—hours work, while equal numbers shuffled in for their turn at the machines, transforming sweat and skill and irreplaceable human lifespan into the wealth of nations.

Today's flow is gentler. A few hundred archie employees, many of them wearing exercise clothes, chat amiably as they leave, heading for scooters and bikes, while a more numerous and colorful host of paper-clad dittos arrives by dinobuses, trooping in the opposite direction.

Some elderly dittos are also departing, homeward bound to inload a day's memories. But most stay, working on till it's time to slip into the recycling vat—armies of bright orange drones, laboring with focus and without resentment, because some *other* self will enjoy fat wages and stock options. It can be kind of spooky if you stop and really think about it. No wonder I never had a factory job. Wrong personality for it. Way wrong.

Even the golem entrance is decorated in eye-soothing tones, with sensoresonant music playing in the background as I wait in line to sign in. There's also a faint vibration, coming through the bottoms of my feet. Somewhere lower down, beneath the grass-covered slopes, giant machines are mixing pre-energized clay, threading it with patented fibers tuned to vibrate at the ultra-complex rhythms of a plucked soul, then kneading and molding it all into dolls that will rise, walk, and talk like real people.

Like me.

Should this feel like coming home? My present, pre-animated body was made here, mere days ago, before being shipped to Albert's storage cooler. If today's snooping expedition takes me down to that factory realm, will I recognize my mother?

Oh, quit it, Al.

I'm me, whether gray or brown. Grasshopper or ant. The only practical difference is how polite I've got to be.

That . . . and expendability. In a sense, I'm freer when I'm gray. I can take risks.

Like the one I'm about to face in moments, when I try to sign in. Will UK security be as lax as the maestra predicts?

I almost hope not. If I'm stopped—or even if the guards ask inconvenient questions—I'll just turn around and leave! Apologize to Gineen and her pals. Send my half-fee home to Nell and spend the rest of my life doing . . . what? Forbidden by contract from inloading memories, or even seeing my rig again, I guess I'd find some other way to pass time. Maybe take in a play. Or stand on a street corner entertaining parents and kids with sleight-of-hand tricks. I haven't done that in a while.

Or maybe I'll visit Pal. Find out what he was so excited about this morning.

All right, I admit it. I'd be disappointed to come so far, and just get turned away. My demilife is targeted now. I have a mission, a purpose, to help my clients find out if Universal Kilns is violating the disclosure law. That seems a worthwhile goal, and well paid.

Approaching the entry kiosk, I find I'm actually nervous, hoping this will work.

Honestly? It was fun for couple of hours—scurrying through outdoor and indoor crowds, ducking through cramped niches, doing quick dye jobs and rapid clothing changes, vanishing and reappearing to fool the omnipresent cameras. In fact, it was today's highlight so far. Doing something you're good at—what else can make you feel more genuinely human?

All right, it's my turn. Here goes.

The big yellow golem on duty at the entry kiosk wears an expression of such ennui, I wonder if it's feigned. Even a ditto tuned for vigilance can get bored, I guess. But maybe he's been bribed. Wammaker and Collins never told me the details, hence my unease. . . .

A beam reaches out to stroke the pellet on my brow. The guard glances at me, then at a screen. His jaw twitches, opening a bit to subvocalize a brief comment, inaudible to me but not to the infrasonic pickup embedded in his throat.

Two items spit from a slot in the kiosk, a small visitor's badge and a slip of paper—a map featuring green arrows, suggesting where I should go. The arrows point up, toward the executive suites, where a different Albert Morris copy had an appointment, hours ago. That me never showed up, but the failure isn't any of my business. *My* interests lie elsewhere.

I mutter reflexive thanks to the guard—unneeded politeness that betrays both my upbringing and my age—then I head for the down escalator.

Whose fault is it if the Universal Kilns mainframe gets two of us mixed up, confusing this me with a completely different me?

■ ■ ■

Normally, at this point in a mission, I'd try to report in. Find a public phone jack—I see one right across the lobby—and dump an encrypted copy of the report I've been dictating almost nonstop since this morning. Let Nell know where I am. Let Albert in on what's been done.

But that's contractually forbidden this time. Gineen Wammaker doesn't even want me to call *her*. Nothing that might be traced to Studio Neo or her strange comrades. One result is a thwarted feeling as I crave to spill the contents of my built-in recorder, like a penitent's impulse to confess.

Well, add it to all the other irritating traits of this oddball mission. I'm riding the down escalator now, dropping into a huge anthill complex underneath the glittering corporate domes, worrying about the next phase—looking for clues that Vic Aeneas Kaolin is illegally withholding scientific breakthroughs.

All right, let's suppose—as the maestra and Queen Irene suspect—
that Universal Kilns has solved a nagging problem of our age, how to
transmit the Standing Wave of human consciousness across distances
greater than a meter. Will there be clues or signs that a layman like me
might recognize? Pairs of giant antennas, facing each other across a
cavernous chamber? Hyperconducting terrahertz cables, thick as a tree
trunk, linking a human original to the distant lump of clay she plans to
animate?

Or might UK executives already have perfected the technology?
Could they be using it right now, in secret, to "beam" copies of themselves all over the planet?

How about the other breakthroughs that Wammaker and Irene and
Collins suspect? Ditto life extension? Ditto-to-ditto copying? Modern
wish-fantasies, but what if they're about to come true?

My employers want me to seek evidence, but the other half of my
job is just as urgent . . . *do nothing illegal.* Whatever I happen to glimpse
by wandering around can be blamed on poor UK security. But I won't
pick any locks for Gineen and her friends.

I could lose my license.

Damn. Something's been bugging me all afternoon. Like an itch that
won't localize. Normally I'd follow the intuition, but there's so *much*
that's unconventional about this job—the non-disclosure contract, the ban
on inloading—plus the fact that I'm working for the maestra, which I
swore I'd never do again. Add that violent episode back at the Rainbow
Lounge and now this tightrope act, trying to a spy on a major corporation
without breaking laws. Any of that would make a guy feel creepy.

So it's strangely easy to dismiss my uneasy feelings. Attribute them
to this assortment of known irritations . . . not something even worse,
glimmering on the edge of awareness . . .

Here's were I should get off. First sublevel. RESEARCH DIVISION, it
says in bright letters over a friendly, campuslike entry portal. Beyond
another simple security kiosk I glimpse high-class gray and black dittos—
even some high-sensory whites—moving about with lively animation,
frenetically busy and apparently enjoying it. Scientists and techies generally love copying, since it lets them run experiments around the clock.
Like creating whole armies of yourself to raid Nature's storehouse, day
and night, grabbing every grain of data while your real brain stays well
rested for theorizing.

Irene said it should be easy to get past security here, too. Yosil Maharal was head of Research and an Albert gray was hired to investigate

the poor man's death, so these folks should expect a visit. Heck, even if they turn me away, I can peer around from the entrance—

Now what are you doing?

Crum, I didn't get off!

I stayed on the moving way, letting it carry me right past the entry portal, downward past Sublevel One, heading deeper underground!

This isn't according to plan. . . .

But it kind of makes sense, right? I think I see what unconscious impulse made me keep going. Won't the Research Department have its own back routes to the deeper caverns, where large-scale experiments can run? Techies *hate* security, so those back routes will be less formal, less guarded than the central shaft. In fact, I'll bet there are no guard-kiosks below at all. Anyway, my cover story will seem more plausible if I wander in through the industrial plant, having gotten "lost" somewhere along the way.

Sounds good. But does it explain why my legs *locked* moments ago, preventing me from getting off? Dammit. Dittotech would be a whole lot more convenient and rational if soul-copying didn't require dragging your whole subconscious along, every time.

More basement levels rise slowly past while I grapple with the question. A wide portal labeled TESTING offers a glimpse into a kind of hell—warrens of experimental chambers where new golem models undergo torturous ordeals, like crash dummies of old, but aware, able to report the effects of every mangling or indignity. And none of the deliberate mutilations can be called immoral, since you'll find eager volunteers for anything nowadays.

Yay, diversity.

Still riding the down escalator, I find that I'm rubbing my side—the long bulge of numb scar tissue covering that wound I got during the fight at the Rainbow Lounge. There's no pain, yet I find it increasingly bothersome. Is the irritation psychocermaic?

I buy grays that are hyper-tuned for concentration, compelled to recite and analyze while roving in the field. Beyond that, all of them partake in Al's quirky subconscious—the part of me that worries, correlates, then worries more. Looking back, it now seems awfully strange how that fellow zeroed in on me at Irene's club . . . coincidentally the same punk that Monday's green ran into last night, on Odeon Square, before taking that walk under the river.

And strange that Queen Irene—eager to see me and with many selves to spare—left me waiting in that violent club, where trouble found me.

Was it *meant* to find me?

I've dropped down to the first industrial level. Sprawling around me now, huge stainless steel tanks array into the distance like regiments of stout, shining giants.

The air fills with pungent, earthy aromas of peptide-soaked clay. Only a fraction comes from new material. The rest gets recycled, delivered every day in great slurry tubes from collection points all over the city—a frothy pureé that only hours ago made up individual humanoid beings, walking and talking, pursuing ambitions and countless distinctive yearnings. Now their physical substance reunites, blending together again in these tanks . . . the ultimate democratic commingling.

Mixing paddles stir as sparkling powders rain into the concoction, seeding nano-coalescent sites that will grow into rox cells, pre-energized for one frenetic day of mayfly activity. My limbs twitch. I can't help picturing the entropy steadily seeping into my *own* cells as they rapidly use up the *élan vital* they absorbed in these same tanks.

In a few hours that depletion will lead to *the pang*. A wish to return, like some ageing salmon, to the one who imprinted me. For inloading, a ditto's only chance at an afterlife, before this body rejoins the everlasting river of recycled clay.

Only there will be no inloading this time. No continuity. Not for me.

The floor rises past me, leading to another subterranean level, bigger and noisier than the last. Those big tanks that I saw—now overhead—funnel their frothy brews to titanic, hissing machines that groan and turn relentlessly. Robot tractors shove huge spools along ceiling tracks, delivering acres of finely woven mesh that shimmers in ways that no natural eye can bear to look upon—the diffraction spectrum of raw soul-stuff. Or the nearest approximation devised by science.

Mesh and prepared clay merge under enormous rotary presses, kneading and forming a pasty union, squeezing out surplus liquid, then popping yet another doughy humanoid shape onto rolling conveyors. On and on they come, pre-dyed to signify cost and built-in abilities. Some roll onward for custom feature installation. Other basic models, state-subsidized, are so cheap that even the poor can afford to replicate, living larger lives than their ancestors could have imagined. Across the globe, similar factories replenish half the ongoing human population, dispatching short-term bodies to a billion home coolers, copiers, and kilns.

A miracle stops being remarkable when you give it to everybody.

Watching titanic presses spit out ditto blanks—hundreds per minute—I'm hit by an absurdity.

Irene and Gineen say I should look for hidden industrial break-throughs here at Universal Kilns. But that can't be the real reason they sent me!

Think, Albert. UK has competitors. Tetragram Limited. Megillar-Ahima'az of Yemen. Fabrique Chelm. Companies who licensed Aeneas Kaolin's original patents, till they expired. Wouldn't *they* care about hidden innovations, more than the maestra and her friends? With greater resources, they could find out dozens of ways . . . like offering top jobs to UK employees. How could Universal Kilns hope to conceal ground-breaking discoveries like those Vic Collins spoke about?

Yes, evil thrives on secrecy. It's what drives Albert on. Expose villainy. Find truth. Yadda. But *is* that what I'm doing, now? Hell, nobody can run a really *big* conspiracy, nowadays, when whistle-blower prizes tempt your henchmen with cash and celebrity status. Countless small-time scams still flourish, keeping me in business. But could anyone hide secrets as major as my employers described?

Why would anyone *bother*?

Suddenly, it's plain what all their talk about "hidden breakthroughs" was about. They were appealing to my vanity! Distracting me with hints of exciting new technology. With intellectual puzzles. *And* with their grating, obnoxious personalities. All manner of irritating digressions, so my general unease could be explained by excitement, or nerves, or personal dislike.

The floor rises past me again, bringing a new layer of the factory to view. At first it looks like more of the same vast assembly line, but these presses are more specialized. Blue police models flop limply onto a conveyor belt, pre-equipped with Peace Talons and loudspeakers. Another grunting unit pops out oversize designs, big-muscled and armor-skinned, dyed in military blur-camouflage. They remind me of Clara, off fighting her war in the desert.

That's an ache I must quash. She'll never concern you again, dittoboy. Concentrate on your own problems. Like why *did* the maestra and her friends hire you?

Not to *penetrate* Universal Kilns, clearly. That was pathetically easy. (Albert should offer Aeneas Kaolin a spec proposal to upgrade security here!) Wammaker and company didn't have to pay a guy like me triple fees just to come and have a look around. Collins and Irene could have sent anyone. They could have come themselves.

No, I already did the hard part—the part they hired me for—before ever reaching the front gate. Dodging all the public cameras out there, changing my appearance a dozen times, skillfully muddying my trail so no one would connect me to my employers.

Could they have a reason, much bigger than the one they gave me?

Glancing at the nearest wall, I spot a recorder-cam. An absorber, the cheapest kind, laying one quickscan frame into a polymer cube every few seconds till it's full and needs replacing monthly. I must've passed a hundred since arriving. And they read my ID pellet at the entry kiosk. So, there's been a record from the moment I arrived. If anyone cares to check, they'll know an Albert Morris gray wandered around. But UK can't complain if I stay legal. So long as all I do is get "lost" and look around.

But what if I do something bad? Maybe without meaning to . . .

Damn! What is this thing?

A small bug—like some kind of gnat—flutters before me. It dodges a swat, darting toward my face. I can't afford distractions, so I use a surge-energy burst to grab the thing, midair, crumpling it in my hand.

Where was I? Wondering if Gineen and the others had some hidden plan. Like maybe for something *else* to happen while I'm in Universal Kilns? The moving way takes me down to another level where yet more machines rumble. Again, I'm rubbing my injury . . . now wondering if the glassy bulge in my side may contain more than scar tissue.

Could that be why the thug-gladiator attacked me, in the Rainbow Lounge? No coincidence, perhaps it was all arranged . . . to make me willing to accept a blank interval during "repairs," when actually—

Another damned bug flutters before me, then makes a kamikaze dive for my face!

Another muscle surge and it crackles in my hand. Can't let pests distract me. What I need is some way to check these crazy suspicions.

Hopping off the moving way, I jog alongside a conveyor belt hauling assorted fresh industrial dittos. Gangly window washers, long-armed fruitpickers, sleek aqua farmers, and burly construction helpers, all made for jobs where mechanization is too inflexible or costly, as inert as dolls, lacking any human spirit to drive them. I may find what I need just ahead, where these specialized blanks get wrapped in cocoons of fluffy-hard airgel CeramWrap for shipment.

There! A worker in UK orange stands near the conveyor, watching a vidboard covered with flashing symbols. *Quality Control,* says a logo stamped in his broad back. Striding forward, I wear a friendly grin while swatting yet another of those pesky, irritating gnat things. (A local industrial infestation?)

"Hello there!"

"Can I help you, sir?" he inquires, puzzled. The few grays who come down here wear UK badges.

"I'm afraid I may be lost. Is this the Research Department?"

A chuckle. "Man, you *are* lost! But all you have to do is get back on the way and—"

"Say, that's a nifty diagnostic station you've got there," I interrupt, trying to stay casual. "Mind if I use it on myself for a sec?"

The tech's puzzlement turns wary. "It's for company business."

"Come on. It won't cost anything but electricity."

His imitation brows purse. "I need it whenever the system detects a flawed blank."

"Which happens how often?" Waving off a persistent gnat, I notice that the orange guy isn't afflicted by the buzzing things.

"Maybe once an hour, but—"

"This'll take a minute. Come on. I'll put in a good word for you upstairs."

Implication? That I'm a VIP visitor. Show me courtesy and I'll add points to his file. Shame on me for fibbing.

"Well . . ." he decided. "Ever used a type-eight Xaminator? I better work the controls. Stand over there. What're we lookin' for?"

Stepping up to a fluorescent screen, I lift my tunic showing the big scar. He stares.

"Well, look at that." Turning curious, the tech starts readying a scan. Only now I'm distracted by two of the cursed gnat things.

What the hell are they, and why are they picking on me?

With uncanny coordination, they dive at the same instant, one for each eye. My right hand snags one, but the other feints, swerves, then streaks for my ear!

Damn, it *hurts*, burrowing inside!

"Give me a few secs," the orange guy says, fiddling controls. "I'm used to inspecting raw blanks. Got to cancel interference from your imprinted soul-field."

Slapping the side of my head . . . I stop when a voice abruptly explodes from within, booming like a wakened god.

"Hi, Albert. Calm down. It's me. Pal."

"P-Pal?"

Stunned, I lower my hand. Can the bug hear me when I speak aloud? "But what—"

"You're in big trouble, dittolad. But I've got your location. I'm heading there now, with one of your greens. We'll get you out of this mess."

"What mess?" I demand. "Do you know what's going on?"

"I'll explain shortly. Just don't do anything!"

The tech glances up from his station.

"Did you say something? We're almost ready here."

"I'm just getting a diagnostic scan," I tell the bug in my ear. "Right here by one of the assembly—"

"Don't do that!" Pal's voice bellows. *"Whatever you're carrying may be primed to go off when you pass a security scanner."*

"But I already passed through one, at the main entrance—"

"Then a second *scan may be the activation signal."*

Abruptly, it makes sense. If Gineen and Irene planted something deadly in me, they'd maximize damage by delaying ignition, either with a timer or by setting it to go off when I pass a second scan, somewhere deep inside . . . say upon entering the research wing, which I almost did just minutes ago.

"Stop!" I cry—as the technician pulls a switch.

■   ■   ■

. . . things . . . happening very fast . . .

. . . apply surge energy . . . shift subjective time . . . trade lifespan for rapid thoughts.

■   ■   ■

Darting aside to escape the beam, I can already tell it's too late. The scan-tingle hits me. The bulge in my side reacts. I brace for an explosion.

"Say, you're right!" the technician says. "There *is* something inside, but—where are you going?"

Running now. A blur of surge action.

It's not a simple bomb, or I'd be a billion flaming pieces now. But *something's* churning within me and I don't like it a bit.

Pal's bug writhes in my ear.

"Head for the loading dock!" it shouts. *"We'll meet you there."*

Ahead, beyond giant machines ship-wrapping ditto blanks in airgel cocoons, I glimpse truck headlights moving through the lowering night.

Picturing the anthill mound of UK HQ, I dare hope—If I can just get outside, will that foil the maestra's plan? Outdoor explosions do less harm.

But it's not a bomb. I sense fizzing heat. The scan set off complex chemical reactions. Programmed synthesis, perhaps manufacturing a tailored nanoparasite or destroyer prion. Running outside might spare UK only to put the city in peril!

Pal shouts in my ear to turn left. So I do.

I can feel the wall cameras, their passive eyes recording. No time to stop and shout my innocence—*I didn't know!* Only actions can speak for Albert Morris now. To keep *him* out of jail, *I* kick in my reserves.

Ahead, the loading docks. Gel-wrapped ditto blanks slide into pneumatic tubes, departing for distant customers with a sucking *whoosh*. Giant forklifts—huffing and puffing—haul larger models onto trucks.

"Over here!"

The yell echoes, both in my ear and across the loading bay. I spy a version of myself, dyed UK Orange, bearing a weasel-like creature on his shoulder. Both dittos bear wounds, still smoking from recent combat.

"Are we glad to see you!" shouts the four-legged mini-Pal. "We had to fight our way inside this place, past some nasty—Hey!"

No time to stop and compare notes. Running by, I share a split-second glance with my other self and recognize this morning's greenie. Looks like I found something more interesting to do today than clean toilets. Good for you, Green.

The churning in my gut is nearing some climax, feeding my crude golem-organs to a chemical frenzy. Some hell is about to burst. I need something massive to contain it.

Shall I dive into the packaging machine? No. Airgel won't do.

So I choose a nearby forklift instead, grunting and farting as it burns extra fuel loading big crates onto a truck. Its diplodocus-head turns, resembling the human who imprinted it.

"What can I do for you?" the low voice rumbles, till I dash under its legs. *"Hey, buddy, what're you—"*

Below the tail, a repellent exhaust spills high-octane fumes, a quivering moist enzyme flatulence from the hardworking clay body. Ignoring all instinct, I plunge both arms between pseudoflesh lips, forcing the waste-sphincter apart in order to . . .

. . . in order to climb within.

The forklift bellows. I sympathize but hold on as he jumps and swerves, trying to shake me out of the worst place I've ever been.

To the best of my knowledge, that is. Some of my other dits may have seen worse. The ones who never made it home . . . though somehow I doubt it.

Worming my way deeper, I hope my built-in recorder survives. Maybe this final act of sacrifice will free Albert from blame. *It's a good thing he won't inload any of this. I'd be traumatized for good.*

The poor forklift writhes. Pulses of foul gas try to blow me out. But I hold on, punching and grabbing fierce handholds. One big contortion culminates in lancing agony as my right foot comes off! Bitten by the frantic golem.

I can't blame him, but it only drives me deeper, holding my breath against the stench, using a final burst of emergency *élan* to climb the sickening cloaca, trying for its heavy center.

Meanwhile, *I'm* being consumed from within. Used as feedstock for some awful reaction as the fulminating contents of my midriff prepare to erupt.

Am I deep enough? Will the huge clay body contain whatever-it-is? *Man, what a day I've—*

2 0

Too Much Reality

. . . as realAlbert learns you can't go home again . . .

Suburbia.

Man, what a wasteland.

Half an hour from Ritu Maharal's place, taking the east ribbonway out of town, we got snagged by a guide beam that took over the Volvo, slaving its engine, rolling us along at a "maxyficient" crawl through a zone of high-density traffic. Cyclists sped past us for much of the way, given priority by computers that prudishly favor real human muscle power over mere dittos in a car.

Beyond and below the ribbonway, a series of 'burbs flowed by, each one garish in its own colorful architectural vogue—from gingerbread castles to Twentieth-Century Kitsch. Village rivalry helps distract people from two generations of high unemployment, so locals and their dittos toil like maniacs to create lavish showpieces, often focusing on an ethnic theme—the hometown pride of some immigrant community that long ago dropped in to join a cultural bouillabaisse.

Some liken Skyroad Ten's elevated carbonite ribbon to some exponentiated version of *It's a Small World,* stretching for more than a hundred kilometers. Globalization never ended human cultural diversity, but it did transform ethnicity into another hobby. Another way for people to find value in themselves, when only the genuinely talented can get authentic jobs. Hey, everyone knows it's phony, like the purple wage. But it beats the alternatives—like boredom, poverty, and realwar.

I felt relieved when we finally made it past the final city greenbelt, plunging into the natural, bone-dry air of actual countryside. Ritu's gray didn't talk much. She must have been in a mood when she imprinted. Hardly surprising, with her father's corpse not even cool yet. Anyway, this trip hadn't been her idea.

To make conversation, I asked her about Vic Aeneas Kaolin.

Ritu had known the tycoon ever since her father joined Universal Kilns, twenty-six years ago. As a girl she used to see the mogul often, until he went hermit, one of the first aristos to stop meeting people in the flesh. Even close friends hadn't seen the man in person for a decade. Nor did most people care. Why should it matter? The Vic still kept appointments, attended parties, even played golf. And those platinum dittos of his were so good they might as well be real.

Ritu, too, must use her UK connections to get high-quality blanks. Even in the dim light, I could tell her gray was supple, realistic, and well textured. Well, after all, I had asked her to send a first-rate copy to help in my investigation.

"I'm not sure which pictures you're talking about," she answered, when I enquired about the missing photos in her father's house—the ones that Kaolin's ditto stole from the wall. Ritu shrugged. "You know how it is. Familiar things become part of the background."

"Still, I appreciate your effort to recall."

She closed her eyelids, covering the uniform blue of her golem-orbs. "I think . . . there may have been a picture of Aeneas and his family, when he was young. Another showed him and my father standing before their first non-humanoid model . . . one of those long-arm fruitpickers, if I recall right." Ritu shook her head. "Sorry. My original may be more help. You can have your rig ask her."

"Maybe." I nodded. No need to let on that the Albert Morris original *was* sitting right next to her. "Can you tell me how Kaolin and your father were getting along recently? Especially just before Yosil disappeared."

"Getting along? They were always great friends and collaborators. Aeneas gave Dad plenty of leeway for his idiosyncratic behavior and long disappearances, and a permanent waiver from the lie-detector sessions the rest of us take, twice a year."

"Twice a year? That must be unpleasant."

Ritu shrugged. "Part of the New Fealty System. Usually they just ask, 'Are you keeping some big secret that might harm the company?' Basic security, without getting nosy, and the screenings apply equally to all levels in the company."

"To *all* levels?"

"Well," Ritu's graydit acquiesced, "I can't recall anyone insisting that Aeneas himself come take a scan in person."

"Out of fear?"

"Courtesy! He's a good employer. If Aeneas doesn't want to meet other people in the flesh, why should anybody in the UK family choose to question his reasons?"

Why indeed? I pondered. *No reason . . . except old-fashioned flaming curiosity! Clearly, it's another case of personality matching your career path. Folks like me just aren't cut out for this new world of fealty oaths and big industrial "families."*

We lapsed into silence after that and I didn't mind. In fact, I needed an excuse to shut down . . . that is, pretend to go into dormant mode. The car would drive itself toward the distant mesa where her father's cabin lay. During those hours, I ought to get some good old organic sleep.

Fortunately, Ritu herself supplied a justification. "I gave this ditto some net research to do during the drive. Would you mind if I proceed now?"

On her lap lay a chador portable workstation, doubtless very sophisticated, with an opaque hood that could be tossed over the head, shoulders, and arms.

"Fine," I said.

"Do you want a privacy screen, in addition to the chador?"

She nodded, repaying me with the same appealing smile that I saw when we first met. "I hope you don't mind."

Some people think courtesy is wasted on dittos, but I never understood their reasoning. I sure appreciate it when I'm clay, or when I'm pretending to be. Anyway, her needs coincided with my own.

"Sure. I'll set the screen for six hours. We should be getting close to the cabin about then, with dawn coming up."

"Thank you . . . Albert." Her smile took on higher wattage, making me flush. I didn't want it to show, so with no more ceremony than a friendly nod, I touched the PS button between our seats, releasing a sheet of nanothreads from overhead, creating a black curtain that quickly solidified into a palpable barrier, separating the car's occupants. I stared at it for a minute, briefly forgetting the real reason why I had impulsively decided to take this trip in person. Then I remembered.

Clara. Oh yeah.

I pulled a sleeping cap out of my valise, laying it over my temples. With its help, a few hours should do just fine.

Ideally, ditRitu would never know.

■   ■   ■

The interrupt call yanked me out of a dream. A true meat-nightmare in which an army of dark figures struggled across a blasted moonscape, too sere to support any life. Yet there I stood, rooted in place like a dying tree, unable to move as towering metallic forms stomped all around me, flourishing blood-drenched claws.

One part of me clenched in terror, wholly subsumed in the mirage. Meanwhile, a more detached portion stood back, as we sometimes do in dreams, abstractly recognizing the scene from a sci-fi holofilm that scared me spitless, back when I was seven. One of the few deliberately cruel things my sister ever did to me, when we were young, was to play that creepy thing for me late one night, despite a "Toxic for Preteens" warning label.

I woke, floundering in the brief disorientation that comes from getting torn out of REM sleep, wondering where I was and how I got there.

"Wha—?" The induction cap fell off as I sat up, heart pounding.

Glancing left, I saw a moonlit desert landscape flowing gently past as the Volvo cruised a two-lane highway, without another vehicle insight. Spiky Joshua trees cast eerie shadows across the dry realm of rattlesnakes, scorpions, and maybe a few hardy tortoises. To my right, the privacy screen stood intact, swallowing light and sound. Fortunately. It kept Ritu from witnessing my undignified and undittolike wakening.

"Well? Are you up?"

The voice—low and directional—came from the car's control panel. A homunculus stared at me with a face like my own, only glossy black, wearing an expression that fell just short of insolent disdain.

"Uh, right." I rubbed my eyes. "What time izzit?"

"Twenty-three forty-six."

So. About three and a half hours since I curled up for a nap. This had better be important.

"What's up?" I croaked with a dry mouth.

"Urgent matters."

Behind the ebony duplicate I saw my home workroom. Every screen was lit, several tuned to news outlets.

"There's been an accident at Universal Kilns. Looks like industrial sabotage. Someone set off a prion-catalyst bomb."

"A . . . what?"

"A cloud of organic replicators designed to spread and permeate the facility, ruining every synthetic soul-mesh in the place."

Blinking in surprise, I must have stared like an idiot.

"Why would anyone—"

"Why isn't our chief concern right now," my jet golem interrupted, sharply and typically. *"It appears that two of our own duplicates were inside UK headquarters at the time. 'Behaving suspiciously' is the phrase I sifted out of a police decrypt. They're arranging warrants right now to come over and seize our records."*

I couldn't believe it.

"Two of them? *Two* of our dits?"

"Plus a couple of Pal's."

"P-Pal? But . . . I haven't even spoken to him in . . . there must be some mistake."

"Perhaps. But I have a bad feeling about this. Both logic and intuition suggest that we're being set up. I suggest you drop present concerns and return at once."

Appalled and mystified, I could only agree. This had much higher priority than nosing around Yosil Maharal's old cabin—or my other impulsive aims for this trip.

"I'm turning around," I said, reaching for the controls. "At top speed I should reach home in about—"

The jetto cut me off abruptly, raising a glossy hand.

"I'm picking up Citywatch—a realtime alert. Unauthorized pyrotechnics, five klicks east of here . . ."

A dreadful pause, then—

"A missile launch. The spectrum matches an Avengerator Six. They're tracking . . ."

Dark eyes met mine.

"It's coming here. ETA ten seconds."

I stammered: "B-but . . ."

With ineffable calm, ebony fingers danced. *"I'm spilling everything to external cache twelve. You concentrate on saving our hide. Then find out who did this and get the bas—"*

Like a doomed mirror, my dark reflection abruptly shattered into millions of glittering shards that swirled briefly in front of me. Then, one by one, they rapidly winked out till only a faint stir of air remained.

The Volvo spoke up with the dull voice tones of silicon.

"YOU ASKED TO BE TOLD OF ANY NEWS EVENTS EXCEEDING PRIORITY LEVEL FIVE THAT AFFECT YOUR HOME NEIGHBORHOOD. I AM PICKING UP FLASH REPORTS OF A LEVEL NINE EMERGENCY ON YOUR BLOCK, CENTERED AT YOUR ADDRESS."

How I envied our ancestors, who were sometimes spared bad tidings for a few hours or days, back in technologically benighted eras when news traveled much slower than light and was channeled through journalists or bureaucrats. I didn't really *want* to see. I barely managed to choke out:

"Show me."

A series of holo images erupted, showing instanews from half a dozen publicams and private voyeur-floaters, programmed to zoom like vultures toward anything unusual, selling their feeds directly to the Net. In this case, the attractive novelty was a conflagration. A house—*my house*—burning wildly and with such heat that a flame funnel had already formed, tipping any unwary cams that fluttered too close.

Stunned, I worked for a while on pure reflex, paying top rates for pan-spectral composites till a clear picture converged out of darkness and flames.

"Damn," I muttered, hating whoever had done this. "They burned my garden, too."

■ ■ ■

I took the car offbeam and turned around, gunning it back toward the city. If I drove at thirty above the speed limit, I figured I could purge all the micro-fines with a public necessity plea. You know, rushing home to help authorities clear up this mess. Anyway, an act of good faith might help convince someone to listen when I proclaim my innocence.

Innocent of what? I still had no clear picture of what happened at Universal Kilns.

Two copies of me . . . and several of Pallie. But which copies? The one that disappeared at Kaolin Manor, presumably. And the gray that cut off communication after accepting a closed contract? Whatever job it took, things must have gone sour in a big way.

News began filtering out of UK headquarters. A prion bomb *had* gone off, but preliminary reports were optimistic. Employees jabbered among themselves about an exceptional stroke of luck. The affected area was small because a brave forklift operator sat on the saboteur at the last moment, quenching the explosion with its huge golembody, limiting the poison's dispersal.

Great, I thought. *But what does it all have to do with me?*

I got no answer on Pallie's phone, or via our secret drop box. Not one of the four dittos I had made Tuesday replied to my ultra-urgent pellet flash. I could only account for one of them—the loyal jetto who stayed at his post, striving until hell plummeted into his lap, converting his damp clay body into drifting ceramic flakes.

I glanced at the privacy screen—the curtain separating me from the car's passenger cell. Should I dissolve it and inform Ritu's gray? But surely, as a senior UK employee, she must have already received an alert about something amiss at her company. Or was her project so narrowly focused that she banished all distractions, like news?

Maybe she *did* know, and preferred to keep the curtain up. Rumors, spreading across the Net, already named me as a likely suspect in the sabotage at Universal Kilns. I debated whether to dissolve the privacy screen from this side and try to explain. Practice my innocent plea, before trying it on the police. . . .

Just then a pair of sharp glints caught my eye. Headlights. Reluctantly, I ratcheted down the Volvo's hell-bent speed . . . then brought it down some more. Something struck me as wrong about the lights. Their position on the road was odd. Maybe the highway swung a bit to the right, up ahead. . . .

Only it didn't seem about to. I kept edging rightward, instinctively planning to pass the headlights on that side, but unexpectedly the road drifted the other way, slightly left! Tapping the brake, I slackened speed some more, hoping to consult the nav computer.

The other car was *close!*

Expecting to finally avoid him on the right, I nearly plowed into the other fellow before comprehending the situation in an instant. The imbecile had pulled onto the shoulder on *my* side, pointing his high beams at oncoming traffic! Only a last-second left swerve took me back onto the road, missing the fool by inches!

The swerve turned into a spin, tires squealing and smoking as the world reeled. I had time to regret a life spent blithely ignoring basic traffic safety rules. No wonder Clara insisted on doing the driving, whenever we went somewhere together. My wonderful, fierce Clara . . . and no ghost of mine to console her.

I envisioned ending up like Yosil Maharal, crumpled at the bottom of a ditch . . . till the whirling spin finally ended with the Volvo squat and safe, sitting in the middle of the two-lane highway, shining its twin beams back at the idiot who almost caused a wreck.

A dark figure stepped from the other car, hard to picture amid the glare. I was about to get out too, and have some choice words with the fellow. Then I saw that he carried something long and heavy. Shading my eyes against the dazzle, I watched him raise the bulky, tubelike thing to his shoulder.

"Pulp!" I cursed, slamming into second gear and pounding the accelerator. Instinct urged me to turn the wheel, frantically swerving to flee whatever weapon he was bringing to bear! Only Albert's forebrain knew better.

Clara explained it to me long ago—a basic military principle.

Sometimes your only hope is to scream defiance, charge ahead; and hope for the best.

Evidently. The tactic sure surprised my attacker, who leaped back, colliding with the hood of his car before trying to steady his aim. I howled, shoving my right foot to the floor, spurring the Volvo's engine to an emergency-power roar.

In that split instant, amid the glare of two converging sets of headlights, I knew several things at once.

Good lord, it's Aeneas Kaolin!

And—*he's going to get his shot off before I reach him.*

And—*no matter what weapon he's got, I'll still have the satisfaction of turning his sorry clay ass into pottery shards.*

That offered small comfort as a bolt of horrid lightning spewed from Kaolin's gun, enveloping my car in fireworks. Pain followed right behind.

Still, through the blinding coruscation I got to see the platinum ditto throw both arms up, venting a last-instant wail of spontaneous despair.

PART II

Remember, I beseech thee, that thou hast made me as
the clay; and wilt thou bring me unto dust again?

—the Book of Job

■

Duplicity

My first clear realization, as I awake, is not about the cramped tube where I find myself confined. I've been ambushed, snared, boxed, and crated so many times, I hardly notice anymore. No, my first thought is that *I should not have been sleeping.* I'm a ditto, after all. With just a ticking enzyme clock, I don't have time for frivolities.

Then it comes rushing back—

I was hurrying along a ragged hedge in an old-fashioned suburban enclave, created for Aeneas Kaolin's servants. Stepping over a bike, I wondered—where did Maharal's ghost hurry off to? Why did the inventor's final golem run off, instead of helping solve its maker's killing?

I hastened around the hedge, only to find—

ditMaharal! The gray stood there, smiling, aiming a weapon with a flared nozzle. . . .

The memory's distressing. Worse, I have a weird impression that more than a little time passed since. Hours. More than I can afford.

It's a good thing I pay to give my ditto blanks phobia blocks, or I'd be having fits right now, pinned inside a narrow cylinder, pickled in a syrup of oily sustaino-fluid. All right, Albert . . . *ditAlbert* . . . quit banging the walls. You'll never break out of here by force. Concentrate!

I remember hurrying to catch up with Maharal's ghost, rounding the corner of a tall hedge, only to find my quarry had turned, pointing spray gun at my face. I plunged into a diving tackle, hoping fresh reflexes would prove quicker than his day-old body.

It must not have worked.

■ ■ ■

How long have I been out? I send a time query to my tracker pellet and the response is a sharp pain—someone must have ripped it from my brow. A throbbing hole gapes when I wriggle up a hand to poke the wound.

In countries with strict laws, pellet removal automatically kills the ditto. In PEZ, the old precautions faded till there's just a cheap transponder and data chip. I can live without it. But my archie will have a hard time retrieving his lost property, which is why bad guys dig the pellets out.

Did they also think to remove the rest of my implants? I can't tell if my auto-recorder is still running. For all I know, this subvocal narration may be futile, words vanishing into entropy, like my thoughts. But I can't stop compulsively reciting. It's built in to keep doing it till this pathetic clay brain dissolves.

■   ■   ■

Wait. Most sustaino-tanks come equipped with a little window, so owners can view their assets. All I see right now is blank metal, but there's light coming from somewhere.

Behind me. Pressing both palms against the tank's inner wall, I rotate slowly . . . and there it is. Beyond a thick sheet of glass, I see a room that resembles some mad scientist's laboratory.

Mine isn't the only preservation cylinder. Dozens lean haphazardly on rough, stony walls. Beyond, I see storage freezers for raw blanks, several imprinting units, and a large kiln for baking fresh duplicates. Every piece of equipment bears the same logo—a *U* followed by a *K*, each letter enclosed by its own circle. Side by side, they blend into something like the symbol for infinity. All over the world, it stands for quality. The genuine article. Kosher. The real McCoy.

Could I be inside the gleaming headquarters of Universal Kilns? Something about the stark rock wall says no. High-bandwidth superconducting cables lay haphazardly draped across cluttered work benches. Shabby dust layers show that no contract janitorial service sends striped golems to clean here. Wherever "here" is.

At a guess, I'd say the loyal Dr. Maharal was pilfering office supplies, and possibly a lot more, before his demise.

Beyond the normal run of dittoing equipment, several machines look unfamiliar, with the open-scaffold look of prototypes. One array of high-pressure tanks and nozzles had been hissing and fuming, obscured in multicolored fog till a few seconds ago, before reaching a climax and abruptly falling silent.

A horizontal panel swings back and clouds of vapor spill away from a naked figure, lying on a cushioned platform—with that fresh, doughy look that you always have when emerging from the kiln. The features are those of Yosil Maharal, resembling the corpse I saw at Kaolin Manor, though hairless and metallic gray, flushed with glimmering reddish undertones.

A sudden jerk and gasp; it starts to breathe, sucking air to feed the catalysis cells. Eyes snap open, dark, without pupils. They turn, as if sensing my gaze.

There is a coldness in their regard. Icy, with an agony. That is, if you can read anything in a ditto's eyes.

Sitting up and swiveling to plant both feet on the floor, Maharal's golem starts toward me. *Limping.* The same uneven gait I once attributed to some recent injury. But that was a different copy. It had to be. This ditto is new. Its uneven gait must have some other explanation. Habit, perhaps.

New? How could it be new? Maharal is dead! There's no template to copy anymore. No soul to lay its impression into clay. Unless he happened to have a few imprinted spares, stored in a fridge. But the machine this creature just stepped out of doesn't look like any fridge or kiln I ever saw.

Even before he speaks, I wonder—Am I looking at some kind of technological marvel? A breakthrough? Project Zoroaster?

Still naked, ditMaharal peers through the small window of my container, as if inspecting a valuable acquisition.

"You appear to be managing well enough." The words enter via a small diaphragm, vibrating the greasy fluid within. *"I hope you're comfortable, Albert."*

How can I answer? I shrug helplessly.

"There is a speaking tube," the gray golem explains. *"Below the window."*

I glance down, groping, and find it. A flexible hose with a mask to fit over the nose and mouth. As soon as I strap it on, suction begins, flushing my throat with water, then air, provoking spasmodic coughing fits. Still, it's a relief to start breathing again. How long has it been?

It also means the enzyme clock resumes ticking.

"So"—coughing again—"so your other gray took a spare out of the fridge and told you who I am before it expired. Big deal."

The Maharal-duplicate grins.

"I did not need to be told. I am that same gray. The one who spoke to your archetype Tuesday morning. The one who stood by my own corpse at noon. The same 'ghost' who shot you Tuesday afternoon."

How can that be? Then I remember the strange-looking machine.

Looking again at the blotches that flicker under a complexion that rather glows as if new . . . I think I get it.

"Ditto-rejuvenation. Is that what it's all about?" After a brief pause, I add, "And Universal Kilns wants to suppress your discovery in order to keep up sales."

ditMaharal's smile hardens.

"A good guess. If only that were all. There would be disruptions. Economic ramifications. But nothing that society couldn't handle."

Thinking hard, I try to grasp what he's implying.

Something more serious than economic disruption? "How . . . how long can a ditto go on acquiring new memories before it gets hard to inload?"

My captor nods.

"The answer depends on the original imprinting personality. But you are on the right track. With enough time, a golem's soul-field starts to drift, transforming into something new."

"A new person," I murmur. "Plenty of folks may worry about that."

ditMaharal is watching me, as if evaluating my reactions. But evaluating for what?

Pondering my present state, I'm struck only by a calm acceptance.

"You've put something in the sustainofluid. A sedative?"

"A relaxing agent. We have tasks ahead of us, you and I. It won't be helpful for you to get upset. You tend to get unpredictable when agitated."

Huh. Clara says the very same thing about me. I'll take it from her, but not from this clown. Sedative or no, I'll get "agitated" whenever I darn well please.

"You talk as if we've done this before."

"Oh yes. Not that you'd remember. The first time we met was long ago and not in this lab. All the other times . . . I disposed of the memories."

How can I react to such news, except by staring? This implies I'm not the first Albert Morris that Maharal has ditnapped. He must have snared several other copies—some of those who mysteriously vanished over the years—and trashed them when he was done . . .

. . . when he was done doing what? The usual perversions don't seem Maharal's style.

I hazard a guess. "Experiments. You've been grabbing my dits and experimenting on them. But why? Why me?"

Maharal's eyes are glassy. I can see my own gray face reflected in them.

"Many reasons. One is your profession. You regularly lose high-quality golems without worrying much about it. As long as your mission goes well—villains are caught and the client pays—you write off a few unexplained losses here and there as part of the job. You don't even report them for insurance."

"But—"

"Of course there's more."

He says it in such a way, one that's both knowing and tired of repetition, as if he's given me the same explanation many times before. It's a notion I find chilling.

Silence stretches. Is he waiting? Testing me? Am I supposed to figure out something, just from evidence before my eyes?

The initial flush of kiln-baking has faded. He stands before me in standard gray tones, looking moderately fresh . . . but not entirely. Some of those under-the-skin blotches haven't gone away. Whatever process he uses to restore *élan vital* must be uneven. Imperfect, like a film doyenne with her latest face-lift. Underneath are signs of irreversible wear and tear.

"There . . . must be a limit. A limit to the number of times you can refresh the cells."

He nods.

"It has always been a mistake to seek salvation solely through continuity of the body. Even the ancients knew this, back when a human spirit had just one home.

"Even they knew—perpetuity is carried not by the body but by the soul."

Despite a vatic tone, I could tell he meant this in a technological as well as a spiritual sense. "Carried by the soul . . . You mean from one body to another." I blinked. "From a ditto to some body *other* than its original?"

It sinks in. "Then you've made another breakthrough. Something even bigger than extending a golem's expiration deadline."

"Go on," he says.

I'm reluctant to speak the words.

"You . . . think you can go on indefinitely, without the real you."

A smile spreads across the steel gray face, showing pleasure at my guess, like a teacher gazing at a favorite pupil. Yet there is chilling harshness in his golem grin.

"Reality is a matter of opinion.

"I am the true Yosil Maharal."

2 2

Mime's the Word

. . . in which Tuesday's green gets yet
another hue . . .

This is my first chance to recite a report since I barely escaped that mess at Universal Kilns.

Talking into an old-fashioned autoscribe feels like a poor use of precious time, especially when I'm on the run. How much more convenient it is for Albert's special-model ditective grays—outfitted with fancy subvocal recorders and built-in compulsions to describe everything they see or think, in realtime present tense! But I'm just a utility green, even after getting several dye jobs. A cheap knockoff. If there's to be an account of my miserable part in all this, I must do it the hard way.

Which brings up the prize question. *An account for whom?*

Not for realAlbert, my maker, who is surely dead. Or the cops, who would as soon dissect me as look at me. As for my gray brothers. Hell, it creeps me out just thinking about them.

So why bother reciting at all? Who will care?

I may be a frankie, but I can't stop picturing Clara, away fighting her war in the desert, unaware that her real lover has been fried by a missile. She deserves the modern consolation—to hear about it from his ghost. That means me, since I'm the only ditto left. Even though I don't really feel like Albert Morris at all.

So here it is, dear Clara. A ghost-written letter to help you get past the first stage of grief. Poor Albert had his faults, but at least he cared. And he had a job.

■   ■   ■

I was there when it happened—the "attack" on Universal Kilns, I mean. Standing on the factory floor not thirty yards away, staring in wonder as gray number two ran by, all blotchy and discolored from something horrid that was roiling his guts, preparing to burst. He sped on past, barely glancing at me, or at Pal's little ferret-ditto on my shoulder, though we had just gone through Hades to sneak inside and rescue him!

Ignoring our shouts, he searched frantically, then found what he was looking for—a place to die without hurting anybody.

Well, anybody except that poor forklift driver, who never understood why a stranger suddenly wanted to burrow up his gloaca. And that was just the fellow's first rude surprise. The giant ditworker let out a bellow, then began *expanding* to several times his former size, like a distended balloon . . . like some cartoon character blowing too hard on his own thumb. I thought the unlucky forklift was about to explode! Then we'd all be finished. Me for sure. Everyone in the factory. Universal Kilns. Maybe every ditto in the city?

(Imagine all the archies having to do everything for themselves! They'd know *how,* of course. But everyone is so used to being many—living several lives in parallel. Being limited to just one at a time would drive folks nuts.)

Lucky for us, the hapless forklift stopped expanding at the last moment. Like a surprised blowfish, he stared about with goggle eyes, as if thinking, *This was never in my contract.* Then the soul-glow extinguished. The clay body shuddered, hardened, and went still.

Man, what a way to go.

There followed a maelstrom of chaos and clamoring alarms. Production machinery shut down. Worker-golems dropped every routine task and the vast factory thronged with emergency teams, converging to contain the damage. I saw displays of reckless courage—or it would have been courage if the crews weren't expendable duplicates. Even so, it took valor to approach the bloated carcass. Faint sprays jetted from the leaking, distended body. Any ditto who brushed even a droplet fell in writhing agony.

But most of the poison was checked, held inside the massive, quivering forklift. As it started to slump and dissolve from within, purple-striped cleaners arrived with long hoses, spraying the area with anti-prion foam.

Company officials followed. No real humans yet, but lots of busy scientific grays in white coats, then some bright blue policedits and a silver-gold Public Safety proctor. Finally, a platinum duplicate of the UK chief himself, Vic Aeneas Kaolin, strode upon the scene demanding answers.

"Come on," Pallie's little ferret-self said from my shoulder. "Let's scram. You're orange right now, but the big guy still may recognize your face."

Despite that, I was tempted to stay and find out what just happened. Maybe help clear Albert's name. Anyway, what awaited me out there in the world? Ten hours of futile head-scratching, listening to the whining recriminations of Gadarene and Lum till my clock ran out and it was my own turn to melt away?

The foam still flowed, bubbling, hissing, and spreading across the factory floor. Imprinted survival instincts *feel* like the real thing, and I joined other onlookers backing away from the stuff. "All right," I sighed at last. "Let's get out of here."

I turned—only to face several burly security types, liveried in pale orange with blue bands. And triple-size ersatz muscles that they flexed menacingly.

"Please come with us," one of them said with an augmented voice of authority, taking my arm in an adamant lock grip. Which I immediately took to be a good sign.

The "please" part, that is.

■　■　■

We were put inside a sealed van—one with plain metal sides that stayed opaque, no matter how hard we stared, which Palloid thought rather rude.

"They could at least give us a view before they start dicing up our brains," groused the ferret with Pal's face, ingratiating himself with the guards in his typical fashion. "Hey, up front! How about letting a fellow consult with his lawyer-program, eh? You want to be held personally liable when I slap a mega-lien on your whole company for ditnapping? Are you aware of the recent ruling in *ditAddison vs. Hughes*? It's no longer an excuse for a golem to say he was 'just following orders.' Remember the Henchman Law. If you switch sides right now, you can help me sue your boss and go swimming in cash!"

Good old Pal, a charmer in whatever form he takes. Not that it mattered. Whether we were "under arrest" in a strictly legal sense was immaterial. As mere property—and possible participants in industrial sabotage—we weren't going to inspire any UK employees to turn whistle-blower over our abused rights.

At least the driver left my armrest entertainment-flasher turned on, so I asked for news. The space in front of me ballooned with holonet bubbles, most of them dealing with a "failed fanatical terrorist attack" at UK. They weren't very informative. Anyway, a short while later another item grabbed top billing as a banner globe erupted, crowding other holos aside.

NORTHSIDE AREA HOUSE DEMOLISHED BY HOODOO MISSILE!

At first I didn't recognize the site of the blazing inferno. But news correlators soon added the address targeted by a clandestine murder rocket.

"Cripes," Pallie muttered near my ear. "That's tough, Albert."

It was home. Or the place where this body of mine got imprinted with memories, before getting set loose into a long, regrettable day. *Damn, they even burned the garden,* I thought, watching flames consume the structure and everything inside.

In one sense, it seemed a mercy. Leading rumor-nets had already begun naming Albert Morris as a chief suspect in the UK attack. He'd be in a real jam if he still lived. Poor guy. It was predictable, I guess, so long as he kept trying to act as a romantic, old-fashioned crusader against evil. Sooner or later he was going to irritate someone much bigger and stronger and get in real trouble. Whoever did all this was being devastatingly thorough.

Trouble didn't even begin to cover what I was in as the van pulled to a stop. The rear door started opening and Pal's raggedy little ferretdit prepared to spring. But the guards were vigilant and quick. One snatched Palloid's neck in a viselike grip. The other took me by an elbow, gently but with enough power to show how futile resistance would be.

We stepped out next to the unlit side portico of a big stone mansion, turning down a dim set of stairs partly hidden behind some truly outstanding chrysanthemums. I might have resisted the guard long enough to try and sniff the flowers, if I had a working nose. Ah well.

At the bottom, an open door led into a sort of lounge where half a dozen figures relaxed at tables and chairs, smoking, talking, and quaffing beverages. At first glance I thought they were real, since all wore varied shades of human-brown under durable cloth garments in rather old-fashioned styles. But an expert glance showed their fleshtones to be dye jobs. Their faces really gave them away—bearing familiar expressions of resigned ennui. These were dittos at the end of a long work day, waiting patiently to expire.

Two of them sat before expensive interface screens, talking to computer-generated AI avatars with faces similar to their own. One was a small, childlike golem, wearing scuffed denim. I couldn't catch any of his words. But the other one, fashioned after a buxom woman with reddish hair, wearing ill-fitting matronly garb, spoke loudly enough to overhear as the guard pulled me along.

"... *with the divorce coming up, there are going to be a lot of changes,*" she told the onscreen face. "*My part will get more complicated while stress-induced submotivations grow increasingly subtle. If we can't have better day-to-day continuity, I wish we could at least be given better data on the original misery indices. Especially since I have to start each day almost from scratch. Fortunately, the situation was so chaotic that consistency isn't much required, or even expected by the subject . . .*"

Her voice was pure professionalism, the words unrelated to any concern of mine. Albert Morris clearly wasn't the only skilled contract laborer hired for obscure projects by an eccentric trillionaire.

Our burly escorts took us to a door beyond the lounge/waiting room. A visible ray scanned their blue-striped foreheads and opened the portal, revealing a huge chamber divided by rows of heavy pillars to support the mansion overhead. We strode quickly through this concrete forest, glimpsing various laboratories on all sides. To my left, the equipment had to do with dittoing, as you'd expect—freezers, imprinting units, kilns, and such, plus a few I didn't recognize. To my right lay the kind of gear involved in human biology and medicine—almost a miniature real people hospital, augmented with the latest brain scanner/analyzers.

That is, I *guessed* they were the latest. Albert is—or was—an interested amateur who studiously read articles about the brain psychopathology of evildoers. A fascination that I, as a frankie, do not seem to share.

The guards escorted us to another waiting area, outside a sealed doorway. Through a narrow window I glimpsed an individual pacing nervously, barking sharp questions at somebody out of sight. The interrogator's skin was burnished-bright and expensive synthetic tendons bunched, almost like a man's. Few could afford bodies like that one, let alone to use them in bulk quantities. It was the second high-class Kaolin-ditto I had seen in an hour. He kept glancing at a nearby wall where multiple bubble displays floated and jostled, ballooning outward in reaction to his gaze, showing events in many time zones.

I noticed that the UK factory was prominent in several bubbles, revealing that emergency teams still moved about, but with less frantic urgency than before, having apparently succeeded at limiting the prion attack. I'd wager that production might resume before dawn, in remote sections of the factory.

Another bubbleview gazed down on the smoldering ruins of a small house—Albert's home, and probably his crematorium. Alas.

"Come away from there, please," said one of my escorts, in a mild tone that implied a second warning would be less courteous. I left the window and joined Palloid, who lay on the slim mattress of a nearby hospital gurney. Pal's little ferret-golem was licking some wounds it received during our brief battle gaining entrance to Universal Kilns.

As realPal expected, the tunnels laboriously dug by fanatic protestor groups—both Lum's and Gadarene's—had already been discovered by someone. Hidden mechanical guardians, vigilant and much longer lasting than clay, pounced when we came through. But clay is versatile. And those robo-wardens never faced a squadron of attacking mini-Pals! By the time I followed close behind, the battle was mostly over. I found one Palloid standing amid shards of its ditto-comrades and melted fragments of the mechanical guards. His refractive fur smoldered and most of the tiny combat beetles it had carried were gone. But enemy sentinels were gone and our path stood clear for a dash into the factory proper, searching for my gray brother, before he was duped into committing a crime.

As it turned out, our warning came too late. Still, the gray must have realized something independently. His last-minute dive into the foul belly of a forklift was courageous and resourceful. At least, I hoped the authorities would see it that way. If they were shown the whole story.

Waiting in the underground anteroom, Pal's little golem soon piped up with a complaint.

"Hey! What does it take to get some *meditcal attention* around here? Anybody notice I'm damaged? How about a pretty nurse? Or a can of spackle and a putty knife?"

One guard stared at him, then muttered into a wrist mike. Soon an orange utility rox showed up, devoid of any features to show the sex of its original, and started applying varied sprays to Palloid's wounds. I, too, had suffered a burn or two skirmishing near the tunnels, but did you see me whining?

Minutes passed. A lot of them. I realized it must be Wednesday already. Great. Maybe I should have spent yesterday at the beach, after all.

While we waited, a messenger-dit came hurrying downstairs from the mansion proper, jogging on long legs, bearing a small Teflon container. Palloid wrinkled his wet nose, sneezing in distaste. "Whatever he's got in that box, it's been disinfected about fifty different ways," he commented. "Smells like a mix of alcohol, benzene, bacteena, and that foam stuff they were using back at UK."

The messenger knocked, then entered. I heard platinum Kaolin grind out, *"Finally!"*—before we were left again to cool our heels, decaying with each passing minute. No sooner did the repair nurse finish patching Palloid than my little friend chirped again, demanding another favor.

"Hey, chum, how's about giving me a reader, eh? Gotta stay productive, right? My rig recently joined a book club. He wants to catch up on *Moby-Dit* for their next meeting. I might as well cover some chapters while we're sitting around."

The nerve of the guy! Suppose he actually got to read a few pages. Did he actually expect to inload anything to realPal? *Yeah sure,* I thought. *As if you and I are ever leaving this place.*

To my surprise, the guard shrugged and went to a cabinet, pulled out a battered net-plaque, and tossed it onto the gurney near Palloid. Soon the little golem was pawing his way through an online fiction index, searching for the latest best-seller about a seagoing golem so huge that its energy cells would take decades to run down . . . a monsterdit imprinted with the tormented soul of a half-crazed savant who must then chase his dire creation as it runs amuck across the seven seas, smashing ships and denouncing its adamant pursuer for about a thousand pages. There's been a rash of stories and films like that lately, featuring dittos in conflict with their archetype originals. I hear this one's well written and full of arty existential angst. But Albert Morris never had a taste for high literature.

In fact, I was kind of surprised to learn that Pal had a weakness for that stuff. A book club, my ceramic ass! He was up to something.

"Come," one of our guards said, answering some hidden signal. "You're wanted now."

"And it's such an honor to be wanted," Pal quipped, always ready with a feel-good remark. Dropping the plaque, he scampered to my shoulder and I strode through the now-open door of the conference room.

A solemn Kaolin-golem awaited us. "Sit," he commanded. I plopped into the chair he indicated—more plush than anything needed by my inexpensive tush. "I am very busy," the magnate's duplicate enounced. "I'll give you ten minutes to explain yourselves. Be exact."

No threats or inducements. No warnings not to lie. Sophisticated neural-net programs would be listening, almost certainly. Although such systems aren't intelligent (in any strict sense of the word), it takes concentration and luck to fool them. Albert had the skill, and I suppose that means I do, too. But sitting there, I lacked the inclination to try.

Anyway, the truth was entertaining enough. Pallie barged right in.

"I guess you could say it started on Monday, when *two* different groups of fanatics came to me, complaining that my friend here"—a ferret-paw waved at me—"was harassing them with late night visits. . . ."

He proceeded to jabber the whole story, including our suspicion that someone was contriving to frame the hapless fanatics—Lum and Gadarene—along with realAlbert, setting them all up to take the blame for this evening's sabotage at UK.

I couldn't fault Palloid's decision to cooperate and tell everything. The sooner investigators were steered onto the right track, the better— one way to clear Albert's name, for whatever good that would do him. (I noticed that the little ferret artfully avoided naming his own rig. realPal was safe, for now.)

And yet, my clay brain roiled with misgivings. Kaolin himself wasn't above suspicion. Sure, I couldn't imagine why a trillionaire might sabotage his own company. But all sorts of twisty conspiracies can look plausible after a day like the one I just had. Wasn't it right here, at Kaolin Manor, that Tuesday's gray number one mysteriously vanished? Anyway, Kaolin was one of the few who possessed the means—both technical and financial—to pull off something so ornate and diabolical.

Foremost in my mind was this: *Why aren't any cops present? This questioning should be handled by professionals.*

It implied that Kaolin had something to hide. Even at risk of thwarting the law.

He could be in real trouble for this, I thought, *if even a single real person was harmed by tonight's attack. True, the only people I saw getting damaged at UK were dittos . . .* The thought hung there, unfinished and unsatisfying.

"Well, well," our platinum host said after Pal's ferret-dit finished its amazing recital about late night visitors, religious fanatics, civil rights nuts, and secret tunnels. The Vic shook his head. "That's quite a tale."

"Thanks!" Palloid panted, wagging his rearmost appendage at the compliment. I almost hit him.

"I would normally find your story preposterous, of course. A tissue of blatant fantasies and obvious distractions." He paused. "On the other hand, it corresponds with additional information I received, a short time ago."

He motioned for the messenger, who had been standing patiently in a corner, to come forward. The yellow golem used disposable gloves to reach into his box and remove a tiny cylinder—the smallest and simplest kind of unpowered audio archive—slipping it into a playback unit on Kaolin's conference table. The sound that emerged wasn't one that our grandparents would have called a *voice*—more like an undulating murmur of grunted clicks and half-tones. That turned into a warbling whine as the messenger dialed the playback unit to higher speed. And yet, I knew this language well. Every word came across perfectly clear.

▪ ▪ ▪

I always hate getting up off the warming tray, grabbing paper garments from a rack . . . knowing I'm the copy-for-a-day. . . .

Ugh. What got me in this mood? Maybe Ritu's news about her father. A reminder that real death still lurks for all.

. . . Some days you're a grasshopper. Some the ant.

▪ ▪ ▪

Recognition went beyond hearing familiar rhythms and phrases. No, the very thoughts themselves struck me with a haunting sense of repetition. The person who had subvocalized this record began his parody of life just minutes before I started mine. Each of us commenced existence Tuesday morning thinking along similar lines, though I wasn't equipped with a gray's fancy features. Made of coarser stuff, *I* rapidly diverged across some strange boundary and soon realized I was a frankie. The first one Albert Morris ever made.

The fellow who recorded this diary was evidently more conventional. Another loyal Albert gray. Dedicated. A real pro. Clever enough to pierce the schemes of your regular, garden-variety evildoer.

But also predictable enough so that some truly devious mind could lay a fiendish trap.

▪ ▪ ▪

. . . I'm in Studio Neo, passing classy establishments, offering services no one imagined before kiln tech appeared. . . .

Wait a sec.

It's the phone. . . . Pal . . . Nell decides to pass the call on to my real self, but I listen in. He wants me to come over . . .

▪ ▪ ▪

"See?" the little ferret-golem on my shoulder jeered. "I *tried* to warn you, Albert!"

"I keep telling you, *I'm not Albert.*" I grated.

We were both caught up in nervous irritation, listening to the super-rapid playback describe a fateful rendezvous.

■ ■ ■

Maestra's executive assistant . . . She beckons me away from Wam-maker's.

"Our meeting concerns sensitive topics . . ."

■ ■ ■

We listened raptly as the "clients"—one claiming to be the maestra herself—explained their need for an untraceable investigator to nose around UK in a surreptitious yet legal manner, seeking clues to seques-tered technologies. Just the sort of thing to tease Albert's vanity and curiosity! I found it especially artful how each of his new employers made certain to act irritating or unpleasant in different ways. Knowing my archetype, he'd overcompensate, not letting dislike influence his de-cision. He'd persevere. Suffer the insufferable out of sheer obstinacy. (Call it "professionalism.")

They were playing him like a fish.

Soon after came his adventure in the Rainbow Lounge, barely sur-viving a *coincidental* encounter with some golem-gladiators. An encoun-ter that left him needing urgent repairs—conveniently provided by the drones of Queen Irene's hive. The gray's present-tense recitation made you want to stand and shout at the warbling voice, demanding that he *wake up* and notice how he was being used!

Well, in hindsight it's easy to recognize a diabolical trick. (Would *I* have seen it under the same circumstances?)

But all sides made mistakes. The enemy—whoever pulled this con-voluted caper—failed to notice gray Albert's hidden realtime recorder, tucked amid the nest of high-density soulfibers in his larynx. Not even when they had him laid out, unconscious, using the pretext of "repairs" to install a vicious prion bomb. No doubt they checked for more sophis-ticated communication and tracking devices, but the tiny archiver used no power source, just tiny throat-flexings to scratch audio at minuscule bit rates. An old-fashioned but virtually undetectable record-keeping sys-tem . . . which is why Albert always installed it in his grays.

No wonder Kaolin's messenger took such precautions against touch-ing the tiny spool! Though disinfected, it had been recovered from a yucky, prion-poisoned slurry on the UK factory floor—the merged remnants of a hapless forklift and a doomed private ditective. The archive might still hold a few catalytic molecules lethal to beings like us, who lack true immune systems.

Still, it was one useful clue, sparkling amid the melted remains. Vital evidence. Perhaps enough to vindicate my late maker.

So why was Kaolin playing it back for *us*—for Palloid and me— instead of the police?

The high-pitched account soon took us to the best part of the gray's day—skillfully evading the Omnipresent Urban Eye, fooling the legion of public and private cameras covering nearly every angle of the modern civic landscape. He'd have enjoyed that. But then, having obscured his path, he entered Universal Kilns.

■ ■ ■

Two items spit forth, a visitor's badge and a map. . . . I head for the down escalator . . . dropping into a huge anthill beneath the corporate domes, looking for signs that Kaolin is illegally withholding scientific breakthroughs. . . .

All right, suppose UK solved how to transmit the Standing Wave across distances greater than a meter. Will there be clues a layman might recognize? . . . Might UK executives already "beam" themselves all over the planet?

■ ■ ■

Palloid and I shared a glance. "Wow," the little golem muttered.

Could *that* be the breakthrough? Remote dittoing would shake up a way of life we've at last started getting used to, after all these rocky years.

We both turned to stare at ditKaolin. His reaction gave nothing away, but what about the first time he heard those words, just minutes ago? Did that platinum complexion flush with anger and dismay?

■ ■ ■

A vibration below . . . giant machines mix organic clay, threading it with fibers tuned to vibrate rhythms of a plucked soul . . . molding dolls that walk and talk . . . and we take it all for granted. . . .

Damn. Something's bugging me. Think . . . how could Universal Kilns conceal anything huge and ground-breaking?

Yes, evil thrives on secrecy. It's what drives Albert on. Expose villainy. Find truth. But is that what I'm doing now?

▪ ▪ ▪

"Finally," I muttered, as the gray started asking the right questions. In fairness, he *did* express doubts earlier. But that made the transcription even more frustrating, listening as he forged ahead, despite all misgivings.

Maybe the gray was defective, like me—a poor-quality copy made by an exhausted original. Not Albert at his best. On the other hand, he had been manipulated by experts. Maybe we never had a chance.

Some kind of gnat dodges a swat, darting toward my face. I use a surge-energy burst to grab . . . crumpling it in my hand.

▪ ▪ ▪

The mini-Pal dug his claws into my pseudoflesh.

"Dammit, Albert. I spent good money on them tiny drones." He glared those ferret eyes, as if the gray's obstinacy were somehow my fault. I might have reacted, sweeping him off my shoulder. But the recording was approaching its deadly climax.

▪ ▪ ▪

It makes sense . . . They'd maximize damage by delaying ignition . . . either with a timer or by setting it to go off when I pass a second security scan. . . .

"Stop!" I cry—

▪ ▪ ▪

From that point, the recitation turned into a rapid, jerky groan, much harder to make out, like words grunted by a hurried runner, or someone trying to concentrate on a desperate task.

Trying to save a lot more than his own measly life.

▪ ▪ ▪

I spy a version of myself bearing a weasel-golem. . . . Looks like today's green found something better to do than clean toilets. Good for you, Green. . . .

▪ ▪ ▪

That made me feel a bit ashamed, for sardonic things I thought about this gray. Could I have tried harder to save him? Might realAl be alive now, if we succeeded?

Regret seemed pointless, with my own clock rapidly ticking out. Why was Kaolin playing this tape for us? To taunt our failure?

▪ ▪ ▪

*The poor forklift writhes . . . can't blame him, but it drives me deeper,
holding my breath . . .*
being consumed . . .
Am I deep enough? Will the huge clay body contain—

■　■　■

The recital ended in a harsh squeal.

Palloid and I turned once again to watch the stolid, almost-human
features of ditAeneas Kaolin, who regarded us for a long time while one
of his hands trembled slightly. Finally, he spoke in a low voice that
sounded more fatigued than a middle-aged golem ought to feel.

"So. Would you two like a chance to find the perverts who did all
this?"

Pal's ditto and I shared a stare of blank surprise.

"You mean," I asked. "You mean you want to *hire* us?"

What, exactly, did Kaolin expect us to accomplish in the ten hours
(or less) that we had left?

2 3

Glazed Buns

. . . as Albert discovers, realtime, how real it
can get . . .

The desert is a lot brighter than they portray in holocinema. Some say
the glare can even penetrate your skull and affect the pineal gland—that
deeply buried "third eye" oldtime mystics used to call a direct link to the
soul. Searing light is said to reveal hidden truths. Or else make you
delirious enough to find cosmic meaning in stark simplicity. No wonder
deserts are the traditional abode of wild-eyed ascetics, seeking the face
of God.

I wouldn't mind running into an ascetic, right about now.

I'd ask to borrow his phone.

■　■　■

Is this thing working? I spent the last couple of hours messing with
a tiny, muscle-powered sound archiver, testing it by reciting an account

of what happened last night. First I had to dig it out of the gray golem I had stored in back of my wrecked Volvo. A gruesome chore, but the ditto was spoiled anyway, along with every bit of electronics in the car, when that platinum Kaolin fired a strange weapon at us on the road.

A subvocal archiver doesn't need electricity—one reason I install them in my grays, scribing microscopic spirals onto a cylinder of neutral-density dolomite. I can't recite in high-speed grunt code, like I do when I'm clay. Still, the little unit should pick up ambient sound, like a spoken voice, while wedged under the skin behind my jaw. Small twitches can provide power. Ritu will think it's a nervous tic, after all we've been through.

She left our cave—a sheltered cleft amid boulders—to drink from a little canyon pool we found. Even dittos need water out here, unless you want to be baked into dinnerware. It gives me an excuse for my own trips to the pool. I'm real, after all. The mark of Adam is on me, covered by makeup and clothing.

Why keep feigning artificiality? As a kindness. Ritu's golem hasn't much chance of getting home to inload. As if her rig would *want* these memories. I, on the other hand, face pretty good odds of getting out of here. Wait till nightfall, then hoof west by moonlight till I reach a road, a house, or some eco group's webcam. Anything to shout an SOS into. Civilization is simply too big to miss nowadays, and a healthy organic body can endure lots, if you don't do anything stupid.

Suppose I do reach a phone. Should I use it? Right now my enemy— Vic Kaolin?—must think I'm dead. *True-dead* from that missile strike against my home. And now all my dittos too. A lot of effort to deny Albert Morris any continuity. Reappearing would only draw attention again.

I need information first. A plan.

And better keep away from the cops, too. Till I can prove I was set up. A little extra suffering—a cross-desert march avoiding cameras all the way—could be worthwhile if it lets me sneak into town undetected.

Am I up to it? Oh, I've withstood a thousand injuries that would've finished any of my ancestors—from incinerations to smotherings to de-capitations. I've died more times than I can count. But a modern person never does any of that in organic form! The real body is for exercise, not anguish.

My tough old twentieth-century grandpa threw *his* body—his only life—off a bridge one time at the end of an elastic band. He suffered unbelievable torment in primitive dental offices. He traveled every day on highways without guidebeams, trusting his entire existence to the uncertain driving skills of total strangers whipping past him in crude vehicles fueled by liquid explosives.

Grampa might've shrugged at this challenge, walking all the way from a desert ravine to the city, without complaint. I'll probably whimper when a pebble gets in my shoe. Still, I'm determined to try. Tonight, after Ritu's golem passes on to where hopeless golems go.

I'll keep her company till then.

She's coming back, so no more reciting. Anything else that gets recorded will have to be picked up from conversation.

■   ■   ■

"Albert, you're back. Did you salvage anything from the car?"

"Not much. Everything's fried, my forensic gear, radio, and locators . . . I figure nobody knows we're here."

"Do you have any idea how we got here?"

"A wild guess. That weapon ditKaolin fired, it killed every bit of electronics and must have been meant to scramble imprinted clay."

"Then why are we still walking about?"

"That old Volvo has more metal than most cars today. We were better sheltered than the poor gray stored in back. Also, I surprised Kaolin by charging right at him, spoiling his aim. That may be why we only blacked out."

"But after! How did we get to the bottom of this gully, surrounded by miles of cactus and scrub. Where's the road?"

"Good question. This time I spotted something at the wreck we didn't notice before, a puddle near the driver's door."

"Puddle?"

"Golem slurry. Remains of our would-be assassin, I guess."

"I . . . still can't believe it's Aeneas. Why would he want us dead?"

"I'm curious about that too. But here's the interesting part, Ritu. The puddle looked too small—about half-sized!"

"Half . . . he must have been torn in two when you smashed into him. But how did the remnants get way out here?"

"My guess? Though ripped apart by the collision, Kaolin must have dragged what was left of himself to the car, climbing to my half-open window. We were knocked out, inside. The engine was running but the doors and the windows frozen. He couldn't squeeze through to finish us with his bare hands. So—"

"So he reached in to grab your side-stick controller . . . the throttle and steering lever . . . piloting us offroad, across open desert, with his half-body dangling all the way."

"He had to get us under cover, so we wouldn't be spotted and rescued. Somewhere surrounded by hot country no ditto can cross by day. We'd be trapped if we did waken. Then, his mission accomplished, ditKaolin ended his torment by dropping off and melting."

"But what's to stop us from walking out after dusk? Oh. Right. Expiration. What time on Tuesday were you imprinted, Albert?"

"Um . . . earlier than you, I expect. Kaolin had reason to think we can't last beyond midnight. He saw us both at your house, remember?"

"Are you *sure* that was the same Aeneas-copy who shot us?"

"Does it matter?"

"Perhaps. If this one was made up to look like him."

"Possible. But those anatomically correct platinums are expensive and hard to manufacture in secret. Put it this way, Ritu. If you had a working phone, is Kaolin the first guy you'd call?"

"I . . . guess not. Still, if we had some idea why—"

"I bet it connects with all the other weird stuff that happened yesterday. Your father's fatal 'accident' not far from here. The disappearance of his ghost at Kaolin Manor, along with one of my grays. Kaolin may have thought Maharal's ghost and my gray were in cahoots."

"In *what*?"

"Then there was the attack on UK. Another of my dittos was involved somehow, according to the scandal channel. Sounds like something set up to discredit me."

"So everything's about you? Is that a bit solipsistic?"

"There's nothing solipsistic about my house getting blown up, Ritu."

"Oh, right. Your archie. Your real . . . I forgot."

"Never mind."

"How can I? You're a *ghost* now. Terrible. And I got you into all this."

"You had no way of knowing—"

"Still, I wish there were something I could do."

"Forget it. Anyway, we can't settle a mystery, stuck here in the desert."

"And that bothers you, Albert. Beyond knowing your life's ended. Beyond the injustice, I sense frustration—wishing to solve one more riddle."

"Well, I *am* a detective. Learning the truth—"

"It drives you, even now?"

"Especially now."

"Then . . . I envy you."

"Me! Your rig lives on. She's in no apparent danger. Kaolin seemed a lot more interested in—"

"No, Albert. What I envy is your passion. The focus, purpose. I've admired it for some time."

"I don't know if it's so—"

"Really. I imagine it adds a special sting to dying—to being a ghost—never knowing why it happened."

"Never is a strong word. I can hope."

"There you go, Albert! Optimistic, even after death. Hoping some plane or satellite will notice that SOS of shredded seat fabric you laid out on the sand. At least it would let you tell everything to the next detective."

"Something like that."

"Even now that the sun is going down, with no rescue copters in sight?"

"A character flaw, I guess."

"A splendid one. I wish I had it."

"You'll continue, Ritu."

"Yes, tomorrow there'll be a Ritu Maharal and no Albert Morris. I know I should be more sensitive saying it—"

"That's all right."

"Can I tell you something, Albert? A secret?"

"Well, Ritu, confiding in me may not be the best—"

"The truth is—I always had trouble with dittos. Mine often head off in ways I don't expect. I didn't want to make this one."

"Sorry."

"And now, to face death out in the desert. Even if it's just one of us who—"

"Can we discuss something other than imminent extinction, Ritu?"

"Sorry, Albert. I keep compulsively returning to the same insensitive topic. What would you like to talk about?"

"How about the work your father was doing, before he died."

"Albert . . . your contract excludes you from enquiring into that subject."

"That was then."

"I see your point. Anyway, who could you tell? All right. For years

Aeneas Kaolin nagged Father to work on one of the hardest questions in soulistics—the non-homologous imprinting problem."

"The what?"

"Transferring a golem's Standing Wave—its remembrance and experience—into a repository other than the human original who made it."

"You mean dumping a day's memory into somebody *else*?"

"Don't laugh. It's been done. Take a hundred pairs of identical twins. Five or so can swap partial memories by exchanging dittos. Most get brutal headaches and disorientation, but a few can do perfect inloads! By using golem intermediaries to share all their life memories, the siblings become, in effect, one person with two organic bodies, two real lifespans plus all the parallel copies they want."

"I heard of that. I thought it was a fluke."

"No one's eager for publicity. The potential for disruption—"

"Your father was trying to make it possible between non-twins? People who aren't related? Egad."

"Don't be too surprised. The notion's been around since dittoing began, inspiring countless bad novels and movieds."

"There are so many, by amateurs and metastudios. I don't try to keep up."

"That's because you've got work. A real job. But the arts are all some people have."

"Um, Ritu? What does this have to do with—"

"Bear with me. Did you see the parasensie called *Twisted*? It was a big phenom, a few years ago."

"Someone made me sit through most of it."

"Remember how the villains went around snatching the dittos of important scientists and officials—"

"Because they had a way to inload memories into a computer. Cute notion for a spy thriller, if impossible. Transistor versus neuron. Math versus metaphor. Didn't someone prove the two worlds can never meet?"

"Bevvisov and Leow showed we're *analog* beings. Physical, not software bits and bytes. But souls can still be copied, like anything else."

"Didn't your father study under Bevvisov?"

"Their team first imprinted a Standing Wave into a doll at Kaolin Klaynamation. And yes, the plot gimmick in *Twisted* was dumb. A computer the size of Florida couldn't absorb a human soul."

"I don't think every story about other-inloading involves computers."

"True. In some dramas they ditnap a golem and dump its memories into a volunteer, to extract secrets. Sometimes the inloaded personality takes over! A scary notion that can really get to an audience. But seriously, what might *actually* happen if we learn to swap memories between people, erasing the boundary between human souls?"

Subvocal note to self. Watching Ritu speak, I realize—she's making light conversation, but her speech rhythms indicate high degrees of stress, carried realistically in the gray. The topic concerns her deeply.

If only I had some of my analytical gear while this is going on!

"Well, Ritu. If people could swap memories, men and women wouldn't be such enigmas to each other anymore. We'd understand the opposite sex."

"Hm. That could have drawbacks. Think how the sexual tension contributes to the spice of . . . oh!"

"What is it?"

"Albert, look at the horizon!"

"Sunset, yah. Pretty."

"I forgot how special this time of day is, in the desert."

"Some of that orange radiance comes from SWETAP. I guess we're going to have to get used to drinking water that glows. . . . Hey, are you getting cold? We could generate heat by walking. It's safe now."

"To what purpose? You were made *before* sunset yesterday, remember? Better save what little *élan* you have left. Unless you can think of something better to do with it."

"Well . . ."

"Let's sit close and share heat."

"All right. Is that better? Um . . . you seemed to be saying that all these bad mo+vieds had something to do with your father's final project."

"In a sense. Holo-story plots always focus on the most *stupid* ways that technology can be abused. But Father had to consider every scenario. Other-inloading has serious moral implications. And yet—"

"Yes?"

"For some reason, I felt that my father already knew a lot about the subject. More than he was letting on."

"Go on, Ritu."

"Are you sure you want me to? Does it matter, with the end rushing closer every minute? One more thing I always found creepy about dittoing. The ticking clock—far better to find some distraction before the final melting away."

"Distraction. Okay. How would *you* like to spend the remaining time, Ritu?"

"I . . . well. . . . What's your personal philosophy about banging pots?"

"I beg your pardon?"

"Clay play. Kneading slip. Do I have to spell it out, Albert?"

"Oh . . . dittosex. Ritu, you surprise me."

"Because I'm being forward? Unladylike? We don't have time to be demure, Albert. Or do you follow some neocelibate creed?"

"No, but—"

"Most of the men I know—and lots of women—subscribed to *Playdit* or *Claymate Monthly* in their tweens, getting that plain-wrapped package once a week containing an imprinted 'expert.' Even when they're older—"

"Ritu, I have a steady girlfriend."

"Yes, I read your profile. A warrior. Impressive. Have you exchanged total vows, or partial?"

"Clara's no prude. We reserve true-true contact for each other—"

"That's sweet. And prudent. But you haven't answered my question."

"Dittosex. Yeah, well. A lot depends on whether you inload."

"Which neither of us seems likely to do tonight."

"I see your point."

"About distraction. I mean, what's the point of inhibition when the world will end in an hour or so. Whatever life can be salvaged—"

"All right! I concede the point. Come here already."

" . . . "

" . . . "

"Oh my."

". . . What?"

"Albert, you spend extra on your grays!"

"You do, too."

"UK offers supertactile enhancement on employee discount—that's nice . . ."

"Yeah. Let's—"

"Uh, wait, there's a rock under me. . . . There. Better. Now, give me your weight. Feel good, Albert. Forget everything."

"All right. It's *so* . . ."

". . . so real. Almost as if . . ."

". . . as if . . . Ah . . . *ch-phlwef!*"

"What was that? Did you just . . . sneeze?"

"I thought you did. I mean the dust . . ."

"You did! You're real, dammit! I can tell!"

"Ritu, let me explain—"

"Get off, you bastard."

"Sure. But . . . what's this dye rubbing off your neck?"

"Shut up."

"And the contacts in your eyes have slipped. I *thought* your texture was too perfect. You're real, too!"

"I thought you were *dead*. A ghost, about to melt away. I was trying to console you."

"I was consoling *you*! What was all that talk about needing distraction?"

"I was talking about *you,* idiot."

"It sounded like you were talking about yourself."

"A likely excuse."

"Hey! Do you think I'd have touched you if I knew? I said, Clara and I—"

"Damn you."

"For what? We *both* lied, okay? I'll tell you my reason for coming disguised, if you tell me yours. Deal?"

"Go to hell!"

"Aren't you glad I *wasn't* in my house when that missile hit? You'd rather I were dead?"

"Of course not. It's just—"

"I could have started walking hours ago. I stayed to—"

"Take advantage!"

"Ritu, each of us thought—aw, what's the point?"

"Damn right!"

" . . . "

" . . . "

"What?"

". . . What?"

"Did you just mutter something?"

"No! That is . . ."

"Yes?"

"I only said it was . . . real nice . . . while it lasted."

"Yeah . . . it was. Oh, now what are you laughing at?"

"I was just picturing us, lying here afterward, feeling pleased having 'consoled' each other . . . then waiting for the other one to start melting. Then waiting some more . . ."

"Heh. That *is* kind of funny. It's kind of too bad we found out so soon."

"Yes. But, Albert?"

"Yes, Ritu?"

"I really am glad you're alive."

"Thanks. That's sweet to say."

"So, now what?"

"Now? I guess we start walking. Get a plastic jug from the car, fill it from the pool, and head west."

"Back to town. Are you sure you don't mean southeast?"

"Southeast?"

"To my father's cabin."

"Urraca Mesa. I don't know, Ritu. I'm in big trouble back home."

"And you have lots to figure out before trying to solve it. The cabin is private, with shielded net-links. You could send out feelers, find out what's going on before you emerge to confront Aeneas . . . or whoever's behind all this."

"I see your point. Can we make it there on foot?"

"There's one way to find out."

"Well . . ."

"And we'll pass near the battle range. Was that why you came in person, instead of sending a ditto?"

"Am I that obvious, Ritu?"

"I'm realistic enough to tell—and be envious—when someone is in love."

"Well, Clara and I . . . we're both shy about commitment. But—"

"All right, then. Let's make your soldier-lass our goal. It's getting dark, but the moon is up and I've got a light-amplifier in my left eye."

"Me too."

"We can do it at a jog. Our ancestors crossed this desert long ago. Anything they could do, we can do, right?"

"If you say so, Ritu. In my experience, people can talk themselves into just about anything."

24

Psycho-Ceramic

. . . Tuesday's surviving gray makes
an impression . . .

I never imagined that being a mad scientist's experimental guinea pig
could be so interesting.

It's been about ten hours since my protein clock starting running
down, triggering the salmon reflex . . . that familiar urge to swim or run
or fly back home, overcoming any obstacle to spill memories from this
mini-life into the copious storage of a real human brain. But that nagging
reflex soon fell away. Every golem-reflex that was pressed into my pseudoflesh, back at the factory, has been worn down by a physical and spiritual pummeling.

"You'll get used to the renewal treatments," ditMaharal explained
after putting me through torments of steam, hot jets, and tingling rays,
leaving torso and limbs all puffy, quivering like those first moments when
you slide out of the kiln.

"It only hurts the first few times," he said.

"How often can you do this, before—"

"Before inevitable wear and tear makes it futile? Clay is still far less
enduring than flesh. This prototype apparatus has done up to thirty renewals. My old team at Universal may have pushed that higher by now.
If Aeneas hasn't terminated the project—which seems rather likely at this
point."

Thirty renewals, I pondered.

Thirty times the normal ditto span. A pittance next to the many tens
of thousands of days you feel entitled to in a modern, multibranched life.
But with fresh *élan* surging through my clay body, I answered Maharal
frankly.

"You'd have my thanks, if this weren't just your way of extending
my captivity."

"Oh come, now. Where there's continuity, there is hope. Just think of
it—thirty days, to hope and scheme for escape!"

"Maybe. But you say I've been here before. Ditnapped and experi-
mented on. Did any of those other Alberts escape?"

"As a matter of fact, three found clever ways to get away. One was stopped by my dogs, just outside. Another melted crossing the desert. And one actually made it to a phone! But you had already zeroed out the poor ditto's credit code, after it was missing for a week. My robotic hunter caught up before it managed to format a message through one of the free-nets."

"I'll be sure and leave the codes active much longer in the future."

"Always the optimist!" Maharal laughed. "I told you about those others in order to show the futility of escape. I fixed the security flaws you exploited those times."

"I'll have to come up with something original, then."

"I also know how you think, Albert. I've studied you for years."

"Yeah? Then why *am* I here, ditYosil? Something about me bugs the hell out of you. Something you need, is that it?"

He looked at me, trapped immobile in his stony laboratory-catacomb, and I swear his golem eyes seemed to glint with a look that lay somewhere between avarice and fear. "I am getting close," he says. "Very close."

"You had better be," I answered. "Even restorative technology can't keep you going forever without a real body. I hold the key, don't I? Some kind of secret that will solve your problem. But *I'll* wear out too, in a matter of days.

"You're in a race against time.

"Then there's Aeneas Kaolin. He was awfully anxious to see you taken to the lab for dissection, Tuesday morning. Why? Does he suspect you've stolen equipment and set up your own clandestine lab, using it to cheat death?"

Maharal's tense expression turned haughty.

"You are clever, as usual, Albert," he replied. "But always there's something missing from your sharp guesswork. You never quite catch onto the truth, even when I lay it all in front of you."

How do you answer when a body says something like that to you? When another person claims to know what you will do even better than you do? Because he remembers many past episodes like this one, tense encounters that you don't recall?

Having no answer, I lapsed silent. Renewal had given me some time, so I bided it.

He pulled a switch and the containment vessel quickly flushed clear of sustaino-fluid, then split open. While my body still quivered, regaining full levels of catalysis, he slipped powered manacles over my wrists and ankles. Using a controller, he used them to force me, marionettelike, onto a machine that looked like a souped-up imprinting unit. Round a corner of the apparatus, I glimpsed a pair of legs, colored bright crimson. A ditto blank. Rather small.

"You want me to make a copy?" I asked. "Let me warn you, dit-Yosil—"

"Just Yosil. I told you, I *am* Maharal, now."

"Yeah right, ditYosil. It's obvious you want to make dit-to-dit copying work. How else can you survive past the thirtieth renewal? But honestly, what kind of a solution is that? The second-order copy always has a flawed soul-imprint. And it gets worse when you copy *that* one. Errors magnify. By the third transfer, you're lucky if it can even walk or talk."

"So they say."

"So they say? Listen, half of my work involves catching copyright violators who ditnap the golems of movied stars and courtesans and such, in order to sell bootleg knockoffs. Force-imprint counterfeiting may work for sex toys, if the customer has low standards, but it's no solution to your problem, Yosil."

"We'll see about that. Now please try to relax and cooperate."

"Why should I? It's *hard* to make a really good imprint from a re-sisting subject. I can make things more difficult for you."

"True. But consider. The better the copy, the more it will share your abilities, your drives, and especially your low opinion of me!" Maharal chuckled. "A quality copy will be your ally in trying to defeat me."

I pondered.

"Those other Alberts you captured . . . they must have tried it both ways."

"True. Only when the copy was poor, I just tried again. And again, till you chose to cooperate. Then we made real progress."

"Your idea of progress doesn't sound like mine."

"Perhaps. Or maybe you can't grasp the long-range benefits of my program, though I tried to explain on other occasions. In any event, your problem now is a pragmatic one, Albert. Shackled, there's little that just one of you can do. Two of you might accomplish more. The logic is inescapable."

"Damn you."

He shrugged. "Think about it for a while, Albert. I have plenty of ditto blanks to experiment with."

Maharal's gray departed, leaving me there to ponder, frustrated be-cause he clearly must have had the same conversation many times before, with other me's, learning through experience which arguments worked.

Man, I wish I'd been more careful to track my missing dittos over the years! I simply assumed that a high rate of loss was unavoidable in this line of work. As long as each case went well, some casualties seemed worthwhile. It's not quite as hard core an attitude as Clara has—sending herselves again and again to gladiatorial battlefields for the sake of PEZ and country, with scant likelihood they'll return unscathed. Even so, I vowed to try harder in the future.

If I ever get out of here.

If I get another chance.

Well, all right. I gave in to Yosil's logic. Concentrating during imprint would ensure my brotherdit emerges from the kiln filled with loathing for all mad scientists.

And I turned out to be right about that.

As if it would make any difference.

▪ ▪ ▪

Well now, for the record, this isn't the first time I remember doing a ditto-to-ditto transfer.

Come on, everybody tries it. Most people are unhappy with the product, which often emerges as a pitifully shallow caricature. It can be painful to watch, like seeing a version of yourself that's drunk, stoned, or damaged beyond medical help. Back in college, some of the guys used to make frankies for laughs. But I never got into that kind of stuff.

Partly because my second-order dits never showed overt signs of degradation. No tremors or apparent memory gaps. No comic reeling or slurring. Boring! I might as well make all my copies directly. It felt more comfortable that way. Anyway, why violate the UK warranty? They can repossess your kiln.

I always knew I was a good copier. A small fraction of folks are gifted that way. I was even part of a research study when I was younger. So? It makes no practical difference. What's the point in dit-to-dit transfer, even if you do it well?

Besides, it feels *odd*. Not at all like inloading. To lie on the *original* side of the machine in *clay* form, especially when the soul-sifter starts probing through you with tendrils that are better tuned to scanning neurons. The tetragramatron has to work harder to grasp the Standing Wave, delicately plucking all the chords of your inner symphony, borrowing and amplifying every note in order to start an identical resonant melody playing in another instrument, nearby.

Funny thing. This time I definitely felt something like an *echo* coming from the new ditto—still a lifeless lump on its warming tray. The sensation of déjà vu that our grandparents used to find so eerie—that we now call a "ripple in the Standing Wave"—swarmed over me then like a chilly breath. A whirling-ghostly wind. A feeling of intimate familiarity with myself that I did not like at all.

Was this part of the experiment? Part of what Maharal was trying to achieve?

"Two centuries ago, William James coined the term 'stream of consciousness,'" Maharal commented happily, while he twiddled dials. "James was referring to the way each of us invests our sense of identity in an illusion. The illusion of continuity—like perceiving a single river, flowing from one source to the sea.

"Even dittotech didn't change this romantic delusion. It only added multiple side branches and tributaries to the river, all of them still flowing back into a single soul, an entity that each person arrogantly chooses to call me.

"But a river is nothing in itself! It's amorphous. A mirage. An ever-changing churn of individual tumbling molecules and moments. Even ancient mystics knew that stepping twice into a stream, from exactly the same spot, will immerse you in completely different 'rivers.' Into different liquids that were peed into the flow by *different* elephants, at different places and times upstream."

"You make philosophy so refreshingly earthy," I muttered, lying there helpless under his monologue.

"Thanks. In fact, that particular metaphor was yours. Another Albert Morris golem expressed it, years ago. Which goes to prove my point, dear fellow. The Standing Wave is something much more than just continuity of memory. It has to be! There must be some kind of connection to a higher—or a lower—level."

I knew his game. Maharal was trying to distract me, so my anger wouldn't interfere with the imprinting process. Yet his voice conveyed something sincere. He cared about the crap he was uttering.

Anyway, the weird sensations had me *wanting* some distraction from those strangely powerful resonant echoes. Though my head was clamped between the sifter probes, I turned my eyes to meet Maharal's.

"You're talking about God, right?"

"Well . . . yes. In a manner of speaking."

"Isn't that just a bit odd, Professor? You've spent your life encroaching on the province of religion, helping make it practical for anyone to duplicate the soul-field, like a cheap photograph. There's hardly anyone the old church conservatives hate more than you."

"I'm not talking about religion," he answered with a biting tone. "All that I and others have done, by introducing this technology, is take another step in a long campaign, pushing back a confused muddle of contradictory superstitions in order to let in more light. First Galileo and Copernicus battled to free astronomy from priests who declared the entire cosmos off limits to human understanding. Then Newton, Boltzmann, and Einstein liberated physics. For a while, religions claimed that *life* was too mysterious for anyone but the Creator Himself to understand—till we analyzed the genome and commenced designing new species in the lab. Today, most babies get some kind of optimizing gene therapy, before or after conception, and nobody objects."

"Why would they?" I asked, momentarily puzzled. "Never mind. Let me guess. You're about to extend this historical trend to consciousness—"

"And the human soul, yes. It was the last bulwark of twentieth-century religion. Let science explain nature's laws, from quasars down to quarks! From geology to biology! So what? Those laws were mere *recipes* and background scenery, concocted long ago by a creator who cares far more about matters of the spirit! That's what they said.

"Only then Jefty Annonas found the soul's vibrating essence, weighed it, measured it—"

"Some still resent her choice of terminology," I pointed out. "They claim there's a *true* soul, beyond the Standing Wave. Intangible—"

"—and ineffable, yes. Something mortals can never detect, that can never be reduced to interacting laws and forces." Maharal barked a laugh. "And so the fighting retreat continues. Each time science advances, a new bastion forms . . . a new line, defining some remnant territory to be kept forever holy, mystical, and vague. Safe from profane hands. Until the next scientific advance, that is."

"Which you seem anxious to provide. But then, why talk about religion—"

"Not *religion,* dear fellow. We spoke of communing with *God.*"

"Uh, the difference—"

"—should be clear enough! Though I always have a hard time explaining it to you."

"Well . . . sorry."

"No, it's all right. I'm used to your obstinate slowness. Rare gifts don't always correlate with intelligence."

I felt a *twang* in the Standing Wave, now vibrating at full pitch between me and the new golem. One thing for sure. It was going to hate this guy just as much as I do.

"Go on," I muttered. "About you and God."

■ ■ ■

But he stopped there.

A small bell gave off a *bing* and I felt the soul-sifter release its invasive grip. The last tendrils slid out of my nose. All at once I was alone again inside my clay head, sagging heavily.

Machinery rumbled as the new golem slipped into a kiln for rapid baking. A short while later I glimpsed it standing up, taking those first, uncertain steps.

Dark red, like Texarkana soil. And *small,* like a child. It looked weak, too. Easier for Maharal to control. Even so, the professor's tall gray ghost cautiously clamped a set of power-manacles over its wrists, even before the puffy afterglow faded.

Such precautions! I must have caused plenty of trouble on other occasions. That offered me a smidgen of consolation.

"We'll be back soon," ditYosil told me. "I want to expose this new ditto to a variety of controlled test experiences, then see how well the memories inload back to you."

"Oh. Can't wait."

Usually, I avoid eye contact with fresh copies that I make. It's uncomfortable and what's the point? But this time, after all those eerie sensations I went through during imprinting, it seemed compulsory to meet the small one's gaze. No window to a golem's soul? Maybe not, but I felt something intense the moment his dark stare met mine. An affinity. I don't have to wait for inloading to know what thoughts course through that maroon body.

Look for your chance, I urged silently.

My other self answered with a curt nod. Then, tugged by Maharal's manacles, he turned and followed our master to another part of this iniquitous lair.

So I wait, lying here where they left me. Wondering and worrying about what my captor has in store for me.

Thirty days is beginning to sound like a very long time. I must find a way to settle this much sooner, whether or not God turns out to be one of Yosil Maharal's personal buddies.

And yet, even if an opportunity presents itself, I must be careful what I do. For instance, what if he leaves a phone within easy reach? Would I summon the cops? In some situations, it's enough for a victim to call for help and wait for professional blue-skin rescuers to arrive. Simple.

But not in this case.

Wracking my brain, I can't see that Maharal has committed even a single felony. At least not to my knowledge. Just a long series of equipment thefts, ditnappings, copyright violations, and unlicensed experiments—the kind of stuff that gets settled nowadays with civil liens and automatic fines. The police don't care very much about this particular kind of villain, not since Deregulation.

Not as much as I do!

As far as I'm concerned, some paltry fines won't make up for any of this.

The real world has its rules, and I have mine.

Ditto-to-ditto, I'm going to make that crazy-evil dirtpile pay.

25

Impassioned Clay

. . . as Frankie revisits a place that he's never been . . .

To my utter surprise, Vic Aeneas Kaolin wanted to hire me as a ditective!

"So. Would you two like a chance to find the perverts who did all this?"

He said it waving at a nearby crowd of holo bubbles, jostling for our attention. Most of them showed the sabotage site at Universal Kilns, now swarming with multicolored repair-dittos, like a hive of busy ants struggling to restore the vast factory to profitable operation.

Other bubbles peered down at the smoldering ruins of a small suburban house.

The trillionaire's offer left me speechless, though Pallie's little weasel-golem took it with aplomb.

"Sure, we can solve this case for you. But we gotta charge quadruple Albert's normal rate. Plus expenses . . . including a new house, to replace the one that just got blown up."

How about getting Albert a new organic body, while we're at it? I pondered caustically. Pal could be amazing sometimes, sweating over minor stuff while ignoring the big picture. Like the fact that Albert Morris no longer existed. So who was legally going to take this case? I had no more legitimate authority than a talking toaster.

Kaolin acted unperturbed. "Those terms are acceptable, but with a condition that payment shall depend entirely on results. And that Mr. Morris truly turns out to have been innocent, as the archive-recording seems to suggest."

"Seems to suggest!" Palloid yelped. "You heard the story. That poor guy was duped! Hoodwinked, chiseled, set up, conned, fooled, frauded, framed, swindled—"

"Pal," I tried to interrupt.

"—cozened, misled, tricked! A patsy. A fool, tool, doofus, dolt, blockhead, pawn—"

"That may be," Kaolin cut him off with a hand gesture. "Or else the archive *might* have been contrived in advance. Pre-recorded in order to offer a plausible alibi."

"That can be checked," I pointed out. "Even buried in the gray's throat, the recorder would have picked up ambient city noise from his surroundings. People talking. A truck's engine on a nearby street. Muffled sounds, but under intense analysis they'll correlate with actual events, recorded on nearby publicams."

"So," Kaolin conceded with a nod. "Not pre-recorded, then. But still perhaps a lie. The gray could have gone through all the motions, reciting as he went, while *pretending* not to be one of the conspirators. Feigning gullibility—"

"—naivete, credulousness, stupidity—"

"Shut up, Pal! I don't"—I shook my head—"I don't think any of this is really our business anymore. Shouldn't you be handing this tape over to the police?"

ditKaolin pursed his expressive, realistic lips. "My attorney says we're right at the borderline, the cusp between civil and criminal law."

Surprise provoked my bitter laugh. "A major act of industrial sabotage—"

"Without a single human victim."

"Without a single . . . What in hell do you call *that*?"

I jabbed a finger at one of the news bubbles, showing an aerial view of my poor burned house. I mean Albert's house. Whatever. Responding to my vehement attention, that bubble swelled in size, jostling others aside and magnifying. Our point of view zoomed toward several black investigator specialdits from the Violent Crimes Unit, who could be seen probing the wreckage. Top professionals, looking for body parts. And missile parts, no doubt.

"There is, as yet, no confirmed link between that tragedy and what happened at UK."

Kaolin said it with such a straight face that I stared at him for several seconds.

"You will only get away with that line for a few hours at best, no matter how good your lawyers are. When the cops find my body . . . I mean Albert's . . . and when testimony is taken from ditnesses and cameras inside UK, your insurance company will have no choice but to co-operate with the authorities. The police will *know* you found something small and important in the foamy mess after the prion attack. If you pretend you didn't find anything, one of your contract employees will—"

"—will likely turn me in, hoping to cash a whistle-blower prize. Please, I'm no fool. I won't try to keep the recording away from the cops. Not for very long, that is. But a short delay may prove helpful."

"Helpful how?"

"I get it!" chirped Pal's mini-ditto with obvious relish, its ferret grin widening. "You want the saboteurs to think they succeeded. Assuming they never knew about the graydit's little recorder, they may think they're safe. That gives us time to go after 'em!"

"Time?" I demanded. "*What time?* Are you all nuts? I was baked almost twenty hours ago! My clock is close to used up. I've barely got enough *time* left to take in dinner and a show. Whatever makes you think I can investigate a case under conditions like this, even if I wanted to?"

At which point Aeneas Kaolin smiled.

"Oh, I may be able to reset that ticking clock of yours."

■　　■　　■

Less than thirty minutes later, I stepped out of the biggest apparatus the mogul had in his laboratory-basement. A hissing, steaming contraption that hammered, zapped, sprayed, and massaged me till I hurt all over . . . like that time Clara made me take an army calisthenics course in realflesh and skivvies. My moist clay pseudoskin fizzed disconcertingly with freshly injected *élan*. If I didn't explode or melt in the next few minutes, I might take on the world.

"This gizmo of yours is gonna change a lot of things," Pal commented from a perch nearby, licking the same puffy glow.

ditKaolin answered, "It has drawbacks—like prohibitive cost—that may prevent commercial development. There were only two prototypes and . . . not all results have been satisfactory."

"Now he tells me," I grumbled. "No, please ignore that. Beggars can't be choosers. Thanks for extending this so-called life."

Looking down, I saw that a color change had been thrown in for free. My third in one day. Now I had the look of a high-quality gray. Well, well. Who *says* you can't advance in life? There can be progress, even for a frankie.

"Where do you plan to go first?" the platinum trillionaire asked, clearly eager to get us on our way. Even though I'm not Albert Morris, I tried to picture what my maker, the professional private eye, would do at this point.

"Queen Irene's place," I decided. "Come on, Pal. We're going to the Rainbow Lounge."

▪ ▪ ▪

Kaolin lent us a sturdy little car from the company fleet, no doubt carrying a transponder to track our movements and a sound tap as well. Palloid had to agree not to inload back into the original Pal, or even contact his archie. In fact, we were under orders not to tell anyone else about what we had learned in the mansion basement.

Whether or not those orders were exactly legal, I felt sure that Kaolin had some way to enforce them, or he'd never let us depart. Maybe it was *my* turn to carry a bomb. Something small, inserted while my body was renewed in that hissing experimental restoration machine? I had no immediate way to check it out . . . or any reason to, so long as our goals were the same.

Getting to the truth, right? That's what we're all interested in, right? Me and Kaolin. Only how could I tell?

Again and again, the same question popped into mind. *Why me?*

Why hire the crude green frankie of a private eye whose behavior must already appear deeply worrisome in Kaolin's eyes? Even if Albert's gray hadn't been one of the conspirators, he was their unwitting dupe—as Pal so colorfully put it.

Either way, it seemed strange for the mogul to trust me.

Then again, who *could* he trust? Kaolin wasn't kidding about the Henchman Law. When first introduced, it soon turned into the quickest way for a fellow to retire early—by tattling on his boss. Whistle-blower prizes grew bigger as one white-collar scam after another collapsed, feeding half of the resulting fines back into new rewards, enticing even more trusted lieutenants, minions, and right-hand men to blab away. To everyone's surprise, a world filled with cameras proved to offer pretty good safety against retribution by most mobs. Many gangs and cabals destroyed themselves simply by *trying* to enforce silence on defectors.

The implacable logic of the Prisoner's Dilemma triggered collapse of one conspiracy after another as informers became public heroes, accelerating the rush for publicity and treasure. For a time it looked as if perfidy had its back to the proverbial wall. Any criminal scheme with more than three members appeared doomed from the start.

Then dittotech arrived.

Nowadays, it's possible once again to have a gang of ruthless accomplices, if all of them are you! Better still if you do find a few trustworthy allies to share the imprinting chores, since they may have skills you lack. But you're still wise to keep the number of original members low. Three or four. Five, tops. Any more and you still have an excellent chance of being betrayed by some trusted aide. A guilty conscience can get plenty of lubrication if the rewards are also big.

Kaolin may have several thousand real employees, who make tens of thousands of proficient and hardworking dittos for him every day. But could he ask any of them to skate the fine edge of the law—as Pallie and I were about to do? The Vic's choices were few. Either do it himself, by sending out his own copies, or hire someone with the right skills. Someone who's already shown a willingness to skulk at the boundaries of legality, and yet with a reputation for keeping his word. Someone also highly motivated to dig quickly to the bottom of this mess.

Having listened to the archive-recording of that hapless gray, Kaolin must figure that I qualify on all counts. I sure wasn't about to complicate matters by mentioning I'm a frankie. He might drop me in the nearest recycler!

Waiting for a driver to bring our loaner car, I resumed bugging Kaolin with questions.

"It would help if I had some idea why somebody wants to wreck your factory."

"Why should concern you less than *who*," he replied sternly.

"Come, sir. Understanding motives can be integral to catching bad guys. Do your competitors resent having to pay royalties on your patents? Do they envy your production efficiency? Could they be trying to knock UK down a notch?"

Kaolin barked a short laugh. "A publicly held firm is under too much scrutiny. And terrorism is risky—not the style of my smug counterparts at Fabrique Chelm or Hayakawa Shobo. Why use bombs when they can cause me far more aggravation with their lawyers?"

"Well, who do you consider desperate enough to use bombs?"

"You mean other than those pathetic fanatics ranting by my gate?" The platinum ditto shrugged. "I don't bother counting my enemies, Mr. Morris. In fact, I would have retired by now, to one of my country estates, were it not for some rather urgent research interests that force me to remain nearby, within easy dit-imprinting range." He sighed. "If you must demand an opinion from me, I can only hazard to guess that this grue-some act of sabotage must be the work of perverts."

"Uh . . . perverts?" I blinked a couple of times in surprise. "When you used that word before, I didn't think you meant *literally*."

"Oh, but I do. It isn't just religious nuts and tolerance fetishists who despise me. Surely you already know about this? I may have helped usher in the age of dittoing, but I've also long opposed ways the technology is misapplied. From the very beginning, I was appalled by some unsavory uses customers came up with."

"Well, innovators often have an idealized view of what will emerge—"

"Do I strike you as a woolly-headed idealist?" Kaolin snapped, sharply. "I realize any new thing gets misused, especially when you share it with the masses. Take the way every new medium, from printing to cinema to the Internet, became a major conduit for pornography almost as soon as it was introduced. Or when lonely weirdos started using dittos for sex, muddying all the boundaries between fantasy, infidelity, and self-abuse."

"Surely that didn't surprise you."

"Not the basic level. Anyone could see this technology would make casual sex between strangers safe again, after several generations of fear. It's a natural pendulum swing, based on deeply embedded animal drives. Hell, the trend of using animated dolls began even before Bevvisov and Leow imprinted the first Standing Wave. I wasn't thrilled to see ditto-swap clubs arise everywhere, but at least that seemed human.

"Only then came the 'modification' movement. Wave after wave of so-called innovations, exaggerations, deliberate mutilations . . ."

"Ah yes. You fought to prevent people from changing the blanks you sold them. But surely that's a dead issue now."

Kaolin conceded with a shrug. "Still, I'm sure the perverts recall how I fought them. And each year I contribute financial support to the Crudity Bill."

"You mean the *Prudity* Bill," Palloid muttered from a balustrade of the mansion's service portico. "Do you *really* want to require that all dittos come out of the factory with their capacity for emotions suppressed?"

"Only feelings that promote violent or hostile behavior."

"But that's half the fun of being a golem! You can do stuff on the edge. Unleash the repressed inner demon—"

"Repression exists for good reasons," Kaolin answered hotly. Palloid sure knew how to goad him. "Social, psychological, and evolutionary reasons. Every year, anthropologists track worrisome trends. People growing more hardened to outrageous levels of violence—"

"—in certain narrowly defined times and places. Like daydreaming about stuff you'd never do in person. There's no conclusive evidence that it translates over to behavior in the real—"

"—becoming callused to mutilations of the human form—"

"—and experiencing firsthand what it feels like to be larger or smaller, crippled, or the opposite sex—"

"—inflicting suffering—"

"—experiencing it—"

"—desensitizing—"

"—gaining new empathy—"

"Enough!" I cried. For a brief time it had been enthralling to watch the platinum golem of a multi-trillionaire get sucked into a shouting match with a ferret-formed creature from dittotown. But Pal's lack of anything like a sense of self-preservation can get unamusing rather quickly. We still existed on this guy's sufferance.

"So you think this attack may have been in revenge for your consistent support of the Crudity Bill?" I asked.

ditKaolin shrugged. "It passed in Farsiana-Indus, last year. That makes twenty-six countries, and the Argentines vote next month. Degenerates may see a worrisome trend, toward a time when our adjunct selves are actually calmer and better than we are—"

"—You mean sexless and boring—"

"—helping to elevate humanity instead of debasing us," Kaolin finished, giving Palloid a scowl that declared the debate over. And my small friend took the hint this time. Or maybe it was the arrival of our car, delivered to the portico by a blank-faced yellow whose only personality trait was a soft melody that he kept humming while holding the driver-side door for me, then as he jogged away, hurrying to catch a jitney cab back to headquarters.

I adjusted the pilot seat and Platinum Kaolin gave me a portaphone with a secure comm number to call, if anything especially urgent came up. Otherwise, I was instructed to send a dictated report to his hi-pri box every three hours, for automatic summarization-transcription.

I was about to shut the door when Pal's little weasel-ditto leaped from my shoulder onto Kaolin's! The silvery golem flinched as Palloid squirmed around his neck. "Incredible texture," crooned the miniature ditto. "So realistic. I been wondering . . ."

It seemed about to give Kaolin a big kiss. Then, without warning, Palloid whirled and sank its gleaming *teeth* into that shimmering neck, just above the collar line!

Twin wounds oozed a pasty grue.

"What the hell?" Pain and anger flushed as Kaolin swept a fist that Palloid dodged easily, vaulting through the car's open window into my arms. Licking shiny-reflective gore off serrated jaws, he spat with distaste.

"Clay! Patooie. Okay, he's fake, after all. Had to check, though. He could've been pretending to be phony."

It was vintage Pal. Authority figures bring out the worst in him. I hurried to mollify our employer.

"Sorry about that, sir. Uh . . . Pal likes to be thorough. And that *is* an awfully realistic-looking body, you must admit."

ditKaolin fumed.

"What if I *had* been in disguise? That goddam thing could have maimed me! Besides, it's none of your bloody business how I choose to present myself! I have a good mind to—"

He stopped abruptly, taking a deep breath. The lacerations ceased oozing after a couple of seconds, turning into hard ceramic crust. Between dittos, this was a trifle, after all.

"Oh, get out of here. Don't bother me again unless you find something interesting."

Pal responded cheerily, "Thanks for a lovely visit! Give my regards to your archety—"

I peeled out of there, cutting off Palloid's clever remise. Passing through the front gate into city traffic, I cast a sharp, disapproving glare at my companion.

"What?" The ferret face grinned back at me. "Tell me *you* weren't curious, looking at such a fancy-realistic golem! There are all those stories. About how nobody's seen his archie in years."

"Curiosity is one thing, Pal—"

"One thing? Hey, at this point it's about the *only* reason I have to keep going. Know what I mean?"

I did, alas. Even though I had been granted an extension—double the lifespan I expected to have yesterday, when I stepped out of the kiln—a day is still only a day. To a frankie or a ghost.

What could I accomplish in that time? Maybe some justice. Or a little revenge on the villains who murdered poor Albert. Those can be satisfying accomplishments. But you can't take them with you beyond the recycling tank.

Curiosity, on the other hand, has a timelessness that no deadline can erase. There are worse things for a man to live for, whether he's born of woman or kiln. It can sustain you, whatever happens and no matter how low your fortunes sink.

"Anyway, Albert. Did you see the *look* on skinny's face when I bit him?"

"Hell, yes, I saw it! You little—" I shook my head. The image of Kaolin's vain countenance still surfed the foamy veneer of my Standing Wave. That expression of affronted shock was—

—hilarious.

I couldn't help but guffaw. Laughter shook us both while I swerved the little cruiser through a yellow light, incurring another four-point infraction to put on our UK expense account. Mirth combined with the fizzing sense of renewal that still permeated my invigorated clay flesh. It left me feeling more alive than I had in, well, hours!

"All right, then," I said at last, trying to concentrate on my driving. We were in Realtown and there might be children about. No time for inattention at the wheel.

"Come on, Pal. Let's see what's happening at Irene's."

■　　■　　■

What was happening was death.

A crowd milled near the entrance to the Rainbow Lounge. All sorts of garishly colored dittos—specialized and home-modified for pleasure or ritual combat—shifted and murmured in confusion, denied entry to their favorite hangout by ribbons of glare tape that shimmered to eye-hurting rhythms, sending *keep away* messages straight to the golem fibers threading their clay bodies.

A female-shaped red stood in the entryway. Wearing dark glasses. Explaining patiently as Palloid and I drew near.

". . . Let me say again, I'm sorry, but you cannot enter. The club will soon be under new management. Till then, you must find another place to pursue your frantic pleasures."

I looked her over. Exaggerated curves seemed to cry out *slutty wait-ress,* while recessed needles under the nails indicated a bouncer's capacity to enforce order, whenever customers got rowdy. This had to be one of the worker drone members of *Irene*—the colony-being we heard de-scribed in grayAlbert's recited diary. She matched the depiction, except for looking haggard and worn, obviously tottering on her last energy stores.

Some customers drifted off, hoping to find another dive open at this hour. One offering as much amusement. I saw grimness in their haste. Especially the dittos with spiky appendages for fighting or exaggerated sexual display. That kind is often made by addicts—experience junkies who need regular fixes of intense recent memories, the more extravagant or violent the better. If these dits fail to bring home the goods, their originals won't take them back. Their chance of continuity-through-inloading depends on finding excitement elsewhere, anywhere.

Still, more customers kept arriving, milling about hopefully or trying to argue with the red bouncer. Would she stand there in the doorway till she melted? From the testimony of Albert's luckless gray, I had an im-pression that Irene took inloading very seriously.

"Let's try around back," Palloid suggested from my shoulder. "Ac-cording to the gray's recording, that's where this hive keeps its queen."

Its queen. I've heard of such things, naturally. Still, it's creepy. Hives and queens, man. Some say we're all heading that way, eventually, by the inherent logic of dittotech.

Interesting times, all right.

"Okay," I told my small comrade. "Let's go back and have a look."

26

Souls on Celluloid

. . . or how realAlbert finds an oasis of the heart . . .

Ritu and I were rather wrinkled and worn after a long night and a morning spent trekking across arid desert.

You might expect that our gray disguises would look much worse than "wrinkled." But fortunately, the best brands of makeup don't clog your natural pores. Instead of blocking perspiration they actually wick it away, maximizing the cooling effects of any passing wind. Dirt and salt crystals work their way outward. In fact, they say the material keeps you cooler and cleaner than exposed skin.

That's fine, so long as you have plenty of water to drink. Which became a problem twice during our long hike south from the ravine where the Volvo had crashed. Each time our carry-jug ran low in the middle of some great expanse, with no civilization in sight, I wondered if the trek was such a good idea after all.

But despite the appearance of lonely desolation, today's desert isn't the same one our ancestors faced. Whenever we ran low on water, something always came up. Like when we came across an area dotted with abandoned squatters' huts, more than a century old, perched on crude cement slabs with rusting steel roofs. One had ancient shag carpeting, so thick with dust that it sported a thriving shade ecosystem. The cabin's clogged plumbing offered a cistern where we managed to refill the jug with scummy rainwater, unappetizing but welcome nonetheless. Another time, Ritu found a drip pool just inside a defunct mineshaft. I wasn't happy about drinking the mineral-steeped brew, but modern chelating treatments should eliminate any toxins, if we made it to civilization promptly.

So, while our trek was an adventure—often miserably uncomfortable—it never became a matter of life-or-death. On several occasions we spotted the glint of a robotic weather station or the dun-colored housing of an eco-webcam. So calling for help was always an option if we got into serious trouble. We had good reasons *not* to call. It was a matter of choice. That made the journey bearable.

In fact, Ritu and I found enough spare energy to pass the time as we trudged along, continuing our conversation about recent dramas and parasensies we had seen. Like the classic cliché you see all the time—a duplicate claims to be the "real one," accusing some imposter of taking over his normal life. On a higher plane, we had both seen *Red Like Me,* the docudrama about a woman whose permanent skin condition made her look unbrown—*unreal* to most people—so she couldn't go anywhere without being treated as a golem. We all put up with being "mere property" much of the time, because it all evens out, right? But this heroine never got to take her turn as citizen/master. The story reminded me of Pal, stuck in his life-support chair, unable to experience the world fully except through dittos. The modern bargain isn't always fair.

That's how I learned why Ritu came on this trip in person, instead of sending a gray. It turns out she's handicapped, too. She can't make reliable copies. They often come out wrong.

All right, millions of folks can't use kilns at all, suffering the disadvantage of just one, linear life. Bigots call them "soulless," thinking it happens to those who lack a true Standing Wave to copy. The heritable deficit can make it hard to get a job or win a mate. Indeed, today's heartless version of capital punishment severs a felon's Bevvisov-nexus, preventing him from imprinting, trapping him forever in the confines of a single body.

Many *tens* of millions can animate only crude, shambling caricatures, able to mow the lawn or paint a fence—but no more than that.

Ritu's problem is different. She imprints dittos of great subtlety and intelligence, but many are frankies, diverging radically. "When I was a teenager, they'd often come out of the kiln resentful, even hating me! Instead of helping to achieve my goals, some tried sabotaging them, or put me in embarrassing situations.

"Only in recent years did I reach a kind of equilibrium. Now, maybe half of my golems do what I want. The rest wander off, mostly harmlessly. Still, I always install strong transponder pellets, to make sure they behave."

The awkward confession came after we'd been walking for hours, fatigue wearing away her reticent shell. I mumbled sympathetically, lacking the nerve to tell her that I never made frankies. (Till yesterday's green sent that strange message, that is. And I'm still not sure I believe it.)

As for Ritu's problem, my professional readings in psychopathology left room for one conclusion—the daughter of Yosil Maharal had deep psychological troubles that stay mute while she's safely confined to her natural skin. But dittoing unleashes them with callous amplification. *A classic case of suppressed self-hatred,* I thought, then chided myself for diagnosing another person on slim evidence.

This explained why she accompanied me in person, Tuesday evening. It was clearly important to help investigate her father's old desert lodge. To ensure it got done right, she must come the old-fashioned way.

A lot of our conversation—including this confession—was recorded on the little transcriber planted under the skin behind my ear. I felt bad about that, but saw no way to stop it. Maybe I'll erase that part later, when I get a chance.

■   ■   ■

The Jesse Helms International Combat Range.
From a distance, it looks like a fairly typical military base in the

desert—a green oasis dotted with swaying palms, tennis courts and resort-scale swimming pools. The barracks for quartering troops during wartime seem appropriately spartan—tree-shaded cabana-style residence bungalows in muted pastels, cloistered near cybersim stations, practice arenas, and zen contemplation gardens. Everything needed by soldiers seeking to hone their martial spirit.

In stark contrast to those stoical training grounds, brash hotels jut skyward near the main gate, serving journalists and fight aficionados who converge in person for each major battle. Killwire barriers keep out reporters and flitting hobbycams, so the warriors inside may concentrate without interruption. Preparing their souls for battle.

Far beyond the oasis, under a natural hillock surrounded by tire ruts, lay the underground bowels of the base—a support complex never viewed by millions of fans who dial in for each televised clash. Below reside all the special weapon fabricators and customized golem-presses required by a modern military. Another subterranean mound, several kilometers away, offers guest facilities to visiting armies who come several times a year to brave weeks of feverish struggle, beyond a range of hills—in the battleground proper.

"Well, it doesn't look as if the war's over," Ritu commented as we took turns peering through a hand-held ocular, one of a few items salvaged from my ruined Volvo. Even standing on a crest five kilometers outside the boundary, you could tell; the grudge match between PEZ and Indonesia still ran hot. Hotel parking areas were full. And the far southern sky glittered with floatcams and relaysats.

Oh, something was going on, below that distant horde of buzzing voyeur-eyes, just behind an escarpment of granite cliffs. Sporadic rumbles—like angry thunder—kept spilling over that craggy barrier. On several occasions, powerful booms made the very air throb around Ritu and me. Those detonations escorted flashes of harsh light so brilliant that brief shadows danced across the sun-drenched terrain.

Something very close to hell was unfolding beyond the escarpment. A fiery maelstrom of death, more violent and merciless than our savage ancestors could have imagined . . . and you'd be hard-pressed to find anyone alive in our crowded world who felt badly about it.

"So," my companion asked. "How do we get in to see your soldier-girlfriend? Do we stroll up to the main gate and have her paged?"

I shook my head. If only it were that easy. All during our hard slog across the desert, this stage weighed heavily on my mind.

"I don't think it'd be a good idea to attract attention."

"No kidding. Last I heard, you were a suspect in a major crime."

"And dead."

"Oh yes, and dead. That could raise a stir when you present your retina for an ID scan. So then. Do you want *me* to do it? I can rent a room. Let us finally scrape off this makeup." She gestured at the gray pseudoskin that covered both of us, looking rather weathered after many hours of sun and harsh wind. "I could take a hot bath while you call your friend."

I shook my head. "Of course it's up to you, Ritu. But I doubt you should reveal yourself, either. Even if the police aren't after you, there's still Aeneas Kaolin to consider."

"*If* that was Aeneas who shot at us, on the highway. Seeing ain't believing, Albert."

"Hm. Will you bet your life it wasn't him? Clearly, Kaolin and your father were engaged in something big. Something disturbing. All signs indicate they had a parting of ways. It may have led to your father's death on the very same highway where we were ambushed—"

Ritu raised a hand. "You convinced me. We need a secure web port to find out what's going on, before letting anyone know we survived."

"And Clara's just the one to arrange it." I raised the ocular again. "Assuming we cross the next few kilometers and get her attention."

"Any ideas how to do that?"

I pointed left, away from the main gate of the base, toward a ramshackle encampment that ran along the killwire fence, some distance beyond the glitzy hotels. Multicolored figures could be seen moving amid a lurid variety of tents, mobile homes, and makeshift arenas, giving the impression of an anarchist's carnival.

"Down there. *That's* where we go next."

27

Shards of Heaven

. . . as Greenie learns there are worse things than dying . . .

Pal's little ferret-ditto rode my shoulder as we retreated from the shuttered front entrance of the Rainbow Lounge, heading around back to find another way inside. A big security fence blocked the service alley, but I didn't have to mess with it. The gate was ajar. It must have been left that way when a large van passed inside. We squeezed through, then sauntered past the vehicle, looking it over.

FINAL OPTIONS, INC.

That was what the hologo banner said, with angelic cherubs beckoning graciously. A great big dish transmitter on the vehicle's roof looked handcrafted, rather ornate and much larger than you need for a satellite data link. As we sidled past, my skin tingled, a bit like the recent fizzing sensation of being renewed.

"A lot of energy in that van," Palloid commented, arching his back, letting the fur bristle.

"Have you heard of these guys?" I asked, shivering till we got past.

"Some. Here and there." Palloid's voice was low and terse.

Chilly cryosteam shrouded thick, insulated cables, snaking between the van and the back door of the building, where kitschy organ music filled the dim interior. Warily, I stepped over the cables into a cavernous chamber where several dozen cloaked forms could be made out, swaying to dirgelike harmonies.

"What're they doing?" Pal asked snidely. "Filming a new episode of *Vincent Price Theater?*"

I was keenly aware of what happened in this place, only yesterday, when these creatures managed to fool one of Albert's best grays, tricking him into letting them plant a fiendish bomb in his gut. If they could manage that, a miserable frankie like me had better be careful. Under my skin-deep dye job, I was still humble green.

Adjusting to the light, I saw that all the robed forms wore the same distinctive reddish shade as the one who barred the front door to the

Rainbow Lounge. All except a central figure lying on a raised dais, who looked so pale that I first assumed it must be an ivory ditto.

But no, the supine shape was a real person, with sparse patches of gray hair sticking out amid clusters of attached electrodes. Silky red cloth covered much of her heavy, flaccid form. Most people today strive to keep their organic bodies in good shape. (Getting enough of a tan to not be mistaken for a pleasure-golem!) But some folks have just one use for the body they were born in—to serve as a memory vessel, passing impressions from one day's set of dittos to the next. Evidently, Irene had been on the cutting edge of this trend. No wonder she ran a popular emporium dedicated to fashionable excess!

And yet, from the requiem sounds reverberating all around, I had to guess that Irene's life—large as it may have been—was finally coming to an end. Her chest rose and fell unevenly beneath the coverlet. Tubes dripped medicinal liquids while a nearby metabolic monitor beeped to a soft, erratic meter.

I saw no kiln. No rows of waiting ditto blanks. So, she wasn't busy making ghosts, as some do when they know they're dying—a final spate of autonomous duplicates to handle last-minute details . . . or to say all those things you never dared to utter while alive. Most of these Irene-copies looked rather elderly. They all might have been present when grayAlbert had his "repairs."

Did Irene stop duplicating herself at the same time, or soon after? A very odd coincidence, if it was one.

Watching from the shadows, I saw one Irene standing aside from the corny threnody ceremony, conversing with a purple golem whose huge eyes and stylishly curved beak resembled those of a hawk.

"Horus," Palloid muttered.

"Horace?"

"Horus!" He gestured at the visitor's bright robe, covered with inscriptions and fancy embroidered figures. "Egyptian god of death and afterlife. Kinda pretentious, by my taste."

Of course, I thought. *Final Options. One of those outfits offering specialized assistance to the dead or dying. If there's a hypothetical service anybody might want, you can find a million of the bored-unemployed eager to provide it.*

I edged closer while hawkface explained items in a glossy brochure.

". . . Here's one of our more popular options. Full cryonic suspension! I have facilities to imbue your archetype's organic body with the right combination of scientifically balanced stabilization agents, then begin reducing its temperature till we can deliver her to our main storage facility in Redlands, which has its own deep geothermal power supply, armored against anything short of a direct cometary impact! All your rig has to do is imprint a release—"

"Cryonic suspension doesn't interest us," replied the red golem, representing her hive. "It has been verified repeatedly that a frozen human brain can't maintain a Standing Wave. It vanishes, never to return."

"But there are *memories*, stored in nearly a quadrillion synapses and intracellular—"

"Memories aren't homologous—not the same thing as *who you are*. Anyway, most of those memories can only be accessed by a functioning copy of the original Standing Wave."

"Well, *dittos* can be frozen. Suppose one accompanies the original head into storage. Then someday, when technology has advanced sufficiently, some combination of—"

"Please," the red Irene cut in. "We aren't interested in science fiction. Let others pay high fees to serve as your experimental guinea pigs. We want a simple service, the reason we called your company.

"We choose the antenna."

"The antenna." The purple hawkman nodded. "I'm required by law to say the technique is unverified, with no confirmed successes, despite many claimed resonance detections—"

"We have reason to believe your past failures resulted from a lack of concentration, desire, focus. These we'll provide, if you do your job as advertised."

Horus straightened.

"The antenna, then. I still need a release. Please have your archetype put her life-imprint here."

He pulled a heavy, flat rectangle out of the folds of his robe, tearing off a filmy plastic covering that released a dense, steamy cloud. The red ditto took the tablet gingerly in both hands by its edges, careful not to touch the moist surface.

"I'll return in a few minutes. There are preparations to complete." Horus spun away toward the van amid a flourish of glittering robes.

Palloid and I watched the red emissary pass through a crowd of her sisters, who parted with no apparent signal. She stepped up to the dais, holding the tablet high over the pale figure lying there. The original, pale-skinned Irene reacted by lifting one hand, then another. *She's conscious,* I realized.

Gently, two dittos approached from opposite sides to restrain her.

Lower came the tablet, closer to that sallow face till her warm breath condensed droplets on the surface. She inhaled deeply, then the red ditto pressed the clay slab down, quickly and with enough force to warp it around realIrene's head . . . holding it there a few seconds, till a near-perfect mask formed—mouth agape in a reflex gasp.

No breath was needed in the short time it took for the raw clay to transform before our eyes, rippling swiftly through several color spectra—including some hues that ancient hermits used to seek in far corners of the world, during the long dark era before soulistics. The mouth area, especially, seemed to flicker briefly with faint lightning.

Then the solid mask lifted away, leaving realIrene ashudder but unharmed.

"I always hate having to do that," Palloid muttered. "Goddam lawyers."

"Signatures can be forged, Pal. Same with fingerprints, cryptociphers, and retinal scans. But a soul-seal is unique."

Irene now had a binding contract with Final Options, to spend the last moments of her organic life buying something else, something she considered more precious. Well, well. Here's to the Big Deregulation. The state has no business getting in between you and your spiritual adviser, especially when it comes to that decisive choice—how to make your final exit.

Too bad poor Albert never had any say in the matter. Partly thanks to Irene, I bet.

Palloid swiveled and grew tense on my shoulder. I turned in time to notice a figure approach us from one side. It was another red ditto, looking a bit ragged like the others, but still formidable. "Mr. Morris." She bowed her head slightly. "Is it you? Or another? Shall I introduce myself?"

"None of the above," I answered, not caring if the cryptic answer confused her. "I know you, Irene. But I'm not the fellow you blew up last night."

She answered with a resigned shrug. "When I saw you, just now, I couldn't help but hope."

"Hope? For what?"

"That the news reports somehow lied. I hoped you were the same ditto that left here yesterday."

"What are you trying to pull? You know what happened to that gray. *You* murdered him. Blew him up inside Universal Kilns! Only his final act of heroism prevented your bomb from ruining the place."

"Our bomb." The red nodded resignedly. "So people will say. But honestly, we thought we were implanting a *spy apparatus,* tuned to sense and evaluate experimental soul-fields in the UK Research Division—"

"Oh, what a pile," Palloid commented.

"No, truly! News of the sabotage attack on UK came as a complete surprise. It showed how fully we were used. Betrayed."

"Right. Tell me about betrayal!"

Oblivious to sarcasm, she nodded. "Oh, I shall. We at once realized that an ally set us up to take the onus for this vicious attack, as part of a multilayered defense, to protect the true villain from retribution. Even if your gray's obscuring tactics had been perfect—even if he masked his trail, cutting all direct links leading back to his employers—a crime of such magnitude would not go unsolved. Universal Kilns will spare no expense to find those responsible. So, after several layers of decoys are peeled back, we were positioned to take ultimate blame.

"Are you the first harbinger of penalization, ditto Morris?"

"Oh, I may be a harbinger all right, but I'm *not* Morris," I muttered, so low she didn't notice.

"We are a bit surprised to see you," the red ditto conceded. "Instead of UK Security, or the police. Perhaps they follow soon? No matter. We'll no longer be here. We are departing shortly, while still able to choose the manner of our going."

I wasn't swallowing it.

"You claim innocence about the prion bomb. What about the attack on realAlbert, slaughtering him in his home?"

"Isn't it obvious?" she asked. "The mastermind behind all of this— our common enemy, it seems—had to cover his own role after using us. That meant leaving no loose ends. He killed you a bit more swiftly than he killed me, but just as ruthlessly. In short order, you and I will both be no more.

"That is, on this plane of reality," she added.

I glanced at the dais, which had been rolled much closer to the van. Hissing cryo-cables were being attached to a dense array of sifter tendrils, piled around the pale head of realIrene. "You're committing some kind of fancy suicide. That'll leave you unable to testify as a full person in a court of law. Are you sure you want to do that? Won't it only benefit your former partner, who betrayed you? Shouldn't you help catch and punish him?"

"Why? Revenge doesn't matter. We were dying anyway . . . a matter of weeks, only. We took part in his scheme as a desperate gamble, hoping

228 ■ D a v i d   B r i n

to stave off that fate. We trusted, gambled, and lost. But at least we still have some choice in the manner of our passing."

Palloid snarled. "Revenge may not matter to *you*, but Albert was my friend. I want to get the bastard who did this."

"And I'm sure we wish you luck," the red sighed. "But this villain is a renowned master at evading accountability."

"Was it that Vic Collins character the gray met?"

She nodded. "You already know him by another name."

With a sinking feeling, I guessed.

"Beta."

"Quite. He was unamused by your raid on his operation in the Teller Building, by the way. That cost him dearly. But the plan to use Albert Morris in this ploy had been brewing for some time."

"And a deeper plan to use *you.*"

"Acknowledged. We saw the collaboration as a clever attempt at industrial espionage. A chance to pirate some first use of the hottest new dittotech, before it went through the cumbersome licensing process."

"Hot new dittotech. You mean *remote* dittoing?" It was the cover story they had told the gray.

"Please. That interested Maestra Wammaker, but it's a minor matter, mentioned only to throw off the scent. I suspect you already know what we were looking for."

"Golem-renewal," Palloid suggested. "A way to make 'em last. Can I guess why? Your archie's memory is *full,* or nearly so."

"Full?" I asked.

"Too many inloads, Albert. Irene here has been duplicating so heavily, taking full memory dumps from every ditto she makes, that she's reached a limit most people only speculate about." He asked the red. "Tell me, how many centuries have you lived in subjective time? A thousand years?"

"Does it matter?"

"It might. To science," I answered. "To help others learn from your mistakes." But I could already see the futility of any altruistic appeal. This person, no matter how old, wasn't going to be moved by anything but her own good. "So you heard rumors about the renewal process and figured that giving your dits a longer span would—"

"—let you put off the inevitable, right?" Palloid rushed on. "And Beta's part in the alliance must've felt logical, too. He sells cheap knock-offs of expensive pleasuredits. Renewal would let him extend the life of his stolen templates. Maybe even switch from sales to lucrative rentals!"

"That's how he explained it to us. Beta seemed a natural ally to help steal this technology. I . . . we still can't figure out what he hoped to gain by destroying Universal Kilns."

"Well, he didn't succeed!" Palloid snapped. "Thanks to Albert outsmarting him at the end."

I wanted to snort. It seemed dubious how far the gray "outsmarted" anybody! But I kept it in. "Whatever Beta's reason, I'm sure he'll try again."

Irene nodded. "Probably. But that will soon be of no concern to us."

Past her shoulder, I saw that preparations were nearing completion. Chilly vapors flowed around the dais and massive high-sensitivity sifters focused around realIrene's gray-haired skull. Her breathing was labored, but her eyes lay open and focused. Soft sounds gurgled and I wondered if she might be trying to speak . . . that is, if she even retained the ability. For so long, she had used other eyes and ears, hands and mouths, to interact with the world.

Horus was back, having changed into a new robe—a blue one with circular mandala motifs. He fussed over the big array of sifter tendrils while red Irene dittos arrayed themselves nearby, like petals of a flower. All of them now wore standard electrode mesh caps.

"Yeesh," Palloid commented. "They're gonna inload back into her all at once! I'd get *such* a headache, doing that."

"She must be used to it," I answered, turning for confirmation to the red we had been talking to. But she was gone! Without comment or salutation she had left to rejoin the others. I hurried after, grabbing her arm. "Wait a sec. I've got more questions."

"And I have an appointment to keep," she answered tersely. "Be quick."

"What about Gineen Wammaker? Was she involved in the plot? Or was that someone else disguised as her?"

The red grinned.

"Oh, isn't our modern era wondrous? I could never tell for sure, Mr. Morris. Not without doing a structural soul analysis. It sure looked and *acted* like the maestra, didn't it? But now I must go—"

"Come on, you owe me!" I demanded. "At least tell me how to find Beta."

She laughed. "You have got to be kidding. Good-bye, Mr. Morris."

The red turned to go, then swiveled when I reached for her arm again. She glared. Needles protruded suddenly from blood-colored fingertips, glistening liquidly . . . with something much stronger than knockout oil,

I suspected. Beyond her, I glimpsed the ceremonial event approaching its climax. Horus was murmuring some mumbo jumbo—about how every soul must eventually upload into the true Original, the source of all souls, way up there in the universe.

I had an inspiration. "Look, you're still seeking some kind of immortality, isn't that right, Irene? The attempt to steal renewal-tech from UK was a bust and cops will be here soon. So you're planning to try something else. Blast your Standing Wave outta here. Pow. Straight into the ether, with all the force of a micro-fusion plant! Apply the neuro-electric surge of organic brain-death to multiply the punch. And use up all your dittos at the same time, like solid rockets, to help the spirit get launched. Am I right?"

"Something like that," she said, backing up warily, toward where a final mesh cap waited, dangling near the dais. "There are raw rhythms out there in space, Mr. Morris. Astronomers detect subspectral similarities to a Soul Standing Wave, only crude, unformed. Like fresh golem clay. The first minds to successfully impose their waveforms might—"

"Might amplify unimaginably, becoming God! Yeah, I heard of that notion," Palloid marveled, leaping off my shoulder and scampering forward, shouting. "This I gotta see!"

I hurried on, talking quickly. "But listen, Irene, didn't all the old religions promise afterlife as a reward for *virtue*? You think technology can replace it. Fine. But what if you're wrong? Did you ever consider that the old-timers might be at least *partly* right? What if some kind of karma or sin or guilt clings to you, like drag on a wing—"

"You are trying to plant doubts," she hissed.

"They're already planted, in the ditto standing before me!" I said. "Maybe you shouldn't add such thoughts to the purity of the hive. You could stay behind and help me. Make up for some of the harm you've done. Lift the burden a bit. Help the rest of the hive by remaining here and atoning—"

Something in what I said triggered a flare of violent emotion.

"No!"

She screamed a curse, swiping at me with her claws, then turning to speed toward the dais . . . only to brake hard when she saw a small, ferretlike form, standing upright amid the crowd of supine red forms. Between glittering teeth, Palloid clutched an electrode mesh cap. The last one. With its cable torn out.

The red ditto howled with such rending despair that I marveled at the implications.

I thought a "hive drone" would have low personal ego, like an ant. Or a worker bee. But Irene is exactly the opposite! Every part of her desperately wants continuity. A roaring, frantic ego was the source of Irene's strength, and her downfall.

Horus looked upset by the disturbance. Some of the other reds were opening their eyes.

"Come on," I urged the one still standing, who quivered as Palloid chewed the mesh cap to bits. Her dark eyes looked wild.

"Help me find Beta," I implored. "It could tip the balance of karma—"

With a cry, she swiveled around—I had to leap back to avoid another swipe of glittering claws—then she spun farther and ran outside, darting over cables into the alley beyond. Soon we heard thumping noises.

"What the hell?" Horus shouted. "Hey, what are you doing? *Get off my van!*"

Chasing after her, the purple left his machinery running as a sharp whine began to rise, aimed at some impending crescendo. I drew closer, both to see what was happening outside and to have a look at realIrene . . . the organic woman who was lying there on the dais, eager to expire in just the right way, so that her Standing Wave might soar, heaven-bound.

How did the red ditto express it?

There are raw rhythms out there in space . . . similar to a Standing Wave . . . like fresh golem clay. . . . The first minds to impose their wave-forms—

Oh, man.

I stepped up to the dais. Outside, the desperate red ditto could be seen climbing on top of the van! Closely followed by Horus, whose robe flapped around bare legs in a rather undignified manner as he clutched after her. Meanwhile, intense energies flowed amid the nest of sparking tendrils that surrounded realIrene's head.

"Mr. Morris—"

It was little more than a moist croak, barely audible above the nucleoelectric whine. Trying not to touch anything, I bent close to the dying woman. Her pale complexion was splotchy and pitted with small pimples. For once, I was glad not to be able to smell.

"Albert—"

This wasn't a person I could like very much. Still, her suffering was genuine and she deserved pity, I suppose.

"Is there anything I can do for you?" I asked, wondering when the machinery was timed to unleash all this pent-up force. It might not be safe to stand there.

"I . . . heard . . . what you said . . . "

"What, about karma and all that? Look, I'm no priest. How should I know—"

"No . . . you're right . . . " She gasped for breath between words. *"Behind the bar . . . unscrew the ketone cap . . . get the son of . . . son of a . . . "*

Her eyelids fluttered.

"Better get outta there, buddy-boy," Palloid urged. He was already standing in the doorway with sunshine on his back. I hurried off the dais to join him, glancing back in time to see an eruption of soft lightnings start to flash. Irene's body convulsed. So did the surrounding cluster of red golems, in perfect synchrony. It wouldn't be long now.

Retreating to the alley, we looked up at the other commotion, going on atop the van. Irene's final ditto, the one who was about to be orphaned, clutched at the big antenna, sobbing quite realistically while Horus held her by an ankle. He, in turn, clung to the cargo rack, trying to drag her off.

"Let go!" he shouted angrily. "You'll wreck it! Do you have *any* idea how long I saved to buy a franchise—"

Palloid leaped onto my shoulder as I stepped away, putting more distance between us and . . . whatever was about to happen.

Thunder seemed to boom within the back room of the Rainbow Lounge, like a pulsing of drums . . . or maybe a million giant bullfrogs with bad thyroid conditions. All right, comparisons fail me, but anyone born in this century would recognize the bass cadence of a hugely amplified Standing Wave. Perhaps a ponderous caricature, impressive but lacking subtlety. Or else a colossally augmented version of the real thing. Who could tell which?

Irene may be able to tell . . . in a few seconds.

Her final golem wailed on the roof of the van, fighting the tug of Horus in order to thrust her head in front of the antenna.

"Don't leave me!" she moaned. "Don't leave me behind!"

Palloid commented dryly, "I didn't think worker ants were s'pozed to care so much about their individual selves."

"I was just wondering the same thing," I replied. "Maybe the hive metaphor isn't right, after all. The human personality best suited to her way of life is *all* ego. She could never let go of even a small part of herself. I guess being large can be just as addictive as—"

Pal's ditto interrupted, "Here it comes!"

We retreated down the alley till I felt the fence against my back, then stared as a sharp light spilled through the rear doors of the Rainbow Lounge, from the chamber where Irene and her copies lay.

The light *seared,* casting shadows even across daylit asphalt. Instinctively, I raised a hand for shade.

The struggle atop the van ended as Horus fell to the ground with a yelp. The very same moment, something *surged* along those superconducting cables. The final red ditto screamed, grappling the antenna desperately, causing the mounts to creak as that glittering surge enveloped the van. Spark-flecked aurorae covered both her and the dish . . . even as her weight bore on the delicate apparatus, causing it to groan—

A visible beam shot forth, blasting through the clay body, which shivered, quickly hardening and sloughing off chunks, then overturned into the delicate parabola, bearing it down, shearing the metal support bolts with staccato pops. I watched with Pal—and poor Horus howled—as the antenna turned . . . then toppled over the side of the van.

A soundless, blinding wave spread outward, like a radiant ripple of pure light. It washed over Pallie and me, driving tremors up my back. Both of my ears popped, loudly and painfully. Arcing static discharges followed the wavefront, blowing the back doors off the van and clouds of equipment into the street.

The transmission finished, not aimed toward the cosmos above, but into the floor of a gritty alley.

Horus slumped, moaning in despair till all was silent.

"You know, Gumby," my small ferret-shaped friend muttered from his perch on my shoulder, when we were both finally able to stir from dazzled shock over the spectacle. "You know, this city is built on some rich layers of pure clay. It's one reason Aeneas Kaolin built his first animation lab here, long ago. So it's not *too* far-fetched to imagine—"

"Shut up, Pal." I didn't want to share whatever perverse notion had just occurred to him. Anyway, the smoke was clearing and I saw no sign of fire. Nobody would prevent us from going back inside the Rainbow Lounge.

"Come on," I said, rubbing my jaw, which hurt below the ears. "Let's see what parting gift Irene left for us."

"Hm? What're you talking about?"

I wasn't sure. Had she said "ketone cap"? Or something about *atonement?*

Anyway, I tried not to think ill of Irene. Despite all she had done, it just didn't seem right. Especially when we crept inside, passing both a barbecued ruin on the dais and surrounding supine heaps of smoldering brick statuary.

I had never seen anyone die quite so thoroughly before.

28

A China Syndrome

. . . as Little Red learns far more than he wanted to know . . .

Yosil Maharal—or rather his gray ghost—appears to be quite proud of his private collection: starting with a unique hoard of cuneiform tablets and cylinder seals from ancient Mesopotamia, the muddy land where writing began more than four thousand years ago.

"This was the very first kind of *magic* that actually worked in a reliable and repeatable way," he told me, holding up an object the shape and hue of a dinner roll, covered with shallow, overlapping wedge incisions. "At last, a kind of immortality could be achieved by anybody who learned the new trick of recording their words and thoughts and stories, by marking impressions in wet clay. The immortality of speaking across time and space, even long after your original body returned to dust."

I may be no genius but I grasped his allusion. For *he* was just such a manifestation of continuity beyond death. A complex cluster of soul-impressions made in clay, speaking on after the original Yosil Maharal had his organic life snuffed out near a lonely culvert, under a desert highway. No wonder he felt a sense of kinship with the little tablets.

Maharal's private collection also includes samples of ancient hand-wrought pottery, like several large amphorae—containers that held wine in a Roman bireme that sank two thousand years ago—recently recovered by explorerdits from the bottom of the Mediterranean. And nearby, in the same display case, lay a setting of rare blue porcelain dinnerware, once carried around the Horn of Africa in the belly of a clipper ship to grace the table of some rich merchant.

Even more precious to my host were several fist-sized human effigies, from an era much earlier than Rome or Babylon. A time before towns or literacy, when all our ancestors roamed roofless, in hunter-gatherer tribes.

One by one, Yosil's gray golem lovingly displayed about a dozen of these "Venus" figurines, molded out of Neolithic river mud, all of them featuring voluminous breasts and copious hips that tapered down from generous thighs to the daintiest of feet. With evident pride, he told me where each little statuette was found and how old it was. Lacking clear faces, most of them looked enigmatic. Anonymous. Mysterious. And prodigiously female.

"Back in the late twentieth century, a spirited postmodern cult organized itself around these effigies," he lectured while tugging a chain around my neck, leading me from one display case to the next.

"Inspired by these tiny sculptures, a few hyperfeminist mystics deduced a delightfully satisfying ideological fantasy—that an Earth-Mother religion preceded every other spiritual belief system, all over the planet. This ubiquitous Neolithic creed must obviously have worshipped a goddess! One whose top traits were fecundity and serene maternal kindliness. That is, till gentle Gaia was toppled by violent bands of macho Jehovah-Zeus-Shiva followers, spurred by an abrupt wave of vile new technologies—metallurgy, agriculture, and literacy—that arrived with concurrent and destabilizing suddenness, all at once shaking the tranquil old ways and toppling the pastoral mother goddess.

"It follows that every crime and catastrophe of recorded history stems from that tragic upheaval."

Maharal's ghost chuckled, rolling one of the Venus figures affectionately in his hand. "Oh, the goddess theory was quite fabulous and creative. Though there is another, far simpler explanation for why these little figurines are found in so many Stone Age sites.

"*Every* human culture has devoted considerable creative effort to crafting exaggerated representations of the fertile female form . . . as erotic art. Or pornography, if you will. I think we can safely assume there were frustrated males back in caveman days, as there are today. They must have 'worshipped' these little Venus figures in ways that we'd find familiar. Rather less lofty than Gaia veneration, but no less human.

"What *has* changed, after all that time, is that today's clay sex idols are far more realistic and satisfying.

"But therein lies a rub."

■　■　■

Standing in chains, wearing a miniature body and forced to listen to this drivel, I could only wonder. Was he being intentionally offensive, in order to gauge my reaction? I mean, why should the great Professor

Maharal care what I think? Anyway, I'm just a cheap quarter-sized reddish-orange golem, imprinted off the gray he captured at Kaolin Manor on Tuesday. What kind of intellectual conversation can he hope to have with the likes of me?

Well, I don't *feel* mentally deficient. Ever since stepping from the kiln, I've checked and found no apparent memory gaps. I can't do a differential equation in my head . . . but Albert himself was only able to manage that for about eight weeks, long ago, when he needed calculus to pass a college course. It took the hard, concentrated work of three ebonies to gain access to that painful beauty, then he flushed it away right after exams, making room amid a hundred billion neurons for more relevant memories.

See? I can even do irony.

All right, apparently I'm better at copy-to-copy imprinting than even I realized—something Yosil Maharal must have known for a long time. Maybe from back when I took part in that high school summer research project. Were my scores really so special? Has he been grabbing my copies to study ever since?

The thought makes me feel creepy. Worse—*violated*. Man, what a jerk.

He claims to have reasons. And yet, don't all fanatics?

■ ■ ■

"Now here is my greatest treasure," Yosil said, leading me to another exhibit. "It was given to me by the Honorary Son of Heaven himself, three years ago, in gratitude for my work at Sian."

Before me, preserved inside a sealed glass case, stood the statue—life-size—of a man with the upright bearing of a soldier, staring straight ahead, ready for action. So detailed was the sculpted handiwork that it portrayed rivets holding together strips of leather armor. A mustache, goatee, and stark cheekbones embellished strong Asiatic features—touched off by hints of whimsy. The entire effigy was made of brown terracotta.

Naturally, I knew of Sian, one of the artistic gems of the world. It would be inconceivable for a private individual to own one of these statues—if there had not been so many of them. Thousands, reclaimed from half a dozen buried regiments, discovered across more than a century, each of the effigies modeled after a particular soldier who served Ch'in, the first emperor, who conquered and united all the lands of the East. The same Ch'in who first built the Great Wall and gave his name to China.

"You know about my recent work there," ditYosil said—not a question but statement of fact. Naturally. He's spoken to other Alberts, giving them the very same guided tour.

To what purpose? I wondered. *Why explain all this, knowing the memories will be lost and that I must be told again, the next time he ditnaps another me to serve as an unwilling subject?*

Unless that's part of what he is trying to test. . . .

"I've read a thing or two about your Sian work, in the journals," I answered guardedly. "You claim to have found soul-traces in some of the clay statues."

"Something like that." ditYosil's thin smile carried evident pride, recalling the worldwide sensation that his discovery provoked. "Some call the evidence ambiguous, though I think it's clear enough to conclude that some kind of primitive imprinting process must have been at work. By what means? We still haven't determined. A fluke, perhaps—or the work of some ancient prodigy—helping to explain the astonishing political events of that era, as well as the terrified awe that his contemporaries held for Ch'in.

"As a direct result of my findings, the present-day Son of Heaven finally agreed to open the colossal Ch'in tomb next year! Some deep mysteries may come to light, having slept for millennia."

"Hm," I answered, a bit incautiously. "Too bad you won't be there to witness it."

"Perhaps not. Or maybe I will. So many delicious contradictions come laden in that one sentence of yours, Albert."

"Uh. What sentence was that?"

"You said 'too bad,' implying values. The word 'you' was directed at me, as a thinking being, the person who is holding you captive right now, right?"

"Uh . . . right."

"Then there are the phrases 'be there' and 'witness it.' Oh, you said a mouthful, all right."

"I don't see—"

"We live at a special time," ditMaharal expounded. "A time when religion and philosophy have become experimental sciences, subject to hands-on manipulation by engineers. Miracles become trademarked products, bottled and sold at discount. The direct descendants of men who used to chip flint spearheads by the riverbank are not only making life but redefining the very meaning of the word! And yet—"

He paused. I finally had to coax him.

"And yet?"

Maharal's gray face twisted. "And yet there are *obstacles!* So many of the outstanding problems in soulistics seem to have no hope of being solved, due to the ineffable complexity of the Standing Wave.

"No computer can model it, Albert. Only the shortest and fattest superconducting cables can convey its subtle majesty, barely well enough to let you press an imprint upon a nearby receptacle of specially prepared clay. Mathematically, it's a horror! Given all the odds, I'm astonished the process works at all.

"In fact, many of today's deepest thinkers suggest that we should just be thankful and accept it as a gift, without understanding it, like intelligence, or music, or laughter."

He shook his head, offering a good facsimile of a disdainful snort.

"But naturally, people on the street know nothing of this. Born with the cantankerous human spirit, they are never satisfied with a marvel—or with their vastly expanded lives. Not at all! They take it for granted, and keep demanding more.

"Make it possible for us to imprint *distant* golems, so we can teleport around the solar system! Give us telepathy, by letting us absorb each other's memories! Never mind what the metamath equations say. We want more! We want to *be* more!

"And of course, people are right. Deep down, they sense the truth."

"What truth do you mean, Doctor?" I asked.

"That human beings are about to *become* very much more! Though not in any of the ways they now imagine."

With that cryptic remark, Maharal carefully put away the last of his dear collectibles—the cuneiform tablets and pottery shards. The ancient amphora vessels and China dinnerware. The enigmatic/erotic Venus statuettes and snow-glazed Dresden figurines. The parchment texts in Hebrew, Sanskrit, and the cryptic coded charts of medieval alchemy. Finally he gave an affectionate nod to the stalwart terracotta soldier, still standing watch with his flickering, barely detectable imbuement of soul. Maharal took obvious comfort from these treasures, as if they proved his work part of a time-honored tradition.

Then, yanking the chain around my neck, he forced me to stumble after him like a small child following a heartless giant, back into the laboratory filled with machines that hissed and whirred and sparked, making the air tingle in frightening ways. I had a hunch that some of the effects might be for show. Yosil had a flair for the dramatic. Unlike some "mad scientists," he knew what he was and clearly relished the role.

A transparent soundproof partition divided the room. Beyond, I glimpsed the table where "I" became aware just an hour or so ago, still warm from the kiln. And nearby, strapped to another platform, lay a gray figure much taller than this body of mine. The self that I had been for several days. The one who provided a template for this narrating consciousness.

Poor gray. Left there to simmer and worry and scheme in vain. At least I had the distraction of an opponent.

"How did you manage to put all this together in secret?" I asked, gesturing around. The sheer amount of material—not to mention the expensive gizmos—would have been difficult to transport to this hidden underground lair (wherever it is) even in the old days of CIA plots and bad moviels about alien autopsies. To find it done today by a single person, somehow evading the all-seeing and all-shared public Eye of Accountability, showed that I was in the hands of a true genius. As if I didn't know it already.

A genius who clearly resented *me* for some reason! Not only was he physically callous toward this body I wore, he kept oscillating between taciturn silence and bouts of sudden talkativeness, as if driven by some inner need to impress me. I recognized clear signs of a Smersh-Foxleitner inferiority complex . . . and wondered what possible good the diagnosis was going to do me.

Mostly, I kept looking for possible ways to escape, knowing that each of my earlier prisoner-incarnations must have done the very same thing. But all they accomplished with their efforts had been to turn Maharal hypercautious—so that now he only imprints experimental copies of me that are too weak to punch their way out of paper manacles.

Fettering me to a chair beneath a machine resembling a giant microscope, he aimed the huge lens at my little reddish-orange head.

"I have access to ample resources, quite near here," Maharal said, answering my question—though unhelpfully. Fiddling with dials and muttering into a computerized votroller, he looked more focused on the task at hand than on me personally. But I knew better by now.

The man worried about me—a disquiet that ran deep. Anything I said could vex him.

"All right, so we ruled out teleportation and telepathy. Even so, you've made impressive breakthroughs, Doctor. Your process to extend a ditto's pseudolifespan, for instance. Wow. Imagine if all golems could replenish their *élan* a week or two . . . it could really hurt the value of Universal Kilns stock, I bet. Is that why you had a falling out with Aeneas Kaolin?"

My remark drew a sharp look. Gray lips pressed together in a line, silent.

"Come on, Doc. Admit it. I could *feel* tension between you two, under all the feigned affection back at Kaolin Manor, when you showed up as a ghost to view your own corpse. The Vic seemed anxious to get his hands on that artificial brain of yours, and dice it to bits. Why? In order to learn more about all this?" I gestured at the big lab with its mysterious stolen equipment. "Or was he trying to hush you?"

Maharal's grimace told me I hit home.

"Is that it? *Did Aeneas Kaolin murder your real self?*"

The police hadn't found any signs of foul play at the desert crash site where real Yosil Maharal had died. But in searching for clues, they only considered today's technology. Aeneas Kaolin possessed tomorrow's.

"As usual, you are thinking small, Mr. Morris. Like poor Aeneas."

"Yeah? Then try explaining, Professor. Starting with why I'm here. All right, so I make great copies. How does that help you solve those great mysteries of soulistics?"

His eyes rolled upward and shoulders shrugged—an expression of fatigued contempt, exactly according to the Smersh-Foxleitner pattern. *Maharal doesn't just envy my ability. He actually fears me! So he must exaggerate the intellectual gulf between us and minimize my humanity.*

Did my other selves notice this? They must have!

"You would not understand," he muttered, returning to his preparations. I heard the crackle of high-power equipment, warming up with me sitting at the focus.

"I'm sure you said that to the other Alberts you captured. But tell me this, did you ever, even once, *try* to explain? Maybe offer me collaboration, instead of unwilling experimental torment? Science isn't meant to be a lonely business, after all. Whatever your reasons for working in isolation—"

"—are my reasons. And they are more than sufficient to justify these means." Maharal turned to regard me tiredly. "Now you'll spout *moral* arguments, about how wrong it is to treat another thinking entity this way. Even though you showed no such regard for your own dittos! Never even bothering to investigate why so many went missing over the years."

"But . . . I'm a private eye. That involves sending myselves into dangerous situations. Taking risks. I came to think of them—"

"—as *disposable* selves. Their loss to be regretted no more than our grandparents would lament the waste of an irritating day. Well, that's your privilege. But then, don't call me a monster if I take advantage."

That gave me pause. "Have I called you a monster?"

Stone-faced. "Several times."

I pondered this a moment.

"Well, then, I have to guess that your . . . *procedure* is gonna hurt. A lot."

"Rather, I'm afraid. Sorry. But there is good news! I have reason to hope things will go much smoother this time."

"Because you've improved your method?"

"In part. And because circumstances have changed. I expect your Standing Wave will be more malleable . . . more *mobile* . . . now that it's no longer anchored to organic reality."

I didn't like the sound of that.

"What do you mean, *no longer anchored?*"

Maharal frowned, but I could tell the expression masked a layer of pleasure. Perhaps he wasn't even aware how much he enjoyed telling me the news.

"I mean that you're dead, Mr. Morris. Your original body was vaporized late Tuesday night, in a missile attack that destroyed your home."

"A . . . what?"

"Yes, my poor fellow artifact. Like me, you are now—as they say—a ghost."

29

Imitation of a Counterfeit Life

. . . Gumby and Pal, poking around . . .

The interior of the Rainbow Lounge lay eerily empty.

Some holoflashers had been left on, illuminating the dance floor and the Grudge Pit with twisted images, like multidimensional Dalí landscapes roamed by erotic figures possessing far too many limbs. But without the intense background beat of CeramoPunk music, the flickering shapes were rather pathetic. This place demanded crowding—a hot press of several hundred brightly colored bodies, hyped to wear their standing waves exposed, ultrasensitive, like the prickly emotions of teenagers.

"I wonder who's gonna take over the Rainbow," Palloid mused. "Do you think Irene had heirs or left a will? Does it all go up for auction?"

"Why? Thinking of becoming a tavernkeeper?"

"It's tempting." He leaped from my shoulder onto the bar, a broad expanse of heavily lacquered teakwood. "But maybe I don't have the personality for it."

"You mean the patience, concentration, or tact," I commented while poking around. The bar featured a dazzling array of tubes, faucets, bottles, and dispensers of intoxicants, euphorics, stimulants, levelers, speeders, slowers, uppers, downers, horizoners, myopics, stigmatics, zealotropics, hystericogens—

"Touché, Albert. Though Irene's idea of tact was rather specialized. The kind used by pimps, bouncers, and cops. Screw 'em all."

"Nihilist," I muttered while scanning labels for a dizzying array of concoctions. My search wasn't going to be easy. The varieties of abuse that you can put a clay body through never cease to amaze me, and almost certainly astonished the inventors of dittotech, back when people started fiddling with home modification kits. You can fine-tune a golem so it will react spectacularly to alcohol or acetone, electric or magnetic fields, sonic or radar stimulation, images or aromatics . . . not to mention a thousand specially designed pseudoparasites. In other words, you can pound, pluck, or molest the Standing Wave in countless ways that would be lethal to your real body, and transfer home vivid memories when the busy day is done.

No wonder there are experience addicts. By comparison, the opiate-alkaloid cocktails that sad folks used to inject in Grandpa's day were like a dose of vitamins.

"Nihilist? You dare call me that? Who's standing here, using up life-span helping you, friend?"

"You call it *help* to squat up there, kibitzing? How about some assistance down here, behind the bar?"

He replied with a desultory snarl, but did leap to ground at the far end, sniffing as he scanned labels, grumbling audibly that I owed him for this. I wasn't buying any of his act, of course. My friend's personal addiction was to poke away at the world's weirdness. After events of the last hour, he never seemed happier.

I hope he gets to inload all this, I thought, recalling the real Pal, imprisoned in his life-sustaining chair. He'd get a kick out of remembering old Horus, toppling onto his butt from the Final Options van. Pal might also help distract Clara from her grief by describing how we spent these haunted hours. . . .

No, I shied away from thinking about her. Anyway, Clara would remember Albert with fondness. That beat most kinds of immortality that I'd heard of. A lot more immortality than *this* particular green frankie was going to get.

Anyway, who wants to live forever?

I kept marveling at the variety of substances stored behind the bar. *Irene must've had real political clout, to get an environmental variance. There are more toxic brews here than in the late state of Delaware.*

"Got it!" Palloid announced, punctuating his triumph with a smug somersault. I hurried over to his end of the bar where a series of large wooden pull levers stood—like those used to serve draft beer in a real people tavern. One of them bore a designation that said: *Ketone Kocktail.*

"Hm, could be. If she had said, 'ketone *tap.*' "

"Are you sure she said 'cap'?"

"Pretty sure." I jiggled the pull lever, not eager to dispense any of the pressurized contents. My cheap green body—even renewed under artificial dyes of orange and gray—couldn't endure most of the exotic mixtures offered for sale here.

"The cap—" Palloid began.

"I know. I'm checking it now." The lever had a large decorative tip, like a tapered brass tube covering the end. I twisted one way, then the other. It gave a little, then no more. Even when I wrenched hard.

I was about to give up, then thought, *Maybe it works in several successive directions, like a Chinese puzzle box.*

I tried combinations of twists, pulls, and shoves, and began making some progress with the cap, confirming my guess. Gradually it worked outward along a complicated, grooved sleeve. A physical storage device, then, like the piezomechanical recorders that Albert always installed in his grays. More secure than anything electronic. Irene clearly grasped that the world of digital data is far too flighty to entrust with any real secrets. Safety-through-encryption is a bad joke. If you must keep something away from prying eyes, put it in hardwriting. Then hide the only copy in a box.

I hope this thing doesn't require any sort of ID check, or involve disarming a self-destruct. When Irene told me about this cache with her final words, I assumed it was an act of deathbed contrition—or perhaps a little karmic insurance. But another explanation was possible. A trap. A petty act of vengeance for interfering with her last red ditto.

If I could sweat, I would have started right about then.

"Better step back, Pal," I urged.

"Already done it, chum," I heard him call from beyond the farthest end of the bar, over a dozen meters removed. "Other than that, I'm with you all the way."

His wry expression of support almost made me chuckle. Almost.

I didn't breathe through the last several twists and turns, operating on storage cells until . . .

. . . the brass cylinder came off at last, revealing a hollow interior with something crammed inside. Exhaling with relief, I tapped it on the bar.

A slim tube of plastic rolled out. *Beta*, said a paper tag, attached to the film with a clip.

"Cool!" Palloid yelped, leaping onto the bar again, using agile paw-hands to pry at other decorative caps. "I bet she had all kinds of stuff hidden away. Maybe Irene had a sideline, blackmailing politicians! She was in the business of catering to perversions and there's still lots of depravities that can cost you votes, if people find out about 'em!"

"Right. Dream on." As if Pallie cared about politics. "Just be careful," I urged. It was my turn to retreat cautiously while he fiddled with one poison dispenser after another. Further warnings would be futile, so I left him there, happily risking his brief existence on a whim.

"I'll be in Irene's office," I said.

We had passed it along the way, a sophisticated-looking data center offering surveillance views into every corner of the establishment. (I chuckled when I saw Palloid barely dodge a spray of some fuming liquid as he kept poking around, looking for more secret hiding places.) There were also some of those hookups the luckless grayAlbert mentioned in his recital-diary—plug-in units designed to let a ditto link directly (well, sort of) to computers. From everything I've read, the advantages are dubious. I'd much rather wear a chador.

Luckily, the office held some regular net-access consoles, too. Irene had left several turned on, indicating rushed departure. I might not have to mess with passwords and such. Hacking is such a retro and tedious chore.

Anyway, my first stop was a simple analog strip reader. The film tube fit perfectly. *Are there any clues here to explain why someone arranged for that vicious attack against Universal Kilns? Or the much worse felony of real-killing Albert Morris?*

As soon as I activated the strip reader, the first holofoto spilled into midair before me. *So that's what "Vic Collins" looked like. Tuesday's hapless gray was right about this character. Plaid clothes over plaid skin . . . ouch!*

Yet it made devilish sense. Some people hide their appearance by looking nondescript. Forgettable. But you can accomplish much the same thing by making it too painful and disgusting to look at you. Still, it was hard to see how this portrait could help answer any of the big questions.

Was Irene right about Vic Collins being a front persona of Beta, the notorious ditnapper?

I recalled that last encounter with one of Beta's rapidly dissolving yellows, stuck in a disposal tube next to the Teller Building, slobbering cryptic remarks about betrayal and somebody called "Emmett." Albert was already tired and distracted by then. And wary toward yet another of Beta's notorious head games.

Sitting in Irene's office, I saw little similarity between that yellowdit and the holo visage in front of me, a squarish face, rather snide, and cross-hatched with a blinding array of intersecting stripes. There were several dozen pictures in Irene's secret archive, date-stamped, every time the conspirators rendezvoused in back of a limousine at some remote location—occasionally with a third party who looked like a cheap ivory of Gineen Wammaker. According to a notation, Collins used a static-disruptor to block sophisticated photo-optical recording devices. These snapshots on old-fashioned chemical emulsion were the best Irene could do as she kept a wary eye on her allies.

Not wary enough, though. Did Irene ever try tracking Collins through the publicam network? I wondered. The first step—following his trail back to the limo rental agency—seemed obvious.

Oh, Albert would have loved the challenge! Starting with these time-and-place fixes, he'd concentrate with all the intensity of a Vingean focus trance, backtracing the plaid Collins-dittos, eager to see what tricks they used to cover their trail, pouncing on any slipup.

I suppose I could have tried to do that, sitting there in Irene's deserted office. But did I *want* to? Just because I inherit Albert's memories, and some skills, that doesn't mean I'm him! Anyway, that missile wrecked more than Al's house. Nell contained all those specialized programs to help Morris follow people and dittos across the vast cityscape.

There are times I wish the citizens of PEZ were less laid back and freedom-loving. Elsewhere, folks put up with higher levels of regulation and supervision. Every golem made in Europe carries a *real* transponder, not a pathetic little pellet tag. Factory-registered to its owner, trackable by satellite from activation to dissolution. There are still ways to cheat, but a detective knows where to start.

On the other hand, I live here for a reason. Tyranny may have only taken a holiday. It could return, first in one corner of the world, then another. And democracy is no absolute guarantee. But in PEZ, the word "authority" has always been so suspect. They'd have to kill everybody first, then start over from scratch.

Turning the film cylinder, I flipped from one holo to the next as Irene and her collaborators met to discuss a stratagem for quasi-legal industrial espionage, or so she thought. But her allies had other plans—manipulating Irene for her resources and Albert Morris for his skills. And the fanatics, Gadarene and Lum, setting them up to take initial blame.

Having met those two, I knew that any first-rate investigator would soon grow suspicious. They just weren't competent enough to sabotage Universal Kilns. And though Gadarene might have a motive to destroy UK, Lum wanted to "liberate slaves," not destroy them. A smart cop would see them as patsies, framed to take the fault. Beta set up Irene to take the heat when that first level failed.

She realized all this when the news broke last night. A knock on the door could come within hours. Oh, she could have stayed and helped investigators peel away more layers. But Beta knew her too well. Revenge wouldn't matter, only arranging with Final Options for a last stab at "immortality."

So, I'm the one left to clean up after her . . . and after Albert, for that matter. And . . .

It seems I'm spending all my lifespan scrubbing toilets after all.

■   ■   ■

Actually, Irene did a good job getting close-ups of Beta with her little microcam—if it really was him. Perhaps my frankie brain viewed things differently, but I was more interested in examining the face than trying to track it from one publicam to another.

All right, I thought. Question number one: was "Vic Collins" really Beta, the infamous ditnapper and copyright thief? The red Irene ditto seemed sure. Maybe they had a long and profitable business relationship. And I could easily picture the pragmatic Gineen Wammaker deciding to stop fighting Beta, joining forces with him instead. Weren't they all in approximately the same trade? Catering to perverse cravings?

I snap-enabled a link from the strip reader to Irene's computer, getting quick response when I asked for some standard image-enhancement programs, then used them to zoom on Collins's features. "Now ain't that interesting," I murmured.

Apparently, Collins used a completely different pattern of plaid design, each of the first five times he sent dits to meet Irene. But on the final three occasions, his skin motif remained the same. *Which element is meaningful?* I wondered. *The earlier variation? Or the fact that he later stopped bothering to change patterns?*

I didn't have resources to do a mathematical-configuration analysis of the interlocking stripes—determining if some code lay embedded in the complex patterns. It would be just like Beta to wear cryptic clues on his very skin, daring foes to decipher them. Vic Kaolin *did* have the resources for such analysis, and I was supposedly working for him at the moment. I could have this evidence forwarded to the mogul in seconds, at a spoken command.

"Zoom in," I said instead, letting the focus of my gaze control where—the plaid skin on the left cheek of the most recent image of "Vic Collins."

I missed Nell. And especially all the wonderful automated tools she kept in her icy core, ready at Albert's disposal. But with some cheap substitutes, fetched via the Internet, I got a pretty good close-up appraisal of the clay surface, which turned out to be finely molded, with supple, kiln-cured texture. Very high quality. Beta could afford fine bodies.

Hell, I knew that. This wasn't significant or new. *So? I'm not Albert Morris. What makes me think I can play private eye?*

Before giving up, I decided to point the same tools at earlier images Irene took when Collins first started meeting her in back of limousines. Was it a hunch?

I stared, blinked, and stammered, "What the—?"

The texture was entirely different! Coarser. And this time it featured a myriad tiny protrusions, like goosebumps, row after row, at least a thousand per linear centimeter. *Pixel emitters,* I realized. Like they weave into smart fabrics that change colors on command. Only these lay flush in normal-looking gray pseudoskin. The plaid pattern was created by these elements; some turned dark, others pale, combining to form an illusion of intersecting stripes.

So. Even if I used old publicam records to follow Collins back in time, say to the limo rental agency, I'd lose him anyway. There'd come some point, a bit earlier, when he'd vanish in a crowd at some carefully scouted blind spot. Tracing farther back, I'd never see a plaid person arrive because he shifted coloration instantly! I bet Collins even had inflatable prosthetics under the skin, to alter his facial contours just as quickly. No need for the quick-change dyes, putty, and cosmetics Albert used.

Oh, old Albert had been proud of his own ability to weave in and out of sight, wiping his trail clean. But Collins—or Beta—had him beat by a mile! It was enough to make me laugh or cry for poor Al, who used to fancy himself as Sherlock to Beta's Moriarty. He was never in the same league.

All very impressive. But why did Beta stop using his quick-change trick, switching to dittos that were more luxurious but less sneaky? And why did he decide to hire an Albert Morris gray to do the old dodge-and-weave during the attack on UK, instead of handling it himself? I checked all the images again. The last three pictures of Collins were different, all right. You could even see it in his facial expression—a smirk that first seemed natural struck me as feigned in the later images.

If only the meetings were held here, at the Rainbow! Irene could have made full holo radar scans, recorded voice patterns, word rhythms, hand mannerisms . . . all the little habits that a man takes along when he copies himself into clay dolls. Cues nearly as individualized as the Standing Wave itself. Did Irene or Wammaker notice any difference? Were they clueless that something had changed?

That yellow who was melting in the recycling tube, next to the Teller Building . . . didn't he claim that some kind of disaster had befallen Beta, even before Blane and I raided the place?

I glanced at a monitor showing the main floor of the Rainbow Lounge. Pal's mini-golem was making a party of it, singing along with a raucous tune that played on the dance floor sound system while he kept poking into every conceivable niche and hiding place, adding to a collection of metal parts torn from various portions of the bar. Only a few small streams of noxious fluid appeared to be leaking onto the floor, so far. But at this rate he might demolish the whole place before his internal clock ran out.

The little mock ferret tapped another decorative cylinder on the bar, peering through it while crooning along to a catchy anthem that had been revered by nihilists long before any of us were born. Rocking back on his haunches, he bayed skyward—

"Life is a lemon and I want my money back!"

Hey, I can relate. In fact, I've felt that way for well over twenty-four hours. But even if I *could* somehow get a refund on this so-called life, whose account would I send it to?

Toggling a switch on the desk, I called down to the lounge. "Pal! You doing okay down there?"

The driving beat automatically faded as he swiveled around, grinning. "Just great, Gumby, old chum! I found some more secret stashes." He held up a holopix tube like the one I had found. "My hunch was right! Irene had nailed herself a couple of local council officials to blackmail."

"Anything juicy?"

"Naw. Local interest, mostly. I keep hoping for something on the President, or maybe the Protector in Chief. But all I found in the last one are pictures of *kids*. Family snaps, not kinkyporn." Palloid shrugged. "What about you? Anything useful?"

Useful? I was about to answer no when another of those odd hunches tweaked an off-resonance in my mutated Standing Wave. I signaled Irene's computer with some rapid eye-wink commands, calling up two images of Collins-Beta—one early and the other late—flicking back and forth between them. "I'm not sure, but I think . . ."

The image on the left showed Beta the chameleon, his gray golemskin studded with a myriad tiny pixel emitters tuned to combine into one of those eye-hurting plaid motifs, but capable of changing instantaneously to some wildly different pattern. The other face, on the right, looked similar at superficial scale. But zooming in close, you could see the tartan pattern was simply *painted* atop normal gray . . .

Wait a minute, I thought, noticing some abrasion marks on the most recent Collins golem, near its left cheek. Nothing unusual there. Clay scratches easily and cannot repair itself. You sometimes end a day pitted and cratered, like some moon. But these tiny scrapes *glittered.* Closer magnification revealed bits of gray surface coating, curling away from a different hue beneath, still metallic-looking, but shinier. Not quite silvery. More of an expensive-looking matte finish, like white gold.

Or else, maybe, platinum.

"Yeah?" Palloid shouted up at me. "What is it you think?"

I didn't want to say more. Who knew what kind of listening devices Vic Aeneas Kaolin planted in me, when he kindly renewed my lease on pseudolife? Heck, I still lacked any clear picture of his underlying motive for sending me out "to find the truth."

Choosing words carefully, I said, "Maybe it's time you and I got out of here, Pal."

"Yeah? And head where?"

I thought about that. We needed a special kind of help. The kind I never knew existed till yesterday, when I was just a few hours old.

30

Apeing Essence

. . . realAlbert gets sympathy from a simian simulacrum . . .

Fortunately, there was a lot of traffic coming and going to the battle range, everything from big supply carryalls and triple-decker tour buses to jitneys and sportcycles. Air travel's tightly restricted though, and the site is far enough from the city that sending a ditto all this way makes little sense. It would only have short time to loiter around before having to head back again.

True aficionados—and news reporters—are better off coming in person, which explains the row of fancy realfolk hotels, amusement centers, and casinos near the main gate, with their high observation towers gazing at the battleground proper. At night, musicians play impromptu arrangements to accompany the flash and bang effects rising over the escarpment.

Like I said, it's a pretty typical military base. Bring the family!

We hitched a ride the final few klicks, flagging down a ramshackle mobile home with twelve wheels and a wheezing catalysis engine that reeked of illegal petrol conversion. The driver, a big fellow, dark brown with greasy locks, welcomed us aboard with a grunt.

"I'm not going all the way to the hotels," he said. "I'll be turnin' offroad to the Candidates Camp."

"We're aimed there as well, sir," I explained with a shallow bow, since he was real while I was pretending not to be. The driver eyed us up and down.

"You don't have the look of soldier-aspirants. What kind of model are you, *strategists?*"

I nodded and the big fellow guffawed. "Some would-be generals, wandering around lost in the desert!" His deriding tone wasn't unfriendly, though.

I now faced yet another problem. As soon as I stepped inside the big van, a small light started flashing in my left eye. For the first time in almost two days, my implant was picking up a useful carrier wave and asking permission to respond. Three tooth clicks and I could be investigating what happened to my burned-out home and why amateur criminalists linked me to a sabotage attempt at Universal Kilns. Above all, in just moments I could be talking to Clara!

But that little flash also signaled a poison. While passive, my implant wouldn't give away my position. But the moment it latched in, others would know I still lived . . . and where to find me.

Ritu and I settled into a back seat while the driver chattered about the war, which had gone through several stunning reverses, a memorable match drawing attention from all over the globe. Soon he pulled off the main highway and down a rutted track leading toward the chaotic encampment I spied earlier.

The Candidates Camp is exactly what you'd expect in an age when war is sport and countless people dream of some way to stand out from the crowd. Amid plumes of trampled dust, you quickly sniff the acrid wafting odors of simmering clay emitted by scores of souped-up porta-kilns, fussed over by aficionados who bray proudly about their special modifications. Crowds gather each time one opens, to stare and criticize as a new monster steps forth, zingularly equipped in ways that could get you arrested or fined in the city. Gargoyles, ogres, and leviathans . . . spiked, fanged, or clawed . . . feral-eyed or dripping caustic poisons from their jaws . . . yet propelled by the ego and soul-stuff of some nerdy hobbyist, woman-born, preening and posing in the background, hoping to be "discovered" by the professionals, just beyond the fence—perhaps even winning a coveted place of glory on the honorable plains of battle.

Our driver grew more talkative as he maneuvered into a parking space at one end of the encampment. "I wasn't gonna come out this time, especially after PEZ got off to such a bad start on Monday. Sure looked as if it was gonna be over quick. Good-bye icebergs and hello again water rationing! In fact, I gotta hand it to the Indonesians for coming up with those sneaky little minidit assassin-golems. They sure played havoc with our first-wave troops. But then came our counterattack on Moesta Heights! Did you ever see anything like it?"

"Wow," I said ambiguously, eager only to get out as soon as he shut down the hissing engine.

"Yah, wow. Anyway, I suddenly realized—I got a perfect battle-mod to counter to those Indie minis! So I figured, come out and give a demo. With any luck, I'll be in the arena soon, making a deal with the Dodecahedron by nightfall!"

"Well, we sure do wish you luck," I mumbled while jiggling the doorknob.

He looked disappointed by my lack of interest. "I had a hunch you two were scouts for the army, but I was wrong about that, wasn't I?"

"Scouts?" Ritu asked, clearly puzzled. "Why would the army have scouts *outside* the battle range?"

"Go on, get outta here," the driver said, yanking a lever and releasing the door, spilling us into the hot afternoon.

"Thanks for the ride." I jumped to ground and quickly headed south, past a cluster of Winnebagos where families gathered together under a striped canopy, chewing barbecued snacks next to a big holo screen showing recent combat updates. If I were a true fan, I'd stop to check the score and see what odds the touts offered. But I only really care about war during the finals, whenever Clara qualifies.

I think she likes that about me.

On one side stood house trailers fronted with fold-down booths selling everything from hand-woven *lumnia* rugs and wondrous cleaning formulas to aromatic funnel cakes. Beyond the usual Elvis Shrine, clusters of monster truck aficionados sweated under their beloved vehicles, preparing for a rally at a nearby offroad course. There were the usual types of real-life weirdos—clippies and stickies and nudies and people walking about shrouded in opaque anonymity chadors—but all of this was secondary. Fringe stuff to the real purpose of this offbeat festival.

I was looking for its core.

Ritu caught up and grabbed my arm, trying to match my rapid pace. "Scouts?" she asked a second time.

"*Talent* scouts, Miss Maharal. The reason for all of this." I encompassed the chaotic encampment with a sweep of one arm. "Wannabes and Trytobes converge here to show off their homemade battle-dits in a makeshift coliseum, hoping the pros will be watching. If army guys see anything they like, they may summon the designer inside the fence. Perhaps make a deal."

"Huh. Does that happen often?"

"Officially, it never happens at all," I replied while turning and seeking my bearings. "Amateur ditviolence has been deemed an undesirable public vice, remember? It's sin-taxed and reproved, like drug addiction. Remember how they yammered against it in school?"

"That doesn't seem to be slowing it down any," she murmured.

"No shit. It's a free country. People do what they want. Still, the military can't be seen officially encouraging the trend."

"But *un*officially?" One eyebrow arched.

We were passing an arcade where carnies touted all sorts of amusement games and joyrides, most of them mechanical and retro, designed to give a safe but scary thrill to trueflesh. Next door, a long tent sheltered stalls for bio-aficionados to exhibit home-geniformed life forms—the modern equivalent of prize bulls and pigs—amid a clamor of grunts, cackles, and braying cries. Lots of color and atmosphere, all the way down to the homey stench.

"Unofficially?" I answered Ritu. "They watch, of course. Half the creativity in the world comes from bored amateurs, nowadays. Open source and fresh clay—that's all folks need. The army'd be stupid to ignore it."

"I was wondering how you planned to get from here into the base proper," she gestured beyond the exhibits and shouting carnies and whirling fun rides to the killwire fence. "Now I get it. You're looking for one of those scouts!"

We were close enough to the killwire to feel its soul-distorting currents along our spines. It *had* to be nearby . . . the centerpiece of this anarchic fairground. The reason for its being.

Just then I caught a glimpse of my goal, beyond a big, grimy tent with slobbery elephant seal noises coming from within. A long line of archies stood patiently outside, waiting their turn to enter. But whatever was going on inside—whether violent or massively erotic—I didn't care, and Ritu quashed her curiosity in order to keep up. I hurried, stepping gingerly past the canvas pavilion with its commotion of loud, clammy grunts.

Looming on the other side of the filthy tent stood a spindly structure of horizontal planks and slanting cables, held up by a single tensegrity spire. Several hundred onlookers crowded the grandstand, setting its spiderweb array jiggling each time they stood to cheer or sat back down with a disappointed collective moan. Their broad posteriors, clad in soft fabrics, showed they were all realfolk, with arms and necks tanned stylishly brown in the desert sun.

Between their cheers and moans came other sounds—howls and bitter snarls echoing from the arena's heart. Defiant insults, hurled by mouths designed for biting instead of speech. Frenzied impacts and moist tearings.

Some think we're going decadent. That all the urban brawlers, the inload-junkies and pseudowars mean we're becoming like Imperial Rome, with its bloody circuses. Immoral, unbalanced, and doomed to fall.

But unlike Rome, this isn't foisted on us from above. A weak government even preaches moderation. No, it rises from below, just another branching of human enthusiasm, unleashed from old constraints.

So, are we decadent? Or going through a phase?

Is it barbarous when the "victims" come willingly and no lasting harm is done?

I honestly had no answer. Who could know?

The arena's main entrance bore an archies-only symbol and a wary guardian—somebody's pet monkey, perched on a stool, armed with a spray bottle of solvent non-toxic to trueflesh. Ritu and I could have slipped inside without harm, except possibly to our makeup. But I still had use for the pretense. So we walked by, seeking a place among the non-citizen onlookers who pressed under the grandstand, peering through a shuffling maze of archie feet. Many of the dittos were combatants, garishly hoofed, taloned, and armored, awaiting their own turns on the gladiatorial grounds.

It *stank* down there. Slobbering, grunting, and farting dense colored puffs from their hyped-up metabolisms, contestants exchanged good-natured jibes while swapping bets and opinions about each round of grotesque slaughter. But not everybody. One fellow was actually *reading* from a cheap web-plaque, through a pair of outsized spectacles perched on his tyrannosaur snout. When a trumpeted blare called him forth to the arena that ersatz dinosaur tossed his lit-plaque to the ground but gently plucked the eyeglasses between two pincers and slipped them onto one plank of the grandstand, between the feet of an archie who picked up the specs and pocketed them without a word.

Well, some people like to make the most of their time, whatever body they happen to be wearing.

Clara had told me about this place, though I never visited during any of my earlier trips from the city to watch her platoon in action. She didn't think highly of the "innovations" that bright amateur designers concoct to show off next to the killwire fence.

"Most are too gaudy, based on legendary monsters or personal nightmares," she said. "They may be fine for a scary movie, but no damned good in combat. A frightening leer won't help much when the enemy has a particle beam weapon sighted between your horns."

That's my girl. Always ready with tender wisdom. I found myself actually breathless with anticipation, getting close to her at last. Beyond just missing Clara, I also knew she'd have insights about my predicament with Kaolin, Maharal, and Universal Kilns. Anyway, I wanted to reach her before word got through that I'd been killed in my home by a terror missile. *Maybe she's been too distracted to watch any news,* I hoped. The last thing I wanted was for her to be worried or in mourning while she still had a job to do for team and country.

"Oh my," Ritu Maharal commented while peering into the arena at a maelstrom of bellowing carnage transpiring within. "I never realized all this could be so—" She fell short, breathless, unable to find words.

I was peering, too. Not at the fight but the surroundings, seeking a particular entity. The object of my quest wouldn't have fangs. It wouldn't be an archie, either. Professionals have better things to do with realtime than attend this amateur exhibition in person.

"You never realized all this could all be so what?" I asked, making conversation absently. There were some big forklift-type dittos on the other side of the ring, assigned to haul away losers before their smoldering bodies could turn into slurry. But no. That was a lot of pseudoflesh to invest. I was betting on something more compact, economical.

"So *exciting*! I always felt a kind of aloof superiority toward this kind of thing. But you know, if I imprinted one of these combat dittos, I bet I'd actually stay interested in the same thing for a day . . . both of me, I mean."

"Hm, great . . . unless your monstrous alter ego turned around and bit you in half," I commented. Rita blanched but I continued to scan. The one I sought would need a good vantage point, yet shouldn't be obvious to all the aficionados flocking round this place. *What if they don't send anybody?* I worried. *Maybe the professionals just use some hidden camera to keep an eye on—*

Then I spotted the guy. I felt sure of it. A small figure, shambling about the edges of the arena, poking at each fallen warrior, reading their pellets with a narrow stick-probe. He looked like a chimp or gibbon. You see little fellows like him all over town, so common they almost fade into the background.

Of course, I thought, *the tax collector.*

"Come on," I told Ritu, pulling at her when she tried to stay and watch the end of a bout. I swear, I almost left her right there, so anxious was I to move on. Fortunately, one contestant struck the other a fatal blow just then, sending its massive body crashing with a thud that set the whole amphitheater vibrating and the crowd frenetically cheering.

"Let's go!" I shouted.

This time she came.

■   ■   ■

The ape grunted and spat when I called to him from behind the arena. He squatted on his haunches atop a wooden pillar, idly watching the next event.

"Go 'way," he muttered, in a voice only a little more clear than a real chimp's.

Naturally, I wasn't the first to have figured out his guise. It must be a nuisance when amateurs come over and try to influence him with direct appeals.

"I need to talk to a member of the 442nd," I said.

"Sure. You an' every other fan, after the assault on Moesta Ridge. But sorry, no autographs till after the war, pal."

"I'm no fan. This message is personal and urgent. She'll want to hear it, believe me!"

The chimp spat again, brown slip with a touch of arsenic glaze. "And why should I believe you?"

Frustration boiled inside, but I kept my voice even.

"Because if Sergeant Clara Gonzales finds out that you kept me from getting through to her, she'll grab you by the archie and give you a memory you'll never get rid of."

The ape blinked at me a couple of times.

"You do sound like you know Clara. Who are you?"

It was a dangerous moment. But what choice did I have?

I told him . . . and those dark eyes stared at me. "So, you're the ghost of poor Albert the ditective, come all this way to bid her good-bye. Damn shame what happened to you, man! Getting torched by a hoodoo missile always hurts. I can't imagine what it must've felt like in person."

"Uh, right. I kind of hoped to reach Clara before she found out about it."

The pseudochimp tsked and shook his head. "I wish you had, fellah. 'Cause you wasted your remaining span coming out here. The minute Clara heard the news, she took off!"

It was my turn to stare in surprise.

"She . . . went AWOL? In the middle of a *war*?"

"Not only that, she snatched a guv'ment copter and flew straight to the city. Our team commander's in a funk over this, let me tell you!"

"I can't believe it." My legs felt weak and my heart beat hard.

"Yeah, ironic. She drops everything rushing to town, only to miss your ghost who rushed out to console her."

The observer-scout leaped off his perch to land next to me and held out a hand. "I'm Gordon Chen, corporal in the 117th Support Company. We met once, I think, when you came down for last year's playoffs."

An image came to mind, of a rather tall half-Oriental fellow with perfect posture and a gentle smile . . . about the least simian-looking human being I ever saw. Yet he wore this body with ease. "Yeah," I answered absently. "At a party after the Uzbek semi-final match. We talked about gardening."

"Uh-huh. So it really is you." His ditto-teeth looked formidable when he grinned. "Gautama! I often wondered how it must feel to be a ghost. Is it weird?" He shook his head. "Forget I asked. Is there's anything I can do for you, Albert? Just ask."

There *was* something he could do for me. But asking could wait a few seconds. Or minutes. I still had to let it all sink in. My disappointment at having missed Clara. Plus surprise that she could be so impulsive. But above all, one transfixing fact.

I always knew she cared for me. We're great friends, good in bed. We make each other laugh.

But for her to pull a crazy stunt like this! Dropping everything to go sift the ashes of my house, hoping and praying that I wasn't there when it blew up . . . Why, she must actually love me!

Over the course of the last two days I had learned that I was both a crime suspect and a target for assassins. I'd been ambushed, left for dead, then endured a harsh desert trek, and faced even more disappointing setbacks. Yet, despite all that, I suddenly found myself feeling rather . . . well . . . happy.

If I survive the efforts of my enemies, and don't wind up a corpse or in jail, I'm going to have to talk to her. Rethink our reluctance to—

Just then, the ongoing background noise of grunting combat gave way to a loud sizzle, followed by a wet-heavy swatting sound. The crowd of ecstatic archies stood up all at once, roaring and setting the spiderweb grandstand jiggling as a spiky round object soared out of the arena in a high arc, dripping trails of gore behind it.

"Sherds!" Corporal Chen cried, leaping back with apelike agility. Ritu and I hurried after, barely dodging as a fanged and glowering head struck just meters away, rolling to a stop near my feet.

Rapid golem-dissolution was already setting in as smoke and slurry poured out both ears, staining the moist sand. The owner of this head better fetch it quick, if he wanted a complete inload. All those barbs and horns and stingers might be part of a hobbyist's loving, homemade combat design, but I sure wasn't bending over to touch the huge, snaggle-toothed thing!

And yet, even after what it had just been through, the head still clung to consciousness. Crocodillian eyes blinked for a few seconds, focusing briefly with an expression more disappointed than tragic. The jaw moved. Trying to speak. Against my better judgment, I bent closer.

"Wow . . ." the head whispered, while light still glinted in those feral eyes. "What . . . a . . . russshhh . . . !"

The chimpanzee soldier snorted, a sound tinged with grudging respect.

Stepping back, I turned to Clara's comrade and asked, "Did you mean what you just said—about being willing to do something for us?"

"Sure, why not?" The ape-ditto shrugged. "Any buddy of Clara's is a bud of mine."

31

Golem Crazy

. . . as Little Red gets ready to make his mark . . .

I stared at the gray ghost of Yosil Maharal, as the news gradually sank in

"A . . . missile attack?"

"That's right. Little remains of your home—and your archie—but a smoking crater. So your only hope now is the same as mine. Successful completion of my experiment."

I reacted with churning fear and dread, naturally. This cheap red body that I wore, though small, was equipped for a full range of emotion. And yet, I've stared death in the face so many times, and till now always managed to put off that final losing match. So why not hope? Maharal could be bluffing. Testing my reactions.

I kept a blank face, turning things around. Testing *him*.

"Continuity, Professor. That's what it's all about. Even with the new technology to refill *élan* cells, your clay body can't be replenished more than a few times. You've got to emulate my copying ability in order to make soul-impressions from one ditto to the next, indefinitely. Without an organic brain to return to, it's your only option."

He nodded. "Go on."

"But something's eluded you. Whatever I do—however I manage to make such good copies—the knack isn't easily duplicated."

"That's right, Morris. I believe it has partly to do with your casual attitude toward the dittos that went missing over the years. An attitude you demonstrate even now. See how relaxed you are, on hearing that your real body was destroyed? Anyone else would be frantic."

I felt anything *but* relaxed. In fact, I was pissed off! But other priorities ranked higher than going orbital and screaming at this fellow. *All my other prisoner-selves would have diagnosed Smersh-Foxleitner syndrome by now. They'd decide to feign a lackadaisical attitude. Act unimpressed. Draw Maharal out.*

Shall I stay with that approach? Or try a new tack in order to surprise him?

At the moment, shackled down, I saw no way to take advantage of surprise. Better save it for later.

"You see," Maharal continued, warming to his subject, "we humans are all still deeply rooted in the animal response set . . . the desperate drive to continue organic existence. Inherited survival instinct played an important role in our evolution, but it can also be an *anchor*, pinning down the Standing Wave. It's one reason why few people make truly first-rate ditto impressions, without affectual holes or memory gaps. They hold back, never letting their entire selves roll fully in the clay."

"Hm. Cute metaphor," I replied. "But there are millions of exceptions. In fact, lots of folks are far more careless with their golems than I am . . . or was. Experience junkies. Org-warriors. Janitors who make commercial throwaway units by the gross. And blue cops who will gladly jump in front of a train to save a cat. Then there are nihilists—"

That word made Yosil wince, his expression briefly pained. A deeply *personal* kind of pain. Something clicked as I put together some disjointed clues from what felt like only yesterday.

"Your daughter," I guessed, stabbing at a hunch.

He nodded, an unsteady jerk. "Ritu might be called a nihilist, of a certain kind. Her dittos are . . . unpredictable. Disloyal. They don't care. At another level I . . . don't think she does, either."

One could easily read guilt in his supple gray features. A hopeful track to follow. A *new* track, since none of my other captive-selves would have met Ritu. Might I use this tenuous personal connection in some way? If I could force Yosil to view me as more of a person . . .

But Maharal only shook his head. His expression hardened. "Let's just say that no simple or single trait explains your ability, Morris. In fact, I consider it a rare combination, perhaps impossible to replicate in another person who remains enmeshed in his own complicated life. The local viewpoint—parochially limited and yet addictive—has long been recognized as an unseverable chain. An anchor, keeping the soul ensnared."

"I don't see—"

"Of *course* you don't see. If you did, your mind would quail from the majestic beauty and terror of it all!"

"I—"

"Oh, it's not your fault." Having surged, his emotion drained away as quickly. "Each of us remains convinced that our own subjective viewpoint is more urgent than anyone else's—indeed, even more valid than the objective matrix that underlies so-called reality. After all, the subjective view is a grand theater. Each of us gets to be hero of an ongoing drama. It's why ideologies and bigotries survive against all evidence or logic.

"Oh, subjective obstinacy had advantages, Morris, when we were busy evolving into nature's champion egotists. It led to human mastery over the planet . . . and several times to our species nearly wiping itself out."

I had a sudden recollection of first meeting this fellow—Maharal's gray ghost—at UK on Tuesday, shortly before his original was found dead in a ruined car. That morning, ditYosil spoke of his archie in surprising terms, describing *real*Yosil as a borderline paranoid, drifting in and out of dark fantasies. Later, he described nightmares about *"tech-*

KILN PEOPLE ■ 261

nology gone mad. . . . The same fear that Fermi and Oppenheimer felt when they watched the first mushroom cloud. . . ."

It seemed easy enough to dismiss at the time. Intriguing, but also melodramatic. Now I wondered. Could father and daughter have different versions of the same underlying tendency? A penchant for unreliable copying? How ironic, then, if one of the founders of modern dittotech was unable to make golems he could depend on!

I started speculating exactly when Yosil Maharal made his great conceptual breakthrough. Last week? Monday? Just hours before his death, when he thought himself quite safe and alone? A growing suspicion made me feel creepy, all up and down my spine.

Meanwhile, the gray golem kept talking. "No, the value of egotistical self-importance cannot be denied, back when individual humans competed with each other and with nature to survive. Only now it's a mixed blessing, fostering waves of social alienation. More fundamentally, it limits the range of plausibility wave functions that we're willing to perceive, or to collapse into reified events that others can share and verify—"

Maharal paused. "But this is going over your head."

"I guess you're right, Doc." I pondered for a moment. "Still, I think I read a popular article a while back. . . . You're talking about the *Observer Effect,* right?"

"Yes!" He took a step forward, enthusiasm briefly winning over his need for scorn. "Years ago, Bevvisov and I argued whether the newly discovered Standing Wave was a manifestation of quantum mechanics, or a completely separate phenomenon that happened to use similar transformation dynamics. Like most scientists of his generation, Bevvisov disliked using the word 'soul' in relation to anything that could be measured or palpably manifested in the physical world. Rather, he believed in a variant of the old Copenhagen quantum interpretation—that every event in the universe arises out of a vast sea of interacting probability amplitudes. Unreified potentialities that only take on tangible effect in the presence of an observer."

"In other words, that 'subjective viewpoint' you were talking about."

"Right again. Someone has to consciously *notice* the effect of an experiment or event, in order for the wave functions to collapse and for it to become real."

"Hm." I was struggling, but tried hard not to show it. "You mean like that *cat inside a box,* who's both alive and dead at the same time, till they open the lid."

"Very good, Albert! Yes. As in the life or death of Schrödinger's cat, every decision state in the universe remains indeterminate till it's reified through observation by a thinking being. Even if that being stands many light-years away, glancing at the sky and casually noting the existence of a new star. In so doing, he can be said to have helped *create* the star, collaboratively, with every other observer who noticed it. The subjective and the objective have a complex relationship, all right! More than anyone imagined."

"I see, Doc. That is, I think I do. And yet . . . this has to do with the Standing Wave . . . how?"

Maharal was too excited to get exasperated. "Long ago, a renowned physicist, Roger Penrose, proposed that consciousness arises out of indeterminate quantum phenomena, acting at the level of tiny organelles that reside inside human brain cells. Some believe it's one reason why no one ever succeeded at the old dream of creating genuine artificial intelligence in a computer. The deterministic logic of the most sophisticated digital system remains fundamentally limited, incapable of simulating, much less replicating, the deeply nested feedback loops and stochastic tonal modes of that hypercomplex system we call a soul-field . . ."

Oog. Now this *was* rapidly going way over my head. But I wanted to keep Maharal talking. In part because he might reveal something useful. And to delay things. Whatever he planned on doing to me next, with all of his mad scientist machinery, I knew by now that it was going to hurt.

A lot. Enough to make me lose my temper.

I really hate it when that happens.

". . . So, each time a human Standing Wave is copied, there remains a deep level of continuing connection—'entanglement,' to use an old-fashioned term from quantum mechanics—between the copy and its original template. Between a ditto and its organic original. Not at a level that anyone normally notices. No actual information gets exchanged while the golem is running around. Nevertheless, a coupling remains, clinging to the duplicate Standing Wave."

"Is that what you mean by an anchor?" I prompted, seeing a connection at last.

"Yes. Those organelles Penrose spoke of *do* exist in brain cells. Only instead of quantum states, they entangle with a similar but entirely separate spectrum of *soulistic* modes. While dittoing, we amplify these myriad states, pressing the combined waveform into a nearby matrix. But even when that new matrix—a fresh golem—stands and walks away, its status as an *observer* continues to be entangled with the original's."

"Even if the golem never returns to inload?"

"Inloading involves retrieving *memories,* Morris. Now I'm talking about something deeper than memory. I'm talking about the sense in which each person is a sovereign observer who alters the universe—who *makes* the universe, by the very act of observing."

Now I was lost again. "You mean each of us—"

"—some of us more than others, apparently," Maharal snapped, and I could tell his anger was back. An envious hatred that I was only now starting to fathom. "Your personality appears more willing, at a deep level, to accept the tentative nature of the world—to deputize your subselves with their own, independent observer status—"

"—and therefore with complete standing waves," I finished for him, struggling to keep a hand in the conversation.

"That's right. At bottom, it has little to do with egotism, nihilism, detachment . . . or intelligence, obviously. Perhaps you simply have a greater willingness to *trust yourself* than most people do."

He shrugged. "Even so, your talents were hampered. Limited. Severely constrained. Their only evident manifestation was a facility at making good copies, even though you should be capable of much more: When it came to moving beyond, into fresh territory, you remained as anchored as the rest of us.

"Then, less than a week ago, I stumbled onto what *must* be the answer. A remarkably simple, though brute-force approach to achieving the end I seek. Ironically, it is the same transforming event that our ancestors associated with release of the soul."

He paused.

And I guessed. It wasn't hard.

"You're talking about death."

Maharal's smile broadened—eager, patronizing, and more than a little hateful.

"Very good, Albert! Indeed, the ancients were right in their dualist belief that a soul can be unlinked from the natural body after death. Only there is so much more to it than they could imagine—"

At that moment, while Maharal droned smugly on, my proper course of action seemed clear as day. I should hold back. Show only reticence and self-control. Continue drawing him out. There were more questions, things to discover. And yet . . .

I couldn't help it. Anger erupted, taking over my small body with surprising force, straining at the shackles.

"*You* fired that missile! You murdered me, you son of a bitch, for the sake of your goddamned theories! You sick, sadistic monster. When I get loose from here—"

Yosil laughed.

"Ah. So, despite a lucid moment or two, the name-calling commences on schedule. You really are a tediously predictable person, Morris. Predictability that I plan to make good use of."

And with that, ditMaharal turned back to his preparations—muttering commands into the votroller and flicking switches—while I lay fuming, torn between the gutter satisfaction of hating him and realizing that the reaction was exactly what he wanted.

Of course, below it all lurked curiosity—wondering where he planned to send me next.

32

Waryware

. . . as Frankie goes over the rainbow,
and undercover . . .

We abandoned the Universal Kilns car that Vic Aeneas Kaolin had given us, figuring it must be bugged.

What other arrangements did the tycoon make? That thought kept recurring as I flagged down an open pullcab outside the shuttered Rainbow Lounge. Hopping into the passenger seat, I asked the driver to take us down Fourth Street.

"And step on it!" my little ferretlike companion urged, panting with eagerness to be off. In a little pouch, Palloid carried some of the treasures he recovered while scrounging behind the bar, where the late Queen Irene had stashed some of her secrets. I think he was already scheming how to sell the material back to its "rightful owners," for a "finder's fee," without having to call it blackmail.

Our cabbie shrugged, dislodging glossy shades from their perch on his forehead and dropping them over his eyes. This revealed a nifty set of little devil horns—probably an implanted compass/locator, cheap enough to supply even to disposable dittos.

"Hold on, gents," he called. Grabbing both arms of the rickshaw yoke, he bore into the pavement with powerful kicks of big-thighed legs, like those of a muscular goat. Only after accelerating beyond thirty klicks-per did he touch a switch engaging the little electric cruise motor, lifting his gleaming ceramic hooves off the ground.

"You got a specific destination in mind?" our Pan-like driver asked me over one shoulder. "Or is an eminent gray like you just visiting? Trawling for memories? Maybe you want a quickie view tour of our fair city?"

It took me a moment to recall that I had been retinted at Kaolin's house, to a high-class "emissary" shade of gray. The driver apparently thought I was from out of town, traveling with a dittopet.

"I know all the historical and secret spots. Market arcades stocked with bootlegs you'll never see back east. Alleys where the law never ventures and no cameras are allowed. Just pay a small vice tax and sign a waiver. Once you're inside, anarchism-paradise!"

"Just keep going down Fourth," I replied. "I'll let you know when we get close." I had a specific destination in mind all right, but wasn't about to say it aloud. Not while we were probably under surveillance, both from outside and within.

He accepted this with a grunt and adjusted his visor, steering lazily with a finger on the tiller. Meanwhile, I took out the flip-phone I'd been given shortly after this body was restored to youthful vigor.

"Who're you calling?" Palloid asked.

"Who do you think? Our employer, of course." Just one number was on the autodialer.

"But I thought—then why did we abandon the car if—"

Those dark little eyes glittered. I could see Pal's suspicious little mind working. "Okay, then. Be sure to give Aeneas my love."

As a cheap green—dyed orange and then gray—I couldn't roll my eyes expressively. So I just ignored him. The phone made old-fashioned *clickety-beep* noises as it hunted for a Kaolin authorized to answer. One of his shiny golems would do . . . or else possibly the real hermit-trillionaire, cowering behind layers of germproof glass in the tower of his manicured mansion. Failing that, a computer-avatar to either take a message or handle routine decisions, perhaps using a fine rendition of Kaolin's own voice.

So I waited. You expect to wait when you're clay. Despite the mayfly timetable, impatience is for those with real lifespan to lose.

Meanwhile, dittotown flowed past, with all of its extravagant fusion of griminess and brilliant color. Some of the older buildings, poorly maintained and no longer inspected, bore condemnation logos forbidding entry by real persons. Yet all around us thronged crowds, oblivious to the rickety surroundings—people built for a day of hard labor, yet far gaudier than their drab makers. The busy worker ants who keep civilization going—every hue and candy-striped combination—bustled in/out of nearby factories and workshops, bearing heavy loads, hurrying to confidential meetings or carrying rush orders on spindly legs.

Traffic snarled for a while, forcing us to wend around an open pit construction site, marked by a broad holo sign:

CITYWIDE ROXTRANSIT PNEUMATIC-TUBE PROJECT:
YOUR TAX DOLLARS AT WORK

A glimmering animated display showed steady progress toward the day when clayfolk and other cargo would zip to every part of town via an extended network of airless tubes, shuttling to any address like so many self-targeted Internet packets, automatically and at hardly any cost. Jitney and brontolorry drivers complained that the completed portions of the project were already spoiling their most lucrative routes. Spates of sabotage occasionally delayed work, reminding folks of the old Luddite days, when unions fought pitched street battles against dittotech. One recent explosion even caused a nearby building to collapse, crushing more than four hundred golems and throwing glass fragments far enough to cut a real person three blocks away, requiring half a dozen stitches. It was a major scandal.

Despite social unrest though, Universal Kilns and the other ditto-makers lobbied hard for tube installation in every city. How better to ensure that customers will receive millions of fresh blanks quickly, helping them get the most out of each imprinted day? The less time a golem spends in transit, or stored in the fridge, the more clients feel they get their money's worth. The more blanks they'll order.

Below the cheery sign, cut-rate epsilon models labored, hauling out baskets of dirt on their speckled-green backs while others descended, bearing lengths of ceramic pipe built to withstand high pressures, deep underground. Epsilons don't even get a full, imprinted personality—no soul-stuff and no salmon reflex—just a simple drive to labor on and on and on, till drawn by the call of a recycling tank.

Squinting at the scene one way, I glimpsed a science-fiction nightmare worse than Fritz Lang's *Metropolis*—slaves and prols laboring for distant masters before toppling to an early death, preordained and unmourned. Squint another way, and it seemed marvelous! A world of free citizens, extending tiny portions of themselves—easily expendable bits—to take turns doing all the necessary drudgery, so everyone can spend their organic lifetimes playing or studying.

Which was true?

Both at the same time?

Should I care?

My own thoughts surprised me.

Is this what happens to a ditto's brain when it lasts beyond a second day? I wondered. *Does* élan-*replenishment make you all dreamy and philosophical? Was it triggered by the events I witnessed at Irene's?*

Or is it because I'm a frankie?

Come on, Kaolin. Answer your damn phone!

Actually, his delay gave me some cause for hope. Maybe Aeneas didn't really care much about me and Palloid. Kaolin might be too busy to bother checking up on us.

Ah, but "busy" doesn't mean what it used to. A rich man can keep imprinting enough fancy dittos to make any job manageable. So there had to be another reason.

We were a block past the pneumo-tube dig when the cabbie suddenly veered, emitting gouts of bitter cursing. I clenched the seat, bracing for collision, but traffic wasn't at fault. No, the driver was fuming over faraway events that had nothing to do with his job.

"Idiots!" he cried. "Couldn't you *guess* they'd be waiting for you around that hill? The Indies must've had it zeroed in from five different angles. Schmucks. PEZ should just give up this match and concede. Send our whole team onto the battlefield in their naked rig hides. We'll be better off starting all over with new talent!"

A faint glimmer shone around the edges of his shades. So, the sunglasses were also vids. Most are.

Still, I wasn't paying to be hauled into a wreck by some sports-distracted coolie. One more unnecessary swerve and I just might slap a civil lien on him—

In whose name? Where would the money go? Poor old Albert had a sister in Georgia, but she owned five patents and didn't need cash. Then I recalled—whatever remained of Al's estate would go to Clara. Whatever the cops didn't seize. Or Kaolin. It all depended on finding someone else to blame for the attack on Universal Kilns.

I had suspicions about that. But first there'd have to be more evidence.

"Hey, fan-boy!" Palloid shouted at the driver, who was still cursing as we dodged some peditstrians then barely missed getting squashed by a huge, eight-legged delivery van. "Forget the score, watch the road!"

The driver muttered something over his shoulder at my friend, who snarled in response, arching his long back and extending claws, as if preparing to leap. I was about to flip the phone shut and intervene when a voice abruptly buzzed in my ear.

"So, it's you. I was wondering when you'd check in," came the tycoon's murmured voice. I couldn't tell which Kaolin it was, though presumably the platinum who gave us our assignment. *"What did you learn at Irene's place?"*

No apology for keeping me waiting. Well, that's a trillionaire for you.

"Irene's true-dead," I replied. "She used one of those soul-antenna services and took all her dittos along with her to the Nirvianosphere, or the Valhallan Belts, or wherever."

"I know. The cops just arrived there and I've got the scene in front of me. Incredible. What a psycho! Do you see what I mean, Morris? The world is filling up with perverts and dittoing only makes it worse. I sometimes wish we never—"

He stopped, then resumed. *"Well, never mind that. Do you think Irene chose this moment to end it all because her conspiracy failed? Because they didn't manage to wreck my factory?"*

Kaolin did an impressive job of feigning confused innocence. I decided to play along.

"Irene was just another dupe, sir. She honestly thought she had hired Albert's gray as a quasi-legal industrial spy."

"You mean all that nonsense about looking for the secret of teleportation?"

I glanced back at the pneumo-tunnel construction project—an awful lot of investment that would lose much of its purpose if remote dittoing ever came true.

"The story seemed plausible enough to deceive an Albert Morris gray. Why not her too? Anyway, by this morning Irene realized she'd been set up to take blame for the prion attack. So she chose to check out under her own terms."

"Another patsy, then. Like you and Lum and Gadarene." Kaolin snorted. *"Did you find any leads to who's behind it all?"*

"Well, her two partners were a plaid ditto who called himself Vic

Collins and another one who claimed to be a copy of the maestra, Gineen Wammaker."

"Is that all? We already knew as much from the gray's tape recording."

I didn't want to say more. Yet Kaolin was still my client . . . at least till I verified some things. I couldn't legally or ethically lie to him.

"Vic Collins was a facade, of course. Irene thought he might really be Beta."

"You mean the golemnapper and counterfeiter? Have you got any proof?" Kaolin's voice grew a bit more excited. *"This could be what I need to bring some real pressure to bear. Force the cops to take that bastard seriously as a real public threat, not just another d-commerce nuisance. We may be able to put him out of business for good!"*

My reply was careful.

"I had a similar thought. I've been after Beta for three years. We've had harsh encounters."

"Yes, I recall. Your narrow escape on Monday, followed by Tuesday morning's raid on his Teller Building operation. There's a lot of bad slip between the two of you."

"Yes, in fact—"

I could see our destination up ahead. I had to make Kaolin feel comfortable enough not to watch my movements too closely for the next few minutes. Timing would be critical.

"That's why I'm heading back toward the Teller Building right now."

Toward. It wasn't a lie, exactly. It fit our present trajectory across dittotown, in case he was tracking.

"Going to look for more clues, eh? Great!" Kaolin said. I heard muffled voices in the background, demanding the platinum's attention. *"Call again when you learn more,"* he told me, then broke the connection without salutation or formality.

Just in time, I noted with some relief.

"Stop here!" I told the cabbie, who was still dividing his attention unnervingly between the road, the war news, and bickering with Pal. *How do guys like this keep their hack license?* I wondered, tossing him a silver coin and hopping out. Fortunately, Palloid kept to his perch on my shoulder, rather than get into a fight. But it was a close call.

Temple of the Ephemerals, flashed the sign in front. Up granite steps I dashed, past all the forlorn dittos hanging about—wounded, damaged, or otherwise derelict, lacking any hope of being welcomed home for inloading. Most looked worn down, near dissolution. Yet I was by far the oldest! The only clay person present who had any direct memory of Tuesday's sermon. Not that I was here to attend services.

Only a short queue of haggard copies stood waiting for emergency repair service, led by a lanky purple with half its left arm torn off. Fortunately, the same dark-haired volunteer was on duty, offering succor to the hopeless and downtrodden. Whatever psychological reason drew her to dedicate precious realtime helping those with little life worth saving, I felt glad of it.

"Yipes!" Palloid gasped a shaky squeak upon catching sight of the volunteer nurse. "It's Alexie."

"What? You know her?"

Pal's mini-ditto answered in a low whisper, "Uh . . . we dated for a while. You don't think she'll recognize me, do you?"

I couldn't help comparing two mental images. One of the *real* Pal—handsome, grizzled, and broad-shouldered, though missing his entire lower half and confined for life to a sustaino-chair—a picture that had little in common with the agile, grinning little weasel creature on my shoulder except when it came to stuff that really mattered, like memory, personality, and soul.

"Maybe not," I answered, stepping past all the waiting dittos, heading for the front of the line. "If you keep your mouth shut."

Several injured golems grumbled as I strode up to Alexie's treatment station, with its unsanitary table surrounded by cheap barrels of golem-grout, ditspackle, and praydough. She glanced at me—and for the first time I noticed she was pretty, in a darkly severe, dedicated-looking way. She began to insist that I wait my turn, but stopped when I raised my shirt, turning to display a long scar of hardened cement on my back.

"Remember your handiwork, Doc? You sure did a great job with that nasty little eater that was chewing out my innards. I recall one of your colleagues said I wouldn't last the day. You should collect on that bet."

She blinked. "I remember you. But . . . but that was *Tues*—"

Alexie stopped, eyes widening. No dummy, she went silent as the implications sank in.

Smart, yeah. But then why did she go out with Pal?

Dropping my shirt, I asked, "Is there a place where we can talk in private?"

She gave a jerky nod and motioned for us to follow her upstairs.

■   ■   ■

Palloid kept uncharacteristically silent as Alexie scanned. She quickly discovered the tracker bugs that Kaolin installed, when he so kindly extended our pseudolives.

She also found the bombs.

Maybe just in time, I thought. *Our employer expects us to report from the Teller Building. He may get upset to find out we've slipped the leash.*

"What pig did this to you?" Alexie cursed, carefully dropping the bombs into a battered-looking containment canister. There *are* special circumstances when golems can be legally required to carry autodestructs, with triggers operated by radio control. But it's pretty rare in PEZ. Naturally, Alexie's group opposes the practice in principle. I refrained from telling her that our bombs were installed by the great slavemaster himself, Vic Kaolin. If she knew, she might go online at once to tell everyone in her community of activists.

I couldn't allow that. Not yet.

Palloid needed a few repairs, too. While she worked on him, I gazed past her balcony at the stained glass window of the main church. The old Christian symbols had been replaced to show a circular rosette, like a flower whose petals all tapered outward before flaring abruptly at the very end, at right angles, to pointed tips. At first, I thought each figure might be a fish, tail thrust outward. *Fish . . . for arti-fishial?* Then I realized, they were square-headed whales—sperm whales, apparently— portrayed gathering together their huge brows in some meeting of cetacean minds.

What was the symbolism? Whales—long-lived, though perpetually endangered—seemed just the opposite of dittos, who faded fast but sprang forth daily in greater numbers, ever replenished by human ingenuity and desire.

It reminded me a bit of the mandala emblem worn by that technician-priest of Final Options, Inc., who presided over the attempted transcendence of Queen Irene. Though clearly different in detail, both groups were struggling with the same problem, how to reconcile soul-imprinting with abiding religious impulse. But who am I to judge?

Okay, I like these Ephemerals folks. Maybe I owe them a couple of favors. Still, I had to play things coy.

Alexie finished and declared us clean. Suddenly, I felt *free* for the first time since . . . well, since I met up with Pal and Lum and Gadarene under the shadows of an ancient skooterboard park, getting snared in all this dirty business.

"Now I can phone home!" Palloid exulted, forgetting his vow of silence. "Wait'll I tell myself what I've seen! It'll be a *rush* of an inload."

Alexie tilted her head, eyes narrowing, perhaps recognizing something about Pal's speech rhythm. I didn't give her time to follow the thought.

"My pa—my little friend and I both need secure web access," I said. "Do you have a couple of chadors we can use?"

After an uncertain pause, she nodded, then pointed to a coatrack. Two black, shapeless garments hung next to a desk. "They've been cleaned recently. No bugs."

"That'll do fine, thanks." I started toward the coatrack.

"Just so you know," she added, "I subscribe to *Waryware Services,* so don't try to pull any scams or illegal stuff while using our access. Take that kind of crap elsewhere."

"Yes, ma'am."

Alexie frowned. "Can I trust you both not to touch anything else up here, while I go back and help more patients?"

Palloid nodded vigorously. "We'll repay this kindness," I assured.

"Hm. Maybe you can explain to me sometime how it is that you're still walking around, so long after you should be slurry."

"Sometime. I will."

She departed with a final dubious look. As her footsteps vanished downstairs, I gave Palloid a questioning glance. "All right!" he answered with a lithe shrug. "So maybe she's better than I deserved. Shall we get on with it now? Kaolin won't stay fooled for long."

My little friend leaped onto the desk and I helped him slip under a chador, so the active hood covered him, adjusting to his strange body plan. I threw the other garment over my head and let its black drapery flow over my arms, down past my waist. From the outside, I now looked like some shrouded creature from those dark days, half a century ago, when a third of the countries on Earth forced women to veil their faces and forms under shapeless tents of muslin and gauze. A repressive move that backfired when the old, confining chador transformed into something completely liberating.

From within—

I was suddenly in another universe. The wonderful cosmos of VR, where data and illusion mix in profusions of color and synthetic depth. Sensors under the garment felt the positions of my arms, fingertips, and each puff of breath, reacting to every grunt from my simulated larynx.

A few muttered commands, and within seconds I had three active globe-worlds set up.

The first one zoomed toward a smoldering ruin where my house . . . *Albert's house* . . . had been. Freeware correlators swooped in from the surrounding webscape begging for permission to fetch data for me about this tragic event. A couple of the agents had good reputations, so I posed a few parameters and unleashed them. At the first curiosity layer, it wouldn't cost a penny and there'd be no possibility of a backtrace. Nothing to distinguish me from millions of other net voyeurs. These were major news events, so my enquiries shouldn't attract any attention till I probed close to bone.

My second bubble skimmed news reports about the sabotage attempt at Universal Kilns. I wanted the official police summary—especially to see if Albert was still a suspect. Also, any event like this one attracted all sorts of conspiracy theories and minority reports, offered by whistleblower clubs, accountability hobbyists, solitary paranoiacs, autonomous *whatif* agents or wandering *yesbut* avatars. And if none of those were on the right track, I might post one of my own! Anonymous rumormongering is a venerable kind of mischief that has its own special place.

realAlbert would be much better at this. And one of his ebonies would be better still.

Me? I'm just a green and a frankie. But I'm all that's left.

While those two bubbles churned at the edges, fizzing with correlative foam, I made ready a third, more dangerous than the others.

The just-in-case cache, where Albert kept his backup files, in case anything happened to our house computer.

Suppose Nell detected the incoming missile . . . even bare seconds before it struck. According to programming, she would have dumped as much data as possible into the remote cache. That record might let me glimpse what my maker was doing—possibly even thinking—the very minutes that he died.

A big prize. But accessing it could be risky. *Whoever sent that missile must've been surveilling the house, in order to be sure Albert was there when it struck. But how intense was the scrutiny? Did they simply prowl around outside with mini-cameras, keeping track of Al's comings and goings? What if they managed to penetrate his privacy shields, say by floating a micro-spy inside the house? It happens now and then. Technology keeps changing and the cams keep getting smaller. Only fools count on their secrets staying safe forever.*

Someone out there may know everything, including the location of the cache. Lurker software could be waiting to pounce on anyone who tries accessing it. A borrowed chador won't mask me for long.

But what choice did I have? My only alternative was to head over to Pal's place and get drunk together till this artificially extended pseudolife finally expired.

Well, feh to that! I typed with waggling fingertips and muttered some phrases under the chador's sheltering drapery, hoping that Albert didn't change passwords on me after learning he had made his first frankie.

Almost at once I found myself looking at a pretty good facsimile of Nell.

Experts claim there's no such thing as true digital intelligence, and never will be. I guess they ought to know by now. It's another of those "failed dreams" from TwenCen science fiction that never came true, like flying saucer aliens. Still, *simulation* has become a high art, and it doesn't take much of an animated program to fool most folks with a well-made talking head . . . at least for a couple of turings.

Her face was originally modeled after a junior professor I had a brief thing for, back in college. Sexy without being overly distracting. A personification of efficiency without imagination. In addition to demanding and verifying the next-level password, the avatar scanned my face and sent a short-range probe to the pellet buried in my forehead.

Normally, that should be enough. But not this time.

"Dissonance. You appear to be Tuesday's green, yet you wear gray dye and should have expired by now. Access to cache denied until a plausible explanation is given."

I nodded. "Fair enough. Here's your explanation. Briefly, the research guys at Universal Kilns have discovered a way to extend ditto lifespan. That explains why I'm talking to you. The breakthrough appears to have triggered some kind of conflict between Vic Aeneas Kaolin and Dr. Yosil Maharal. It's possible this led to Maharal's murder. And the murder of Albert Morris."

The animated face contorted—a caricature of doubt. I had to remind myself, this wasn't the Nell I remembered. Only a phantom, a replica that had been stashed in some corner of the vast datasphere, operating in a patch of rented memory.

"Your explanation of the discrepancy in your lifespan is deemed plausible, given other information that was cached by Tuesday's ebony before the explosion. However, a new dissonance must be resolved before I can give you access."

"What new dissonance?"

Nell's phantom did a good approximation of her disapproving frown, a familiar programmed nuance that I never cared for. It generally appeared at times when I was being particularly dense.

"There is no convincing evidence that Albert Morris was murdered."

If I were real, I'd have coughed and sputtered. "No convincing—? What kind of smoking gun do you need? Isn't it murder when somebody blows you up in a bloody missile attack?"

I had to remind myself, this wasn't a real or clay person to be argued with—or even a top-level AI. For a software-cache phantom, the shadow-Nell looked good. But it must be damaged, or caught in a semantic bind.

"The missile attack is irrelevant to the dissonant issue at hand— Albert Morris's putative murder," the face replied.

I stared, repeating a single dismaying word.

"Ir—irrelevant?"

The semantic bind must be severe. Damn. I might not be able to gain access at all. "How . . . could the murder weapon be irrelevant?"

"Organic citizen Albert Morris has been missing for just over a day. No trace of him has appeared on the Web, or on the Streetcam Network, or—"

"Well, of course not—"

"But the disappearance was expected. Moreover, it has no direct relation to the destruction of his home."

Amazed, I could only let this sink in. Expected? No relation to the destruction?

As if compelled, I turned to gaze at the bubbleview that peered down upon the house on Sycamore Avenue. Several hovering voyeur-eyes and newscams contributed to a highly textured image that ballooned larger when I stared, offering a vivid overhead view of blackened timbers and collapsed masonry walls. The remnant chimney jutted like a defiant finger. The back porch, its wrought-iron balustrade curled into a cork-screw by recent heat, led to rose trellises that were reduced to charred stumps.

Police flickertape kept gawkers at bay—both realfolk and dittos who might try for souvenirs. I spotted several teams of ebony specialists inside the cordon, crouching with scanners and samplers, sifting for evidence. Other figures could be seen stepping amid the debris.

While I was busy speaking to the cache-phantom, those correlator agents that I hired had been busy gathering info about the missile attack, lining that bubble's edges with summaries and flowcharts. I stabbed one reporting on the weapon that had done all this. The exact model type was unknown but clearly sophisticated, delivering lots of punch in a small package. That helped explain how it could be smuggled into dittotown and set up without detection. More impressive was the way it launched amid wild gyrations and a dense cloud of obscuring chaff, masking its point of origin as five semi-abandoned houses burned in its wake, erasing any clues to whoever planted the damned thing. Worse, a scarcity of publicams in the area made it extra hard for the cops establish a reverse-time shakeout. They might never pin down who planted it.

I wondered, in awe, *Who would have access to such a weapon? And why use it on a measly local private eye?*

The first half of my question had a ready answer. Oh, the police were keeping mum, but professional circumspection didn't have any hold over thousands of amateur analysts and retired experts out there with time on their hands. After intensely poring over the available information, they reached a consensus.

It must have been *military* hardware. And not the normal variety used by our national teams in ritual battles, before mass audiences on the International Combat Range. Naturally, nations keep their best stuff hidden away, just-in-case. This had to be one of those nasty items, put on the shelf amid hopes that it would never be used.

This explained why so many ebonies were crawling over the site. They probably cared much more about the weapon than poor old Albert.

There were other anomalies. Opinions sputtered and fizzed at the bubble's fringe.

This Morris guy was supposedly involved somehow in that attempt to sabotage Universal Kilns, Tuesday night. Obviously they took revenge on him . . .

Within just a couple of hours? Ridiculous! It took days or weeks to set up the missile carefully enough to obscure its emplacement from back-tracing . . .

Right! Morris was obviously framed! The missile was meant to in-cinerate him so he couldn't testify . . .

That could be. Still, there's something fishy about all this. Why haven't they found a body? . . .

What body? It was vaporized . . .

Blown to smithereens . . .

Oh yeah? Then where's the organic residue? . . .

There's plenty of DNA traces, identical to Morris's profile . . .

That's right, traces! Hell, if you blew up my house while I was away, you'd find lots of bits . . . skin cells, dandruff, hairs. Take the pillow on your bed—a tenth of its weight consists of stuff that flaked off your head after a thousand nights . . .

Ew, disgusting!

. . . so it's no good just to say they found the guy's DNA in the same house where he lived. To confirm death, show me differentiated tissue! Even if he was puréed, you'd find bits of bone, blood, intestinal cells. . . .

That rocked me. Partly because I should have thought of it! Even as a green-frankie. After all, I still had Albert's memories. His training.

What could this mean?

Probably I'd have reached the obvious conclusion in another second or two. But suddenly I was distracted by the sight of a single figure moving across the smoldering ruins, poking embers with a stick. Something about the slender physique drew me, and the globeworld responded by zooming closer.

Dressed in neutral dungarees, with hair bundled under a cap, it seemed at first to be a high-class ditto, especially with her face smeared gray by ash. But when an ebony bowed out of her way, I realized, she must be real. And her movements were those of an athlete.

A small identifier label popped up next to her as the camera view zoomed closer:

VICTIM'S ASSIGNED HEIR

My emotions were stronger than expected, given the cheapness of the body I wore.

"Clara," I murmured as her face came into focus, wearing a grim expression, one that combined grief and anger with extreme puzzlement.

"Final password accepted," said a voice—Nell's phantom, responding to the single word I had spoken.

"Access to cache allowed."

I glanced to my right. Nell's computerized image was gone, replaced by a list that scrolled down, showing a catalogue of contents. Nell's simulated voice continued.

"The first item, by relevance, is one that you requested in your present golem form on Tuesday, at thirteen forty-five hours. You asked for a trace of the waiter-contractor who was fired from his job at Tour Vanadium restaurant. Despite being handicapped in this primitive form, I managed to complete the trace. The waiter's name and life summary are

given below. He has lodged a protest with the Labor Subcontractors Association, disclaiming any responsibility for the incident that led to his termination. . . ."

Waiter? I wondered. Restaurant? Oh. I had forgotten about all that. A trivial matter now.

"There were other items in queue, just before the explosion," Nell's phantom continued. *"Unanswered calls and messages from Malachai Montmorillin, Inspector Blane, Gineen Wammaker, Thomas Facks . . ."*

It was a long list, and ironic. If only Albert had taken that call from Pal, trying to warn him about a plot involving Tuesday's second gray—a plot to frame him with the attack on Universal Kilns—I might not even be here now. I might have spent the rest of my short span as a liberated frankie, detached from Albert's concerns, juggling for kids on a street-corner or trying to find that clumsy waiter. Until at last I fell apart.

"I can also replay a recording of the final call your original made, to Ritu Maharal, arranging a joint trip to investigate her father's cabin in the desert."

What was that? A trip, together?

I trembled suddenly. A trip with Ritu Maharal . . . to the desert? Abruptly I saw a glimmer, an outline of what could have happened. How Albert might have departed *in person,* under the guise of a ditto!

If he did, was it because he suspected the house was under surveillance by assassins? If so, the ploy worked. He sure fooled everyone into believing his real self was still there. I had to absorb this stunning notion. There could be a flaw . . . but Albert might not be dead, after all!

Good news, right? It'd liberate me from a heavy burden—sole obligation to uncover the truth. For all I knew, right now Al and a dozen of his loyal copies were already hard on the trail of the villains, closing in with grim determination to avenge his incinerated garden.

And yet . . . the idea also brought with it a sense of letdown. For a while, I had actually felt important. As if this little sliver of existence somehow *mattered* on the grand scale of things. Justice seemed to depend on me. On what I chose to do.

Now?

Well, my duty's clear. To report, of course. To describe everything I've learned and offer my services to my betters.

But it's nowhere near as romantic as fighting on, alone.

▪ ▪ ▪

I decided what to do while watching Clara poke through the ruins, apparently far more concerned with uncovering Albert's fate than taking part in her war. If Al *was* alive, he hadn't even bothered to contact her. Not even to let her know he was all right!

Maybe he preferred the company of the beautiful heiress, Ritu Maharal.

Bastard.

Sometimes you only see yourself clearly by standing on the outside. Or better yet, by becoming someone new.

■   ■   ■

All right, that brings me up to the present. My story's done. I'll submit one copy for the cache . . . in case there are any Alberts running around who care to listen.

And I'll send an abbreviated report to Miss Ritu Maharal. She was Albert's final employer, just before the missile attack, so I guess she deserves to be told that I think Aeneas Kaolin has gone murderously insane.

But I'm really doing it for Clara. She's the reason why I stood here under this chador for ten extra minutes, rapid-reciting a first-person narration of everything I've seen and done for the last couple of days, leading all the way to this moment. Doing it despite entreaties from Pal's little ferret-ditto, warning that each added second exposed us to danger. Either from Kaolin or some unknown enemy, maybe even worse.

Whatever. My report probably won't matter. I've uncovered only a few pieces of the puzzle, after all. Far from enough to solve the case, for sure.

Maybe I just duplicated work that's already been done by other, much better versions of "me."

Hell, I don't even know where I'll go next . . . though I do have a few ideas.

Still, I can tell you one thing, Clara.

As long as this small patch of soul continues, I'll remember you. Till the recycling tank finally claims me, I've got something . . . and someone . . . to live for.

33

Lasting Impressions

Wow.

This place is amazing.

I really must switch to realtime, in order to describe what I'm seeing right now.

Even so, can I begin to do it justice? Especially having to grunt into a tiny recorder-implant that I borrowed from a dead golem. An implant that may not even be functioning properly?

And yet, what can I do except try? Not many people get to witness this spectacle. Not without getting their brains wiped clear of the memory, right afterward.

An entire *army* stands at attention before me, divided by rank and specialty into squads, platoons, companies, and regiments. Casting long shadows in the dim light, row after row of sturdy figures extends into the distance. Neither living nor quite lifeless, silent in the chilly dry air of a deep subterranean cavern that must stretch for kilometers, each soldier abides sealed by a thin layer of gel-wrap to maintain freshness, awaiting an order that may never come—a command to turn on the lights and fire up nearby kilns, rousing a clay legion from its sleep.

Corporal Chen says they have a motto in this corps—*Open, bake, serve . . . and protect.*

That touch of whimsy—a note of self-deprecating humor—reassures me. A bit. I guess.

Oh, it's not too much of a surprise. There have always been rumors of a secret stash—or more than one—where the nation's real military power is kept, dormant but ever ready. Surely the generals and planners in the Dodecahedron know that twenty little reserve battalions, like Clara's, won't suffice if *real* war ever returns. Everyone assumes that those gladiator-entertainer units represent the tip of the iceberg.

Yeah, but to see it now, with my own eyes. . . .

"Come on," says ditto-Chen, motioning for us to follow his apelike form. "This way to that secure dataport I promised."

Ritu's been wiping her face with a cleanser towel to remove ragged leftovers of gray makeup ever since we entered a tunnel leading deep under the vast military complex. Only now the towel hangs from a limp hand as she stares at endless ranks of golem-soldiery, standing watch in their filmy, shrink-wrap cocoons.

"Amazing. I can see why they would build such a facility here, under the surface base, so the warriors who train up there can readily imprint spare copies for this stockpile force. But I still don't understand." She waves at the rigid brigades standing before us. "Why do you need so *many*?"

With a shrug, Chen resigns himself to the role of tour guide.

"Because the other side may have made even more." He takes a bowlegged step toward us. "Think about it, Miss. It's cheap to dig holes. So is making an army of pre-imprinted dittos. You don't have to spend anything on food or training. No insurance or pensions and very little maintenance. We have good intelligence that it's been done in over a dozen other countries, some of them unfriendly. The Indies have their force in a big cave under Java. The Southern Han, the Guats, and the Gujarats all have mega-hordes tucked away underground. After all, who could resist the temptation? Imagine having available a military force bigger than the Prussians fielded at the Marne—one that can be mobilized and transported across the world within hours. With every trooper fully prepared, carrying the skills and experience of a battle-hardened veteran."

"It's scary as hell," I answer.

Chen nods in agreement. "So we gotta have the same thing—a corps of defenders, ready to rise from the ground at a few hours' notice. At one level, it's simply a matter of outditting the enemy."

"I mean the whole *situation* is scary. This kind of insane arms race—"

"Arms, legs, torsos . . . don't quibble. Call it diterrence—making sure the other guy knows he'll get hurt bad if he ever tries to throw us a first strike. The same logic worked for our ancestors, way back in the age of nukes, or we wouldn't be here now talking."

"Well, I think it stinks," Ritu comments.

"Amen, Miss. But till the politicians finally get around to negotiating a treaty—one with real teeth for onsite inspections—what else can we do?"

It's my turn to pose a question.

"What about the secrecy. How can it be maintained in this day and age? The Henchman Law . . ."

". . . is designed to bring out whistle-blowers. True enough. Yet no insider's tattled openly about this buried army. And the reason is simple,

Albert. The Henchman Law is aimed against *criminal activity.* But don't you think the brass in the Dodecahedron went over the legalities carefully? They never denied having a reserve defense force. There's nothing heinous or illicit—no real people have been hurt in any way—so there's no 'whistle-blower' reward. What good will it do anybody to reveal this place, then? All he'd get for the trouble is a lien slapped against his lifetime earnings, to help pay the cost of moving our golem corps to a new site."

Chen looks at Ritu and me archly.

"And that holds for you two, by the way, in case you're getting any self-righteous notions. We don't mind private rumors. Go ahead and blab generalities and exaggerations to your friends, if you like. Just don't put any pix or location details on the Net, or you could wind up deep in debt, making monthly payments to the Dodec. For life."

The very moment that he said that, I was using the implant in my left eye to snap-record a scene. *For private use,* I rationalized.

Maybe I should erase it.

"Now," Chen insists. "Let's get you to that secure portal I promised."

Still a bit numb from the corporal's slanted threat, Ritu and I follow him silently past more rows of modern janissaries, silent as statues, most of them dyed in blur-pattern camouflage. Up close, you can see how *big* these combat-golems are! Half-again normal size, with much of the difference consisting of extra power cells, for strength, endurance, and to operate enhanced sensoria.

Though most of the figures are thick-limbed and broad-shouldered, I keep looking for Clara's face. Surely she would have been asked to be among the templates, imbuing her skill and battle spirit into hundreds, maybe even thousands of these duplicates. I feel miffed that she never told me . . . at least not about the *scale* of all this!

Ritu continues pressing Chen as we walk.

"It seems to me there's a danger beyond that of foreign adversaries. Isn't this legion something of a temptation to those holding the keys? What if the Dodecs—or the President or even the Protector in Chief— ever decide that democracy is too damned inconvenient? Imagine a million fully equipped battle-golems spilling out of the ground like angry ants, capturing every city in a coup—"

"Wasn't there a thriller about that exact scenario, a few years back? Good effects and lots of cool action, I recall. Hordes of ceramic monsters, marching about stiff-limbed, shouting in stilted voices, blasting everything in sight . . . except the hero, of course. Somehow they kept missing him!"

Laughing, Chen waves a long arm at the companies surrounding us. "But honestly, it's pretty far-fetched. Because every one of these dough-boys was imprinted by a licensed citizen reservist, strictly according to regulations. They have our memories and values. And it's kind of hard to stage a coup when all your grunts are made from guys like me—and Clara—who happen to think democracy's just fine.

"Also there are coded autodestructs, with the ciphers distributed to—"

Chen stops, shaking his head. "No, forget all the safeguards. If you can't have faith in procedures and professionalism, then consider logic."

"What logic is that, Corporal?"

Chen pats the plastic-sheathed flank of a nearby war-golem, perhaps one containing a duplicate of his own soul.

"The logic of expiration, Miss. Even augmented with extra fuel, a battledit like this one can't last more than five days. A week, tops. I defy you to come up with a way to hold onto those captive cities, after that. No small group of conspirators could imprint enough replacements. And no large group could possibly keep such an undertaking secret nowadays.

"No, the purpose of this army is to absorb the first shock of an enemy surprise attack. After that, it'll be up to the *people* to defend themselves and their civilization. Only they can provide enough fresh souls and raw courage to throw into an extended conflict."

Chen shrugs. "But that was true way back in Grandpa's day, and his grandpa before him."

■　■　■

Ritu has no ready answer for this and I manage to keep silent. So Chen turns again to lead us rapidly past more regiments, one perfectly arrayed unit after another, till we lose count of their serried ranks, awed by the vast hall of mute guardians.

Ritu's especially uncomfortable here. Edgy and distant, unlike the easy companionship of our trek across the desert together. Part of it may have to do with her own trouble in making dittos—never able to predict what will happen when she imprints. Sometimes everything goes nor-mally—the Ritu-golem emerges enough like her to share the same am-bitions and perform assigned chores, then return at day's end for routine inloading. Other copies vanish mysteriously, only to send back cryptic taunting messages.

"Can you imagine what it's like to be mocked by someone who knows every intimate thing you've ever done or thought?"

"Then why imprint at all?" I asked, during our long walk together across the wilderness.

"Don't you see? I work at Universal Kilns! I grew up in the clay-namation trade. It's what I know. And to do business nowadays you have to copy. So I kiln a couple of golems each morning and hope for the best.

"Still, whenever it's an urgent appointment—or something has to be done right—I try to handle it in person."

Like this trip to investigate her father's cabin—and the nearby site where he died. When I invited Ritu, she decided to invest a day of real lifespan. Only now we've been sidetracked for several, ever since that wretched "Kaolin" ambushed us on the highway. Stuck far from town, out of contact and only slowly nearing our goal. It must be frustrating for her . . .

. . . as it is for me. To come all this way and find Clara's gone AWOL, having dashed off to poke at the ruins of my house while I'm stuck in the boonies. Dammit, I hope we reach that secure portal of Chen's soon. I have *got* to find a way to get in touch—

At last!

The columns of clay soldiery finally come to an end. We emerge from the silent host, only to pass under bigger shadows—row after row of towering autokilns, presently idle, but primed to fire up quickly and bake freshly unwrapped warriors in giant batches, stimulating their *élan* storage cells into vigorous activity, sending whole divisions to self-sacrifice and glory.

Corporate brand logos loom over us, embossed proudly on these mechanical behemoths. No symbol is more prominent than the circled *U* and circled *K*. Yet Ritu doesn't seem proud, just nervous, rubbing her shoulders and arms, her eyes darting left and right. Her jaw is set and tense, as if walking is an exercise of pure willpower.

Now Chen leads us through a sliding gate into yet another vast chamber where innumerable suits of *armor* dangle on hooks from the tracked ceiling. A forest of duralite helmet-and-carapace combos, ready to slip over bodies still puffy from the oven. We have to sidle along a narrow avenue between tracks, our shoulders brushing metal livery and leggings, jostling sets of refractory coveralls into ghostly motion.

I can't help feeling dwarfed, like we're children, tiptoeing through a dressing room for giants. This chamber's even more intimidating than the assembly of golem-soldiers. Maybe because there's no *soul* here. That ditto-army was human, after all. Well, a kind of human. But this armory has the chill impersonality of gears and silicon. Empty, the suits remind me disquietingly of robots—deadly unaccountable, and free of anything like conscience.

Fortunately, we make good time. Minutes later, we're on the other side, and I'm glad to be out of there!

No sooner do we emerge from the "dressing room" than Chen beckons me to join him at the rail of a balcony. "Albert, you've got to see this! You'll find it interesting, if Clara's been any kind of influence on you."

Joining him at the rail, I find the terrace overlooks yet a third immense gallery, some distance below this one, containing the greatest hoard of weapons I ever saw. Everything from small arms to flame guns to personal helico/raptors can be seen arrayed in neat stacks and or piled on shelves—like a huge emporium of destruction. A central library of war.

Chen shakes his head, clearly wistful.

"They insist on keeping the best stuff down here, in reserve. Just-in-case, they say. But I sure wish we could use this gear topside, during some of our regular matches. Like against those Indies we're fighting this week. Tough bastards. It'd be great if—"

The ditcorporal stops abruptly, arching his simian head to one side.

"Did you just hear something?"

For a second I'm sure he's pulling my leg. This eerie place seems perfect for a haunting.

Only then . . . Yes, a faint murmur. I hear it now.

Scanning below, I finally glimpse figures moving down there amid a distant row of shelves. Some are jet black and others the color of steel, carrying instruments and clipboards, peering amid stacks of warehoused killing apparatus.

Chen whispers a curse. "Shards! They must be doing an audit! But why now?"

"I think I can guess."

He looks at me with dark eyes under heavy, apelike ridges. Abruptly, comprehension dawns.

"The hoodoo missile! The one that fried your archie and your home. I figured it for another homemade job, like urban punks and criminals make in their basements. But the brass must suspect that it was stolen from here. Damn, I should have thought of that!"

What can I say? The possibility occurred to me a while ago. But I didn't want to spook Chen when he's being helpful.

"Why would anyone in the military would want me dead? I admit, Clara's threatened to break my arm a few times . . ."

The joke goes flat. Chen's ape-ditto writhes.

"We gotta get out of here. Right now!"

"But you promised to take us—"

"That was when I thought the place'd be empty! And before it occurred to me that military hardware might be involved. I'm sure not takin' you straight into a team of tight-ass rule enforcers!" Chen grabs my arm. "Let's get Miss Maharal and—"

The sentence falls flat as we both turn and stare.

Ritu had been right behind us.

Now she's gone. The only vestige is a rustling commotion along one long row of hanging armor coveralls—a fading wavelet in a rippling sea of shrugging torsos and helmets that nod and bow politely in her wake.

34

Fishing Real

. . . as Little Red gets jerked around . . .

It can be hard to penetrate the mind of a genius.

That's usually no cause for worry, since true brilliance has a well-known positive correlation with decency, much of the time—a fact the rest of us rely on, more than we ever know. The real world doesn't roil with as many crazed artists, psychotic generals, dyspeptic writers, maniacal statesmen, insatiable tycoons, or mad scientists as you see in dramas.

Still, the exceptions give genius its public image as a mixed blessing—vivid, dramatic, somewhat crazy, and more than a little dangerous. It helps promote the romantic notion, popular among borderline types, that you must be outrageous to be gifted. Insufferable to be remembered. Arrogant to be taken seriously.

Yosil Maharal must have watched too many bad movieds while growing up, for he swallowed that cliché whole. Alone in his secret stronghold, without anyone to answer to—not even his real self—he can ham up the mad scientist role, to the hilt. Worse, he thinks something about me offers the key to a puzzle—his sole chance at eternal life.

Trapped in his laboratory, helplessly shackled down, I start to feel a well-known pull—the salmon reflex. A familiar call that most high-level golems feel at the end of a long day. The urge to hurry home for inloading, only now amplified many times by strange machinery.

I've always been able to shrug it off, when necessary. But this time the reflex is intense. An agonizing need, as I yank against the bonds holding me down, struggling heedless of any damage to my straining limbs. A million years of instinct tell me to protect the body I'm wearing. But the *call* is stronger. It says this body doesn't matter any more than a cheap set of paper clothes. Memories are what count. . . .

No. Not memories. Something more. It's . . .

I don't have a scientist's terminology. All I know right now is craving. To return. To get back into my real brain.

A brain that no longer exists, according to ditYosil, who informed me a while ago that the real body of Albert Morris—the body my mother spilled into the world more than twelve thousand days ago—was blown to bits late Tuesday. Along with my house and garden. Along with my school report cards and Cub Scout uniform. Along with my athletic trophies and the master's thesis I always meant to finish someday . . . and souvenirs from more than a hundred cases that I solved, helping to expose villains, sending the worst of them to therapy or jail.

Along with the bullet scar in my left shoulder that Clara used to stroke during lovemaking, sometimes adding toothmarks that would fade gradually from my resilient realflesh. Flesh that is no more. So I'm told.

I have no way to know if Maharal is telling the truth about this calamity. But why lie to a helpless prisoner?

Damn. I worked *hard* on that garden. The sweet-pit apricots would've ripened next week.

Good, I'm getting somewhere with this approach—distracting myself with useless internal chatter. It's a way to fight back. But how long can I keep it up before the amplified homing reflex tears me apart?

Worse, the golem-Maharal is talking too. Jabbering on while he labors at his console. Maybe he does it for his nerves. Or as part of a devilish plot to harass mine.

". . . so you see it all started *decades* before Jefty Annonas discovered the Standing Wave. Two fellows named Newberg and d'Aquili traced variations in human neural function, using primitive, turn-of-the-century imaging machines. They were especially interested in differences that appeared in the orientation area, at the top rear of the brain, during meditation and prayer.

"They discovered that spiritual adepts—from Buddhist monks to ecstatic evangelicals—all apparently learned how to quell activity in this special neural zone, whose function is to weave sensory data together, creating a feeling of where the self ends and the rest of the world begins.

"What these religious seekers were able to do was *eliminate* the perception of a boundary or separation between self and world. One effect—a presentiment of cosmic union or oneness with the universe—came accompanied by release of endorphins and other pleasure chemicals, reinforcing a desire to return to the same state again and again.

"In other words, prayer and meditation induced a physicochemical *addiction* to holiness and unity with God!

"Meanwhile, other investigators plumbed for the seat of *consciousness,* or the imaginary locus where we envision our essential selves to exist. Westerners tend to picture this locale centered behind the eyes, looking out through them, like a tiny homunculus-self riding around inside the head. But some non-Western tribes had a different image—believing that their true selves dwelled in the chest, near the beating heart. Experimenters found they could persuade individuals to shift this sense of locality, where self or soul resides. You could be trained to envision it *outside* your body. Riding some nearby object . . . even a doll made of clay!"

Amid this ongoing rant, the professor occasionally pauses to offer me a smile.

"Think of the excitement, Albert! At first, these clues came with no apparent connection. But soon, brave visionaries began realizing what they were onto! Pieces of a great puzzle. Then a *gateway* to a realm fully as vast as the grand universe of physics . . . and just as full of possibilities."

Helplessly, I watch as he cranks a big dial up another notch. The machine above me gives a preliminary groan, then sends yet another jolt into my little red-orange head. I manage to choke back a moan, not wanting to give him any satisfaction. For distraction, I keep mumbling this running commentary . . . even though I have no recorder and the words are futile, vanishing into entropy as I think them.

That's beside the point. I keep telling myself to *find a habitual be-havior and stick to it!* Venerable advice for the helpless prisoner, offered long ago by a survivor of far worse torment than Maharal could ever dish out. Advice that helps me now as—

Another jolt impales my skull! My back arches in spasms. Writhing, I feel wracked by a *need* to return.

But return where? How? And *why* is he doing this to me?

Suddenly I notice something through the pane of glass dividing Yosil's lab. On the other side I see grayAlbert. The ditto who was captured at the Kaolin Estate on Monday. The one who was brought here, replen-ished and then used as a template to make *me*.

Each time this body of mine wrenches, so does the gray!

Is Maharal doing the same thing to us both, simultaneously? I see no big machine like this one aimed at the gray.

That means something else is happening. That ditto is somehow feel-ing what I feel! We must be—agh!

That was a bad one. I bit down so hard I might have broken a tooth, if I were real.

Got to speak. Before the next jolt.

"Rem—em—emo—"

"What is that, Albert? Are you trying to say something?"

Yosil's ditto hovers near, offering faux sympathy. "Come on, Albert. You can do it!"

"Remo—tuh. . . . Re-mote! Y-you're t-tryin-ing to do r-r-r—"

"Remote-imprinting?" My captor chuckles. "You *always* guess the same thing. No, old friend. It's nothing as mundane as that old dream. What I'm trying to achieve is much more ambitious. Phase-synchronizing the pseudo-quantum soul states of two related but spatially separated standing waves. Exploiting the deep entanglement of your Shared Ob-server Unification Locus. Does that mean anything to you?"

Shivering. Jaws chattering.

"Sh-shar-shared observ—"

"We talked about this before. The fact that each person helps to make the universe happen by acting as an observer, collapsing the probability amplitudes and . . . oh, never mind. Let's just say that all copies of a Standing Wave remain entangled with the original version. Even yours, Albert, though you give your golems remarkable leeway.

"I want to *use* the connection! Ironically, that requires severing the original link, the only way it can be severed . . . by eliminating the tem-plate prototype."

"Y-you k-killed—"

"The original Albert Morris, using a stolen missile? Of course. Didn't we already cover that?"

"Yourself. You killed yourself!"

This time, the gray golem before me winces.

"Yes, well . . . that, too. And it wasn't easy, believe me. But I had reasons."

"R-reasons . . . ?"

"Had to act fast, too. Before I realized fully what I was up to. Even so, I nearly got away from me, speeding along that desert highway."

It's getting harder to talk . . . even to grind out single words . . . especially each time another spasm strikes. The relentless pummeling of the machine, plucking the chords of my Standing Wave with a sharp *twang* . . . makes me cry out to escape . . . to rush back for inloading . . . to a home brain that no longer exists.

Uhn! That was bad. How much worse can it get?

All right, think! Suppose the real me is gone. What about the gray in the next room? Can I dump this soul back into *him?* Without inloading apparatus to connect us, he might as well be on the Moon.

Unless . . .

. . . unless Maharal expects something else to happen. Something— *uhn!*—unconventional.

Can it . . . can it be that I'm expected to *send* something . . . some essence of me . . . across the room and through that glass wall to my gray, without any thick cryo-cables or any of the normal inloading junk connecting us?

Before I can even begin to ask, I sense another jolt gathering strength, a big one, readying to strike.

Damn, this one's gonna hurt . . .

35

Glazed and Confused

... as Tuesday's gray gets the urge ...

Damn. What was that?

Did I just imagine a wave of something, passing through me, like a hot wind?

I could be making it up. Strapped to a table, unable to move, sentenced to the worst fate possible.

Thinking.

Ever since Maharal made me imprint that little red-orange copy and left me here to stew, I've been trying to come up with a clever escape plan. Something all those other captive Alberts never tried before. Or, failing that, some way to get a message out to real-me. A warning about Yosil's techno-horror show.

Yeah, I know. As if. But scheming, no matter how futile, helps pass the time.

Only now I'm getting surges of weird anxiety. Flickering almost-images, too brief to recall, like fragments of a dream. When I chase them using free association, all that comes to mind is a vast row of silent figures ... like the statues of Easter Island. Or pieces on a giant chessboard.

Every few minutes, there's another episode of wild, claustrophobic *need*. To leave this prison. To go home. To flee this stifling body I'm wearing and get back into the one that counts. One made of nearly immortal flesh.

And now, something like an ugly rumor whispers, *There's no me any longer to go home to anymore.*

36

Kiln Street Blues

. . . Greenie goes gallivanting . . .

Dittotown? Sherds!

Departing the Temple of the Ephemerals, Palloid and I hurried down Fourth Avenue past dinobuses that bellowed and snorted, hauling in cheap factory laborers, round the clock. Truckbills and brontolorries grunted at each other, jostling to deliver their wares, while errand boys sprinted by on gangly legs, stepping over the bowed heads of stubby epsilons, who marched to underground workpits without a thought or care. Obsessive little dit-devils scurried about, sweeping up any debris or trash, keeping the street spotless. And striding imperiously amid all these disposables were lordly grays, ivories, and ebonies, carrying the most precious cargo of all—*memories* that real human beings may actually want to inload at day's end.

Dittotown is part of modern life, so why did it feel so unfamiliar this time? Because of all I've learned as a frankie, at the ripe old age of almost two?

Ducking past the Teller Building, where Tuesday's raid led poor Albert into troubles beyond his ability to cope, I hurried down a "shortcut" recommended by the little weasel-shaped fellow riding on my shoulder. Soon we left the commercial district with its bustling factories and offices, and plunged south into the backstreet area—a world of decaying structures, reckless whims, and short-term prospects.

The dittos that you'll find in that area were sent on missions that have little to do with business or industry.

One flashing sign yelled E-VISCERAL! Touts stood outside, dyed in garish colors, beckoning passersby to enter for "the trip of your lives." Through gutted walls I saw that a twenty-story building had been converted into one giant thrill ride . . . a wildly gyrating roller coaster without straps or safety backups, and with the added feature that many customers had guns—trading shots with those streaking past them in other cars. What fun.

Next came a row of mud-pimperies and d-brothels—with exaggerated holems of all kinds leering out of brightly curtained windows—for those who can't afford to have their fantasies special-made and delivered to their door.

There followed some of the same soot-wracked battle lanes that I visited as a teen, still marked with flickertape risk warnings and cheap kiosks renting weapons to those who neglect to bring their own. *Free head-collection,* yammered one flasher-ad, as if any of these places would dare charge for the traditional service. *Let Us Stage Your Gang Rumble!* another yelled. *Discounts for Birthday Parties!*

You know. The usual ditritus. Embarrassing reminders of youth.

It was distracting for another reason. My skin had started *shedding*. The gray coating that had seemed so posh and high-class back at Kaolin Manor, when I got my renewal treatment for another day of life, was apparently no more than a cheap spray-on. Once it started peeling, the whole thing came away in strips, taking away the red-orange layer underneath. Rubbing away the itchy stuff, I found myself rapidly regaining this body's original hue—utility green. Good for mowing the lawn and cleaning the bathroom. Not for playing detective.

"Turn left here, then right at the next intersection," Palloid urged. His claws dug in. "But watch out for Capulets."

"Watch out for *what?*"

I saw what he meant in a few minutes, rounding a corner, then stopping in surprise to stare down a street that had been expensively transformed since the last time I ventured this far into dittotown—an entire city block, meticulously rebuilt as a lost fragment of Renaissance Italy, from cobblestones all the way to a garish Brunelleschi fountain in the grand piazza, facing a romanesque church. Towering at both ends were two ornate fortress-mansions, their balconies festooned with the fluttering banners of competing noble houses. Multicolored bravos leaned from terraces to shout at those passing below, or swaggered on patrol, sporting flounces over gartered tights and bulging codpieces. Buxom females dragged around tents of ornate silken fabric, strolling past shopkeepers hawking tastefully archaic merchandise.

Such a lavishly expensive recreation seemed rather much for dittotown, where the whole thing might be wrecked the next time a nearby golemwar got out of hand, spilling bazookafire over the border. But I soon realized, risk was the very justification for its existence. The reason for its inditgenous population.

Shouting broke out near the fountain. One fellow in red and white stripes nudged another whose skin and clothes both featured polka-dot motifs ... each the livery of a feuding house. Bright rapiers abruptly whistled, clanging like harsh bells, while a crowd gathered to cheer and wager in faux-Shakespearean lingo.

Ugh, I thought, getting it. *One of them must be Romeo. I wonder if all members of the club take turns with the role, or if it's a matter of seniority. Maybe they auction off the honor daily, to finance this place.*

Unemployed and bored with cautious play-acting in the suburbs, these aficionados must get up early to send dittos here each crack of dawn, then spend all restless day at home, eagerly awaiting another headful of drama—whether dead or alive. Nothing they might legally experience in realflesh could match the vivid, alternate life they led here.

And I thought *Irene* was weird!

Easy, Albert, a part of me chided. *You have a job and lots more. The real world has meaning to you. Others aren't so lucky.*

Oh yeah? answered another inner voice. *Shut up, twit. I'm not Albert.*

Several polka-dot bravos turned away from the duel to eye Palloid and me, as we passed under a nearby flowered colonnade. They glowered, hands drifting to pommels.

Must be Capulets, I realized, offering a quick, inoffensive bow and hurrying onward, with averted eyes.

Thanks, Pal. Some shortcut.

Some *trend.* I soon learned that whole sector of dittotown had been given over to simulations, whole stretches of abandoned buildings finding new life as imitation worlds. The next block had a Wild West theme, complete with sauntering gunslingers dyed in every shade of the Painted Desert. Another streetscape followed some glassy-metallic sci-fi scenario that I didn't have time to figure out as we hustled by. The common touch was danger, of course. Oh sure, *digital* virtual reality offers an even wider range of weird locales, vividly rendered in the privacy of your own chador. But not even touchie attachments can make VR feel *real.* Not like this. No wonder the cyber realm is mostly for cyberfarts.

The next zone was the grandest of all, and most terrifying.

It spanned six whole blocks, with giant holo screens at both ends, fostering the illusion of an endless, sweeping cityscape. A *cruel* cityscape of dilapidated tenements and chilling familiarity. A world my parents used to describe to me. The Transition Perdition. That era of fear and war and rationing was nearly over by the time I was born, when the dittoboom began delivering its cornucopia, along with the purple wage. But mental scars from the Perdition still afflict my folks' generation, even now.

Why? I wondered, while staring at the vast imitation. Why would anyone go to so much expense and care, trying to recreate a hell we so narrowly escaped? Even the air seemed hazy with something acrid that stung the eyes. "Smog," I think it was called. Talk about verisimilitude.

"We're almost there," Palloid urged. "Third brownstone on the left. Then head upstairs."

I followed his directions, taking the front steps of a run-down brick apartment building two at a time. The realistic lobby featured water dripping into a bucket and peeling, old-fashioned wallpaper. I'm sure I would have smelled urine, had I been equipped with full senses.

No one was out and about as I climbed three flights. But I heard noises behind closed doors—angry, eager, passionate, or violent sounds— even the yelling of children. *Most of it is probably computer-generated, for realism,* I thought. *In order to make the place appear crowded to customers.* Still, why would anyone want to experience such a life, even on a whim?

My companion pointed down a dingy hallway. "I rented one of these little flats a few months ago, to serve as a safehouse for special meetings. Best to have our rendezvous here, instead of my real home. Anyway, it's closer."

He aimed me to a door with the number 2-B spelled in flaking decals. I knocked.

"Enter!" a familiar voice shouted.

The knob turned under my hand—expensively machined metal parts, lavishly rusted to give a satisfying squeak. So did the hinges, as I pushed into a room decorated in Early Bachelor Shabby.

Several people stood when I entered, except of course the one I'd come to see. Pal's life-support chair whirred as it rolled forward and lifted to two wheels, a modern techno-anomaly amid all this ersatz poverty.

"Gumby! I gave up on you—till I got that report of yours an hour ago. What an adventure! Fighting your way into Universal Kilns! A prion attack! Did you really see a Morris gray climb up the ass of a *forklift?*" He guffawed. "Then a face-off with Aeneas Kaolin. And I can't wait to inload all that fun stuff at Irene's!"

Pal's burly hands reached for the ferretlike ditto, but Palloid suddenly went shy, backing around my neck to the other shoulder. "That can wait," the littler version of my friend snapped. "First, why is Gadarene here, and who are these other guys?"

I had also recognized the golem-hating fundamentalist. His presence in dittotown was like the Pope coming to Gehenna. The poor fellow must be desperate and it showed on his real face.

A green stood opposite Gadarene and I figured it could only be Lum, the emancipation fanatic. This cheap clay visage bore only a passing resemblance to his wide-cheeked original, but it nodded with polite familiarity.

"So you made it out of UK, ditMorris! I was skeptical when Mr. Montmorillin urged us to hurry down here for a meeting. Naturally, I'd love to know how you got your extended lifespan. This could be a real boon to the oppressed!"

"Nice to see you, too," I answered. "And explanations will come in due time. First, who is he?"

I pointed to Pal's third guest. A golem dyed in mauve shades, with a risqué tan stripe spiraling around from the top of his head all the way down. The ditto's chosen face was unfamiliar, but the *smile* gave me a sudden sense of worrisome familiarity.

"So we meet again, Morris," the spiraled copy said, in a speech rhythm that scraped raw memories. "If our paths keep crossing, I'll start to think you're following me."

"Yeah, right. And greetings to you too, Beta." Much as I hated this guy, I sure needed to ask him some questions.

"I think it's time we talk about Aeneas Kaolin."

37

Ditrayal

. . . realAlbert hurts a digit . . .

I finally gave up trying to subvocalize in realtime. It was too exhausting, using that little jaw-powered recorder. My real body isn't designed for it! Anyway, things got way too busy, right after Ritu abandoned us in that vast underground base, disappearing amid a great army of silent defender dolls.

At first, Corporal Chen and I could only stare in amazement. Where did she go? Why on earth would she leave us, especially in that spooky cavern of all places?

Chen was torn. He wanted to drag me out of there, now that he had seen auditors sniffing around, perhaps investigating who stole the missile that had "killed" me. On the other hand, the ditto-corporal couldn't just abandon Ritu Maharal, letting a civilian—a real one—roam around the hidden base unescorted.

"Do you have any gear that can track residual body heat?" I asked in a low whisper, gesturing at the suits of battle armor hanging in neat rows that stretched forever. "Or something that'll pick up metabolic by-products?"

My apelike companion glowered.

"If I admit that, you could have a whistle to blow."

"I might? Oh, yeah." The golem army is supposed to shield us against *other* golem armies. It might be harder to justify stockpiling stuff that can hunt down *real* people. Only the police are supposed to have things like that, under lock and key.

I shrugged. "I guess we'll just let Ritu wander around, then. If she gets lost, she can use one of those big machines to wake some soldier and ask directions. Did I mention she works for Universal Kilns?"

Chen growled. "Dammit! Okay. Follow me."

He swiveled around and hurried, striding bowlegged toward one end of the vast dressing room.

Most of the helm-and-coverall suits were measured for outsized bodies like those we'd seen in the Hall of Guardians. How did this particular Corporal Chen hoped to fit in one? I soon got my answer. The last few dozen rows held an assortment of garments, in all sizes, featuring wildly varying numbers of limbs and appendages. Apparently, there were specialized combat-dittos we never saw on TV, even in major league wars.

"The suits with green and amber stripes are scout models," he explained. "They have adaptive camouflage and full sensoria . . . including some that might serve our needs in tracking down . . . um . . . in finding and helping Miss Maharal."

Chen was clearly nervous about this. His eyes darted and I could guess what he was thinking. It might have been simpler if Ritu kept her disguise on, as I did. But the makeup made her skin itch and she'd wiped it off.

"Could a real person use one of these?" I asked, fingering the sleeve of one armored uniform, hanging nearby.

"Could a—oh, I get you. If *Ritu* climbed into a suit and sealed up properly, she wouldn't leave an organic residuals trail after that. Yeah. First thing I should check is whether she came this way."

Chen grabbed a scout ensemble—much shorter than average, to

roughly fit his simian dittobody—and began working the zippers. I stood behind, reaching out, as if to help . . .

. . . and seized him round the shoulders with my left arm, grabbing his head tightly with my right, bearing down hard.

I had a couple of things going in my favor—strong realhuman muscles and the element of surprise. But how many fractions of a second before his soldier training kicked in, erasing the advantage?

"Wha—?" He dropped the garment and grabbed at my arms, crying out, trying to whirl, clutching for a hold.

Chen might be a pro, but I knew a thing or two about betrayal and murder. And his tax collector body wasn't top-of-the-line. The neck snapped, just in time, as he yanked hard on my thumb, causing an incendiary eruption of pain.

"Ow!" I yelped, letting go and shaking the offended digit.

The golem slipped out of my arms and fell to the floor. Supine and paralyzed, he was still able to watch me curse and dance and suck my thumb.

I saw realization fill his eyes.

Chen knows I'm real. And that he hurt me.

Even as the light of consciousness began to fade, the ditto's mouth moved, forming a single word, without air to give it voice.

"Sorry," he mouthed.

Then the active Standing Wave went flat. I could see it . . . almost feel it go away.

■   ■   ■

My next move was obvious. I still needed that secure web port Chen first promised, and he had just shown me how to get there safely, by wearing one of those "scout" ensembles. Its sensor array should help me detect and avoid those Dodecahedron auditors we spotted. And perhaps catch Ritu's trail, if I was lucky.

Frankly, her disappearance wasn't my biggest concern. As soon as I got properly zip-sealed and was sure of air, I bent over to pick up the clay figure at my feet. Poor ditChen. I'd like to say my aim was to get him to a freezer, and save the day's mortal memories. But I just needed a place to stash the decaying clay out of sight, preferably an anonymous recycling bin.

Anyway, the real Corporal Chen wouldn't benefit by downloading what had happened here today. The best favor I could do for him was erase his involvement.

All right, maybe that was rationalization. I had cut him down for one reason, above all. As soon as he donned a scout suit, he would have begun scanning for a real human . . . and would've found one standing right next to him. Damn inconvenient for me. I couldn't allow it.

I think he understood, at the end.

There was no recycling bin nearby, so I pried out his dogtag pellet and stuffed the rest of him into a refuse can.

I'll make it up to Chen, if I ever get out of this mess. Someday I'll insist on buying him dinner. Though he'll never have any idea why.

■ ■ ■

It took only a few minutes to get a feel for the scout gear and adjust the camouflage settings to background light levels. Like a squid or octopus, the light-sensitive skin rippled to match whatever lay on the other side of me. A blurry rendition, to be sure. Not true invisibility, but a much better version than you can buy nowadays at the Hobby Store. Good enough to fool most edge-and-movement pattern recognition systems—digital, organic, or clay.

Yup. Even after the Big Deregulation, the guvvies still manage to spend our tax dollars developing cool things.

With the sensors of my scout uniform set to maximum wariness, I set out for the site where Chen had spotted those auditors. Maybe I'd try to eavesdrop for a while and find out why they suspected that stolen military hardware was used in my assassination. Even more important, that secure net-access port must lie somewhere beyond the weapons hall.

I also hoped to find a snack machine. Surely real people came down here *sometimes!* Being organic is nice, but it has disadvantages. By that point, I was so hungry that even self-hypnosis couldn't drive away the pangs anymore.

It made me thankful the scout uniform had sound dampers. My growling stomach seemed loud enough to wake the sleeping army next door!

Here's to high technology.

38

I, Amphorum

Like a container—or several—spilling over at the rim, I fill up.
My only desire? To empty all these vessels that I am!

■   ■   ■

The urge to reunite . . . to recombine . . . to rejoin, overwhelms me.
But *which* me?
What me?
Why, when, and *where* me?
All the famed journalistic double-U questions, turning around to bite the reporter.
Double-U. Double-yous. Identical, yet *different.* For one of me knows things the other doesn't.
One has seen clay jars from shipwrecks two thousand years old. Mother- or whore-goddess figures that were molded out of river mud twenty millennia ago. Wedgelike symbols, pressed by hand, way back when hands first learned to scribble thoughts . . .
One has seen all those things. The other me writhes, wondering where all these images are coming from. Not memories, but fresh, immanent, experience in the raw and actual.

■   ■   ■

I know what Maharal is doing. How could I *not* know?
Yet the aim of all this torment remains obscure. Has he gone mad? Do all dittos face the same fate when they become ghosts, cast adrift without the anchor of a soul-home?
Or is he exploring a new way for the Standing Wave to vibrate? Multifariously.
I do feel less like an individual actor. More like an entire cast. An arena.
I am a forum.

■   ■   ■

Ack! This isn't at all like the familiar sensation of inloading we all know—passively absorbing memories as a soul-wave replica flows back to combine with the original. Instead, two waves seem to stand in parallel, gray and red but equal in status, both interfering and reinforcing, jostling toward mutual coherence . . .

And droning in the background, like a bad tour guide or a hated lecturer, the voice of ditYosil tells me, over and over again, that *observers make the universe.* Oh, he teases and taunts with every rising throb of the salmon reflex, urging me to "go home" to a self-base that longer exist.

"Answer me a riddle, Morris," my tormentor asks.

"How can you be in two places at once, when you're not anywhere at all?"

PART III

With earth's first clay they did the last man knead,
 There of the last harvest sowed the seed,
 And what the first morning of creation wrote,
 The last dawn of reckoning shall read.

—Edward Fitzgerald,
Rubáiyat of Omar
Khayyám

39

Only Some Lads

. . . as Greenie has an escapade . . .

The golem with the tan spiral offered some personal recollections to prove he was Beta . . . things only he and Albert Morris should know from past encounters between two adversaries. Actions, deceptions, insults, and secret details from times when I barely escaped his clutches— or he mine.

"It sounds like you two have been engaged in an ongoing role-claying game," remarked Lum.

"A childish one," commented the soul-conservative, Gadarene.

"Perhaps," Beta's ditto answered. "But a game with serious money at stake. One reason I had to expand my business was in order to set aside enough cash to pay off the accumulating fines. In case Albert here finally caught the real me."

"Don't blame Albert for your career as a ditnapping thief," I grumbled. "Anyway, I'd wager everything I own that you've got bigger troubles now. A whole lot worse than civil liens for copyright violation. You've attracted new enemies, haven't you? More dangerous than any local private eye."

Beta conceded the point with a nod. "For months, I felt a hot breath on my neck. One by one, my operations were meticulously targeted by someone who would break in suddenly, using prion bombs to slaughter my copies—and the templates I'd stolen—or else he'd take over the operation for a few days, before burning it all to cover the evidence."

"Huh. That explains something that happened at the Teller Building," I commented. "On Monday, you temporarily captured my green scout. At least I thought it was you. But my captors seemed more vicious, even kind of frantic. They actually tried using *torture*—"

"That wasn't me," Beta assured grimly.

"Hm, well, I escaped, barely. And on Tuesday morning I returned with Inspector Blane and some LSA enforcers to raid the joint. That went well. But later, around back of the building, I ran into a decaying yellow who claimed to be you, muttering something about how a competitor was 'taking over.'

"Do you have any idea who's been doing all this?"

"At first I suspected *you,* Morris. Then I realized it had to be someone really competent—" Beta glanced at me, but I refused the bait, keeping a poker face. So the sardonic ditto resumed. "Someone who was able to track down my clandestine copying centers, one by one, despite every precaution. As a desperate measure, I used my best evasion methods to stash emergency backups in secret portakilns, programmed to thaw after some delay."

"You are one of those pre-imprinted copies?" Lum asked. "How old are your memories? When were you made?"

Beta's ditto grimaced. "More than two weeks ago! I might have stayed dormant in that tiny niche forever, if Albert's news hadn't arrived, triggering reanimation. At that point, I contacted Mr. Montmorillin here, who kindly invited me to this meeting." The spiral golem indicated Pal.

I sat up. "You say, 'Albert's news—' "

The other realperson present, James Gadarene, stomped a foot. "Whoa! First let's establish something, this Beta person, a notorious underworld figure, really was engaged in a plot with 'Queen' Irene and Gineen Wammaker—"

"We haven't yet determined if the maestra herself—"

Gadarene shot me a glare. Remembering my place, I grunted apologetically and shut up.

"So," he resumed. "We're expected to believe that Beta and Irene and Wammaker really were planning to invade UK in a semi-innocent effort to uncover hoarded technologies. Even if that's true, I doubt they had the public's benefit in mind. More likely extortion! A scheme to blackmail Aeneas Kaolin into buying their silence."

Beta conceded with a shrug. "Cash is nice. We also wanted the new ditto-extension technique. Irene was running out of organic memory and needed to slow her inloads. Wammaker and I saw commercial benefits to extending the duration of our copies—her legal ones and my pirated rip-offs." Beta laughed. "Our alliance was one of temporary convenience."

"Never mind that." Gadarene leaned forward. "In order to carry out your espionage mission, you planned to hire your ongoing nemesis, Ditective Albert Morris. Wasn't that risky?"

Beta nodded. "It's why I pretended to be that Vic Collins character. Anyway, why *not* hire Albert? The job suited his abilities."

"Only some enemy hunted you down first. He *replaced* you, then changed the aim of the mission. Is that what we're expected to believe?"

A high-pitched version of Pal's voice called from a table nearby. The little ferret-golem—Palloid—manipulated a holo viewer. "I've got that film roll we found at Irene's. Ready to show 'em what you discovered, Gumby?"

I nodded. Images erupted from the viewer, showing a series of clandestine meetings in limousines, between Irene and her confederates. I told the others about my close-in analysis of the plaid dye patterns worn by "Vic Collins."

Beta grinned at the compliment when I said, "That was a neat trick, using tiny pixel emitters to change your skin motifs in a flash. It explains how you slipped my grasp a number of times. Apparently, your enemy didn't know about the technique. Or else he didn't care. Because when he took over, he just copied your latest dye job and moved right in. Irene never noticed.

"It was a simple matter, then, for this enemy to alter your plan. Replace the espionage gear that you three intended to plant in Albert's gray, inserting a bomb instead, changing the goal from industrial espionage to sabotage. Is that right?"

Beta's golem shrugged. "My memories are two weeks old, so I can't testify about recent events . . . except to say that's consistent with what I feared. My nemesis must have completed his takeover of my entire operation." He smacked his palm angrily. "If only I had a clue who it was!"

Would it be wrong to confess feeling gratification at seeing Beta suffer, in the same way Albert had, for years—wondering and worrying about the identity of his arch foe?

"Well, I can't claim that I'm *competent,* Beta. But if it's a *clue* you want . . ."

At my nod, Palloid switched to the very last slide, showing a later "Vic Collins" with its stolid, unchanging tartan-styled skin. Only when the view zoomed closer . . . much closer . . . we could all see micro-peeling where the surface disguise gave away, revealing a different coloration underneath. A shimmering glint, like metal, only much brighter than steel. Lum's green golem walked closer, rubbing his chin as if he had a beard to scratch. "Why, that looks . . ."

His ideological opposite, Gadarene, finished for him. "It looks like white gold or platinum. Hey, you aren't trying to tell us *Aeneas Kaolin—*" The man gaped. "But why would a tycoon get his hands dirty, messing with scum like this?"

Gadarene gestured dismissively at Beta, who sat up, offended.

"More to the point," Pal added, scratching his own very real two-day beard. "What would he gain by sabotaging his own factory?"

"An insurance scam?" Lum guessed. "A way to write off obsolete stock?"

"No," Gadarene said, his teeth clenching. "It was a plot to eliminate all of his enemies, at once."

I nodded. "Consider the multiple layers of blame we have here. First, by completing your foolish tunnels into the UK complex, both of your groups"—I gestured at Lum and Gadarene—"dug yourselves a trap. The perfect scapegoats. Especially after someone sent those dittos, made up to resemble the apparent bomber, to meet with you the night before. Even if you manage to avoid jail or fines, you've suffered a major humiliation. Discredited, you look like fools."

"Huh, thanks," Lum grunted. Gadarene glowered silently.

"Then Kaolin had to get rid Albert, too," Pal said. "Is that why you got blown up, old friend? To keep you from denying involvement? Rather harsh! For one thing, the police take murder a lot more seriously than slaughtering a bunch of dittos."

I agreed.

"That part still doesn't make much sense. Anyway, what did poor Albert ever do to him?

"But the *next* layer fits everything we've heard this afternoon. Queen Irene realized, just as soon as she heard about the sabotage attack, that everything had gone horribly wrong. She arranged an exit under her own terms, leaving her partners, Vic Collins and Gineen Wammaker, to serve as the ultimate fall guys."

"And Irene left evidence indicating that *Collins* was *Beta,*" Palloid added.

"Yeah. And that's where the trail would have ended. With an infamous ditnapper and a renowned 'pervert' implicated at the bottom layer, caught in a fiendish alliance that went horribly wrong. A neat package, implicating or embarrassing a whole swathe of folks Kaolin hated—or merely found irritating."

Beta's spiral golem nodded.

"And the scheme might have worked, if not for these pictures Irene took, and some clever ditective work on your part. *Surprisingly* clever, Morris."

I could only shake my head. "Charming, to the last."

Pal rolled forward, inspecting the holo image. "This ain't a whole lot of evidence to go on. Especially when you're throwing accusations at a trillionaire."

"We don't need convincing evidence," Palloid snapped at his original. "Just enough probable cause to open a full investigation. With this, we can subpoena UK's inner camera network. Offer a Henchman Prize. Get the police in on it. Demand to see Kaolin himself, in the flesh—"

That's when it happened.

Something passed through me—it felt like a warm sigh of wind— urging me to turn around and *listen.*

I did, and immediately picked up a strange sound . . . a soft scraping at the door.

Then the door exploded.

■   ■   ■

Because I saw it coming, I barely dodged a huge splinter of wood, hurtling through the space where my head had been. Then the first armed invader charged through whirling smoke, guns ablaze.

Shifting to emergency speed, I threw myself at the wide-eyed James Gadarene, who yelped as I covered him with my body, bearing him to the ground. Accidents can happen during a melee, and whoever was barging in might not expect to find any real people here in dittotown, where the rule is often "shoot whatever moves." Gadarene kicked back with panicky strength, as if *I* were an attacker! So it took at least four seconds to bury the fool under a couch. By then, a red-hot battle raged.

The invaders wore crisscross stripes—gang colors. Wax Warriors, if I recalled right. And it *could* have just been a few lads, dropping by to have some fun—except for the coincidence of timing. Rising up, I saw that several assailants had already fallen at the door, cut down by Pal's uncannily swift reflexes—and the viciously effective scattergun he now held, pumping wide sprays of high-velocity pellets at the ruined entryway.

He wasn't alone. Pal's little ferret-duplicate stood on his right shoulder, firing a mini-pistol, their intrapersonal differences apparently forgotten. And Beta was busy, too. The spiral-patterned ditto had whipped out a slender blowgun with a forty-round magazine. With each puff of breath, he dispatched a self-targeting smart-dart toward a foe's ceramic eyes, bearing small payloads of trenchant enzymes.

Bodies piled near the shattered door, but more assailants kept spilling though, clambering or leaping over fallen comrades, firing as they came. Lamps and fixtures shattered all around.

"Gumby, catch!"

Pal tossed me the scattergun, grabbing another that popped from some recess in the mobile chair as I joined the fight. We fired together, just in time to thwart another rush.

A new clamor made me turn, catching movement outside the apartment window. More invaders teetered on the rickety fire escape, preparing to smash in.

"Lum!" I cried at the cheap green, sent to our meeting by the emancipation fetishist. "Guard the window!"

Lum spread his hands. "I'm unarmed!"

"Go!" I yelled, diving toward the front door and firing another blast as I rolled up by several steaming bodies. Grabbing a weapon from one still-twitching hand, I tossed it in a high arc toward the green mancie, hoping Lum would catch it and know what to do. "Beta, help Lum!" I shouted, dashing forward again.

Pressed against the wall, right next to the shattered door frame, I was suddenly in position to blast down the hallway in one direction, taking out a whole row of nasties who were waiting to charge in. The scattergun mowed them down like clay dolls slumping before a hose. Of course, that let the other half of the attacking force know exactly where I was.

A *thump* told me when someone slapped an object on the other side of the wall that I leaned against. I hurriedly backed away, two secs before an explosion showered the interior with debris, smashing a new opening four meters wide.

The window blew at the same moment. Glass sprayed everywhere. I heard gunfire from that quarter and hoped Lum would give a good account of himself.

My new position let me ambush about half of the new wave pouring in from the hall. A good ratio, if they cared about losses. Which they didn't, continuing their charge heedless of casualties. Palloid's mini-gun emptied and with no time to get another, the miniature golem leaped, flinging himself at the throat of a foe who reacted with reflexive surprise, stumbling backward into several fellows. The kamikaze attack kept that bunch busy for precious seconds while I blasted those behind. But the gesture ended predictably, with poor little Palloid smashed to bits.

That pissed me off, but not as much as Pal.

"Dammit, I wanted those memories!" he screamed, flinging his scattergun and grabbing another weapon from some recess of his chair. One glimpse made me quail. It was an evaporator.

Even battle-hardened gang members reacted with dismay, diving for cover. One was too late as a lump of unstable crystal collapsed in the firing chamber, sending a coherent blast of tuned microwaves boring right through him—*and* the wall behind.

Another pair arrived as reinforcements, stared at Pal, turned to flee . . . only to join a second wall section evaporating into oblivion.

"Behind you!" I screamed, standing to shoot my comparative popgun toward the window as Lum's hapless greenie was trampled by fresh invaders. No sign of Beta. No surprise there.

Swiveling his chair, Pal reloaded, then blasted another bolt of disintegrating microwaves at the newcomers, vaporizing one of them plus half of another—along with the window frame and part of the fire escape beyond.

To my relief, nobody fired back at him, even though he was in the open.

They can tell he's real and they don't want cops involved. The most they'll do to Pal is grab his gun and throw a tarp over him. Maybe try to force a forget-sniff up his nose, to erase the last hour or so.

Of course, that meant all the gunners turned on *me.* Bullets struck all around, edging closer, till Pal finished levering another crystal into place and waved the ray tube, preparing another blast. The Waxers scattered, dropping for cover, briefly giving me a respite.

Pal's eyes met mine, releasing me from my golem duty to defend any realfolks. These gangers were playing by the rules. "I'm safe," he growled, snatching my roll of film from the nearby holo reader and tossing it to me. "Go!"

With a quick nod to my friend, I rolled to one side, scrambled up, then dashed across the room, taking a shallow dive behind the kitchen counter just in time as sprays of pellets tore the faux-wood panels, ricocheting amid pots and pans. Thank heavens the place came furnished.

"Come on, bastards!" Pal screamed while charging his semi-illegal weapon one more time. "Pathetic, punks. *Shoot me!"*

There was a sob in his voice—a pain that even his best friend rarely heard. And yes, part of me sympathized, hoping Pal would finally get the kind of death he wanted. With a bang, no whimper.

They were closing in. Surely his Big Gun must be running out of fist-size charges. My own weapon had just a few rounds. I heard skirmishers approaching from three sides. It looked bad.

Then the wall *behind* me evaporated in a sudden cloud of hot, expanding gases.

"Gumby, run!" Pal cried.

I was already through, pounding past surprised tenants of the apartment next door—a simulacrum family who stared at me goggle-eyed, cowering behind their sofa while a cheap TV in the corner blared theme music for the *Cassius and Henry Show.*

Fortunately, they were all dittos, play-acting life in a more adventurous age. So I charged past them guilt-free. Any fines resulting from this interruption will be simple. Damages only. No punitives.

Anyway, who are they gonna bill?

40

Friends in Knead

. . . as realAlbert finds a connection . . .

There is something quaintly sweet and old-timey about the electronic world of "artificial intelligence" and computer-generated images.

All right, my generation tends to look down on antique hackers and cybergeezers, many of them still clinging to their vain faith in digital transcendence—a miscarried dream of super-smart machines, downloaded personalities, and virtual worlds more real than reality. It's become a joke.

Worse, it's turned into another hobby.

Yet, I confess that I do love this stuff. Cruising the Old Web in search of hidden info-troves. Skating from one camera view to the next. Setting up little micro-avatars to go plunging into databases that are so thick and sedimentary with more than a century's layered gigabytes that your software emissaries come equipped with pickaxes and headlamps. You nearly always have to specify exactly what you're looking for in order for them to draw anything useful at all.

Still, pluck and persistence *can* bring up gems. Like the fact that Yosil Maharal served as a highly paid consultant for the Dodecahedron.

It fits—he was a world-renowned expert in soulistics, known for original thinking. Naturally, the Dodecs—and perhaps even the President's team in the Glasshouse—would've consulted Maharal, in order to plumb the next stage. Get a handle on what's coming. Scope out what new technologies may already be in the hands of potential enemies. He was also a chief adviser and designer when they planted this giant reserve army of battle-golems deep under the Jesse Helms Range.

I learned about all this while using the secure dataport that Chen's ditto had been leading us toward, before Ritu vanished and I had to make the little, apelike tax collector go away. Things felt bleak now, without company, though solitude allowed me to concentrate without interruption.

It seems they pretty much gave Maharal carte blanche, I realized, waggling my fingers and hands beneath an ultra-secure, government-issue chador. Several viewglobes grew and shrank, responding to my flitting eyes. One conveyed a surface map of the region, portraying the army base with its training, relaxation, tanning, and imprinting facilities, along with nearby four-star hotels that cater to avid fight fans. Some distance southwest, beyond a sheer escarpment, lay the battleground itself, where national teams fight for glory and to settle disputes without bloodshed. In a region as cratered as the Moon, a patch of desert had been sacrificed for sport, and to spare the rest of the planet from war.

That much the public knew.

Only now I could also follow a maze of tunnels and caverns *below* the base, heading in the opposite direction. A secret fortress created for a vast army of ready-to-serve warriors. Some portions were openly labeled. Other areas were mere vague outlines on the map, shaded to indicate stronger layers of secrecy, requiring passwords and ID verifiers I lacked. Nor did I care about that. Matters of national security didn't interest me. What riveted my attention was the fact that this network of man-made caves appeared to stretch quite some distance eastward, beyond the formal military zone, deep below state and private lands.

Toward Urraca Mesa—I saw—*the destination Ritu and I were aiming for when we first set out, Tuesday night.*

Coincidence? I had already begun to suspect that Yosil Maharal chose the site of his "vacation cabin" with great care, many years ago.

Bodily pangs forced me to shrug off the chador and switch to old-fashioned viewscreens, in order to drink and eat while I worked. Fortunately, this part of the cavern was also a National Leadership Enclave—a habitat set aside for high government officials, in case of some dire emergency. Food and other provisions lay plentifully stacked on nearby shelves. At first sight, the cans and packages looked untouched, but quite a few were missing in back, as if someone had been raiding the larder, carefully rearranging intact goods up front to hide the pilferage. I availed myself of my first fully satisfying meal in two days—my tax dollars well spent, I figure—plus a double mug of fizzy Liquid Sleep. That helped a lot. Still, I found myself wishing I were black instead of organic brown. I concentrate much better when I'm ebony.

"Superimpose the location of the mountain cabin owned by Yosil Maharal," I ordered.

The spot instantly glimmered onscreen—a flashing amber speck at the end of a winding road. If I asked to zoom closer, the computer would retrieve recent skyviews showing the house and drive, or even catalogue nearby foliage by species and chlorophyll reflectivity profiles. The cabin lay a few kilometers beyond the easternmost extension of the underground golem base, separated from my present map locale by a single oblong plateau.

I no longer believed in coincidence.

"So, what d'you figure, Al?" I mumbled to myself. "Did Maharal *commute* all the way around that furshluginer mesa, in order to come down here through the front door? Naw, that wasn't the Professor's style. Come and go without a trace, that was Dr. Yosil! Even a back door would've left him open to detection and observation every time he came down here to raid the government's larder, or to pick up nifty items for his cloak-and-dagger scheme . . . whatever it was. Hell, some war fan with a wandering voyeur drone might have spotted him, if he came across the surface."

No, I went on silently. *If Professor Maharal had been sneaking into this base, he'd want to come all the way under concealment.*

Jabbing my finger repeatedly at the map-globe, I commanded, "Avatar, find microseismic data for the subregion indicated. Use a Schulman-Watanabe tomographic correlation to sift for unmapped subterranean passages, connecting *this* location and *that* one."

The military intelligence program I had hijacked was a pretty good one. Yet it balked, unable or unwilling to comply:

"The area in question was last given a detailed seismic survey eight years ago. At that time, no subterranean passages existed in the area you indicated. Since then, systematic seismometry in the specified region has been limited to watching for attempted area penetration by unauthorized interlopers. No inward-directed tunneling has been detected."

So. There had been no hidden passageways through the mesa when the secret base was established, and no sign of outsiders trying to get in since then. Was I barking up the wrong tree?

"Wait a minute. What about digging activity from *within* the base, aimed outward?"

I had to rephrase the question several times, forcing the avatar to reexamine the security system's record of micro-temblors and sonic vibrations in surrounding rock layers.

"What about areas on the base perimeter with seismic activity levels well above normal?"

"There have been no unexplained activity levels more than fifteen percent above normal."

Rats. So much for that idea. Too bad. It seemed a good one.

I was about to give up . . . then decided to follow this line just a bit farther. "Show me the highest-level activity loci *with* accepted explanations."

The map of the underground facility and its surroundings now bloomed with overlapping bands of color, showing peak levels of sonic and seismic noise during the last few years. "There," I pointed. An area at the perimeter zoomed toward me, haloed by ripples of red and orange. Appended was a notification—sealed and date-stamped—explaining that an ongoing program of boreholes had been ordered, for the purpose of groundwater quality sampling.

But a cross-check with the base environmental protection office showed no data from these samples! Moreover, the area in question happened to be at the exact spot closest to Urraca Mesa.

Bingo.

"So, Ritu. Your dad hacked the military's security system and forged approval for a seismic variance. All the cover he needed to burrow away to his heart's content. Impressive!

"Of course, it still meant having to dig *outward* from the interior, instead of coming in from the outside. What did Maharal do, smuggle in tunneling equipment?"

No, there was a better explanation. An easier way to get the job done.

I thought of checking the base master inventory, to see if someone had been pilfering from the golem stores, taking some of the raw soldier blanks away to use as mining labor. But those auditors Chen had spotted in the armory . . . they'd be accessing the inventory system right now for their tallies. They might notice if I snooped that database at the same time, secure portal or no.

Better go in person, then. See where this trail takes me.

I started to sign off, but hesitated, my eyes darting among the beautiful viewglobes floating above the desk, each of them responding to my attention by ballooning larger, eagerly, voluptuously. Linked to the wide world again, I felt it draw me, call to me, tempt me with opportunities—

To contact Clara and let her know I was alive.

To access Nell's emergency cache.

To communicate with Inspector Blane and find out what was new in the Beta Case.

To check police and insurance company reports about the sabotage attempt at Universal Kilns, and find out if I was still a "top suspect."

To get in touch with Pal and have him send a whole army of his wonderful sneak-and-grab dittos, to help me as I headed—vulnerably real—into hazardous territory.

I had meant to do all of those things, and more, when I first asked Chen's little ape-dit to find me a safe access port. Only now I held back.

Contacting Clara might only serve to implicate her in my actions, perhaps ruining her career.

Nell's cache? What could it contain that I didn't already know? All of my dittos vanished days ago. The last one—a sarcastic ebony—was blasted into supersonic pottery shards on Tuesday, around midnight. Since no one else knew how to access the cache, checking it would be a waste of time. Worse, it might alert my enemies.

As for the UK attack, blame seemed to be shifting already. Open news reports were now showing a raid—led by the LSA's Blane, of all people—breaking down the doors of a recently shuttered kink bar in dittotown, the Rainbow Lounge. A lurid tale of conspiracy, double-cross, and ritual suicide was rapidly unfolding. One disturbing image showed a cremated woman, surrounded by her own crisped dittos, like the pyre of some Viking potentate departing for Valhalla with an escort of sacrificed thralls.

Another view hovered over the maestra of Studio Neo, Gineen Wammaker, who swatted at voyeurcams that buzzed around her elegant head while denying that she had any part of the conspiracy, crying out, "I was framed!"

That made me chuckle . . .

. . . till I recalled what it meant. I wasn't the sole patsy, or the only person set up as a fall guy. Reputations were toppling all over town, from religious nuts to the ditto Emancipation movement, to purveyors of perversion like the maestra. Yet no one mentioned the three names that worried me most.

Beta. Kaolin. Maharal.

Seared in memory, I could still see that platinum golem suddenly appearing along a desert highway to bushwhack me. Because of something I knew? Or perhaps something I was *about* to find out—probably having to do with Kaolin's ex-partner and friend, with whom he was now at war. Somehow, I had become caught up in a desperate struggle between mad geniuses. And it didn't even matter that Yosil Maharal was dead! Nowadays, mere death offers no guarantees. In fact, I could *feel* Maharal's reach, extending beyond the grave, keeping the war hot. Driving the tycoon to desperate measures.

More to the point, Maharal had helped to design this very facility I was sitting in. Given his aptitude for skulduggery, Ritu's father might have laid any number of traps for the unwary. Especially if you stopped in one place too long.

Better to stay a moving target. Much as I wanted to linger and study the news, probing the Web for details, it really was time to get on.

I folded the government-issue chador under my belt, then headed east along a corridor I'd seen on the map—a passageway that supposedly should end about a hundred and fifty meters from there in a large storage room—followed by solid rock.

■   ■   ■

Only it wasn't just a storage room.

True, there were shelves, piled endlessly with machine parts and tools, followed by freezers containing hundreds of ditto blanks, still doughy and unimprinted, ready to be used by the Prexy and Dodecs, should they ever come down here to hide.

To the naked eye, it all seemed above board.

My eyes weren't nude, however. The scout uniform that I wore had lovely infrared scanners, pattern detectors and Dopplers that showed swirls and eddies in the way air gusted across the room. I was no expert at using all that stuff, but I wasn't exactly clueless, either. I learned as I searched. Anyway, it was obvious which wall to go to.

The seismic anomalies emanated from somewhere around here.

I didn't expect to find any obvious signs of a tunneling operation, but the place was actually spotless. Banks of tall, locked cabinets covered the wall in question, with no sign of anything behind them but native stone.

Which cupboard should this little doggie try? I pondered. *Even if I choose correctly, how do I get through? And what defenses might lie on the other side?*

Instrument readings didn't show much difference from one cabinet to the next. No swirls of cold, subterranean air leaking from the other side. No telltale heat signatures.

Maharal would've made sure that routine security patrols saw nothing to raise suspicions. Even in his arrogance, did the Professor imagine he could take on PEZ and the entire United States of America? Concealment was Yosil's only friend. No wonder he worked so hard at developing the skill.

I fingered the small sidearm that came with the scout uniform—a laser that could be adjusted into a tool for either a machinist or a sniper. Cutting through the locks would be no problem . . . and then through the backing of each cabinet till I struck a hidden passageway—or else learned the flaw in all my fancy reasoning.

What about sensors or booby traps? Could I find a way through without alerting whoever lurked on the other side of Urraca Mesa?

You keep thinking and acting as if Maharal is still alive!

Any tunnel was probably dusty and unused, ever since the professor crashed and burned way back on Monday. His residual golems would've decayed soon after that, leaving a silent sanctuary, with no one left to defend its secrets.

Sounds logical. Are you sure enough to stake your life on it?

Even if Maharal was dead, *Kaolin* had proved himself active, inimical, and willing to do almost anything. What if the trillionaire was already there, waiting at the other side?

Another notion occurred to me as I stood contemplating my next move—a piece of advice Clara once offered:

"When in doubt, try not to think like the dumb hero of some silly movied."

Charging into danger was one of those overused cinematic clichés, religiously adhered to by eight generations of brain-dead producers and directors. Another went: *A hero must always assume that the authorities are evil, or useless, or bound to misunderstand. It helps keep the plot rolling if your protagonist never thinks of calling for help.*

I had been operating under that assumption for two days. And, well, after all, the cops were after me! Officially as a "material witness," but clearly I had been set up to be blamed for the sabotage attempt at Universal Kilns. Not to mention the fact that someone had tried to blow me up.

Twice!

Still, things were changing. The police and military were clearly upset about the missile attack on my home. Surely some of them were honest and competent enough to realize there were layers to this whole affair, running below surface appearances. What if I showed them how Maharal had hacked the system here at the base, abusing their trust and creating a back entrance for his personal use? It might help clear my name. There could even be a whistle-blower award!

Suppose I were to phone up my attorney. Have her call a meeting. Bring the base commandant together with a commissioner from the Human Protection Unit and a licensed Fair Witness, to make sure nothing can get hidden away. . . . It *would* be a profound relief to tell all. The whole story, as far as I knew it. Just recount everything. Let battalions of professionals take over from there.

And yet, my gut churned at the thought. *It wouldn't feel right!*

I was still running on a high of anger and combat hormones—nothing else could have sustained me across the last few days. Indignation is a drug that burns long and hot. And it can only be properly experienced in your real body.

Me against Beta. Me against Kaolin. Me against Maharal. Bad guys, all of them, each in his own brilliantly evil way. Didn't their hatred make *me* the hero? Their equal?

That sardonic crack helped me step back.

It helped me decide what I had to do.

"A hero is someone who gets the job done, Albert," Clara once said. "Bravely when necessary. Courage is an admirable last resort, for when intelligence fails."

Okay, okay, I thought, feeling humility wash over me with a sense of cleansing relief.

A man's got to know his limitations, and I've gone way beyond mine.

Hell, I'm not even a match for Beta! Kaolin and Maharal are clearly out of my league.

All right. Time to be a citizen. Let's do it.

Already bracing for the inevitable long interrogation ahead, I reached for my borrowed chador-telephone and started to turn around—

—only to stagger back in surprise as a tall figure loomed toward me, out of the shadows!

■　　■　　■

The oversized humanoid shape emerged from around the corner of a nearby autokiln, lumbering at me with both arms outstretched.

The visor of the scout uniform flared with threat diagrams, covering the golem's silhouette with flaring auras and juttering symbols that might have meant something to a trained soldier. But the garish flood of data only smothered me in clouds of confusion. I threw back the visor from my face—

—and was immediately struck by waves of odor. New-baked clay, rather sour. The harsh smell might have warned me, if I hadn't been relying on borrowed army equipment, instead of my own senses.

"Stop!" I warned, dropping the chador, which got tangled on the holster of my sidearm. Finally pulling the laser free, I frantically tried to find the safety switch. My wounded thumb, slippery with sweat, worked badly and the gloves didn't help.

"Don't come any closer. I'll shoot!"

The golem kept shambling forward, emitting a low groan. Something was wrong with it—perhaps faulty imprinting or too-rapid baking. Whatever the cause, it wasn't slowing down or pausing for rational discussion!

I faced a sudden choice.

Try to dodge. Or shoot. You can't do both.

The safety clicked. The pistol abruptly throbbed with reassuring power. I chose.

A hot beam tore through the golem, slicing off one arm, biting the torso.

It reacted with a roar, and charged. The heavy figure crashed into me as I threw up an arm.

Wrong choice.

41

Oh No, Mr. Hands!

. . . a mixture in red and gray . . .

Did you know, Albert, that the very first life forms may have been made of clay?"

Yosil's damned ghost won't stop talking. It just keeps yattering while the torment inflicted by his soul-stretching device gets worse by the hour. I yearn desperately to stifle his gray specter. Exorcise its unnatural haunting. Dispatch it to rejoin the maker it betrayed and destroyed, days ago.

Of course, that's what it wants—my anger! To give me a focus. Pain will be a center for me to revolve around, while everything else crumbles.

"A Scotsman came up with the idea, Albert, almost a century ago, and it really was quite clever.

"By that time, biologists agreed that a rich soup of organic compounds must have formed on Earth, almost as soon as the planet cooled enough for liquid oceans. But what happened next? How did all those drifting amino acids and such get organized into tidy, self-replicating units? Cells, containing DNA and the machinery for reproduction, didn't just happen! Something got them jump-started!

"That something may have been vast beds of semi-porous clay, spanning whole sea bottoms, offering an enormous array of patterned surfaces to protect growing molecular clusters. Providing templates for the earliest organisms. Setting a few on the road to greatness."

Maharal's gray ghost preens, slapping its chest.

"Only now the road is coming full circle, as we return to our original form! *No longer organic, but creatures sculpted out of Mother Earth's own mineral flesh! Don't you find that interesting?"*

What interests me is getting out of here, especially each time the machinery sends another wave of compulsion down my spine, propelling me against the straps, heaving to get these hands of mine around ditYosil's neck. I'd grind his undead bones so fine, none of the atoms would ever find each other again!

From somewhere nearby . . . closer than nearby . . . comes a resonant reply.

Amen, brother.

The voice is no figment. I know it's the little orange-red golem, the one Maharal imprinted from me a few hours ago. Now its thoughts come flooding in, swelling and fading, merging with mine. It must be part of ditYosil's complicated experiment and he seems greatly pleased. Now that a link has been established, the next phase is a memory test. How well can I remember things that "I" never learned?

With the wave of a hand, he sends about a hundred image bubbles floating in front of my eyes, depicting everything from lunar landscapes to the latest robohockey game. My gaze can't help flitting among the pictures, involuntarily focusing on a few that look familiar. Certain bubbles flare as I recognize their contents . . .

. . . a Grecian urn that held wine from the age of Pericles . . .

. . . a buxom Venus figure from the Paleolithic era . . .

. . . a full-sized terracotta statute of an ancient Chinese soldier, given to Yosil by the grateful Son of Heaven, for his work at the excavations in Sian . . .

I not only recognize these images, I *remember* being shown the originals, in Maharal's private museum. Somehow, Little Red is feeding me memories, without benefit of a brain-sifter or thick cryo-cables! We're inloading each other, back and forth, despite being separated by twenty meters and a thick glass wall.

So, this isn't just about wanting to make dit-to-dit copies. Not another industrial process for Universal Kilns. Maharal is trying for another breakthrough. Something bigger!

The gray ghost chatters in excitement over results from the memory test. For a time it pleases him even more than lecturing to me about evolutionary claydistics. Clamping down, I try hard to shut out the sound of his yammering voice. Quash the irritation and anger! He obviously wants me distracted by *hate*—an easy emotional state to model and control. One so pure that it may breach the containment of a single vessel. A single body.

I must resist. Only it's so hard *not* to hate. Every few minutes, his loathsome machinery scrapes my pseudoneural array, prodding agonizingly at my ersatz body, provoking the salmon reflex—that craving to go home. To return. To my original. *An original he destroyed with a missile, around midnight on Tuesday.*

It's what he told Little Red. That he murdered me. In order to make this experiment work, he removed the "anchor" of my organic self, hoping it would force two copies of me toward each other, instead.

I get it. His aim is to set one Standing Wave reverberating across open space. It's an accomplishment, all right. Like making an electron occupy an entire room with a single, prodigious quantum state. But why? What's the goal?

He can't be after a Nobel Prize. Not when it took both suicide and murder to reach this point. Is he crazy enough to hope he can maintain secrecy indefinitely? Secrets are like snowflakes, nowadays—rare and hard to keep for very long.

There's got to be more at stake. Something he plans to bring to a fruition, soon.

I feel agreement from Little Red—my other half. Each time the big machines pulse, we feel closer. More like a single person, reunited. And yet—

—and yet, there's something else. Something *outside of us.* Something both familiar and strange at the same time. I keep picking up what feel like *echoes* . . . like glinting reflections, scattered off distant pools. Are they part of ditYosil's plan?

Maybe not.

I take some hope in that.

■ ■ ■

"Very good, Albert," the mad gray croons, peering at several read-outs. "Your observer state profiles are excellent, old friend!"

He leans over me, trying to meet my gaze.

"I've performed this experiment countless times, Albert, trying to create a self-sustaining soul-resonance between two nearly identical dittos. But my own copies never worked out—the ego field is flawed, you see. Too much self-distrust. An inherited trait, I'm afraid. One that's often associated with genius."

"Even if you do say so yourself," I reply. But Yosil ignores the dig in order to press on.

"No, my own golem-selves would never do. The first thing I needed was somebody who copies *cleanly*. That's why I started grabbing your dittos, years ago. But it wasn't easy, especially at first. I almost blew it several times and had to destroy your grays, rather than let them get away. You forced me to learn a whole new suite of sneaky skills, Albert. But eventually we were able to start serious work.

"And we made good progress, didn't we?"

He pats my cheek and I must redouble my efforts to keep rage at bay.

"Of course, you don't remember, Albert. But in my hands, you explored new spiritual territory. We seemed destined to make history together, the two of us.

"Only then we hit a barrier! The Observer Effect I told you about, remember? Your original kept remotely influencing the soul-field, anchoring you to this plane of reality, interfering whenever I tried to raise the paired-state resonance to a new level. Eventually, I realized what was needed in order to solve the problem.

"I had to eliminate the organic Albert Morris!"

ditYosil shakes his head ruefully.

"Only I found that I couldn't do it. Not while my own organic brain came burdened with so many hang-ups—conscience, empathy, ethical principles—along with gutless worries about getting caught. It was terribly frustrating. I hated myself for it! Here I was, with a possible solution and tools to do the job, ready at hand, but lacking the will!"

"My . . . deepest sympathy for your problem."

"Thank you. Nor was that even the worst of it. Soon, my *partner* and *friend,* Aeneas Kaolin, started putting pressure on. Demanding results. Making threats. Stoking my natural bent toward feelings of paranoia and pessimism. And don't let anyone tell you that recognizing and acknowledging such feelings makes them go away! Illogical or not, they eat away at you.

"I started having *dreams,* Morris. Dreams about a possible way around my dilemma. Dreams about death and resurrection. They both frightened and thrilled me! I wondered—what was my subconscious trying to tell me?

"Then, last Sunday, I realized abruptly what the dreams meant. It came to me while I was imprinting a new copy . . . *this* copy, Albert." ditYosil slaps his chest again. "In a moment I saw the whole picture, in all its glory, and knew what must be done."

Through gritted teeth, I manage to growl a reply.

"*real*Yosil saw it, too. At the same time, I'll bet."

The gray laughs.

"Oh, that's true, Albert. And it must've terrified him, because he kept his distance after that, avoiding this copy. Even while we worked together down here in the lab. Soon, he made an excuse to head up to the cabin. But I knew what was on his mind. How could I *not* know?

"I could sense that my maker was preparing to run."

An overtone of amazement thrums the Standing Wave, vibrating painfully between me and Little Red. Even though I/we suspected something like this . . . to hear it verified openly is positively weird.

Poor, doomed realYosil! It's one thing to see death coming at the hands of your own creation. That's part of the human epic tradition, after all. Oedipus and his father. Baron Frankenstein and his monster. William Henry Gates and Windows '09.

But to realize that your slayer will be *your own self.* A being who shares every memory, understands your every motive, and *agrees* with you about nearly all of it. Every subvibration of the Standing Wave—identical!

And yet, something was unleashed in clay that could never fully emerge in flesh. Something ruthless, at a level I could not imagine.

"You . . . are genuinely insane . . ." I pant. "You need . . . help."

In response, the gray ghost simply nods, almost amiably.

"Uh-huh. That sounds about right. At least by society's standards.

Only results can possibly justify the extreme measures I've taken.

"I'll tell you what, Albert. If my experiment fails, I'll turn myself in for compulsory therapy. Does that sound fair?"

He laughs. "For now, though, let's operate on the assumption that I know what I'm doing, eh?"

Before I can answer, an especially strong pulse of the soul-stretching machinery throws me into a spasm, my back arching in pain.

Through it all, part of me remains calm, observant. I can see ditYosil working now to prepare the next phase of his grand experiment. First by pushing aside the glass partition that divided the laboratory and replacing it with some kind of hanging platform, suspended by cables from the ceiling. Carefully he centers the platform, midway between me and my alter ego, Little Red. It sways back and forth like a pendulum, bisecting the room.

After a few seconds, the quivering aftereffects of that last pulse begin to fade, enough for me to blurt the question foremost on my mind.

"Wh . . . what . . . is it you're trying to accomplish?"

Only when he's fully satisfied with the placement of the swaying platform does the renegade golem turn to face me again, now with a thoughtful expression, sounding almost sincere. Enthralled, even.

"What am I trying to accomplish, Albert? Why, my purpose here is evident. To fulfill my life's work.

"I aim to invent the perfect copying machine."

42

Diteriorata

. . . as Greenie flees and finds . . .

Dusk was falling over the city as I burst onto the tenement roof, closely chased by a mob of candy-striped Waxers, howling to blast me into pottery shards. Turning at the exit door, I spent one of my last scattergun shells, emptying it down the stairwell, taking out the nearest pursuer along with several wooden steps, three feet of bannister, and a huge gout of ancient plaster. The rest of them backed off, darn fast.

Catching my breath, I saw it was a pretty good defensive position, for the moment. Still, they seemed to have plenty of reinforcements, and ways to outflank me, given time. ·

Time was one of many things I lacked—along with allies and ammo. Not to mention my fast-draining supply of *élan vital,* which was due to run out in a few hours, at best.

I'm getting way too old for this kind of thing, I pondered, feeling stale as a loaf of bread several days out of the oven. Those multicolored basdits were still down there. I could hear scuttle movements below. And whispers, urgently debating ways to get at me.

Why me?

All this was rather over the top for a typical gang raid. Nor could I imagine any reason to spend so much expense trying to annihilate the cheap utility-greenie of a dead private eye.

Unless Kaolin is cheesed at me for missing our appointment.

It did appear rather eerie, I recalled. The attackers struck just after Palloid—poor little guy—mentioned slapping Aeneas with a transparency subpoena, forcing the reclusive trillionaire to open his books and camera records, perhaps even requiring him to appear in person. Could *that* be driving the hermit to desperate measures?

Maybe Kaolin didn't send these goons after me, but to recover the pictures.

In my pocket lay the spool of photos Queen Irene took, during her meetings with "Vic Collins" . . . the co-conspirator she thought was Beta, but who later revealed hints of platinum skin under all that clever makeup. Instinctively, I had grabbed the spool from Pal when shooting broke out. Save the evidence—a good reflex for a gumshoe. But maybe the Waxers wouldn't be pursuing me right now, if I had left the pictures behind!

Palloid should've been the one to snatch the film and run! They'd never have caught the lithe ferret-ditto. Only retreat wasn't part of my friend's basic nature. And now Pal would never get those memories.

Too bad. We may have been a couple of disposables, but we sure had some times, Palloid and me.

I kicked the door in frustration. *There's gotta be a way off this roof!*

Still listening for another attack, I stepped away from the edge a bit, turning to look around at twilight in dittotown . . . perhaps my last view of the world. Off to the west and north, realfolk would be sitting on balconies and verandas right about now, sipping cool drinks and watching the sun set while awaiting their other halves—the selves they sent forth to work this morning, with a promise of downloaded continuity as reward for a hard day's labor.

That's fine. It's fair. Only where was a home that *I* could go to?

Grumbles down the stairwell turned into loud argument. Good. Maybe their command structure had been messed up by the carnage Pal and I dished out, back in the apartment. Or it could just be a ruse, while they prepared a flanking maneuver.

Taking a chance, I hurried over to one parapet and glanced down at the rusting fire escape. No one there. At least not yet.

The opposite end of the roof supported a rickety shed made largely of wire mesh. Small gray shapes bobbed and cooed within. A pigeon coop. Two humanoid figures could be made out beyond—an adult and child, working together at repairing part of the enclosure. Both wore threadbare clothes, suitable for the slum environment, but their skin color was a drably realistic dun shade . . . almost brown. Probably an illusion in the rapidly dimming light. Still, I beat a hasty retreat just in case. If they were real, I had no business drawing danger toward them.

Returning to the stairwell, I arrived in time to catch two of the red and pink–striped gladiators trying to sneak past the shattered steps by slithering up ropes attached to the ceiling by shock grapnels. They opened fire when I appeared, but the swaying cables spoiled their aim. So I blasted them to fragments that fell, tumbling, six stories to the atrium below.

Only one shell left, I thought, checking the scattergun. It also occurred to me that this artfully contrived slum wasn't quite as accurate as the designers hoped. Even in the worst of the old days, there were cops who would show up, eventually, if gunfire went on for very long. But here and now, nobody would come.

Well, you had your chance, Gumby. You could have called Inspector Blane. Had him send a bunch of LSA enforcers to pick you up. But you're too much like Pal. He can't turn down a fight, while you gotta try and outsmart the forces of darkness. All by yourself, if possible.

Even when you haven't got a clue.

It was true! More than I had realized. My mood at that particular moment gave it away. Despite everything, I felt strangely . . . happy.

Oh, there's no high quite like getting the focused attention of powerful enemies. Nothing is better guaranteed to make you feel important in the world, which may be why conspiracy theories are so popular among frustrated underachievers. In this case, it wasn't an illusion. The mighty Aeneas Kaolin was apparently willing to spend loads just to get my little green porcelain ass.

Well, bring 'em on! Hey, nothing beats the drama of a last stand.

Maybe . . ., I thought, though it galled me to admit it. *Maybe I am Albert Morris, after all.*

In fact, just one thing was spoiling the smug intensity of the moment. Not the fact that everything might end soon, in a blaze of battle. I could accept that.

No, it was another of those strange, brief headaches that had begun coming over me during the last few hours . . . starting almost too mild to notice, but recurring lately with greater intensity. They would blow in like a hot wind and last only a minute or so, filling me with unexplained feelings of claustrophobia and helplessness, then vanish, leaving no residue. Perhaps it was a side effect of dittolife extension. I had no idea what to expect when the rejuvenation finally wore out. Only that the extra day had been rather more interesting than dissolving into slurry.

Thanks, Aeneas.

A faint clatter drew my attention away to the east, where I hurried to look over the parapet. There, on the fire escape, I now saw a dozen Waxers trying to climb quietly. Only the rusted metal framework kept creaking and popping, spoiling their stealth. It looked so rickety, with any luck the whole thing might give way, sending them crashing to the alley below.

Should I try to help luck along? I wondered. A blast from the scattergun, aimed just right, could remove several bolts from the brickwork, causing a chain reaction, maybe unzipping the whole rickety thing.

Or maybe not. I decided to hold back my last shell, for at least a minute or two.

A quick dash to the south end showed another bunch of ditbulls clambering upward. These were equipped with finger and toe spikes, doing it the hard way, ascending laboriously hand-over-hand by jabbing the sharp tines into crumbly mortarwork. More than ever, I felt flattered by their attention. And eager to return the favor.

A low wall surrounded the roof, looking rather decrepit and ready to go. So I pushed . . . and had the rapid contentment of feeling the whole mass give way. More than a meter of brickwork collapsed over the side, followed by a satisfying scream below. I ran along, kicking and shoving, sending more sections of wall toppling onto climbers, then turned and hurried back to the stairwell.

Half a dozen figures dived for cover as I brandished the scattergun. That won me about a minute's reprieve, I figured. Spinning around, I rushed to check the east-side fire escape again.

That group was much closer now. So close, I no longer had any choice. While bullets pelted the rim of the wall, I cocked the hammer and chose a target, firing my final shot where it'd do the most good.

Two warrior-golems screamed and rusty latticework groaned as a bolt popped free . . . then another.

But the fire escape didn't collapse. Those ancients built well, dammit.

No time left. What should I do now? Try to hide Irene's film? They'd search every square centimeter, as soon as I was squashed . . .

I suddenly thought of the pigeon coop. Maybe I could tie the spool to the leg of a bird, send it flapping away, only to return after the goons departed—

Bullets abruptly splattered the roof nearby. I spied a head and arms poking over the west parapet. Dodging behind the stairhouse, I evaded that threat only to see more hands fumble over the rim on the east side.

Just one thing to do, then. Run for the edge while I still can! Some passerby may see me splat. With any luck, they'll grab the film spool, and perhaps my head, hoping for a finder's fee. My pellet code would lead to Albert . . . or Clara. . . .

It was a damn thin hope, but all I could muster as voices converged inside the stairhouse less than a meter away. Bullets smacked from nearly all directions now, encroaching on my narrow umbra of shelter, splattering me with sharp slivers.

I gathered my legs, preparing to spring for the precipice—

—then *stopped* as a new sound arose, burgeoning from nothing to noisy in seconds.

A groaning whine of engines.

The battle-dit who had been shooting at me turned around, stared, then lost his grip with a cry.

A new shape rose to take his place. Compact, sleek, and powerful—a blue and white coupe with downthrusting engines at three corners and a logo in jaunty letters that spelled HARLEY along the nose.

The trim skycycle turned as its cowling opened, revealing a figure who waved insouciantly, his beige spiral motif resembling that of a spinning propeller.

Beta, I thought. *So that's where you vanished during the fighting!*

Grinning, my erstwhile nemesis offered a small space behind the pilot seat. "Well, Morris? Coming?"

Believe it or not, I hesitated for a split instant, wondering if the pavement might be a better bet.

Then, dodging bullets all the way, I ran hard to dive for the sanctuary offered by my longtime foe.

43

Kidnapped by Ditsies

. . . as realAlbert gets carried away . . .

Picture the inimitable Fay Wray, wriggling vainly in the adamant grasp of King Kong. That's how I must've looked as the giant golem hauled me from the underground storage area under its one remaining arm. I gave up prying uselessly at the behemoth and tried instead to gain calm . . . to slow my pounding heart and chill the hormones surging through my veins. It wasn't easy.

A caveman, in danger, never wondered, *Am I real enough to matter?* But I often do. If the answer is, *Not really,* I can greet death with an aplomb that only heroes used to know. But if the answer is yes, fear multiplies! Right at that moment I could taste bile surging from my gut. Having seen my house and garden burn, I had no wish to make Clara grieve for me twice.

"Where . . . are you taking me?" I asked, catching my breath. The monster barely acknowledged with a low grunt. A conversationalist. He also *stank,* from some kind of spoilage either before or during imprinting.

Moving away from the wall, with its row of locked storage cabinets, he carried me through the enormous storage room past shelves piled endlessly with tools and equipment . . . all the kinds of stuff you might need if, say, a few dozen important VIPs wanted to take shelter underground from some nuclear-bio-cyber-ceramo calamity up at the surface, forever. We were nearly at the door leading out of the storeroom when a drumming sound arrived from the hall outside. My captor paused in his tracks.

He listened. I listened. It sounded like marching footsteps.

Something more than dumb grunts stirred in the monster's head. Making a decision, he stepped to one side, shifting into shadows before a procession of clay soldiers trooped into view.

They entered in a column, one after another, wearing army camouflage colors and still glowing from the autokiln. Golems—big ones—dressed and equipped for battle.

Did someone activate one of the reserve units? To look for *me* perhaps? I felt tempted to shout and wave, in case they included a Clara.

Only I didn't see her among them.

You learn to look for signs . . . a certain carriage or bearing or maybe a sashay of the hips. I've been able to pick out Clara, on the flickering image of a battlefield sportscam, amid a squad of mud-encrusted quadrupeds covered with refractory plates of stegasauroid armor. Mere costumery doesn't matter. Something in the way she moves, I guess.

No, she wasn't in this bunch. In fact, they all moved pretty much the same, swaggering in a manner that seemed as brash as hers, only more arrogant. And maybe a bit mean. There *was* a sense of familiarity, without being able to pin it down.

I didn't shout. The troop of thirty or so combat golems passed by, heading deeper into the storage room, toward the place where I was standing before the monster abducted me. And for the first time, I wondered, was the thing actually trying to *help* me?

Soon I heard sounds of tearing metal! My captor moved out from the shadows, far enough for us to glimpse the demolition of several wall cabinets! War-dittos attacked them, ripping off doors and tossing the contents aside, searching . . . searching . . .

. . . till one let out a cry. The back of one cabinet split open with a loud *hiss*, exposing blank emptiness where a stone wall was legally supposed to be.

I knew it!

Of course, my satisfaction was mixed. This showed I was a still a pretty good private eye. It also meant I was an idiot for not calling the authorities before! Now . . .

Now?

I wondered as the big golem shifted me under its good arm and headed the other way, out of the storage room, into the hall.

ThHhHhHhHhHhH-mmmmmph!

Behind us, I heard laser and phase-maser fire! Low, menacing hums followed by the rapid pops and cracks of spalling rock . . . and the *splat* of warm, moist clay hitting some wall. The battle-dits must have encountered something inside the tunnel. Defenses. Strong ones.

And you were going to just charge on through. Fool, I chided myself.

If only I could make that call! But the chador was gone. Anyway, the big monster was carrying me in the opposite direction, down a long hallway toward the fresh smell of newly baked souls.

■ ■ ■

We entered a chamber containing deluxe freezers and kilns—the kind used by elites, equipped with the highest quality Standing Wave sifters.

More stuff for the gummint cream to use if they ever had to hide down here while the rest of us were getting snuffed out, far above. Several freezers gaped open, with their contents recently looted. A high-speed kiln hissed, the machinery chugging through final warmdown after having just processed a large batch—presumably the pack of warriors I just saw. The ones now fighting their way into a tunnel under Urraca Mesa.

But where was the archetype source, the archie? The one who did the imprinting? Clearly, this was not the military police at work. I tried to look around for the copier machine itself. We rounded a corner.

From my position, pinned under that giant arm, I caught a blurry glimpse. One figure lay stretched out on the original platten of the copier, while a second shape bent over, holding some ominous instrument.

The big golem who was carrying me let out a bellow and charged!

The standing figure turned, grabbing for a weapon—but the three of us crashed together before the pistol came to bear, tumbling in a pile.

"My" golem needed its arm in order to fight the thick-limbed soldier-dit, so I rolled free, scooting away as fast as I could, then scrambling to my feet while rubbing my bruised rib cage. The battle surged as two monstrous roxes pounded each other, rolling back and forth amid horrendous roars!

Real people first, I thought, remembering lessons from school. I hurried to the figure who lay supine on the platten . . . and gasped to find *Ritu Maharal!* She lay there, conscious—you have to be, in order to make decent copies—but her eyes didn't track at first as I tugged at the cruel straps holding her down.

"Al . . ." she choked. "Al—bert . . . !"

"What bastard did this to you!" I cursed, hating whoever it was. Involuntary copying—soul-stealing—is an especially nasty kind of rape. As soon as the straps were loose, I hauled her off the table and to a far corner, as far as possible from the battling titans. She clung to me hard, burying her head in my shoulder, sobbing as her warm skin shivered.

"I'm here. It'll be okay," I assured, not sure the promise could be kept. Eyeing possible ways to exit the room as "my" one-armed monster battled the other big golem. The one who had been tightening Ritu's straps, preparing to—

I glanced at the floor where an implement lay fallen from that ditto's fingers. Not some torture device but a *med-sprayer,* filled with some purple concoction. I wondered . . . could appearances be deceiving. What if this was only a doctor, trying to help Ritu?

The fallen laser clattered across the floor, kicked to and fro as the giants bellowed, strained, and tore at each other. Should I try to grab the weapon? Not easy, amid those heaving limbs. And suppose I did manage to recover the weapon. Should I shoot the first ditto, or the second?

As Ritu quivered in my arms, the issue was settled with a double *crack* of finality. Both of the struggling war-golems suddenly shuddered and went still.

"Well, I'll be a . . ."

It took a moment to disentangle poor, disheveled Ritu and guide her back, taking a few steps toward the two bodies, already starting to smolder on the floor. I approached cautiously, though she tried to hold me back, till I could see them clearly on the ground, beyond the imprinting tables.

My captor—the rox with one arm—lay atop the other one, apparently lifeless.

The one beneath, who had been standing over Ritu preparing to inject either medicine or poison, lay with its neck twisted at a creepy angle. But a spark remained. The eyes glittered, staring directly into mine, beckoning.

Against my better judgment—and Ritu's frantic tugging—I approached.

One of the eyes winked.

"Hello . . . Morris," came individual raspy words. "You . . . really . . . have to stop . . . following . . . me around like this."

A chill coursed my spine.

"*Beta?* Great Rava of Prague! What are *you* doing here?"

A chuckle. Snide and superior. I knew it all too well.

"Oh, Morris . . . you can be . . . so dense." The effigy of my enemy coughed, spitting slip with an ugly, deathlike glaze. "Why don't you ask *her* what . . . I'm doing here?"

The glittering eyes moved to Ritu.

I glanced up at Yosil Maharal's daughter, who moaned in response.

"Me? Why should I know anything about this monster!"

ditBeta coughed again. This time the words came mixed in a chalky death rattle.

"Why indeed . . . Betty . . ." Then all light vanished from its eyes.

I guess, long ago, there used to be some gratification from having your worst enemy die in front of you. A sense of completion, at least. But Beta and I had done this to each other—gasped our cryptic last in each other's arms—so many times that I could only view it now with utter frustration.

"Damn!" I kicked the one-armed golem on top. The mute one who apparently had been intent on rescuing me and Ritu, all along. "Why'd you have to kill it? I had questions!"

I turned back to Ritu, still shivering in reaction and clearly in no shape to be interrogated.

Just then a nearby autokiln hummed back into active mode, hissing and rumbling.

Nobody had asked it to, as far as I could tell.

I didn't like the sound.

44

The Dit and the Pendulum

. . . as gray combines with red . . .

Echoes . . . the weird ones from outside . . . keep getting stronger, recurring every few minutes. Whenever the big machine triggers another "resonance" mode, I/we pick up hints of something that seems both *other* and *familiar*. At once oddly reassuring and strangely terrifying.

Aw, man . . . we/I had just started getting used to being combined. A twinned state . . . one mind sharing two bodies—gray and little red—sloshing back and forth, continuously imprinting each other. Two emulated brains, linked not only by a common soul-template, but the same active Standing Wave, thrumming through the empty space between us.

A space where Yosil Maharal's gray ghost is preparing to sit, on a swaying platform that swings back and forth, passing between Gray and Little Red at regular intervals.

There's something familiar about the *period* of the pendulum . . . linked to the pattern of our rhythmic soul-bursts. No coincidence, I bet.

No bet, I feel Little Red agree, from outside my gray skull, feeling no different than any of the many internal voices that a person conjures up, in the course of a day.

Weird.

■ ■ ■

"You said you were making the perfect copier," I prompt ditMaharal, trying to get him talking. Even his smarmy lecturing beats the dread of waiting. Or maybe I'm just claying for time.

He looks up from his preparations, glancing toward me. Busy, but never too busy to pontificate.

"I call it a 'glazier,' " he says, with evident pride.

"A . . . what?"

"G-L-A-Z-I-E-R," he spells. "It stands for God-Level Amplification by Zeitgeist Intensification and Ego Refraction. Do you like the name?"

"Like it? I—"

Starting to answer, I feel the latest amplification wave strike, triggering another spasm as I strain against the bindings that hold me down. It's painful, and rife with those strange echoes, but fortunately quick. Actually, I'm kind of getting used to the hits.

I've started noticing something in them other than just agony. Something queerly like *music*.

When the wave ebbs, I can resume answering ditMaharal's question.

"I . . . hate it. What . . . whatever made you pick such an awful name?"

The golem that assassinated its own maker—and mine—reacts to my goading by laughing aloud. "Well, I admit there was a touch of whimsy involved. You see, I wanted to make a parallel with—"

"—with a *laser*. I'm not stupid, Maharal."

He winces in evident surprise.

"And what else have you figured out, Albert?"

"The two of us . . . we two Morris dittos . . . the gray and red . . . we're like the *mirrors* at both ends of a laser, is that it? And the important stuff . . . whatever's supposed to be *amplified* . . . goes in between."

"Very good! So you did go to school."

"Kid stuff," I growl. "And don't patronize me. If I'm gonna provide the instrument for making a god out of you, show some respect."

ditYosil's eyes widen for just a moment, then he nods.

"I never quite looked at it that way. So be it, then. Let me explain without patronizing.

"It's all about the *Standing Wave* that Jefty Anonnas found glimmering in that region of phase space between neuron and molecule, between body and mind. The so-called soul-essence that Bevvisov learned to press into clay, proving that the ancient Sumerians had an inkling of a lost truth. The *motivational* essence that Bevvisov and I then imprinted onto

Aeneas Kaolin's wonderful claynamation automatons, with results that stunned us all and transformed the world."

"So? What does this have to do with—"

"I'm getting to that. Sustained by fields and atoms, like everything else, the Standing Wave is nevertheless so much more than the sum of our parts—our memories and reflexes, our instincts and drives—in much the same way that ripples on a sea show only the surface portions of a vastly complex tug and pull below."

I'm feeling another pulse approach. Watching the suspended platform, I've realized that it swings back and forth exactly twenty-three times between each painful throb of the machine.

"All of that sounds awfully pretty," I tell ditYosil. "But what about this experiment? So you've got *my* Standing Wave bouncing back and forth, with the *two of me* acting as mirrors. Because I'm such a good copier that—"

The next pulse hits, hard! I grunt and strain. Sometimes the effect is worse, like plucking harmonies out of catgut while it's still inside the cat. Then, abruptly, another of those echoes comes over me . . .

. . . and I briefly find myself envisioning a moonlit landscape of dark plains and ravines, covered with opal glows and shadows, rolling along below me, as if viewed by a creature of the air.

Then it passes.

I try to hold my train of thought, using the conversation as an anchor . . . since my *real* anchor, the organic Albert Morris, is dead, I'm told.

"So, you use my Standing Wave . . . because I'm such a good copier. And you're a bloody awful one. Is that right, Yosil?"

"Impudent, but correct. You see, it's fundamentally a matter of *accounting*—"

"Of what?"

"Accounting, the way physicists and soulists do it. Adding up, arranging, or counting assortments of identical particles. Or anything else, for that matter! Grab a bunch of marbles out of a bag . . . does it matter which one is which, if they all look alike? How many different ways can you sort them, if they're all the same? It turns out the statistics are totally different if each marble has something unique about it! A nick, a scratch, a label. . . ."

"What the hell are you talking—"

"This distinction is especially important at the quantum level. Particles can be counted in two ways—as *fermions* and *bosons*. Protons and electrons sort as fermions, which are forced to stay apart from one another by an exclusion principle that's more fundamental than entropy. Even if they seem identical and come from the same source, they have to be counted individually and occupy states that are quantum-separated by a certain minimum amount.

"But bosons love to mingle, overlap, merge, combine, march in step—for example, in the amplified and coherent light waves generated by a laser. Photons are bosons, and they are anything *but* aloof! Happily identical, they join together, superimpose—"

"Get to the point, will you?" I shout, or this could go on all night.

Yosil's ghost frowns at me.

"The point? Even though a golem-copy can be very much like its original, something always prevents the soul-duplicate from being truly identical . . . or being counted with Bose statistics. That means it cannot be coherence-*multiplied,* the way light is in a laser. That is, it couldn't be, till I found a way! Starting with an excellent copier and an ego of just the right ductility—"

"So it's like a laser and you're using two of me to supply your mirror. What's *your* role in all this?"

He grins.

"You'll supply the pure carrier waveform, Morris, since you're good at that. But the substance of the *soul* we're amplifying will be mine."

Hearing this and looking at his facial expression—oh, he's got Smersh-Foxleitner, all right. Stage four at least. Amoral, paranoid, and profoundly self-deceptive. The worst sufferers can believe seventeen different things before breakfast . . . and sometimes brilliantly weave the incompatible notions together by noon!

"What about the *god-level* part of your machine's stupid name?" I ask, not expecting to like the answer. "Isn't that unscientific? Even mystical?"

"Don't be rude, Albert. It's a metaphor, of course. At present we have no words to describe what I'm about to achieve. It transcends today's language the way Hamlet outsoliloquies a bonobo chimp."

"Yeah, yeah. There have been Neo Age rumors about such 'transcendence' for as long as I can remember. Soul-projection machines and wild-eyed schemes to *upload people* straight to heaven. You and Kaolin were pestered by such nonsense for decades. Now you're telling me there's a core of truth?"

"I am, though using true science rather than wishful thinking. When your own Standing Wave becomes a Bose condensate—"

ditYosil pauses, cocking his head, as if curious about a sound. Then, shaking his head, he seems ready to go on, enthusiastically describing his ambition to become something new—something much bigger or better than the mere run of mortals. He opens his mouth—

—as a noise penetrates the underground chamber, now clearly audible. A distant rumble from beyond one stony wall.

An instrument panel erupts with warning glows, some red, others amber. *"Interlopers,"* a cyber voice announces. *"Interlopers in the tunnel . . ."*

An image globe resolves in thin air, growing larger as we both feed it with our attention. Inside, we see dim figures marching along a murky corridor of undressed limestone. Sudden flashes pour from an outcrop, slicing one of the figures in half, but the rest of the armed force respond with uncanny quickness, swinging weapons up to fire, blasting hidden robo-sentinels. Soon the way is clear and they resume their steady march.

"Estimated arrival at this locale in forty-eight minutes . . ."

Maharal's gray ghost shakes its head.

"I hoped for more time, but it can be done."

He hurries away, abandoning our conversation, returning to his preparations. Preparations that would use me—

—*use us!* Little Red insists.

—use us to help elevate his soul, amplifying it to some grandiose level of power. Typical bloody Smersh-Foxleitner. The mad scientist's disease.

I wonder. Could this really work? Might the ghost of a dead professor manage to transform himself beyond any need for an organic brain, or even a physical link to the world? Perhaps rising so high that life on a mere planet becomes trivial and boring? I could picture such a macro-Maharal entity just heading off, seeking cosmic-scale adventures among the stars. Which'd be cool by me, I guess, so long as he went away and left this world alone.

But I have an uneasy feeling that ditYosil has in mind a more local kind of deification. Both more provincial and deeply controlling.

Many of the folks I know won't like what he'd become.

Oh, and the process will probably use up the "mirrors" of his . . . glazier. Whatever the outcome, I don't figure i/we (gray/red) will much enjoy serving as Yosil's vehicle to reach this personal nirvana of his.

"You know—" I began, hoping to distract him.

Only then another pulse struck.

45

Desert Rox

Tuesday's child is full of grace—
Wednesday's child is full of woe—
Thursday's child has far to go, and—

And? I wondered. After my eventful and generously extended span on Earth—more than two whole days—what next?

Not much, at the rate my body was starting to decay. I could feel the familiar signs of golem senescence creeping in, plus glimmerings of the salmon reflex, that urge to report home for memory inloading. To escape oblivion by returning to the one real organic brain where *I* might yet live on.

A brain that might actually still exist! Just when I had grown accustomed to the idea that it was blown to bits, I wondered. *Suppose Albert Morris lives, and I could somehow reach him before I dissolve. Would he have me back?*

Assuming he still lived?

As Beta flew his agile little Harley through the night, that seemed a growing possibility! According to web reports I viewed while crammed behind Beta's pilot seat.

"That settles it," one of the amateur deduction mavens announced. *"They never found enough protoplasmic residue in that burnt house for a whole body!"*

"And see how the police are behaving. Munitions auditors still swarm all over, but the Human Protection Division is gone! That means no one was killed there."

I should be glad. Yet, if Albert did exist, he probably commanded a whole army of himselves, using high-class grays and ebonies to track down the villain who destroyed my . . . our . . . his garden. Why, in that case, should he welcome back a stray green who refused to mow the lawn?

Good question—and moot if I couldn't find him! Where *was* Albert when the missile struck? And where was he *now*?

Beta tossed a theory at me, turning his head to be heard over the engines. "See what some hobbyist ditectives found in Tuesday's streetcam data." His domed head gestured to a display globe showing the Sycamore Avenue house, before it was destroyed. Leaning my chin on Beta's pilot seat, I watched the garage door open in soft pre-twilight. The Volvo crept out.

"He left! Then why did everybody think he was still there when the missile . . . Oh, I see."

As the car turned down Sycamore, one camera got a fine view of the driver. It was an Albert Morris *gray*. Bald and glossy—the perfect golem. By implication, realAl must still be in the house.

Beta knew better. "Appearances mean nothing. Your archie is nearly as good at disguises as I am." Strong praise from a master of deception. "But then where . . . ? I spent lavishly for a top freelance voyeur. She tracked the car from camview to camview along the Skyway Highway, to this camera-blank road." ditBeta waved past the windshield at a slender desert lane below. Moonlight painted wan, lonely tones—a different world than the ditto-clogged city, or suburbs where comfortably unemployed realfolk distract themselves by pursuing a million hobbies. Below, nature reigned . . . subject to advice and consent from the Department of Environments.

"What could Albert be up to, coming out this way?" I wondered aloud. Our memories were the same Tuesday noon. Something must have happened since.

"You have no idea?"

"Well . . . after I was made, Ritu Maharal phoned with news that her father was killed in an auto wreck. My next move would've been to study the crash site."

"Let's see." Beta twiddled chords on a controller. Images rippled, zooming to a rocky desolation, underneath a highway viaduct. Police and rescue cruisers surrounded a ruin of twisted metal. "You're right," Beta announced. "It's not far from here, and yet . . . odd. Albert drove some distance *past* the crash site; we're already fifty klicks south."

"What could be south, except . . ."

Abruptly I knew. *The battle range. He was heading to see Clara.*

Beta asked. "Did you say something?"

"Nothing."

Albert's love life wasn't any of this character's business. Anyway, I had seen Clara today, rummaging through the ruins. So they must not have connected, after all. Something was fishy, all right.

After flying in silence for a while, I asked Beta for a chador. He took a compact model from the glove compartment and passed it back. Wriggling in the cramped space, I slipped the holo-luminescent folds over my head and spent a while rapid-reciting a report, summarizing what happened since the last time I filed, not caring if Beta listened in. He already knew all about events that took place after Palloid and I left the Ephemerals Temple.

"Who're you sending the report to?" he asked casually when I removed the chador. A keypad glowed nearby, ready for any net address. The in-box of the chief of police. The whistle-blowers page of the *Times*. Or the fan/junkmail queue of one of those golem astronauts who were on Titan right now, taking turns exploring for a day or two, then dissolving to save on food and fuel till the next replacement came out of storage.

I asked myself the same question. *If I send an encrypted file to Albert's cache, there's no guarantee Beta won't tag it with a parasite-follower.*

Clara, then? What about Pal?

Assuming the Waxers hadn't hurt my friend amid all that mayhem, he'd be in a helluva state—either steaming mad over the loss of Palloid's memories or else in a stupor if they made him take a forget-sniff. Either way, Pal didn't know how to be discreet.

Then I thought of someone fitting . . . with the added virtue that it'd gall Beta. "Inspector Blane of the Labor Subcontractors Association," I told the transmitter unit, with an eye to my companion's reaction. Beta merely smiled and fussed over the controls while my report went out.

"Include a copy of the film," he suggested. "Those pictures Irene took."

"They implicate you—"

"In Class D industrial espionage. A trifling civil matter. But the sabotage attempt at UK was serious! Realfolk might have been endangered. Those pictures prove Kaolin—"

"We don't *know* it was him. Why sabotage his own factory?"

"For insurance? An excuse to write off capital equipment? He strove hard to blame all his enemies—Gadarene, Wammaker, Lum, and me."

I'd been thinking about Kaolin. *What's in the Research Division that he might want to destroy? A program he couldn't justify shutting down . . . unless it were ruined by some act beyond his control?*

Or one he didn't want to share?

I knew firsthand of one breakthrough—golem-rejuvenation—that gave me this extra, eventful day. Suppose I kept loyal to Aeneas for that, bringing *him* the film. Would my reward me be another extension? I guess it's to my credit that I never felt tempted. The habit of a lifetime . . . thinking yourself expendable when you're in clay.

Still, why suppress the new replenishment technology? To keep people buying lots of ditto blanks?

Not necessarily. Kilns and freezers and imprinters were the big-ticket items, and sales had tapered off. There was also talk of "conservation"— how we may deplete the best golem-quality clay beds in a generation or two. What could be more profitable than for UK to act responsibly . . . and make billions . . . by manufacturing and selling replenishers? Anyway, suppose he did wipe out every ditto in the Research Division. Word of the breakthrough would leak anyway, in a matter of months.

He *must* have had a reason, though. One I hadn't fathomed yet.

"The film could exonerate me—and you," Beta urged. "I have a scanner here. Just feed it in and send." He indicated a slot in the control panel.

"No," I said, feeling wary. "Not yet."

"But in seconds Blane could have a copy and—"

"Later." I felt another of those weird headaches coming on—brief but intensely disorienting, accompanied by queasy, claustrophobic feelings, as if I weren't here at all, but someplace cramped, confining. Probably a side effect of my overextended existence. "Are we getting close?"

"The Volvo's last trace was about there." Beta pointed to a curvy stretch of desert road. "Then no further sightings. It never showed up where the next camview covers the highway. I've been circling, looking for signs, but Albert disconnected his car-transponder, naughty boy. And there'd be no pellet in his brow if he was real. I'm at a loss."

"Unless—"

"Yeah?"

"—he set forth with a spare in the trunk."

"A spare?" Beta ruminated. "Even if it wasn't baked yet, the *pellet* would respond if we broadcast a close enough coding. Great. Let me just take a reading of *your* pellet for comparison. . . ."

Reaching around, Beta pushed a portable scanner. The reasoning—if Albert took a spare, it could be from the same factory batch as me. Similar codes, unless he scrambled them. And he was often too lazy to bother.

"Good idea." But I warded off the scanner. "Just don't play games. You already read my code. I felt it when I hopped aboard."

Beta offered his usual grin. "Fair enough. A little paranoia suits you, Morris."

I'm not Morris, I thought. But the protest, which seemed proud on Tuesday, felt weary now.

"Let's see if we can find that ditto spare," the pilot murmured, turning back to his instruments. The skycycle leaped powerfully at his bidding.

It must pay to be a copyright pirate. Even after Beta's enemy wrecked his bootlegging empire, he still has enough loot stashed away for an emergency backup copy to ride in style.

"Got it," Beta said minutes later. "The resonance is . . . damn! The car headed east, into the badlands. Why would Albert drive cross-country in a Volvo?"

I shrugged, unable to guess as the signal grew stronger. Such a long-range fix would be impossible in the city, with so many pellets all around. Here, it positively throbbed just ahead.

"Careful, this is rough country," I urged. The lower ravines lacked even moonlight. Beta let instruments take over, doing what computers and software are best at, performing simple procedures with utter precision. A minute later, amid a roar, a shuddering bump, and then a tapering sigh, we landed in a narrow canyon with the Harley's headlight shining at the canted wreckage of a battered land car. Not as badly smashed as Maharal's, but trapped just as surely.

How did this happen? Could Albert be dead, after all?

I had to wait for Beta to open the canopy and exit first, waving his scanner around, then followed to verify there were no real bodies. So Albert either walked away or was taken. Good. I didn't relish burying my maker.

"Every piece of electronic apparatus is ruined. Some kind of pulse weapon could do that," Beta commented. "Best guess, almost two days ago."

"And no one spotted the car in all that time." I glanced up to see how narrow the ravine was.

"Here's the ditspare." The trunk of the wrecked auto groaned wide to reveal a small portakiln and a CeramWrap cocoon that lay split open. The golembody had never been heat-activated. Instead of dissolving, it slumped like a corroding clay figurine, cracking in the desert heat. A latent life—a potential Albert—who never got a chance to stand or comment sardonically on the ironies of existence.

In the skycycle's beam, I saw a deep gouge at the base of the ditto's throat. *The little recitation-recorder. I give them to every gray, to narrate investigations in realtime. Someone cut it out. Only Albert would know it was there.*

Beta, using a torch to examine every inch of the passenger compartment, cursed colorfully. "Where could she have gone off to from here? Did someone pick them up? Was she trying to reach . . ."

"She? There was a passenger?"

Contempt filled Beta's voice, replacing his recent cordiality. "Always two steps behind, Morris. Did you think I'd go to all this trouble just to find your missing rig?"

I thought quickly. "Maharal's daughter. She hired Albert to investigate her father's accident . . . Albert must've headed out with her to look over the crash site. Or else—"

"Go on."

"Or else to the place Maharal fled *from* when he died. Some place Ritu knew about."

Beta nodded. "What I can't figure is why Morris went in person. And in disguise. Did he know his house was being targeted?"

I had an idea about that, from the way Albert felt when he made me. Lonely, tired, and thinking of Clara, whose battalion waged war not too far from here.

"What do *you* know of the assassins?" I asked, changing the subject.

"Me? Why, nothing."

You know something! I could tell. *Not the whole story, maybe. But you have suspicions.*

Time to tread carefully. "Tuesday, after helping Blane raid your Teller operation, I met a decaying yellow in a back-alley disposal tube. It spoke convincingly like you, claiming that a big new enemy was taking over. Then it blurted a request that I *go to Betzalel* . . . and *protect someone named Emmett* . . . or maybe *the emet.* Can you explain what you meant?"

"The yellow was desperate, Morris, if he asked *you* for a favor."

Ah, the familiar, insulting Beta. But I was playing for time, checking my surroundings in case things went abruptly sour.

"I was too exhausted to think much about it. Still, the words sounded familiar. Then I recalled. They refer to the *original* Golem legend, back in the sixteenth century, when Rabbi Loew of Prague was said to have created a powerful creature out of clay in order to protect the Jews of that city from persecution.

"The *emet* was a sacred word, either written on the creature's brow or placed in its mouth. In Hebrew, it means 'truth,' but it can represent the *source* or wellspring—all things arising from one root."

"I went to school too, y'know," Beta stifled a yawn. "And Betzalel was another of those golem-making rabbis. So?"

"So, tell me why you're following the trail of Yosil Maharal's daughter so avidly."

He blinked. "I have reasons."

"No doubt. First I thought you meant to grab her as a template for your ditto-piracy trade. But she's no phaedomasochistic vamp, like Wammaker, with an established clientele. Ritu's pretty, but physical attributes are trivial with golemtech. It's the personality—the unique Standing Wave—that makes one template special compared to another." I shook my head. "No, you're tracking Ritu to find the source. *Her father.* To find whatever secret frightened Yosil Maharal into studying the arts of deception. It's one so terrifying that he fled across the desert Monday night, fleeing something that chased and finally killed him."

Greeted by silence, I insisted. "What game are you involved in? How do you fit in between Maharal and Aeneas Kaolin—"

Beta's golem threw back its head and laughed. "You're just fishing. You really don't have a clue."

"Oh? Then please explain, great Moriarty! What can it hurt to tell me?"

He stared a moment.

"Let's make a trade. You transmit those pictures. Then I'll tell a story."

"Irene's pictures? From the Rainbow Lounge?"

"You know what pictures I mean. Dispatch them to Inspector Blane. He knows how you got 'em, from the report you just sent. Transmit and verify. Then we'll talk."

It was my turn to pause. *He rescued me from that rooftop in order to help track down realAlbert . . . and thus Ritu Maharal . . . and thus her father's secret hideaway.*

Now he has no further use for me, except to send the pictures.

"You want me to be the one who transmits them . . . for the sake of credibility."

"You *have* credibility, Morris—more than you realize. Despite ham-handed efforts to frame you, nobody in high places considered you a likely saboteur. The pics you found at the Rainbow will clinch it, help exonerate you—"

"And you!"

"So? They implicate Kaolin. But if I send them, well, who will believe an infamous ditnapper? They'll say I faked 'em."

This explained why Beta hadn't simply taken the film away from me. But his patience was wearing thin. "I know you, Morris. You think this gives you leverage. But don't press it. I have bigger concerns."

Resignation washed over me. "So, in exchange for lending a little credibility to the theory that Kaolin sabotaged his own factory, you'll tell me a few glimmers of useless information that will vanish when this body dissolves soon. Not much of a deal."

"It's the only one you're being offered. At least your notorious curiosity will be fed."

How inconvenient it is, to have an enemy who knows you so well.

■ ■ ■

He never let me out of sight, or easy reach of his younger, stronger arms.

"Send no messages," Beta warned, standing next to the Harley's open cockpit, uncovering the slot of the reader-scanner for me to slip in the spool of pictures. "Just transmit, verify, and sign off."

He punched in Blane's mailbox at LSA headquarters. A nearby screen asked: *Validate Sender ID*. Then a single number flashed:

6

Too quickly for conscious thought, I impulsively jabbed a response:

4

The unit responded with 8 . . . and I stabbed 3.

It went back and forth like that, rapidfire, two dozen more times, feeling entirely random to me. It *wasn't* random, of course, but a kind of encryption that's hard to crack or feign, based on a partial copy of Albert's personal Soul Standing Wave that Blane keeps secure in a hard-baked ceramium—a kind of cypher key that can be used many times. Any particular give-and-take pattern of number cues would be different, unique, yet show a high correlation with the sender's personality—

—assuming it didn't matter that I was a frankie! Nor my overwrought emotional state, scared and suspicious as hell. It actually surprised me when the screen flashed ACCEPTED, taking no longer than usual. Beta's spiral ditto grunted approval.

"Good, now step away from the cockpit."

I did so, watching a slim gun—one of his fingers, removed and reversed to aim a narrow muzzle, waved for me to move back. "I'd love to stay and chat, as promised," said the nine-digited golem. "But I've wasted too much time on you already."

"Do you have a particular destination in mind?"

Keeping the mini-gun trained on me, he climbed into the skycycle. "I found two sets of footprints, heading south. I have a pretty good notion where they're going now. You'd just slow me down."

"So you won't explain about Maharal and Kaolin?"

"If I told you more I'd have to shoot you, against the slim chance that someone might come by and rescue you. As things stand, you're clueless as usual. I'll leave you to dissolve in peace."

"Big of you. I owe you one."

Beta's grin showed that he knew how I meant it. "If it matters any, I'm not the one who tried to kill your rig, Morris. I doubt it was Kaolin, either. In fact, I hope the real you survives what's about to happen."

What's about to happen. He expressed it that way deliberately, to frustrate me. But I kept silent, not giving him any satisfaction. Only action would accomplish anything now.

"Good-bye, Morris," ditBeta said, closing the glass bubble, revving the engine to a rising pitch. I stepped back, thinking furiously.

What are my choices?

I still had the cautious option—wait a bit, burn the Volvo's fuel and hope to attract attention before I melt.

But no. I'd lose his scent. My reason for living.

The skycycle drove dust-billows down the narrow canyon defiles. ditBeta offered a jaunty wave, then turned his corkscrew head back to the job of taking off.

It was my cue. In that split second, as the Harley swung about and began climbing atop three pillars of superheated thrust, I ran forward and *leaped.*

There was pain, of course. I knew there would be pain.

46

All Fired Up

. . . as realAlbert gets earthy . . .

There wasn't much choice except to follow. Back to the storage room. Back to the dark opening where I had seen a small army of clay soldier-figures go plunging into a tunnel of death.

■ ■ ■

Ritu was still shivering in my arms, recovering her composure from the violation that my enemy inflicted on her—by forcing her onto an imprinting machine against her will. I wanted to ask Ritu about that. To find out how and why Beta (if it really *had* been a copy of the infamous ditnapper) grabbed her in the deep underground sanctuary of a supposedly secure military base.

Before I could begin, a series of loud tones reverberated around us from rank after rank of nearby rapid-bake kilns, announcing the emergence of yet more battle-dittos, sliding forth red and glowing with freshly sparked enzyme catalysis—special models that had been stored here at taxpayer expense, blank but ready to be imprinted with the souls of reserve warriors like Clara, only now hijacked by an infamous criminal for some reason I couldn't fathom.

If there had been just one or two of them, I could handle the situation quickly. Even a war-golem is helpless during those first moments after sliding from the activation oven. But a glance down the aisle of towering machines showed there were too many—dozens—already beginning to stand on trembling legs . . . legs like tree trunks . . . and stretching arms that could crush a small car. In moments their eyes would focus on Ritu and me. Eyes fired up with some purpose that I didn't want any part of.

And there were more bell-like tones, from tall ovens even farther away, ringing their birth announcements till they merged like some rippling call of destiny. *Do not ask for whom the kiln tolls,* commented a wry little voice within.

Time to get out.

"Let's go," I urged Ritu, and she nodded, as eager as I was to leave that place.

Together we fled in the only direction available, back toward the storeroom where that huge, silent mystery golem grabbed me less than half an hour ago and saved my life—though I didn't know its motive at the time. Departing, I glanced at the dissolving corpse of my benefactor, wondering who he was and how he knew that I needed help at that particular moment.

Then we were running past dark, fearsome-looking figures, molded and augmented for war. Terracotta forms that turned to glare at us, clumsily reaching out, but slowed by uneven peptide activation. Thank heavens. Fleeing their ranks, I led Ritu back down the corridor of shelves, looking for some weapon big enough to make a difference against their numbers. I'd settle for a simple phone to call up Base Security!

But nothing useful lay in sight—just tons of freeze-dried gourmet foods, stacked here against some doomsday scenario, meant to feed a governmental elite whose tax-paid job it is to stave off all varieties of doomsday.

There didn't seem to be any good hiding places, either. Not as a platoon of counterfeit warriors began entering the storage room after us, grunting and shuffling as they came. *Quick-imprinted,* I diagnosed. *Beta doesn't need quality, but speed and large numbers.*

A nagging sense of doubt yammered at me, screaming that none of it made sense. The golem that rescued me. Beta's sudden appearance here. The two waves of war-dittos that he created for some unexplained reason. The grabbing and force-imprinting of Ritu. It all had to mean something!

But there wasn't time to sort it out, only a series of rapid decisions. Like where to flee. Inexorably, we had but one choice.

Ritu balked at the tunnel entrance. "Where does it go?" she demanded.

"I think it leads under Urraca Mesa, to your father's cabin."

Her eyes widened and her feet planted hard, refusing to budge. I glanced beyond her shoulder to see those shuffling pseudosoldiers approach, still fifty meters away but closing.

"Ritu—" Despite rising anxiety, I restrained myself from tugging at her arm. She had already been subjected to more force today than anyone should endure.

At last her eyes cleared, coming around to focus on mine. With a grim tightening of the jaw, she nodded.

"All right, Albert. I'm ready."

Ritu took my offered hand. Together we plunged into the tunnel's stony-cold womb.

47

Vasic Instinct

. . . as gray and red expand by acclaymation . . .

Like a capacious, ever-expanding jar—this soul contains many.

It feels bottomless, able to absorb a gathering, a plenitude, a *forum* of standing waves, uniting in a resonant chorus of superposed frequencies, combining toward some culmination of ultimate power.

It isn't just the two of us anymore—the Albert Morris gray who was ditnapped from Kaolin Manor, plus the little red copy-of-a-copy who visited the Maharal's private museum for a memory test. Gray and red are linked, serving as mirrors in a mad scientist's wondrously terrifying "glazier" machine. And now there is more, much more.

No longer confined to a single skull—or even a pair of them—we/i expand into the vacant space between, filling its sterile void with a compellingly intricate melody . . . an ever-growing song of *me*.

A song heading for its crescendo.

Oh, some kind of amplification is happening, all right, as Yosil's demented ghost predicted. A multiplication of soul-rhythms on a scale I never imagined, though cults and mystics have chattered about such a possibility ever since the Golem Age began. It could be an egomaniac's sublime nirvana state—the self, exponentiated by countless virtual duplicates that reflect and resonate in perfect harmony, preparing to burst through, en masse, to a splendid new level of spiritual reification.

I always dismissed the notion as metaphysical nonsense, just another version of the age-old romantic-transcendentalist fantasy—like stone circles, UFO hallucinations, and "singularity" mirages were to other generations who kept yearning for a way to rise above this gritty plain. For a doorway to some realm beyond.

Only now it seems that one of the founders of this era, the legendary Professor Maharal, found a way . . . though something about his method drove him mad with fear.

Is that why ditYosil needs the soul of Albert Morris, to use as raw material? Because nothing about golemtech frightens me? Self-duplication always felt natural to Albert, like picking something comfortable to wear from the closet. Hell, I'm not even bothered much anymore by all the *pain* inflicted by this brutal machinery—some clever modification of the standard tetragramatron. *Creative* machinery that will soon nudge a zillion overlapping copies of my Standing Wave to unite in perfect unison, as light rays do in a laser, joining as collusive bosons rather than independent/bickering fermions . . .

Whatever that means. I can already feel the process working. In fact, there's a strong temptation to stop thinking and just let go . . . wallow in the simplicity . . . in the glorious *me*-ness of it all. Memory and reason feel like impediments, sullying the purity of a Standing Wave that multiplies on and on, filling an ever-expanding vessel.

I, amphorum . . .

Fortunately, there come respites when fierce, machine-driven energies aren't pummeling and stretching me/us according to plan, when cogent thought remains possible . . . even enhanced with a peculiar kind of focus. For example, right now I can perceive ditYosil bustling about nearby, sensing his presence in ways that go beyond mere sound or vision. The intensity of his desire. His growing excitement and confidence as a life-long goal draws near.

Above all, I feel ditYosil's burning concentration, enhanced by the genius that so often accompanies Smersh-Foxleitner syndrome . . . a concentration so fixed, he can ignore a rain of dust that falls from the cave's ceiling each time the stone walls shudder from some distant, booming explosion, as war-golems claw their way closer, ever closer to this buried lair.

They're still too far away for me to decipher much about their soul-harmonies. Could they even be me? It's tempting to imagine realAlbert, accompanied by an army of himselves . . . and maybe a whole bunch of Pal's wonderful/nasty specialty dittos . . . fighting their way up that tunnel, coming to the rescue.

But no. I forgot. I'm *dead.* ditYosil says he killed me. The real, organic Albert Morris had to die, so he wouldn't "anchor" my quantum-soul observer state to the material world—whatever that means.

Still puttering and preparing, Maharal's ghost fine-tunes a large pendulum that sways slowly back and forth between my red and gray cranium-mirrors, raising soul-ripples with each passage. Ripples that *thrum* to the lowest sound you ever heard—like the voice heard by Moses on Sinai . . .

I lack the proper technical vocabulary, but it's easy to imagine what'll happen when ditYosil steps aboard that rocking platform. Those ripples will *take over*. He plans to use my purified-amplified presence as a carrier wave, to boost his own essence higher. I'm to be *spent,* the same way that an expendable rocket is splurged, drained, and discarded in order to hurl an expensive probe toward the black abyss of space. Only the cargo I'm assigned to carry will be Maharal's soul-pattern . . . launching it toward something like godhood.

Everything makes sense, in a perverse way, except for one puzzling thing.

Wasn't I supposed to be losing my sense of identity by now? ditYosil predicted that my ego would be overwhelmed by the sheer ecstasy of amplification, removing all of Albert Morris's personal hang-ups and desires, leaving just Albert's talent for duplication, distilled, expanded, exponentiated. The purest of all booster rockets.

Is that happening? *Ego Reduction?* It . . . doesn't feel that way. Yes, I can sense the glazier machinery trying to achieve that. But my footing isn't loose. Albert's memories feel intact!

Moreover, what about all these echoes that i/we keep picking up? Musically resonant echoes that feel like they come from *outside?* Yosil never mentioned anything about that . . . and I don't plan on bringing it up.

For one thing, he's dismissed me as a cipher, a beast of burden, talented at copying but unworthy of respect.

But there's another reason.

I . . . we . . . are . . . am starting to enjoy this.

48

Mortar Enemies

. . . as Tuesday's frankie takes a turn as baked goods . . .

They say that golemtech arrived in Japan with much less upheaval than in the West, almost as if they expected it. The Japanese had no trouble with the idea of duplicating souls, in much the same way that Americans embraced the Internet, seeing it as a fundamental expression of their national will to *talk.* According to legend, all you had to do was give something eyes—a boat, a house, a robot, or even the fluffy *AnpanMan* who hawked pastry in cute TV commercials.

When it came to investing an object with soul, eyes mattered above all.

I thought about that while clinging to the bottom of Beta's skycycle, sheltering my face from a terrible wind that kept alternating between fire and ice. *Protect the eyes*, I told myself, desperately clutching a pair of slim handholds while my feet pressed hard against the landing skids. *Protect the eyes and brain. And never regret that you chose this way to die.*

During level flight my chief problem was wind chill, sucking warmth out of every exposed catalysis cell. But that was a picnic compared to the agony whenever the Harley banked or turned. Without warning, one or another of the thrust nozzles would swivel, grazing me with jets of collimated flame. All I could do then was swing my head to the other side of the narrow fuselage and try to squirm out of the way, reminding myself over and over why I had put myself in this fix . . . because it seemed like a pretty good idea at the time.

The alternative—to stay behind at the wrecked Volvo and make some kind of signal, then wait around for help—might have made sense if I were real, without a ticking expiration clock that could lapse any time in the next hour or so. But my logic had to be ditto logic. When Beta took off, I felt just one imperative more urgent than what little remained of my life.

Don't lose the scent.

I now realized Beta was key to understanding all that had happened during this bizarre week, starting from the moment I slinked into the basement of the Teller Building to uncover his pirate copying facility, with its stolen Wammaker template. That operation had already been hijacked by some enemy, presumably Aeneas Kaolin. Or so Beta claimed; Aeneas told a different story, portraying himself as the victim of perverted conspiracies. Then there were the dark, paranoid musings that Yosil Maharal had muttered on Tuesday morning, after he was already dead.

Who told the truth? All I knew for certain was that three brilliant and unscrupulous men—all of them much smarter than poor Albert Morris—were engaged in some kind of desperate, secretive, triangular struggle. And the secretive part was what impressed me most.

Nowadays, it takes power, money, and genuine cleverness to keep anything out of the public glare—a scrutinizing glare that was supposed to have banished all those awful, dark, twentieth-century clichés, like conniving moguls, mad scientists, and elite master criminals. Yet here were all three of those archetypes, battling each other while colluding to keep their conflict hidden from media, government, and the public. No wonder poor Albert was out of his league!

No wonder I had no choice but to follow the trail, whatever the cost. As Beta's skycycle sped through the night, just forty meters or so above the desert floor, I knew that one cost was going to be this body of mine, which kept getting baked each time those narrow torch-jets shifted to adjust course. Especially the portion of me that stuck out the most, my hapless clay ass. I could feel colloidal/pseudo-organic constituents react to the heat by fizzing and popping, sometimes loud enough to hear above the wind's tumult, gradually transforming supple lifeclay to the hard consistency of porcelain dinnerware.

Let me add, as a cheap utility greenie with an unbuffered Standing Wave, that it also hurt like hell! So much for the advantages of soulistic verisimilitude. I tried to find distraction by imagining our destination—presumably the goal that realAlbert and Ritu Maharal had been heading toward when the Volvo got ambushed. Some cryptic desert hideaway, where her father lurked during the weeks he went missing from Universal Kilns? Beta apparently knew where to go—which made me wonder.

He's trying to follow Ritu. But why, if not to reveal Yosil's hiding place? What other use could Beta have for her?

I tried to concentrate, but it's hard to do when your butt keeps getting singed every minute or two by sonocollimated heat. I found myself returning over and over to the image of poor little Palloid, my ferret-ditto companion, who got smashed before unhappy Pal could harvest memories of our long day together. *That was my sole chance to be remembered,* I thought glumly. *At this rate, all that'll be left of me is a pile of shattered statuary when Beta lands.*

For solace, I tried conjuring up an image of Clara's face—but that only increased the pain. *Her war must be approaching its big climax by now,* I thought, picturing how close we were to the Jesse Helms Combat Range. Beta would turn aside before then, of course. Still, I wondered about the coincidence . . . and hoped that Clara wouldn't get in too much trouble for going AWOL when Albert's house was destroyed. We had assigned each other survivor benefits, so maybe the army would understand.

If Albert truly is still alive, they may still have a chance to be happy together . . .

Anyway, something else was happening as the Harley sped through a night where even the stars seemed out of joint. My soul-wave kept doing unsettling things, jittering wildly . . . up-down, in-out . . . and through some of those weird directions that nobody has ever named properly—self-contained dimensions of spirit that Leow and others only began mapping a generation ago, exploring the newest *terra incognita* or final frontier. At first, the disturbances were almost too brief to notice. But those periodic tumults grew progressively stronger as the awful flight went on. Spikes of egotistical self-importance alternated with troughs of utter abnegation when I felt less than dust grain. Later, the effect was one of brief but intensely focused *awe*. When it passed, I wondered—

What next? Zen-like detachment?

Feelings of unity with the universe?

Or will I hear the booming voice of God?

Every culture has had what William James called "varieties of religious experience." They bloom whenever a person's Standing Wave plucks certain chords in the parietal nexus, Broca's area, or the spiritual-paraphrase juncture of the right temporal lobe. Of course, you can get similar sensations in clay—a soul is a soul—but the feelings are almost never as compelling as in trueflesh.

Or unless you get replenished and given one more whole day of life? Could *this* be why Aeneas Kaolin sabotaged his own Research Division? Because the new trick of extending ditto endurance had a side effect? Might it *convert* golemfolk, eventually sparking a holy revival among billions of artificial men? What if dittos stopped going home for inloading each night, abandoning their archies to seek their own, separate highway to redemption?

What a bizarre thought! Perhaps it was provoked by my visits to the affably crackpot Ephemerals. Or else by the blazing agony of being half-roasted alive! Maybe.

Still, I couldn't shake a growing impression that something or someone accompanied me during that tormented ride across a fractured sky, keeping pace nearby or within, between the fiery hell of my lower body and my wind-chilled face. Now and then, a half-heard echo seemed to urge me to *hang in there . . .*

The blustering gale abated a little, letting me glimpse a rough terrain of plateaus and deep ravines, steeply shadowed by a setting moon. The Harley began losing altitude, its wan beams lending the fractal landscape a kind of jagged beauty. Hollows loomed upward like gaping maws, eager to swallow me whole.

Maneuvering jets roared, swiveling to vertical, surrounding me in a cage of throbbing flame. I had to release one grip in order to throw an arm over my eyes. That left just two feet and a hand pressed against the skid supports, bearing my entire weight while those fingers and toes gradually cooked, hardening into crispy things.

As for the noise, it grew tolerable soon . . . I guess because I had nothing to hear with anymore. *Hold on,* an internal voice said, probably some tenacious part of Albert Morris that never learned to quit. I'll give him credit for that much, old Albert. Tenacious bastard.

Hold on just a little while—

Shivering reverberations rattled me like a mud doll. Some remote bits snapped! My stubborn grip failed at last and I fell . . .

(Time to rejoin the Earth already?)

. . . only the plummet was much shorter than expected. About half a meter or thereabouts. I barely felt a jolt as my seared backside hit the rocky desert floor.

Engines sputtered to a stop. Heat and ruction faded. Dimly, I knew— *we've landed.*

Still, it took several tries before I managed to command an arm to move, uncovering my last undamaged sense organs, and at first all I could see were clouds of agitated dust—then dim outlines of one landing skid. It took hard work to turn my head and look the other way. My neck seemed to be coated with a hard crust, something that resisted movement, cracking and giving way grudgingly, after strenuous effort.

Ah, there he is . . .

I spied a pair of legs turning to step away from the skycycle. There was no mistaking the spiral pattern motif covering the ditto's entire body. Ascending a dirt path, bordered by pale stone, Beta strode with a confident swagger.

I once moved like that. Yesterday, when I was young.

Now, broiled, abraded, and near expiration, I felt lucky to drag myself with one arm and half of another, grateful that the skycycle had plenty of ground clearance.

Once fully clear of the hot fuselage, I struggled to sit up and assess the damage.

That is, I *tried* to sit up. A few pseudomuscles responded down there, but they failed to make anything bend properly. With my good hand I reached down to tap along my hard-glazed back and buttocks. I clanked.

Well, well. It always seemed a quixotic-doomed gesture to leap through flaming jets and grab the departing skycycle. Yet here I was! Not exactly kicking, but still in motion. Still in the game. Sort of.

Beta had passed out of sight, vanishing among the varied shades of blackness. But now at least I could dimly make out his goal—a low, boxy outline nestled in the flank of an imposing desert mesa. Under starlight, it seemed little more than a modest, one-story structure. Perhaps a vacation cabin, or a long-abandoned shack.

Resting next to the slowly cooling Harley, I felt one more of those periodic *otherness* waves swarm by again. Only now, instead of preaching at me to persevere, or tantalizing with hints of infinity, the strange half-presence seemed more curious . . . questioning . . . as if it wondered, wordlessly, what business I had there.

Beats me, I thought, answering the vague feeling. *When I figure that one out, you'll be the first to know.*

4 9

Ditbulls at the Gate

. . . realAlbert is caught between rox and a
hard place . . .

It was a rather tight pickle that Ritu and I found ourselves in, squeezed by two squadrons of battle-golems who were marching in the same direction. The first armed contingent, just ahead, battled their way forward against stiff resistance while a second band of ditto-warrior reinforcements drew up behind, ready to take over when the first bunch were depleted. Ritu and I had to step along carefully in order to stay between the two advancing groups, forging ahead through that awful, dank tunnel. Only a few dim glowbulbs, tacked onto bare stone walls, kept us from stumbling in the dark.

"Well, there's one thing we can find satisfying," I quipped, trying to lift my companion's spirits. "At least our destination is near."

Ritu didn't seem amused by the irony, or cheered that we were finally approaching the goal we set out to visit Tuesday evening—the mountain villa where she spent weeks as a child, vacationing with her father. The trip had taken much longer than promised, by a route more circuitous and traumatic than either of us expected.

I kept searching for an alcove or crevice, any refuge to avoid being herded toward the harsh echoes of fighting—detonations and clanging ricochets—as the first squadron of battle-golems advanced against bitter resistance. But though Yosil Maharal's secret access shaft twisted enough to take advantage of softer layers in the rock, it never offered a safe place to duck and hide.

Lacking that, I'd give anything for a simple phone! I kept trying to use my implant, dialing for Base Security. But there weren't any public links within line of sight and the tiny transceiver in my skull couldn't transmit through stone. We were probably outside the boundaries of the Military Enclave by now, traversing deep under Urraca Mesa.

Serves you right, I thought. *You could have called for help ages ago. But no, you had to play go-it-alone sleuth. Smart guy.*

Ritu wasn't much help offering alternatives. Still, I tried to keep up one side of a conversation, talking to her in a low voice as we hurried along.

"What puzzles me is how Beta penetrated the Defense Zone without someone like Chen to escort him inside. And how did he even know we were here?"

Ritu seemed unsteady, perched halfway between listlessness and tears after her recent ruthless treatment. It made me hesitate before asking, "Do you have any idea what Beta wanted you for?"

I saw conflict in her eyes—a wish to confide, battling against a habitual terror of something that must never be said aloud. When she finally spoke, the words came haltingly and tinged with bitterness.

"What does Beta want me for? Is that your question, Albert? What's the ultimate thing that any male animal wants a female for?"

Her question made me blink. The answer might have seemed obvious a century ago, but sex just isn't the all-transfixing force that it was in Grandpa's day. How could it be? That urge is no harder to satisfy now than any other inherited Stone Age hunger, like the yearning for salt or fatty snack foods.

So, if not sex, what else could she be talking about? "Ritu, we don't have time for riddles."

Even in the dark, I saw symptoms of a carefully buttressed facade collapsing. The corners of her mouth moved—halfway between a tremor and a sardonic smile. Ritu wanted to divulge, but had to do it on her own terms, preserving a sliver of pride. A measure of distance and . . . yes . . . that old superiority.

"Albert, do you know what happens inside a chrysalis?"

"A chrys . . . you mean a *cocoon*? Like when a caterpillar—"

"—turns into a butterfly. People envision a simple transformation: the caterpillar's legs turn into the butterfly's legs, for instance. Seems logical, no? That the caterpillar's head and brain would serve the butterfly in much the same way? Continuity of memory and being. Metamorphosis was seen as a cosmetic change of outer tools and coverings, while the entity within—"

"Ritu, what does any of this have to do with Beta?" I honestly couldn't see a connection. The infamous ditnapper made his fortune offering cheap copies of highly coveted—and copyrighted—personalities like Gineen Wammaker. Ritu Maharal certainly had her own quirks, as unique as the maestra's. But who would *pay* for bootleg copies of an administrator at Universal Kilns? What profit could Beta see in it?

Ritu ignored my interruption.

"People think the caterpillar changes *into* a butterfly, but that doesn't happen! After spinning a chrysalis around itself, the caterpillar dissolves! The whole creature melts into nutrient soup, serving only to nourish a tiny embryo that feeds and grows into something else. Something altogether different!"

I glanced back nervously, weighing the distance of marching footsteps. "Ritu, I don't get what you're—"

"Caterpillar and butterfly share a lineage of chromosomes, Albert. But their genomes are separate, coexisting in parallel. They need each other the same way that a man needs a woman . . . to *reproduce*. Other than that—"

Ritu stopped walking because *I* had stopped, halting suddenly, my feet unable to move as I stared without blinking. Her revelation burst in my brain at last, just like a bomb.

Now, don't get me wrong. I'm usually calm about new ideas. In fact, I've always tried to be a skeptic, especially when I'm walking around in realflesh. An archie-debunker, you might say. But right then, her words and their implications *hurt* so much that I wanted desperately to push them away, and all understanding with them.

"Ritu, you . . . can't be saying . . ."

". . . that they're paired creatures. Caterpillar and butterfly need each other, yet have in common no desires or values. No loves."

I could hear the second contingent of war-golems coming up from behind, even more intimidating now that I had some inkling of their inner nature. Still, I couldn't move without asking one more question. I met Ritu's eyes. In the dimness, everything was gray.

"Which are you?" I asked.

She laughed, a bitter sound that bounced harshly off the tunnel walls.

"Oh, I'm the butterfly, Albert! Can't you tell? I'm the one who gets to flutter in the sunlight, reproducing in blithe and blissful ignorance.

"That is, I used to be. Till last month, when I started to realize what was going on."

My mouth felt dry as I followed up. "And Beta?"

The strain showed in her short, barked laugh. Ritu's head jerked toward the sound of marching feet.

"Him? Oh, Beta works hard, I'll give him that much. He's the one with hungers. Ambitions. Voracious appetites.

"And one more thing," she added. "He gets to remember."

50

Through a Simulacrum, Darkly

. . . or, a glazier in the glass . . .

I should feel honored. This really is genius-level stuff.

It's apparent in the amplified Standing Wave that I'm now part of, filling a space far greater than the body-limited ripples that are contained within a typical golem. It pulses and throbs with power that I never before imagined.

Yosil Maharal must have known that he was on the verge of an epochal breakthrough, both beautiful and terrifying. And that terror did its work on him . . . on the solipsistic cowardice that comes embedded with Smersh-Foxleitner syndrome. Naked fear battled the awe-drenched draw of an unparalleled opportunity to change the world, and that conflict tipped him the rest of the way into madness.

A madness that his ghost manifests in spades, ranting as he cranks up the soul-stretching machinery, preparing me/us for my/our assigned role as a *carrier wave*—a finely tuned vehicle for transporting the Yosil-soul to Olympian grandeur . . .

. . . even as echoes of distant gunfire penetrate from some nearby subterranean passageway, creeping closer by the minute.

■   ■   ■

"You know, Morris, it's awful how people take miracles for granted. TwenCenners adapted to *faster* lives, because of jets and cars. Our grandparents could fetch any book by Internet. We got used to living in *par-*

allel—the convenience of being in several places at once. For two generations we've just tweaked golemtech, making minor improvements, never pushing beyond the physique-limited vision of Aeneas Kaolin's clay dolls.

"Such banality! People receive a splendid gift, then lack the will or vision to exploit it fully!"

■   ■   ■

Ah yes, contempt for the masses, one of the lovelier Smersh-Foxleitner symptoms. Better not answer, though. He thinks I'm already largely subsumed into the giant, amplified waveform of the glazier beam—the augmented spiritual field that he designed to utilize the perfect duplicating talent of Albert Morris, while deleting the ego-consciousness that made Albert special to himself.

Something's gone wrong with his plan. It must have, since *I* am still here. Smeared thin, rolled up, sliced, and then mirror-multiplied ten thousandfold . . . in fact, there seems to be more me than ever! Tickled and driven by electric currents. Vibrating in a dozen dimensions and sensitive to countless things I never before noticed before—like a myriad flakes of crystalline mica, floating like glittery diatoms within the surrounding ocean of stone.

It *is* an ocean, of magma that flowed here ages ago. The mountains are waves. I feel this one still moving, slower now, having cooled and congealed. But everywhere, still in motion.

I can even start to stretch my perceptions beyond this mountain, reaching out toward polyspectral sparkles that seem to glimmer in the distance, just beyond clear reckoning, like tendrils of delicate smoke . . . or like fireflies that tremble at my touch. . . .

Metaphors fail me. Am I sensing other people? Other *souls* beyond this underground lab?

It's an austere, terrifying sensation. A reminder of something we all suppress most of the time, because it hurts so much.

The stark loneliness of individuality.

The essential *alienness* of others.

And of the universe itself.

■   ■   ■

"The real driver is pleasure," ditYosil continues while nudging instrument settings toward perfect synchronization. "Take the entertainment industry back in one-body days. People wanted to watch *what* they wanted, *when* they wanted. Demand brought analog videotape into being, three decades before digital technology was ready to do the job right. A ridiculous, kludge solution using magnetic heads and noisy whirling parts, yet VCRs sold by the millions so that people could copy and play whatever they desired.

"Doesn't that sound like dittoing in our time, Morris? A clumsy, ornate industry that ships hundreds of millions of intricate clay-analog devices all over the world, every day. The complexity! The resources and cash flow! Yet people pay, gladly, because it lets them be wherever they want, whenever they desire.

"A fabulous, flamboyant industry, and my good friend Aeneas Kaolin counts on it going on forever.

"But it will end soon, won't it, Morris? Because the crucial breakthroughs are ready at last. Like digital finally overwhelming analog recording. Like jet planes outracing the horse. After we're done tonight, things will never be the same."

■   ■   ■

The pendulum sways, rhythmically cutting through my/our amplified Standing Wave, plucking complex harmonies with every sweep. Soon, ditYosil will climb aboard and his ghastly personality will start drawing all the stored-up power, taming it, preparing to ride the glazier beam toward deification.

If only that were all that lay at stake, I'd almost be happy to help. I'm expendable—a golem knows it. And much as I dislike Maharal's ghost for its callous smugness, the scientific wonder of this experiment might make my sacrifice seem almost reasonable. At one level I know he's right. Humanity has been marking time, mired in an orgy of self-involvement, squandering vast resources on teeny personal satisfactions that don't add up to much at all.

There's something much bigger awaiting us. I can tell, sensing it now with growing certainty as the glazier amplification mounts. Maharal—no matter how twisted by sickness—had the vision to know this. And the brilliance to hunt down a hidden door.

Yes, he's made a mistake of some sort. My ego hasn't gone away as planned. Instead of leaving only a perfect copying template behind—a healthy root substrate for his diseased soul to graft onto—my sense of selfness seems to grow and expand with each passing minute, in ways that no longer seem painful but more akin to voluptuous bliss.

And for the first time it occurs to me . . . this may not be a bad thing. In fact—

In fact, I'm starting to wonder. Who is in the best position to exploit this magnificent glazier, when it finally attains full power? Its inventor? The one who understands the theory?

Or the one who dwells *within* the ever-growing Standing Wave? The one who makes it possible by virtue of raw duplicating talent? The one who, you might say, was born for it?

Hey, theoretical understanding is overrated. Anyway, as we/I amplify, grow, and spread, I can start to feel Maharal's knowledge, like a riffling breeze of index cards, all aflurry nearby, close enough to reach out and access—

Who says *he* should be the rider and *I* the steed?

Why not the other way around?

51

Ceiling Fate

. . . as Greenie falls in . . .

It's kind of hard to move about when half of you has fallen off or broken down.

Crushed and burned, shrunken and diminished, I had only partial function in one leg to help me haul myself upward along the fuselage of the skycycle, perching next to its cockpit, leaning in to fumble at whatever buttons I could reach. I was trying for the radio, to transmit a general distress call. But after a few encouraging bloops and beeps and instrument flashes, what I somehow triggered was the autopilot!

"Emergency escape procedure activated," a voice announced, loud enough to make out through seared and blasted ears. My torso felt a rumble as the engine reignited. *"Closing canopy. Prepare for lift."*

I was still dazed and muddled from the nightmare ride that brought me here, so it took a couple of seconds to realize—or notice the glass bubble swinging down. I managed to pull my head back in time, but not my left arm, which got pinned in that moment of indecision.

Damn! I was used to pain by then, but this crushing sensation was ghastly as the transparent canopy tried to squeeze shut. For some reason it didn't sense my arm was in the way. A malfunction? Or did Beta program the unit not to care about trivial clay limbs when a quick getaway was at stake? All I could do—while the lift ducts sandblasted grit into the air—was send commands for my trapped left hand to keep stabbing buttons, hoping to shut it off.

Instead, my efforts gave the Harley conniptions! It bucked and jittered, with each jerk tearing agonizingly at my arm as the glass bubble tried to close. Why couldn't the idiot machine sense that no one was aboard! Perhaps it also served Beta as a pilotless courier, conveying small objects, like severed heads.

What little feeling I had in my left leg sensed the ground's queasy departure. I was flying again!

More buttons and switches fell before my chopping hand, which kept swinging long after an organic arm would have nerves and circulation pinched off. All the clay version needed was some residual connection for me to order a splurge of all its remaining *élan.* The limb flung wildly, seeking things to twist and pull, until the canopy's steady guillotine pressure finally tore through.

The weight of my body did the rest. I looked down—

—about fifteen or twenty meters, almost straight down to the roof of Maharal's cabin.

Frantically twisting during my plummet, I managed to strike the shingles first with my useless right leg.

Did you ever have that feeling of viewing life through the wrong end of a telescope? Everything from the moment of impact seemed to happen in a fog of dulled senses—the noise and jarring force were distant things, happening to someone else. Even time felt softened as another of those eerie *otherness* waves came over me. I could swear the substance of that termite-eaten roof dissolved as I passed right through, floating toward the floor amid cottony clouds of splinters, dust, insects, and other debris.

Landing on my back, I heard an awful thud. But other senses disagreed. To touch, it felt like rebounding off the surface tension of a soap bubble, hardly jarring at all. An illusion, of course, for I could tell that more chunks of me had broken off.

Bottomed out at last, I stared up at a ragged circle of sky—rimmed by still-crumbling rafters. Soon the dust haze cleared enough to glimpse Beta's poor skyscooter almost directly overhead, brighter but more frantic than the surrounding stars. Flaming extravagantly, the damaged machine fought to right itself, then turned laboriously to head off. *Westward,* I guessed from a glimpse of Sagittarius, and from the orientation of the cabin walls. *A good choice, if you're trying to get help . . . or to be destroyed.*

Speaking of destruction, I saw little option but to write off this particular branching of the multilimbed life tree of one Albert Morris. Tiredness didn't begin to describe how I felt. What little of me could feel anything at all.

There was no "salmon urge" anymore. Just the siren song of slurry . . . the beckoning of the recycling bin, calling me to rejoin the great clay circle, in confident hope that my physical substance may yet find some better use, in a luckier ditto.

But not one who's seen or done more with its life, I thought, finding consolation. It had been interesting, the last few days. I had few regrets.

Except that Clara will never hear the whole story . . .

Yeah. That was too bad, I agreed.

. . . and now the bad guys will win.

Aw, man. Whatever nagging inner voice had to put in that last bit? What guilt-tripping nag? If I could, I'd tear it out! Just shut up and let me die, I groused.

You gonna just lie there and let 'em get away with it?

Crap. I didn't have to take this from some obsessive soul corner of a cheap-model golem who was misborn a frankie . . . became a ghost . . . and any moment was about to graduate to melting corpse.

Who's a corpse? Speak for yourself.

Stunning wit, that triple irony. Speak for myself, indeed. And though I tried hard to ignore the little voice, something surprising happened. My right hand and arm *moved,* lifting slowly till five trembling fingers came within sight of my good eye. Then my left leg twitched. Without conscious command, but reacting to imprinted habits a million years old, they started cooperating with each other, fumbling to shift my weight, then pushing to turn me over.

Oh well. Might as well help.

As I've said, Albert was always pigheaded, obstinate, persistent— and I guess that endearing trait came through on Tuesday morning when he made me, rolling his soul into this inert doll and willing it to move . . . with much the same sanguine hopefulness as ancient Sumerian scribes who long ago held that each clay impression manifested something sacred and magical. A brief but potent shove back against the surrounding darkness.

So I crawled, using one arm and a half-usable leg to haul what was left of me past broken furniture and tattered western-motif rugs, through an open door with a shattered lock and then over fresh footprints that led down a long, dusty hallway—a corridor that seemed to push right into the mountain. Following Beta.

What else could I do, since it seemed quite clear that I was too stubborn to die?

52

Prototypes

. . . as realAI peels away layers . . .

There had been clues. Too subtle for the likes of me, but somebody smarter might have caught on ages ago.

Beta—the name implied "number two" or a second version. Ritu's middle name was *Lizabetha.* And in mythology, Maharal—the name her father chose to adopt before she was born—had been a title given to the greatest late medieval maker of golems . . . while another reverent appellation for one with that skill was Betalel or Betzalel.

And so it went, on and on. The sort of childish puzzle-hints that made you groan, both over your own stupidity and the comic book immaturity of it all.

Another reason I never caught on? Maybe because I'm old-fashioned at heart. The gender difference between lovely-reserved Ritu and the prodigally flamboyant Beta shouldn't have fooled a worldly fellow like me, who's seen plenty of ostentatious cross-roxing in his time. The fact that it did trick me proves what a conservative old fart I really am, dammit. Unwarranted assumptions are the bane of any private eye.

I still had trouble absorbing this, trying desperately to recall what I've learned over the years about Multiple Personality Disorder, or MPD.

It's not an either-or thing. Most people experience the fluid overlap of amorphous subselves from time to time, debating or contesting internally when awkward decisions have to be made—imagining inner dialogues till the conflict is resolved. They do this without engendering any lasting fracture or disturbing the illusion of a single, unified identity. At the opposite extreme are those with mental schisms that are rigid, adamant, and even self-hateful, erecting permanent personas who hold opposing values, voices, and names, battling each other over control.

You seldom ran across truly blatant examples back in pre-kilning days, outside of a few famous case studies and some movie exaggerations, because one body and brain don't offer enough room! Confined to a single cranium, one dominant character-facade usually held fierce command. If others lurked—products of trauma perhaps, or neural injury—they'd be reduced to waging guerrilla wars of spite or life sabotage from below.

Dittoing changed all that. Though MPD is still rare, I've seen imprinting unleash the unexpected from time to time. Some peculiarity that lay dormant or suppressed in the original would burst forth in a duplicate, unleashed to manifest in ditto form.

But never anything as extreme as this Ritu/Beta flipflop! One in which the original person—a seemingly competent professional—somehow remained unaware of the very existence of her alter ego, even though it hijacked nearly every ditto that she made.

As a mere criminalist, I'm no expert psych-diagnostician. Guessing, I pondered a possible link to Yang-Pimintel disease. Possibly a variant of Smersh-Foxleitner, or a rare and dangerous variety of Moral Orthogonality syndrome. Frightening stuff! Especially since a few of these disorders show significant association with the worst kind of genius. The persuasively self-deceptive kind, fashioning brilliantly amoral rationalizations for any crime.

History shows that some of these psychopathologies have been heritable, passing from one generation to the next. It could explain why I've been outclassed from the very start.

▪   ▪   ▪

Much of this raced through my mind a few seconds after Ritu obliquely revealed the truth through her *parable of the chrysalis.* I wanted to stand and stare, to blink in a fugue of dismayed realization, stammering incoherent questions—in other words, all the time-honored ways that folks react to extreme surprise. But there wasn't time to do any of that, only to resume our hurried march. What choice did we have, with one platoon of Betas in front of us, fighting their ahead way through the tunnel, and a contingent of reinforcements pressing close behind?

I finally understood why the two groups of Beta-drones had left us alone so far, allowing the gap around us to remain intact. Ritu—their archie and reproducer—was now safely pinned right where they wanted, available in case more dittos had to be made. Till then, they had no reason to harass her any further. Indeed, they would be fiercely devoted to protecting her physical welfare.

I tried frantically to make sense of this.

Ritu always had the power to destroy Beta, by staying off copying machines! If the butterfly refused to lay any more eggs, there'd soon be no more chomping caterpillars.

To protect against that, paranoid Beta would have stashed extra frozen copies all over town. I met one of them behind the Teller Building, after Tuesday's raid, when it spoke about someone *"taking over my operations. . . ."* Did one of those backup copies follow us here to force Ritu onto an imprinter?

Why, in all the time since we set out on Tuesday night, did Ritu never warn me about this!

All right, at one point she mentioned that her dittos were "unreliable," that most of them went missing, unaccountably. Even the fraction who loyally performed their assigned chores only brought home partial memories, because—I now knew—the missing experiences were seized and stored away by the proto-Beta personality, hiding in her brain. From Ritu's point of view, dittoing must have seemed a horribly inefficient and unsatisfying process, even before she learned the truth about Beta.

In that case, I wondered, *why do it at all?*

Rationalizations. People are talented at coming up with reasons to keep doing stupid things. Perhaps she worried about the modern bigotry toward those who cannot ditto—the unkind implication that such folks are barren, with no soul to copy.

Or she might have kept imprinting because an official of Universal Kilns *has* to send out duplicates, even if it takes four tries to make one that goes where it's told. Certainly she could afford the cost.

Maybe she needed desperately to pretend she was like everybody else.

I guessed one more reason. A compulsion from below. Inner pressure that could only be satisfied by laying between the soul-probes, feeling them palp and massage, pressing her Standing Wave sensually into wet clay. Something like an addiction, along with the denial blindness *to* addiction that has always plagued junkies, of every kind.

No wonder it took years for her to admit her problem aloud.

I had been wondering how Beta managed to track us across open desert, then follow us past every security screen into a buried national security redoubt. The answer hit me. He did nothing of the sort! Beta simply lay quiescent *inside* Ritu, building pressure within her till the strain grew intolerable. At which point she slipped away from me and Corporal Chen, rushing to one of the giant military autokilns we had seen. Loathing herself, like any addict giving in to a foul habit, she laid herself down, seeking relief between the floating tetragramatron tendrils, surrendering to her insistent, stronger half—a master thief and desperate character, the sort of devil-may-care who dared all and defied every authority of the lawful outer world.

No wonder I was never able to connect Beta to a real person! Oh, the endless hours I spent in ebony form, laboriously noting and encoding fragments of Beta's speech and other personality quirks, sieving the Net in search of someone who used similar patterns of phrasing, syntax, and emphasis—the sort of arduous slog that lets a plodding detective track down even the shrewdest arch criminal, given enough time.

Only all that work was wasted in this case. Because the villain had a perfect hiding place, and Ritu spoke with a voice-manner that was nothing at all like Beta's.

At last, here was my nemesis, my Moriarty, walking beside me in the dark corridor, shivering with both dread and shame in her dark eyes. How long did this secret personality alternation go on before Ritu finally grew suspicious, then fully aware of her gangster other half?

Was that why she first decided to hire me? In order to have Beta's expert adversary on retainer? Finding her missing father probably had little to do with it, at first. Not till Yosil Maharal was found dead on the highway.

And yet, there *had* to be more of a connection than that.

Shaking my head, I found it hard to concentrate because of sheer emotion. Because by this point I was positively boiling with anger!

Ritu had known what was going on—the potential for extreme danger—by the time we set out together Tuesday evening. *So why didn't she warn me?* All those hours and days in the desert, then underground, and never once did she mention the pressure that must have been building up inside her. The clutch of demon's eggs that she carried, ready to hatch as soon as there was an opportunity.

Damn her selfish, self-centered—

Something in my attitude may have crossed the short space between us. Or maybe the fierce reality of our situation tore away Ritu's last

illusions. For whatever reason, after minutes of silent walking my companion spoke at last.

"I'm . . . so sorry, Albert," she whispered.

Glancing at her face I could see what tormented courage it took to
form that simple apology. Yet I was in no mood to let her off the hook
so easy. Because we both knew what Beta would do—what he *had* to
do—in order to survive.

If Ritu got away now, she might finally acknowledge the gravity of
her condition and seek cloistered refuge at a hospital resort while Beta's
supply of secretly cached ditsicles slowly expired, their memories growing ever more useless and obsolete. Under expert therapy, her secondary
personality would be summoned forth, challenged, forced to justify itself
or else face drastic treatment.

Even if denial set in again and Ritu avoided getting help, I'd surely
report the situation to both her employer and her personal physician.
Anyway, with or without therapy, Beta would be washed up as a criminal
mastermind. Because notoriety would subject Ritu Lisabetha Maharal to
ongoing scrutiny by the World Eye . . . by free networks of amateurs
who'd never let her dittos out of sight. Not for years to come. Underworld
figures hate that sort of illumination. They find it hampering, as we
learned in the years following the Big Heist.

To avoid that, Beta couldn't let either of us go free. He must find a way
to keep Ritu prisoner, a slave to this weird reproduction cycle forever—a
kind of self-rape that would have given me utter willies, if I weren't even
more worried about myself.

Because my old foe Beta had no reason to keep me alive at all.

Trying to fit the pieces, I thought, *Beta must've been the one who
tried to kill me with that missile strike on my home. Did he realize I was
hot on the trail of . . .*

*. . . but that makes no sense! Wasn't a copy of Aeneas Kaolin nosing
around the Maharal house, late on Tuesday? He was skulking about,
looking for stuff while eager to avoid being caught in the act by Ritu's
gray.*

*And it was Kaolin who shot at Ritu and me, as were drove through
the desert.*

*He must have grown wise to the link between Ritu and Beta, maybe
even earlier than she did.*

Was he the one "taking over" Beta's operations?

I remembered my first meeting with Ritu and her boss in that fabulous
Yugo limousine. They had both seemed united and sincere about hiring

me to help find the missing Professor Maharal. Under the surface, each of them must have also been thinking about using my expertise to help control the Beta persona . . . and maybe to exploit it . . .

But all that changed by Tuesday evening. Something spooked Aeneas. Was it the prion attack at Universal Kilns? Or maybe something else, having to do with Ritu's father.

That could explain why he sent one of his platinums to attack us on the highway. Ritu and I were both disguised as grays. Kaolin might have thought that I was making an alliance with Beta, and we were both on our way to rendezvous with—

My mind was thrashing about, grabbing threads from all directions. But before these floundering thoughts could coalesce into a new picture, I abruptly noticed something far more pressing. Something offering a ray of hope that our luck had changed.

On the left appeared a branching passageway. A possible way out.

▪   ▪   ▪

This smaller tunnel cut backward at a sharp angle, close to the one we had been following till now. My impression—it seemed aimed toward another part of the nearby military base we had just departed. Professor Maharal must have had more than one target when he delved for hidden treasure down here, helping himself to a nation's hoard of secret, high-tech marvels.

This new hole looked even more dank and narrow than the first. But it offered a slim chance and I took it without hesitation, grabbing Ritu's arm and tugging her after me.

She made no complaint, coccooned again in her blanket of passive resignation. *No wonder Ritu could be bullied around by a figment of her own imagination,* I thought—admittedly a churlish remark. *How strange that the aggressive, stronger-willed part of her was suppressed, only to be released through dittoing. She must have had a strange childhood.*

Progress grew difficult. This tunnel was much rougher and so cramped that we had to stoop much of the time. Less effort had been taken to flatten the floor, as if the builder didn't expect to need this passage very long. Glowbulbs were fewer and most seemed to have been shot out in recent fighting. Fragments of robotic cockatrice guardians lay everywhere, mingling with pools of recently dissolved golem slurry. Surrogates of clay and silicon had waged a brief, bitter struggle down this narrow lane.

Were there survivors? More important, were they still tuned to avoid injuring beings made of flesh? Or did such legalistic distinctions matter anymore?

I lost track of time and distance. (My implant wasn't working down there, of course.) Still, a sense of hope grew as Ritu and I hurried. We *must* be getting near the base again—whatever part of it Yosil spent so many golem-years digging to reach. Once inside, I'd waste no time making that phone call—

Suddenly, I tripped over something in the shadows, stumbling past a squishy obstruction. A *body* groaned and reached for me with massive arms, but I managed to jump out of the way. And the supine battle-golem couldn't pursue because three quarters of it had been blown away.

That was the good news.

The bad news: now Ritu and I were on opposite sides of the crippled warrior-doll, which turned what was left of a smoldering head to peer at us at us before it asked—

"Making a break for it, Morrissss?"

The raspy, slobbery voice wasn't too bad, for someone with just half a face. Most dittos would disintegrate after such injuries, their Standing Waves unraveling like spun candy in a thunderstorm. But gladiatorial models are sturdy.

"You don't want to go that way." The head nodded in the direction I had been heading.

"Why not?" I asked. "Were the defenses too strong, Beta? Couldn't blast your way through?"

The fractured figure shrugged. "No, we made it. But Yossie had already grabbed the stuff. He's holding out in his lab. I shudder to think what he plans to do with—"

"Whoa! What are you talking about? Maharal is dead!"

A dry chuckle. "You think so?"

I spat to get rid of a sudden foul taste. "The police coroner was thorough. Yosil Maharal died in that car wreck. And by now any ghosts would have—"

"Any ghosts would still be around, Morris. But Alpha never told you about that, did she?"

Alpha. Beta's nickname for Ritu, naturally. In the dim light her face seemed gaunt, sickened by the figure on the ground, by its injuries and flippant attitude, but above all by the Mirror Effect—disgust at seeing a reflection of yourself that you despise. She had it bad.

"What's he talking about?" I demanded. But Ritu only backed away two steps, shaking her head.

The shattered golem laughed. "Go on, tell him! Tell Morris about Project Zoroaster and its multifaceted assault on the status quo. Like the new method to replenish dittos, so they last weeks or even months—"

"But that would . . . ."

"—or the research into making better imprints from one ditto to another. That's the part I was interested in professionally, of course, to make piracy really pay. I needed details that Ritu never learned at her day job, way up in the UK management dome, and for some finicky reason she refused to go down to R&D, no matter how hard I prodded. So I came up with a nifty espionage plan instead . . . one that used you, Morris.

"Only it must've backfired, I guess. Seems I finally offended somebody powerful. Someone with the resources to track me down and—"

"Powerful. You mean Kaolin?"

A shrug. "Who else? He was already upset when Yosil vanished, taking all his records and prototypes. Maybe Aeneas decided it was time to clean house, to purge Project Zoroaster . . . and get rid of all his enemies while he was at it.

"But your guess about that is as good as mine. This is the first chance I've had to incarnate for weeks! When it comes to recent events, all I know is what Ritu's seen and heard. If only I had time, I'd put out feelers. Verify what I think panicked Aeneas. Maybe plan some revenge.

"But now—"

Tremors shook the remnant golem. Clay skin that once seemed nearly as supple as the real thing now cracked, rapidly mimicking the onset of age. Struggling, ditBeta grunted a few words at a time.

"Now . . . there's a much . . . more critical matter . . . to deal with."

I shook my head.

"You mean Yosil's ghost is trying to do something—"

"—that must be stopped!" The clay soldier used its good arm to grab at at Ritu. "Go on . . . Tell Morris . . . what it's about. Tell him what . . . Father is trying to do.

"Tell him!"

A wild look filled Ritu's eyes. She treated two more steps the way we came, back toward Urraca Mesa and the hidden sanctuary of Yosil Maharal. I could only make out the whites of her eyes as I called.

"Wait! Beta's trying to spook you . . . to herd you back among the others. But this one's harmless, look!" I struck with my foot and the arm flew off, shattering as it hit the ground.

"Come this way," I urged, holding out my hand to help her to step over the decaying war-doll. "We can escape—"

"Eshcape!" Beta's putrefying ditto was down to a corroded half-face and part of a torso, yet it maintained enough force of will to emit guttural laughter.

"Jussst go to the end . . . of thiss tunnel . . . Morrissss . . . and see your *esh—cape!*"

The golem's final cackle was the last straw for Ritu. With a moan of dread and self-revulsion, she swiveled about and ran back the way we came, toward the main tunnel. None of my shouts availed.

You can't reason with blind panic. Not that I blame her.

Soon—predictably—I heard Ritu's despairing cry as she ran headlong into our pursuers. More Betas, no more pleasant than the version at my feet. Only these would be intact.

I couldn't help her now. My sole chance was to turn and flee as the nearest Beta liquefied at last. His final laughter flayed at me, driving my haste as it had Ritu's, even after the last audible echoes faded.

A real battle must have raged here, I observed. Machines set up by Yosil Maharal fought bitterly against clay automatons bearing one aspect of his daughter's many-faced personality. The treasure they vied over must be important! Hurrying, I heard a distant drum of pursuing footsteps, drawing closer from behind.

At last, the crude tunnel came to an abrupt end. A metal wall stretched left and right before me—armor that was clearly meant to keep trespassers out. The barrier should have worked. It *might* have, if the base guardians had listened for approaching moles. They meant to, I knew. They established all the proper instruments and vigilant watch programs. Only someone much smarter managed to hack the defense system, fooling the mechanical wardens of this secret redoubt into ignoring blatant sounds of digging.

A broad face of high-tech steel had been exposed, then a jagged-slanted section removed, carefully avoiding embedded continuity detectors. More evidence of an inside job, planned by someone in the know. Of course this was all short term. It wouldn't take long to track down the culprit, once Base Security services were roused. The thief had only a little time to execute his plan, whatever it was.

Approaching the wall fissure—a centimeter thick, I noted—the implant in my left eye scanned for ambush by any leftover cockatrice-bots, though all I saw were fragments. It also got busy trying to put through that phone call to Base Security, but no link was in line-of-sight yet. I'd have to step inside and hope . . .

Then I saw the emblem:

BIOHAZARD
EXTREME DANGER TO ORGANIC LIFE

The armored room was supposed to have just one entrance. I saw it opposite from me—a heavy airlock with massive, overlapping closures. Almost as imposing were a dozen bulky refrigerators, each of them triple-locked and covered with ribbon seals to show any trace of tampering.

Somebody *had* tampered, though, carefully bypassing the alarm wiring on two storage units, then slicing new openings to avoid the locks. Frosty condensation exhaled from the gaps as laboring heat pumps strove to keep up. But that cold was nothing compared to the chill passing through my heart as I glimpsed all the burglary detritus strewn across the floor—abandoned metal trays and torn plastic coverings showing more of those frightening BIOHAZARD symbols. Without any conscious will on my part, the implant zoomed till I could read some ripped tags, carrying names like *Airborne Saringenia and Tumoformia Phiddipidesia: Advanced Strain.*

Clara once told me about *Saringenia*—a truly nasty organic plague that had been tested during the Fizzle War. As for *Phiddipidesia,* a mild version that escaped ten years ago caused the SouthWestern Eco-Toxic Aquifer Plume. I shuddered to imagine what an "advanced" strain could do.

According to solemn treaty, stocks were supposed to have been destroyed long ago.

Naturally, web cynics have always spun lurid tales about dark conspiracies. Vaults like this one had to exist, they claimed. It just isn't in human nature to throw away a weapon.

I stood there, half-astride the gap in the metal wall, gazing into whistle-blower's paradise, pondering the huge tattler's bounty if I reported all this to the open nets . . . and wondering how the Dodecs ever managed to keep it secret in this day and age. That is, I *would* have pondered such things, I'm sure, if I weren't paralyzed with mind-numbing terror. Especially when I noticed a spray of glittering slivers on the floor . . . bits of glass from vials that had fallen during the hurried robbery.

It was already way too late to start holding my breath.

How long I stood there, blankly staring at death's shiny frosting, I cannot imagine. What finally stirred me from blank fixation was a sound—drumming footbeats announcing the approach of a more familiar and tangible threat. One the mind could grasp.

"Well, Morris. Here you are." Beta's voice rocked me off the cusp of fear. "Now you see what's at stake. So why don't you be a good little shamus and back away from there, hm?" From the shadows behind me emerged half a dozen of the burly war-dittos Beta had hijacked from the reserve armory, advancing under the tunnel's low ceiling in a stooped crouch.

As they drew near, I felt something precious start to vanish—my power to act. To affect events. I don't know about you, but to me that power can mean more than one measly life, even a real one. In this case, a whole lot more.

I jumped the rest of the way into the storage room and began running for the door at the other end. "No!" the nearest Beta cried. "Let me handle this! You don't know what you're doing. Your body heat could set off—"

I strained to turn the big wheel controlling eight big steel pins that sealed the hatch shut. No codes or locks should be needed to turn it from the *inside,* right? I felt it start to move . . .

Battle-golems are fast, though. They were on me before the wheel turned thirty degrees. Implacable hands pried loose my grip, further abusing my sore thumb, then a jumbo-sized Beta slung me under one arm—a sensation I was really starting to hate. Writhing and kicking, I flailed frantically as he carried me away from the big hatch, till we passed the cool surface of a storage refrigerator. When my hand brushed strands of luminescent ribbon I spasmodically *grabbed,* yanking and tearing clumps from their moorings.

That had results! Abruptly, the ambient lighting switched from muted white to alert red. Shrill blarings resounded.

"That tears it," one Beta muttered.

"We'll bring him along anyway," my bearer answered, bending over to reenter the cramped tunnel while hauling me like a slab of meat. Soon we were racing along, driven by augmented ceramic muscles that felt uncomfortably hot near my skin, especially after leaving that refrigerated room. All I could do was watch stony walls tear by in a blur, inches from my face, growing disoriented, as if in a fever.

Was I already infected with some fast-acting plague? More likely, motion sickness was being amplified by hopelessness and an overactive imagination. But who knew yet?

Emerging back in the main tunnel, we found ourselves amid a swarm of other battle-golems. The Beta who was hauling me turned left, hurrying toward the hidden stronghold of Yosil Maharal—at least that's what I presumed. I also spied Ritu in their midst, now more closely guarded than before, looking glassy-eyed and withdrawn amid the creatures she had imprinted—giant, terrifying dolls that were propelled by a part of her she loathed.

The spatter of gunfire sounded closer than before, but seemed to be tapering off. Apparently the reinforcements had been called forward to mop up Yosil's final layer of defense.

Well before we arrived at that front however, a second fractious murmur came up from the rear—distant, surprised shouts followed by sharp detonations. I saw the nearby Betas consult each other in brief, worried tones. Some turned to face this new threat, setting up firing positions, while the rest of them pushed Ritu and me forward.

Apparently our little task force was surrounded. Enemies behind us now, as well as ahead.

Great, I thought, succumbing to fever, or else to gloom.

Better not let the travel nets learn about this lovely Place. Or every maso-tourist in the world will want to come.

53

Soulscape

. . . as gray and red combine to explore
a rainbow . . .

Who says Yosil should get to be the rider?

His mad ghost yammers on, using pompous braggadocio to convince himself he's still in charge, but I've stopped listening. Poor old ditYosil hasn't got a clue yet that something's gone terribly wrong with his plan.

The glazier amplified me from the measly ditective who was seized from Kaolin Manor. Countless boson-duplicates combine like droplets in a mighty wave. That's *all* I was supposed to be, a simple carrier wave with all the "me-ness" rubbed out.

But I'm here! Peering along new dimensions. Learning fast.

■   ■   ■

For example, I've been studying those "echoes" that I noticed earlier. They are *other people.* I behold them flickering nervously at some undefinable distance.

Here one burns with a bitter tang that reminds me of anger. Over there shimmers a wavering flame with the acidic color of regret. But the common trait appears to be aching *isolation*—each a lonely outpost, forlorn, incommunicado, a solitary spark burning on an arid plain.

Even when I happen on a crowd of millions—a nearby metropolis?—the premier feature of this realm is melancholy sparseness. Cityscapes always seemed crowded—all those jostling bodies of flesh and clay, accoutered with clothes and tools and brash voices. But here, viewing them stripped down to their cores, you realize that a few million souls amount to almost nothing, like widely scattered blades of grass, desperately calling themselves a lawn.

No, they're even less. Consider specks of algae, dotting a barren shore, touching only the barest fringe of an enormous, vacant continent. It's a dour view of the human condition. Yet I find the austere panorama exciting. For I can touch them!

■ ■ ■

One corner of me still feels compelled to recite and describe, even though I know that metaphors of sight and sound mislead. Yosil was right—new perceptions call for new vocabularies. Space and proximity have different qualities on this alternate plane, where location is based on *affinity*. Love or hatred or obsession can move two soul-flickers closer together for a while. Side by side, a pair will sometimes kindle a new glimmer that ignites in abrupt hopefulness. *Marriage*, I figure, giving the phenomenon a comfortably familiar name, *and children.*

Not all of these collaborations are lasting or happy. Still, gentle aromas of joy waft from some.

It gives new meaning to the phrase "soul mate." How many wistful teens have yearned to find that one special other with all the right complementarities to blend in perfect union? The romantic notion always seemed foolish, ignoring the work and compromise that genuine love requires. But while scanning this strange landscape, I spot patterns and textures of character that seem to complement each other, suggesting harmonious blends, if only they meet.

What a business opportunity, if some enterprising entrepreneur ever used this technique to offer a new, improved dating service . . .

. . . but Yosil Maharal had something more profound in mind when he designed this window to a deeper layer of reality. Take what happens when a flicker starts to waver and then fade. In the so-called real world, we have a name for it. Death.

A few of these dwindling embers smolder with unmistakable courage, while others fume what I can only call despair. And, at the very last moment, some make a fleeting, ecstatic effort to go *elsewhere.*

There's one! A dying speck launches itself across the solemn expanse like a dandelion seed that sparkles briefly, auspiciously . . .

. . . before tumbling back to the sere plain, guttering out, leaving behind a dusty imprint. A great many burnt indentations mark the landscape in all directions. More than I could ever count. Most of them feel *old.*

It happens again, and again. The dying repeat this futile effort, one after another. Why do they bother, when it's always unavailing? Do they sense a goal worth striving for, no matter how bleak the odds?

There is something . . . I can tell with my new senses. It must be the same allure that underlay religions—a *potential* for some phase beyond egg and child, beyond larva and youth. Beyond adult woman or man. Hope for continuity, proliferation—perhaps even endless propagation across a vast new dominion. The potentiality is evident to me now!

Then what holds them back? Lack of faith? Divine judgment?

No. Those old excuses won't suffice. They never did. For where's the logic in basing salvation on a creator's capricious whim or craving for praise? Or on prayer-incantations that vary from culture to culture? That's not consistent or scientific. It's not how the rest of nature works.

Think, Albert. Look back at all the tragedies that marred human life, ever since our dim beginnings. Sickness stole your loved ones. Starvation scythed your tribe. Blighted by ignorance and coarse of speech, you couldn't even share what little you managed to learn. Or take the frustrating clumsiness of your hands and slowness of feet. Or the curse of having to be just one place at a time, when innumerable things needed doing! None of these problems were solved by the prescriptions of shamans and priests. Not by patronizing mystics or condescending monks.

Technology. That's what made things better! In fits and starts—and often horribly abused along the way—that's where we found answers that were consistent, dependable, uncapricious. Answers that applied to lord and vassal alike. Answers that improved life across the board and never went away.

So, why not use technology to solve the greatest age-old riddle— immortality for the soul?

I admit, I'm starting to understand what drove Yosil Maharal. Heaven help me, I can grasp his dream.

■   ■   ■

With each passing moment, I learn more. Explicit facts and abstract theorizations pour in, sponged out of ditYosil as he works unsuspecting nearby, striving to finish before attackers break in. His knowledge—the work of a lifetime—comes to me unearned and disjointed. I can encompass the glazier's beauty, for example, at an aesthetic level, before the underlying equations make any sense. The uneven pace of understanding is one reason why I've held back from meddling. So far.

Examining all those fragile glimmers out there, I believe I know what holds them apart—a raw dread of losing individuality! Of being smeared out. Of getting lost. People approach and then avoid each other in a mad dance, fearful of *both* too much isolation and too much intimacy.

I remember that dance, too well. But the fear is gone now, burned out by my ordeal in Maharal's tormenting machinery. In becoming many, I no longer dread the prospect of sharing a Standing Wave.

Am I like some bodhisattva, then, returning from Nirvana with compassionate aid for the unenlightened? *Is* it compassion I feel, so eager to intervene?

I yearn to reach out, to embrace all those dismayed flickers, to waken and encourage and liberate them. To stoke their wan fires and *force* them to acknowledge the starkness all around.

It's not the humble version of compassion we've been taught to admire. Unlike a buddha, I brim with ambition for myself and all of my benighted species!

Some honest corner of me calls this "arrogant."

So? Doesn't that very honesty help qualify me for the job?

For sure, I'll make a better god than ditYosil.

■   ■   ■

Algae on a barren shore. Increasingly, I find that metaphor apt. For we seem very much like the first creatures that climbed awkwardly from the sea to colonize bare land, underneath a blazing sun.

The nearly empty soulscape beckons, like a new frontier. One filled with far more potential than sterile outer space with its mere planets and galaxies. Science and religion only hinted at the immense potential here! If we can make it happen.

I can make it happen! I suspect this with growing excitement. There are just a few things to figure out first. . . .

■   ■   ■

Wait. I see it now! A truth that Professor Maharal realized weeks ago. His ghost actually tried to explain it to me, with analogies from quantum mechanics. I never understood then, but now it seems so clear—

The body is an anchor.

That paragon of organic evolution, the breakthrough marvel of human flesh and brain that made self-awareness, abstraction, and the Standing Wave all possible—the body comes well equipped for those wonders, but also saddled with animal instincts and needs, like individuality, craving the insulation of *I and thou* the way a fish needs the surrounding stroke of water.

To finish climbing ashore, leaving the sea for good, we must abandon the carapace of flesh!

This realization must have terrified Professor Maharal, triggering a split between his rig and rox, between man and golem, copy and archetype, ditto and master. realYosil saw self-murder looming as a natural consequence of his own research. He may even have agreed, in abstract. But the body would defend itself, flooding his real brain with panic hormones, sending him plunging across the desert in blind and futile flight.

Of course then realAlbert had to follow him in death. Both the rider and the mirrors must be un-anchored. Another small price of deification. I see it now.

Only suddenly I fathom something else.

It won't be enough to sever just two body links.

More souls have to be cut loose, soon, in order to feed the glazier's hungry process.

More murder . . . on a grand scale.

Images pour into me . . . things ditYosil had pushed to a corner of his mind. I glimpse a symbol—a trefoil of blood red scythes—accompanied by words: *airborne contagion.* Then another quick impression of *missiles* . . . trim, efficient rockets, stolen and assembled, ready to fire on an urban trajectory. At a moment that's approaching soon.

■　■　■

I need to know more!

Whatever ditYosil has planned *may* be justifiable. Evolution doesn't happen without pain or loss. A lot of fish died, in order for a few to stand. The price may be worthwhile . . .

. . . but only if the benefits can actually be achieved!

Yosil has already been much too careless. The experiment veered off its planned course, or else why would I feel this growing tide of power and ambition as the number of my perfect duplicates keeps multiplying, gathering energy like magma under a volcano? *I* am the one getting ready to ride the Big Wave . . . something ditYosil never anticipated.

If he made one mistake, he might have made others. I'd better check, and quick.

He really shouldn't be allowed to slaughter so many innocents.

At least, not till I'm sure there's a high probability of success.

5 4

Like a Brick

. . . as Gumby becomes partly useful . . .

Crawling slowly after a trail of footprints in the dust, propelled through blazing agony by little more than stubbornness, dragging the dead weight of this dying body with just one good arm and a half-functioning leg . . . I couldn't help wondering what I ditto deserve this.

My aim was to chase Beta, to catch the basdit before this body of mine dissolved, to thwart his evil scheme—whatever it might be. And if that proved to much to ask? Well, then, maybe I could inconvenience him a little. By biting him around the ankles, if nothing else.

All right, it wasn't much of a plan. But my other motivation, curiosity, which had kept me going for two grinding days, didn't serve anymore. I no longer cared about the secret struggle among three geniuses—Beta, Kaolin, and Maharal—only that they all must think they were rid of this cheap green copy by now, and damn if I wasn't going to show them otherwise!

Anyway, that's how it felt as I crawled past the main part of the old vacation house and into the mountain, following Beta's footprints across the uneven floor of a cave . . . a natural limestone grotto that must have attracted Maharal to build here in the first place, erecting his cabin over the entrance, then using the cavern to establish a clandestine scientific redoubt.

Glowbulbs cast long shadows across stalactites and other drip features that shimmered along their dewey flanks. Water beads glistened as they fell. If my ears were functioning, I'd surely have heard a rhythmically pleasant plinking as the drops struck cloudy pools. One sound did penetrate, a low vibration I felt through my belly while creeping across the stone floor, growing more intense as I pursued Beta's trail downward at a shallow angle . . . easier for me than climbing, I suppose.

Soon I passed by a wall that had been chipped and smoothed by human hands. My good eye glimpsed figures, etched in the rocky face by strike-flaking, one chiseled nick at a time. Petroglyphs, incised by some long-ago native people who deemed this cave a sacred place of power, where nature's forces might be implored and miracles invoked. Humanoid shapes with sticklike arms and legs brandished spears toward rough-drawn beasts—simpler dreams, but no less ambitious or sincere than anything we hope for today.

Let me thrive and prevail, the magic on the wall beseeched.

I agreed, *amen.*

For about a hundred meters there weren't any more distractions. Dragging myself along with one arm and a bad leg became so normal, I found it hard to recall any other mode of existence. Then, blinking in confusion, I found myself confronting a decision: a fork in the trail.

Left—a small niche room contained humming machinery. Familiar mechanisms, a freezer, imprinter, and kiln combination. Automated and ready-to-use.

Ahead—a well-lit ramp lunged downward, to the belly of the mountain. The vibrations came from there. It was also the direction taken by Beta's footprints. The focus of big events. Probably the doctor's secret lab, in all its glory.

I didn't bother examining the third path, leading to the right. And upward, yuck. I had enough trouble deciding between just two options. Should I keep following Beta, or try something really daring?

The autokiln beckoned, its ready lights all gleaming the same color that I first wore when Albert made me long ago. It sure was a lot closer than trying to catch Beta by slithering after him. How alluring to contemplate swapping a ruined, expiring body for a fresh one!

Alas, there was no guarantee I could manage to pull myself onto the imprinting platform with just one arm and a bum leg, let alone fumble the controls correctly, setting golem-creation in motion.

Disadvantage number two: everybody knows that it's non-warranty for a copy to try making copies. True, Albert was—or is—an excellent copier. But trying ditto-to-ditto using *me* as a template? At best a cheap frankie, now a complete ruin, how could I make anything but a mindless, shambling thing? Anyway, the exertion of reaching the perceptron platform would likely finish this body.

On the other hand, straight ahead lay a smooth downhill path to the center of all secrets . . .

That isn't the way.

I winced. It was the damned external voice again. The bedeviling scold.

You may want to go right.

Upward.

It could be important.

Obstinate anger nearly overwhelmed me. I didn't need a termagant hounding the last moments of my pitiful existence!

Oh, but perhaps you do.

And to my surprise, I realized something about the statement rang true.

I could not—and still cannot—explain what made me decide to accept that advice against all evidence and reason, abandoning two known options to invest all that I had left in a final daunting climb.

Perhaps it amounted to—*why not?*

Turning away from the tempting autokiln . . . and Beta's hated footprints . . . I started to drag myself up the crude stairs.

55

A Family Spat

. . . as realAlbert comes to appreciate his simple upbringing . . .

Ritu and I were trapped in that awful tunnel under Urraca Mesa, with one band of enemies battling toward us from behind while others blocked further progress ahead. We could only crouch in the narrow passageway while gunfire echoes pinged around us from both directions.

Beta seemed to be running out of fighters. Only one damaged drone was assigned to watch over us. Still, he seemed quite capable of guarding two scared organics.

"I should have made more of myself when I had the chance," groused the giant golem.

Ritu winced. She was already worn out from imprinting so many dittos with the alternate personality carried around inside her head, obliged to do so by a compulsion stronger than addiction. The thought of copying more would only deepen her self-loathing. I worried in the dim half-light that Ritu might suddenly leap up and try to end her misery by dashing toward the combat zone, throwing her body into the melee before warriors of both sides could cease fire.

Lacking any other way to be helpful—and badly needing distraction from my own worries—I tried asking questions.

"When did you realize about Beta?"

She seemed at first not to hear, chewing a lip, eyes darting nervously. I repeated the question. Finally, Ritu answered without looking back directly.

"Even as a kid, I knew something was wrong with me. Some inner conflict made me do or say things I didn't intend or that I'd later regret, sabotaging relationships and . . ." Ritu shook her head. "I guess a lot of adolescents might describe the very same problem. But it got far worse when I started imprinting. Dittos wandered off, or returned only to inload fragmented memories. Can you imagine how frustrating and unfair it felt? I was *born* into this business. I know dittoing better than most of the UK development guys! I kept telling myself it must be a glitch in the machinery. It would clear up with next year's model."

She turned to look at me.

"That must have been denial, I suppose."

No kidding. It was like calling the ocean wet.

"Did you ever seek help?"

She turned haunted eyes downward. "Do you think I need help?"

It took hard effort to squelch a reflexive, horrified laugh. The force of repression within her must be incredible to even ask such a question while we cowered in this awful place.

"When did I start to understand?" Ritu continued after a few seconds. "Weeks ago, I overheard my father and Aeneas argue fiercely over whether to announce some new breakthroughs, like extending ditto lifespan. Aeneas called the methods unready and complained how much of Yosil's research aimed at mystical areas like non-homologous imprinting. . . ."

I made an earnest effort to listen as Ritu's story poured out at last. I was interested, really. But the tunnel felt so stifling and hot . . . I couldn't help wondering, were my sweats a symptom of some vile plague, contracted during my brief visit to the germ warfare room? Were superfast pathogens already tearing through my flesh?

I did *not* want to think about that! Like Ritu, I sought distraction from helplessness in dialogue.

"Um . . . could those quarrels with Aeneas explain why your father went into hiding?"

"I guess so . . . but they had *always* fought like brothers, ever since Aeneas bought the Bevvisov-Maharal process to animate his movie-effex dolls. The two of them usually calmed down and sorted things out."

"Not this time though," I prompted. "Kaolin—"

"—accused Yosil of stealing files and equipment! I could tell Aeneas was furious. Yet he kept his anger bottled, as if Father had some power over him. Something that kept even the chairman of Universal Kilns from interfering, no matter how mad he got."

"Blackmail?" I suggested. "Kaolin's ditto was snooping around your father's house when you and I met there Tuesday evening. Maybe he was looking for evidence to destroy, right after knocking off Yosil—"

"No." Ritu shook her head. "Before he departed for the last time, I overheard Father tell Aeneas, '*I'm your only hope, so get out of my way if you haven't the guts to help.*' That sounds rather scary, I admit, but not like blackmail. Anyway, I still can't believe Aeneas would murder anyone."

"Well, *some* Kaolin dit-alike shot at us later that night, on the desert highway."

As if on cue, several loud bangs resonated where Beta's rear guard still fought off unnamed enemies. Panic reignited in Ritu's eyes . . . till she pushed the dread away one more time. In her own way, she was showing real courage.

"I . . . thought about that. Aeneas wasn't only worried about my father, you know. He also had a growing obsession about . . . *Beta*." Ritu spat the word in distaste. "Aeneas spent a fortune on insurance and security, trying to plug Beta's access to UK technologies and material. I guess somehow along the way he must have finally discovered the truth about my other half." She jerked her head toward the nearby guard-golem.

"It would have galled Aeneas to realize that Beta knew everything that I know about the company. He couldn't even prosecute or take revenge without hurting me . . . the same Ritu Maharal he always treated like a daughter. Nor could he talk to me about the problem. That would only *warn* Beta, so I was kept out of the loop."

"Even worse," I added, "Kaolin would worry about the possibility that Beta and Yosil Maharal had forged an alliance."

Ritu's head jerked. "The very idea would drive Aeneas crazy."

"Then his golem shot us on the highway because he thought you were Beta," I concluded. "You *were* wearing that ditto-disguise. And all this time I thought he had it in for *me!* But then, who shot a missile at my house and—"

A far-traveling bullet came zinging by, interrupting as it ricocheted off the ceiling. Ritu winced. For the fourth or fifth time, she tried crouching closer to me. Amid this fracas, the most natural thing would be for us to hold each other. But I edged back, keeping distant, since I might be carrying some foul virus.

The alternative was to keep talking. I tilted my head to fix contact with her eyes.

"What about your father?" I demanded. "What was he doing down here that frightened Kaolin? Why steal golems and arms from the government. And germ warfare agents, for God's sake!

"Ritu, what is *still* going on here, days after he died?"

My intensity made her draw back. Ritu clamped both hands against her head. Her voice cracked.

"I *don't know* about any of that!"

Someone else joined in at that point.

"Leave her alone, Morris. You're badgering the wrong me."

It was the wounded battle-golem assigned to guard us, so stolid till now that we had been sheltering behind it like a stone. The square-jawed face looked down, regarding me with barely any expression. Still, I sensed the familiar contempt of my longtime foe. Even knowing, at last, that it was born of neurotic overcompensation didn't help much. I still hated the guy.

Beta spoke in a deep-gravelly voice, but with the same snide tone.

"As you suspect, we did have an arrangement, Yosil and I. He slipped me a limitless supply of specialty golem blanks, straight from Research, with all sorts of great features like pixelated skin that can change color patterns on command."

"You're kidding."

"Nope. Yosil helped ship them directly into Ritu's supply fridge while I worked from inside, to ensure she never examined her blanks closely. Together, we made it seem that a number of her dittos were doing exactly what she wanted them to do, minimizing her worries and suspicions. It was a big help in my operations and worked well . . . till just a short time ago."

"And what did Maharal get in return?"

"I taught him the fine art of evasion! How to dodge and weave and evade the World Eye. My underworld contacts were a big help. It became sort of a father-and-son pastime." The ditto winked at Ritu, who shuddered and turned away, so Beta turned the knowing smile toward me.

"I suspect Dad always wanted a boy," he said.

Sibling cruelty can be disgusting. So is destructive self-hatred. This lay somewhere viciously in between.

"I have to admit," Beta went on, "that she put up quite a fight the last few weeks. Ever since learning about me, she stopped imprinting and killed every Beta that approached her for inloading. I was running out of delay-release versions!"

"The decaying ditto that I found in a Dumpster behind the house—"

"Bang." Beta used a finger to mime a pistol firing. "Ritu terminated it. Then she grabbed Dad's makeup kit in the house and disguised herself to look just like that gray, hoping the pretense would let her come south with you and . . ." Beta shook his head. "Well, I have to admit her forcefulness surprised me. I was only able to interfere a little, from inside. Good for you, Alpha!"

"How touching," I answered for Ritu, who looked too angry for speech. "So Father liked you best. Is that why you're fighting your way into good old Dad's sanctuary right now?"

Before Beta could answer, something clicked in my thoughts.

"The lab *isn't* dormant, guarded by leftover robot sentries. Somebody's inside, right now, planning to use stolen germ weapons in some grisly scheme. Is it Yosil's murderer? Are you breaking in to avenge your father?"

Beta paused, then acknowledged, "In a manner of speaking, Morris. But as long as buried truths are coming out, you might as well know"—he nodded toward Ritu—"that we have more in common with our father than you'd ever imagine."

Ritu blinked, looking directly at the golem for the first time. "You mean—"

"I mean that a genius like his could never be contained within a single personality, or confined to one human brain. In Yosil, the divisions were less explicit. Still—"

I let out a grunt of realization, recalling some bad movied plots Ritu and I'd discussed during our desert trek. How many focused on the same old nightmare, couched in contemporary terms—the fear of being conquered by your own creation, by your own darker half? In Ritu, technology brought an inner nightmare to life, amplifying an irksome personality trait into a fully reified arch criminal.

How much further might the same syndrome go, if unleashed by a virtuoso?

"Then Maharal—"

Before I could finish, a shrill whistle echoed down the corridor. Beta grunted with satisfaction. "It's about time!" The big war-ditto stood up awkwardly, favoring a gravely wounded left side, motioning for Ritu and me to follow. "The way is clear ahead."

When Ritu shivered, the golem soothed.

"Picture it as a family reunion. Let's go see what Father has become."

56

Top of the Line

. . . a green doughboy tries to rise . . .

There weren't any glowbulbs in the crude staircase and I had no way to judge the time spent dragging up one rough step then another, hauled along by a single good arm and a half-functional leg, leaving bits of me crumbling along the way. The ascent seemed measureless except for rhythmic throbs each time my battered form heaved upward. I counted one hundred and forty of these pulses. A hundred and forty opportunities to relax into darkness forever—till the utter blackness around me started to give way.

Attenuated light slid down the stairs, tentatively liquid in quality, actually cheering me a bit. It's hard to feel completely hopeless during that special moment when you first catch sight of dawn.

It *was* daybreak, I soon verified, pouring through a rough cut in the far wall of a modest room that was nearly filled by a bulky machine.

Crawling nearer, I saw a funnel-track slanting toward the narrow window. A rugged frame held more than a dozen slender tubes bearing dorsal and pectoral fins, as if to maneuver with agility through water or air.

My good eye glimpsed ominous cutlass-shaped symbols marking the sleek forward tips; still realization came slowly.

Missiles, I thought, fighting expiration fatigue. *Stacked in an automatic launching system.*

And . . . I further noted when a row of electronic displays came alight . . .

And the machinery just turned on.

57

Bosons in the Circuit

. . . or the importance of being Emet . . .

As I grow larger, as knowledge floods into me, I grow more appreciative of the grand vision that drew my tormentor to this place and hour. Yet the closer he came to greatness in recent months, the more it intimidated poor Yosil Maharal. No wonder, for he stood alone atop a vaulting arch that had been built across the millennia by humanity's greatest minds, each of them battling darkness in his or her own way, against all odds.

The struggle went slowly at first, with more false starts than progress. After all, what could primitive women and men accomplish, what secrets could they pierce without fire or electricity, lacking biochemistry or soulistics? Sensing there must be *something* more to life than tooth and claw, the earliest sages focused on their one precocious gift—a capacity for *words.* Words of persuasion, illusion, or magical power. Words that preached love and moral improvement. Words of supplicating prayer. Call it magic or call it faith. Well endowed with hope—or wishful thinking—but little else, they imagined that words alone would suffice, if uttered sincerely enough, in proper incantations, accompanying pure thoughts and deeds.

Later successors, unbaring the splendor of mathematics, supposed *that* was the key. From Pythagorean harmonies and numerological puzzles like Kabbalah to elegant superstring theories, math seemed to be God's own language, the code He used to write creation's plan. Like quantum mechanics—the elegant sorting of aloof fermions and gregarious bosons—all the proud equations added to a growing edifice. They were foundations, gorgeously true.

But not enough. For the stars we yearned to touch remained much too far away. Math and physics could only measure the vast gulf, not cross it.

Same with the vaunted digital realm. Computers briefly tantalized, hinting that software models might prove better than reality. Enthusiasts promised new-improved minds, telepathic perception, even transcendent power. But cyberstuff fell short of opening grand portals. It became another useful tool set, just another incremental brick in the arch.

Back in Grandma's time, *biology* was the queen science. Decipher the genome, the proteome, and their subtle interplay with phenotype! Solve ecology's riddle and achieve sustainability in nature! These were attainments every bit as vital as harnessing flame or kicking the habit of all-out war.

Yet where were answers to the truly *deep* questions?

Religion promised those, though always in vague terms, while retreating from one line in the sand to the next. *Don't look past this boundary,* they told Galileo, then Hutton, Darwin, Von Neumann, and Crick, always retreating with great dignity before the latest scientific advance, then drawing the next holy perimeter at the shadowy rim of knowledge.

From here on is God's domain, where only faith will take us. Though you may have penetrated the secrets of matter and time, made life in a test tube, even covered Earth with thronging duplicates, man will never infiltrate the realm of the immortal soul.

Only now we're crossing that line, Yosil and I, armed not with virtue but skill, utilizing every insight gathered by *Homo technologicus* during ten thousand years of painful struggle against nescient darkness.

One matter remains to settle before the adventure can begin.

Which of us will carry . . . and which will ride?

■　■　■

Oh, there is another issue.

Can such a bold endeavor properly commence, if it begins with a terrible crime?

■　■　■

ditYosil pulls the pendulum aside now, preparing to climb aboard and launch his final dittobody into the glazier, right between the mirrors. No more nervous yammering about philosophy and metaphysics—I can sense the basso drumbeat of fear in his Standing Wave, so shuddering that it robs the poor gray's power of speech. A fear like realYosil must have felt on Monday, when he saw things getting out of hand, with no way to avoid paying the ultimate price of hubris.

A fear intensified by pressing events, as the last mechanical defenders fall before that army in the tunnel . . .

. . . and instruments show ditYosil at last that something's gone wrong with his precious plan. The glazier readings aren't what he imagined they'd be at this point. He may finally suspect that I'm still here, not erased at all but riding the tsunami! Growing mightier by the second.

▪ ▪ ▪

The pendulum is aimed to slice right through the glazier, at its very heart. Suddenly I realize—*this will hurt.* In fact, it could be worse than anything I endured as an organic, or dittoing one copy at a time.

I can see how it's supposed to work . . . how ditYosil's inner fire may spark the glazier's heightened energies, seeding his own imprint with each pass, like rolling a cylinder seal over and over again in soft clay. Despite everything that's gone wrong with his plan—despite my lingering presence—it just might work. He may succeed in taking over, wiping me out!

Or else, we may cancel each other, leaving behind a wild, self-feeding beam of spiritual essence that could burst out of here unguided, like an all-consuming storm. A psychlone . . .

I didn't think that anything could still frighten me. I was wrong.

Right now all I want is to go back. Return to the sere beauty of the soulscape. Contemplate again those virgin territories, more vast than any unexplored continent, more promising than a galaxy, though as-yet barely colonized by a mere few billion minuscule algae flecks along the shore— flecks who barely suspect their own latent destiny.

Especially one cluster of unsuspecting algae—a few million—who've been targeted for a special fate, to make the ultimate sacrifice. Like hand-servants accompanying a Babylonian monarch to his tomb, their supporting role is to die, offering their soul-energies, contributing potency to the glazier beam, propelling the Standing Wave to new levels.

Ancients would have called this "necromancy," drawing magical force from the mysterious power of death itself. However named, it will be a ghastly crime . . .

. . . and I've almost reconciled myself to it. All those waning embers that I witnessed earlier—dying human souls striving at their very last moments to fly free, then guttering out, falling to leave ashen impressions on the barren plain—this will make their dashed hopes worthwhile, right?

After gazing across the Continent of Immortal Will, beckoned by its wealth of possibilities, how seriously should I worry about a few doomed algae on the shore?

Except—

Except that one of those tiny flickers has begun to annoy me, like a stone in my shoe. Like a pebble in my saddle. The soulscape doesn't count distance in meters, but affinity, and this spark was too close to notice, clinging to me like a shadow. Only now do I turn to examine the irritation and discover that . . .

. . . it's me!

Or rather, it's the living, breathing Albert Morris—source of the Standing Wave that I've amplified profoundly. I can sense him sneaking closer in physical space, filled with all those old organic fears, drives, and sympathies. Nervous and yet dogged as ever, so near we might actually touch.

How could this happen?

ditYosil claimed to have killed Morris with a stolen missile! Death of the body should release the anchor, liberating the soul. I saw news reports—the burning house and garden—yet he survived.

This must be why my personality never succumbed to erasure! The wave kept reimprinting somehow, from the original source, till it grew self-sustaining.

That's great. I'm glad to be here. But now what? Will Albert's presence interfere? Will his biotic anchor pin the glazier to "reality" when the crucial moment comes to fly free?

■　■　■

Yosil's ghost has finished strapping himself in. With enemy soldier-dits breaking down the final door, he can't procrastinate anymore. Preparing to let the pendulum fly, he gathers nerve for a vocal command.

"Initiate final stage!" he shouts to a control computer. "Launch the rockets!"

So. Preparing for battle, I can feel reassured. Whatever is about to happen to the city isn't my fault. The mass murder of so many won't be *my* doing. Their karma can't affect me.

I'm as much a victim as anybody else, right?

I will make their sacrifice worthwhile.

58

Claylight

. . . as something dawns on Greenie . . .

A single wan star gleamed through the roughcut window, twinkling like the panel lights of a dark machine that nearly filled the room at the top of the stairs. I felt ominous vibrations through the ground, rather than my ruined ears, as the mechanism awoke. Slim objects tightened formation in the feeder magazine, each bearing scythelike crimson symbols. I wasn't too far gone yet to recognize an automatic launching system. Damn. Not good.

No, it isn't.

Perhaps you should stop it.

Instead of nagging, what I needed were ideas how. *How* was I supposed to stop it!

Buttons glowed, about the height of a standing man's shoulder. One of them might cut the launcher from its remote controller. But how to get up there? The weapon's flank, military-smooth, offered no gripholds suitable for a one-armed man sprawled on the floor, even more hopeless than trying to climb aboard that autokiln downstairs.

"I . . . can't . . ." came a hoarse whisper from my throat. "It's too far."

Then improvise.

I looked around, seeing no convenient ledge or chair to clamber on. No handy tools, or even bits of stone to throw. The cheap clothes that Aeneas Kaolin gave me, half a lifetime ago, were mostly gone, shredded to useless ribbons.

TARGETING COMMANDS ACCEPTED, said a row of dire words. COMPUTING TRAJECTORIES. There followed a series of numbers. Even in my dismal state I could recognize range and heading data.

Some maniac is shooting at the city!

I guessed Beta. Doubtless he murdered Professor Maharal in order to take over this facility. Why? Desperate because all his ditnapping schemes were collapsing, I guessed. My old foe must hope to wreak such havoc, the authorities will have more urgent chores than chasing down a copyright thief.

Frustrated and supine on the floor, I knew my theory made no sense, and didn't care. What mattered was stopping him. I'd give anything. My pitiful life, certainly. I already surrendered my left arm to the cause. What else could I possibly . . .

A shout escaped my corroding mouth. Some things are only obvious after you think of them.

I did have one tool that might work, if I hurried.

It wasn't going to be easy . . . but what is?

5 9

Divine Flu

. . . as realAlbert confronts unpleasant news . . .

The self-made army of stolen war-golems finally broke through. While Ritu and I were shepherded over the last shattered robot defenders, a dozen of Beta's scarred veterans hurried the other way, rushing to help the rear guard. How long could they resist the force battling toward us from the Base?

Not long. I had a feeling things would start happening fast.

They had better. I may not have much time.

Smoke fumed around the edges of an armored door with a big hole burned through. Waves of heat still poured from recently molten metal as we passed into what must be the buried lair of Yosil Maharal. Ritu and I found ourselves standing on a parapet overlooking a scene that was altogether bizarre—a grotto filled to bursting with equipment, much of it jerry-rigged by stringing together hardware with familiar UK logos.

Surely this must be the hoard of electroceramic gear that Kaolin accused Maharal of swiping from work. *What on Earth was he trying to accomplish here?* I wondered. *No doubt some avenue of research that Aeneas forbade him to pursue in the company's R&D department.*

Flooding to me came foreboding words, *"the curse of Frankenstein,"* followed by a clipped image of a mushroom cloud.

Huge antennalike coils funneled from all angles toward a pair of humanoid figures, splayed at opposite ends of the room, facing each other with arms pinioned wide. One of these dittos was dark red, the other a specialized shade of a gray that I sometimes wear myself. Ornate inloading apparatus festooned all over their clay bodies, though I couldn't imagine what so many souped-up linkages could be for.

Between the pair of dittos, some kind of giant clockwork mechanism kept time to the swaying of a huge pendulum. And damn if there wasn't a golem there too, riding back and forth like a child on a swing!

That one was yelling its head off.

■ ■ ■

Those were some of the features my *eyes* saw. More interesting were things that eyes weren't meant to see.

First, was I already dying of some awful fever? I had felt better crossing into the lab's bright light and cooler air after that bloody tunnel. Only now, nausea waves skewered my viscera, like those gut-churning sensations that astronauts used to report, back when realfolk actually risked their lives in space. Bowels clenched, nearly as hard as my teeth, which barely let escape a reedy moan.

This is it, I thought. *Some fast-acting super-virus. Death in minutes. Too bad. I came so close to finding out what was going on here.*

Should I have stayed home instead, and get blown up? At least it would have been quick. I never achieved my real goal, setting out on Tuesday night.

Clara, I'm sorry. I really tried—

More symptoms teemed, clouding the senses. I could swear the space between the captive golems, which had seemed as clear as air moments ago, now rippled and fluttered like some dense fluid! The undulations had a dreamlike quality, impossible to pin down, like a smoke-sculptor's interpretation of manic mood swings.

I had a brief impression that battalions of identical ghostly entities occupied the confined zone, thronging in limitless multitudes, yet somehow uncrowded, with plenty of room in their well-ordered ranks for more. Except when the pendulum passed through. Then brusque waves roiled, transforming many of the marching figures, giving them a face.

Floating before me, I pictured the visage of Yosil Maharal.

"Albert, are you all right?" Ritu murmured, but I shook her hand away. Let her take it as anger for getting me into this fix. I just didn't want to infect her.

I didn't want *anybody* infected. So, despite stomach convulsions, apparitions, and disorientation, I forced myself to look away from shenanigans in the center of the lab, aiming instead at the support machinery lining the grotto walls, seeking any clue about those germ agents. They were all that mattered.

There.

Bleary-eyed, I spotted a computer. One of those expensive AI-XIX models. Damn smart for silicon. One of Maharal's chief tools, surely, maybe even a master process controller. And just the sort of thing that a fellow like me could smash to bits, without having to know specifics of how or why.

Can I make it all the way down there and do it quickly?

At least it was a goal.

A nearby Beta—perhaps the very same war-dit who spoke to us in the tunnel—grabbed the balcony rail and shouted in a voice whose suddenly plaintive tone surprised me. I never heard the like from Beta before.

"Yosil! Father, stop . . . we had a deal!"

60

Mixed Glazes

. . . grinding glazier beams . . .

Damn this compulsion to recite, built into one of the golembodies that serve as mirrors to enclose the growing waveform.

A new kind of Standing Wave surges between the glazier poles. Soon it will escape confinement, bursting through these porcelain dolls with enough power to endure for weeks over a dying city, feeding on death manna from millions of extinguishing spirit flames—a meal sufficient to complete the transition from created to Creator.

While that countdown ticks, a desperate struggle rages. What imprint will the glazier-made god carry? Whose core personality? Right now the waveform oscillates between two possible states—two discordant definitions of *I am.*

Yosil is with me now, our borders overlapping in unhappy swirls, like immiscible fluids. We both howl against this unnatural merging! It's like trying to inload someone else's ditto, a calamity that no one attempts twice. How can you share without agreeing on *dimensions* like left-right? Up-down? In-out? It's all subjective on the soulistic plane. My versions dart away at angles that have nothing in common with his.

Communion *will* come, when I finally arc over this landscape as an all-transforming deity. I'll establish fair metrics that are simple, universal, then invite all to join me in a vast new cosmos! Using raw material more basic than vacuum, together we'll make stars, planets, whole new Earths.

But first, to win control.

I was here first, growing immeasurably during the last few hours. But my adversary knows more theory. He also has the advantage of position. With each rhythmic pass, the pendulum cuts like a blade, slicing through the glazier's soft center, the most energetic and impressionable spot.

Worse, I feel yanked by the presence of *realAlbert,* so close that his image enters me now through a set of eyes. The red ditto can actually see him, leaning on a bannister rail as he descends from a western parapet. *realAlbert looks like hell. Sweaty and pale. Shaking. A mess.*

With each footstep nigh, the glazier shudders!

He's my archetype . . . the reason I survived erasure to reach this point. Now he's getting in the way.

Poor Albert may have to go.

61

Extremities

. . . as Greenie goes out on a limb . . .

Ever try to rip your own leg off? You need motivation.

It helps if you're already falling apart.

Even so, pulling hard with my one good hand and arm, I made little progress while the nearby missile launcher ticked through its final check sequence.

Let me offer a suggestion.

Nag that it was, the voice had steered me right so far. Soon I felt a touch along my crusted skin, and within.

The appendage is no longer part of you.
Envision that.
Draw yourself back from it.
Trigger these enzymes as you go.
Like this...

My knowledge of chemistry was rudimentary, at best. Yet somehow the instructions made sense, like recalling a lost skill. *Naturally, that's how to do it,* I thought, ignoring for now that the instructions came from an imaginary friend. *Simple. I must remember this.*

All pain and fatigue fled from the leg. Amid that growing numbness, every dram of leftover energy spent itself, not melting but *hardening* as if in a quick oven.

My next hard tug was rewarded by a brittle cracking. Again I pulled, and the limb snapped off below the hip, trailing gooey bits of shredded soul-fabric that sparked and glittered.

In my hand now—a near-perfect replica of a human limb in baked terracotta, bent at the knee. I hefted the thing. It was handsome, but hardly aerodynamic.

TARGET LOCKED, announced the launch-controller screen. Missile number one slid into place with its dire crimson warhead.

ARMED. PREPARING TO FIRE.

As the machine's hum rose in pitch, I knew I had one chance.

62

The Clay's the Thing...

... an ensemble in twenty seconds ...

Descending from the parapet, my feet were like blunt clubs at the end of mushy noodles. Waves of nausea whelmed over me as I clutched the bannister from one sweaty grip to the next. Dry-retching, I'd vomit if my stomach had been fed more than a few protein bars during the last few days. Hunger and exhaustion were factors, of course, but such a fierce decline must come from something else—surely a rapid war plague that some arrogant Dodecs stashed at the bottom of an armored hole for safekeeping. A tool of genocide, banned by solemn treaty. But who ever throws a weapon away?

Was my agony a taste of things to come, for millions? I had no clue what was happening in the center of the lab with all those antennas and humming tubes and pendulums swinging between crucified dittos, like some nightmare painting by Hieronymus Bosch. *But I do know it involves germs, so it's gotta be evil.*

That made things simple. *I've got to interfere.*

Only how?

My old friend Pal had a philosophy: "When you lack understanding, or subtlety, you can still get your argument across with a monkey wrench."

A simplistic, often foolish credo, but right now rather compelling. *If I disrupt things enough, Clara and her friends may have time to find out about this place. They'll come do the rest . . . sort it all out. So, whatever the hell is going on, just find a way to interfere.*

Even a futile resolve is something to cling to. As nausea worsened with each downward step, I pictured the AI-XIX computer . . . and a metal folding chair that stood nearby. Just the thing, in lieu of a monkey wrench. Assuming I could still lift furniture when I got there.

Which seemed doubtful as my symptoms worsened. Halfway down those rickety stairs I felt surrounded by nasty invisible creatures with stingers and claws, leaving flesh quivering after each phantom slash. *Figments,* I diagnosed. *Your brain is making up stories to explain unpleasant signals from a dying body, Keep moving.*

Fine. But two steps later the imaginary pests were joined by unsettling bursts of vivid recollection—sensory waves that made me stagger on the stairs.

> The unmistakable floral aroma of Chavez Avenue Park.
> Spears and shields displayed above a dead man's open coffin.
> Ritu in tears, consoled by a figure with skin like luminous tin.
> Sneaking past a trio of boys tormenting each other in a yard—
> —then turning to see a gun in the hand of grinning ghost . . .

These unsorted memories didn't rise from personal experience, or any ditto I recall inloading. They had to be delusions. Yet their déjà vu familiarity was hurtfully intense, like the first time I ever rolled my Standing Wave in clay, or witnessed a scene from several points of view, or looked directly into my own eyes without a camera or mirror.

> Awakening trapped in a liquid-filled vessel.
> Viewing cuneiform tablets and Venus figurines—
> —and pain *liked I never imagined,*
> machine-generated, amplifying my soul-undertone,
> while rubbing to erase everything else about me—

Stumbling under this barrage of frenzied images, I could also hear people yelling across the room. Beta and Ritu for sure, and maybe others, all of them sounding so-slow as time seemed to creep more gradually with each passing second. Few of their frantic words were clear. Anyway, their passions seemed immaterial as I paused on the bottommost stair, a foot wavering above the laboratory floor.

Somehow I knew that one more step would make things even worse. Glancing left, I saw that I was almost lined up with the gray and red golems—spreadeagled across from each other while the pendulum crisscrossed slowly between them. The nearest ditto—dark gray—turned its head quarter-profile toward me, looking almost familiar to my bleary eyes.

Then, unexpected and unbeckoned, quavering words entered my head.

▪   ▪   ▪

realAlbert looks like hell. Sweaty and pale. Shaking. A mess.
What was that? Another symptom?

No distractions, I vowed. Got to keep my rendezvous with a folding chair, just meters away.

Taking another step dropped me down those final inches to the floor—

—completing the alignment.

And suddenly the sky seemed to crash on me! The intruding voice went basso profundo, filling my head with urgent-compulsive commentary in present tense:

▪   ▪   ▪

Is realAlbert Dying?
Will He Perish Soon? What If My Organic "Anchor" Suddenly Lets Go During These Final Moments Before the Glazier Peaks?
▪   ▪   ▪

Estimating . . .
It Seems the Death Whiplash Could Give My Waveform a Boost
Against Yosil. It Might Even Hurl His Obnoxious Specter out of Here!

■　■　■

What the hell? Stabbing pain shot through my parietal lobes. I swayed
from the bizarre thoughts pouring through me. It felt like ditto-inloading,
only far more intense and alien.

■　■　■

My Foe's Attacks Grow More Desperate with Each Pendulum Swing.
No Compromise. If He Can't Have the Prize No One Will!
Yosil and I May Annihilate Each Other, Spewing the Glazier Forth Un-
guided, Rampaging on a Plane of Reality That Society's Defenses Aren't
Even Equipped to Detect. All Those Doomed People in the City, About to
Suffer Writhing Deaths . . . I Can't Let Them Be Sacrificed in Vain.

■　■　■

Daunted by the sheer size of this entity, by its booming thoughts, I
wondered, How could it have anything to do with me?
Then again, how could it not? You don't read the minds of other
people. Only different versions of yourself.

■　■　■

realAlbert Begins to Understand! I'll Help Him, Before the Pendulum
Swings Back.
He's Dying Anyway. When He Sees What's at Stake, He'll Do the
Right Thing.
How Fitting If My Creator Joins Me the Very Moment When It Will
Do the Most Good!

■　■　■

That thundering narration, like foam on a tidal wave, was only the surface layer of a mammoth inloading. I cried out, clutching my head as events
of several days flooded my battered brain across a link that was unbuffered,
unprotected. Coalescing from the raucous clamor were key data—
—what became of my graydit that went missing at Kaolin Manor,
back on Tuesday. Enhanced and multiplied a million-fold, it now stood
as part of a great machine whose terrifying purpose was starting to dawn
on me—

—and who torched my house and garden, a rogue ditto who murdered its own rig. The very one now riding that pendulum, screaming its head off. In a fraction of a second, I grasped why . . . and what it means to be an "anchor"—

—and what I was being offered . . .

—and the cost.

■ ■ ■

Our Patterns Mesh. Despite a Befuddled Brain, realAl Partakes of My New Vision. With Growing Awe, He Perceives the Soulscape in Its Fallow Beauty, Barely Touched by Some Algae Flecks Along the Shore.

Look Deeper, Albert. See How the Soulscape Emerged from the Limitless Inherent Potentialities of the Dirac Sea. Dormant for Ten Billion Years, It Awaits an Entity Who Can Observe. Someone Able to Collapse All the Quantum Probabilities with a Finesse Never Imagined by Theorists . . .

■ ■ ■

Stop!

All That Technobabble Comes from ditYosil! While His Specter Slices Through the Standing Wave, He Keeps Trying to Impose His Viewpoint on the Divine.

How Many More Cycles Before Our Conflict Shatters Everything?

■ ■ ■

Resolution Depends on realAlbert.

Decide! I Tell the Small Organic Man That I Once Was. Decide Now!

■ ■ ■

Our thoughts weren't in synch. Time operated differently for that altered and amplified version of "me," its voice surging and then muting in waves. I needed several intense seconds of instruction before my slower organic mind grasped the outlines—the elegant discovery made by Ritu's genius father. And his plan to fulfill the life arc of a species.

How many times have I scorned those fringe mystics who took the word "soulistics" literally? Beyond our banal power to live parallel lives, they saw implicit hope—or tacit dread—that humanity had crossed a line, embarking on a new destiny. And here I was, being offered a key role in the greatest thing since the Big Bang!

To earn it, all I must do was die.

Isn't That Happening Anyway? Just Hasten It by a Few Minutes, I felt urged.

Grab Any Tool. A Bludgeon Will Do.

Wavering on my feet, I spotted a sharp pencil on a nearby console.

Before even willing it—and maybe I didn't—the slender thing was in my hand, the tip approaching my right eye.

One hard shove and a new age would be born.

"Oh God," I groaned.

And my own voice came right back, emerging from my mouth with a reply.

"Yes. I Am Here. And Be Assured, This Will Serve Me Well."

63

Catch the Conscience . . .

. . . five fateful seconds . . .

Lying on a cold stone floor as chilly dawn broke through an open window, I hefted my sole weapon—the bent and baked leg that I wrenched from my own body.

I'd have one chance to hurl it right.

Clickety went the missile launcher while a screen glowed READY.

The meddlesome voice that had guided me here was gone. I kind of missed having an audience for my effort.

Here goes, I thought. My one functioning limb—a hand and arm—throbbed with all its might as I threw . . .

64

...of the King

...and another twenty...

The pencil tip approached my eye. Groaning an oath, I felt quick encouragement from the nearby god-machine. One good shove and a new age would be born, fulfilling a myriad forlorn dreams.

Anyway, I've slain myself many times, ever since I turned sixteen, right?

But those were dittos.

■　■　■

My *org-body* protested against the plan. It bawled to survive!

The same clash with instinct repelled realMaharal from his own project a week ago, fleeing recklessly across the desert night.

"But You're Made of Sterner Stuff," my own mouth answered. *"Unite with Me. It Will Be Just Like Inloading."*

A day is enough for a ditto, when it knows it will rejoin a larger self. Wasn't this the same sort of thing? Saints walked into ovens with less assurance than I was being offered.

Okay, I thought, as determination flowed into my arm.

The pencil tip trembled—

Suddenly a flare of amber warning lights erupted nearby, drawing my reflex gaze.

WARNING! WARNING!
MISSILE LAUNCHER MALFUNCTION
FIRING SEQUENCE INTERRUPTED

Holo diagnostics zoomed toward an awkward-looking foreign object, obstructing a tilted ramp. News of this sabotage provoked sharp resonance between the gray, the red, and all their virtual copies.

■　■　■

Why Aren't the Rockets Flying?
Ah, Here's the Cause—Another Me!
Tuesday's Green, Made for Cleaning Toilets and Mowing Lawns...
the Dull Thing Shouldn't Even Exist Anymore!

■ ■ ■

A green? The one who called himself a "frankie," then sauntered off to seek self-fulfillment? I wondered. How could it be here?

The AI-XIX screen displayed new letters:

REPAIRS INITIATED

"Ignore the Distraction," my own voice muttered. *"The Launcher Will Repair Itself. Get Back to the Business at Hand."*

The business *in* my hand—achieving immortality the way Escher and Einstein did, with a pencil. Adrenaline surged and my heartbeat pounded. Reptile, primate, cave dweller, and urban man all tried to mutiny. But now spiritual resolve felt much stronger than instinct.

It would be just like inloading, I thought, gathering strength.

Only *another* diversion yanked the makeshift weapon back again.

This time it was pain. Brilliant, dazzling, coruscating pain.

■ ■ ■

Yosil Has Seen My Plan—How realAlbert's Death Whiplash May Eject Him!

■ ■ ■

Yosil Reacts, Channeling a Blast of Refined Agony to Knock Albert out of Alignment.

Poor Albert Moans at Sudden Images of Fire and Brimstone. Hellish Pangs Abet the Animal Portions That Always Come Embedded in True-flesh, Rousing Them to Flee or Fight.

■ ■ ■

Now Yosil's Golem Shouts from His Swinging Perch, Calling for His Daughter to Rush Downstairs—for Her to Push Albert Aside and Take His Place in the Beam!

This Will Keep Their Agreement, He Vows. But She Must Hurry.

With Seconds Left, I Must Draw Albert Back into Focus. Show Him That Pain Is an Illusion.

■ ■ ■

"Pain Is an Illusion," my own voice soothed. The mouth spoke words from outside the brain. *"Pain Is a Mirage Compared to the Hyper-Reality of the Great Soulscape.*

"Gaze upon It Now, Albert.

"Behold!"

All at once, the panorama of that vast new realm spread open before me, wider and more gorgeous than any Earthly horizon, beckoning me away from a hellish abyss, replacing it with appealing cross sections from every "heaven" ever imagined.

The pleasures of sensual paradise!

The bliss of unreserved acceptance and love.

And the nameless serenity that comes with detachment from the Great Wheel. All of these heavens and more—tendered without trickery or deceit—would soon be mine.

Ours, I thought, imagining a better a world for all. All people. All life.

It worked! The visions soothed my "animal" parts, calming resistance, easing the way.

And yet—

While reaching out, I also felt the green ditto's flickering presence nearby, now a barely mobile lump sprawled on the floor of a cold chamber somewhere upstairs in this very labyrinth, watching helplessly as the missile launcher deployed robotic repair units to dislodge a pitiful ceramic limb. The golem's brave sacrifice had bought only a little time for the city. Minutes, at best.

Of course he knew nothing of the broader ramifications, or the greater good that would come out of all this, or the inviting immensity that awaited us in the vast soulscape.

And yet—

And yet—

There was something about the greenie lying there, so pathetic after making that grand, futile gesture.

Feelings rose unbidden within me. First a soft touch, then a tickle at the back of my throat.

A tickle that burst forth as a surprised snicker.

Then a chuckle at the hapless, one-limbed, decaying parody of me—flopping about on the floor, all wretched and friendless, without even another leg to throw, but still trying to intervene.

The image was poignant, touching . . . and funny!

Both tears and guffaws flowed like uncorked magma, not from mind but gut. I laughed at the piteous thing—at its courage and misfortune and utter slapstick obstinacy. Moreover, in that raw moment I knew with perfect clarity:

I'm not meant to be a god.

All those heavenly perspectives I'd been shown. They were true possibilities, ripe for reification. Only now I realized what was missing. Not one of them had a place for humor!

How could they? Any "perfect" world would eliminate tragedy, right? That meant giving up the gritty-human *answer* to tragedy, the defiant levity that can make even a futile gesture worthwhile, even—especially— in the face of unbearable injustice.

Aw, man. I had more in common with that ragged green than any pompous, puffed-up, deified gray.

This one insight seemed to push great billows of fog away. Suddenly feeling whole again, I hurled the stupid pencil across the room with a derisive chortle.

Then I started looking for that folding chair.

■   ■   ■

Incredible. He Refused the Offer!

Worse, realAlbert Hopes to Interfere.

I Can Stop Him. Just Reach out and Tweak His Beating Heart. Burst an Artery. Disrupt the Sodium Channels in a Few Million Well-Chosen Neurons.

I'll Be Doing Him a Favor.

To Win the Prize, It Seems That I Must Not Only Defeat Yosil. I Must Also Imitate Him.

I Must Crush My Other Selves.

■   ■   ■

With a bit more spring in my step, I turned away from the great soul-amplifying apparatus and saw what I was looking for, a much simpler machine, right there in front of me. Grabbing and lifting the chair with both hands, I figured Pal would approve of my monkey wrench. It had pleasant heft. I felt stronger and filled with purpose as I brought it swinging down, first at the computer's holo array.

REPAIRS 60% COMPLETE, it flashed as the fragile display blew apart, filling the air with sparkling meshtrodes. Satisfying? Sure, but that was just a holo unit. The true superconducting heart of AI-XIX lay beneath, in a pressed phenolic casing.

The chair swung up again as someone yelled. Was it Ritu or Beta, approaching as the stretched seconds ticked slowly by? Did it matter?

On the next downstroke I felt swarmed by unpleasant sensations. Palpitations in the chest. Throbbings in my arm. I might have called it painful, except I'd been taught there's no such thing!

The CPU casing cracked under my first blow. It might take several, plus a prayer that Professor Maharal never spent extra for remote backup. I raised the chair once more—even as my lips moved, once again muttering on behalf of the mega-entity in the glazier beam.

"Albert . . . Yosil and I Agree on This . . . You Must Be Stopped."

I wanted to shout back—the hell you say!—but a tight fist clamped around my heart, sending me reeling.

Still, the mouthed words came.

"Sorry . . . About This. . . . It Must . . . and Will Be Done."

That was when another voice broke in, reverberant and strange, as if out of nowhere.

Oh no, it won't.

As suddenly as it came, the pressure in my chest vanished, leaving me to stagger, nearly blanking out. Consciousness wavered. But I couldn't give up now. Not after witnessing the example set by that poor greenie.

I can do anything that I can do.

Gritting my teeth and grunting hard, I brought the chair down again with all my might.

65

Ready to Rock . . .

. . . Gumby is almost equipped to play

first base . . .

Did it work?

I wondered after throwing my former leg at the launcher ramp. Then, for about a minute, I felt exultant as the machine halted, groaning and complaining.

FIRING SEQUENCE INTERRUPTED, the small display blared.

Only my triumph was short-lived. For that message was followed by a second that I liked much less.

REPAIRS INITIATED, said the screen as half a dozen maintenance dronelets deployed from recesses in the machinery. Scurrying like worker ants toward the source of the problem, they started tugging and pulling at my bygone ceramic limb. Two of them ignited small cutting torches.

Meanwhile, the first missile hummed in its place at the bottom of the ramp. If I didn't know better, I'd swear it seemed impatient.

Although it was harder to move than ever, I tried using my one arm to drag myself closer. Maybe I could distract the drones by shouting or bluffing a voice of command . . .

. . . but only a hoarse croak emerged. Well, after all, I was a wreck.

Helpless to do anything but watch, I wondered about this germ warfare attack—*why would Beta want to do such a thing? Yes, a deadly act of terrorism might distract the authorities for a while, making them too busy to pursue a notorious ditnapper and copyright thief. They might even forget all about the prion attack on Universal Kilns. . . .*

Still, it made no sense! Only a stupid crook bets everything on the cops remaining ignorant forever. There are too many ways to leave inadvertent clues in the modern era, no matter how careful you are. Anyway, this didn't sound like Beta.

Maybe it isn't, I thought. A ditective should always be ready to revise or discard his working theory.

Well? If the pilot of that Harley wasn't Beta, who else then?

Someone eager to follow Ritu Maharal and discover the whereabouts of her father's cabin.

Someone who found it suspiciously easy to track down the Volvo, out there in the desert.

Someone who must have studied Beta well, in order to mimic my arch foe's mannerisms, and who knew all about what happened at Queen Irene's.

Someone who quickly found out about the meeting that Palloid and I arranged in dittotown with Pal and Lum and Gadarene . . . someone who showed up surprisingly well prepared.

There seemed only one reasonable explanation for how "Beta" and I escaped from the Waxer attack on Pal's safehouse apartment. We were *meant* to get away. It was all arranged in advance, hence the convenient manner that he reappeared, with an air scooter, in the nick of time. That had already been clear to me, only now—

I blinked (though one eyelid was already coming off), feeling close, very close to the answer.

In fact—

■   ■   ■

I sagged. Did any of it matter now? When those missiles fired, people in the city—maybe the whole world—would care little about the details. Only raw survival.

And it wouldn't be long now.

REPAIRS 80% COMPLETE, the display read.

Ah, well.

Lying there, I knew it was way past my rendezvous to check out—to stop fighting the insistent call of the slurry bin. Dissolution would come as a relief.

Time to become an untidy stain on the floor.

I made ready to let go. . . .

Then held back as amber words, high above, turned into flashing red.

HARDWARE failure at command source

The missile launcher's display monitor seemed resentful somehow, as it continued reporting.

UNABLE to confirm reestablishment
OF launch code certificates
REMINDER: protocols demand repeated high-level
VERIFICATION for weapon targeting
OUTSIDE of a publicly sanctioned battlefield zone
RETRY or query alternate server?

Snippy machine. Yet I approved wholeheartedly as the thing began shutting down. Crimson-tipped rockets reengaged their safeties, rolling back into their storage magazine, and I wondered, *Does this mean it's over?*

Not quite. The repair drones were still hard at work, carving up my erstwhile leg and disposing of the bits. Moreover, the remote link could be restored, setting all firing codes and proceeding with the countdown, at any minute.

There'd be no way for me to stop it next time.

Oh yes there will be.

Huh?

I thought my imaginary Nag had vanished.

Are you back, then?

Then? Now?

Present and past do not matter.

What counts is that you get moving again.

Moving? Where? And more important . . . *how?*

There seemed no point in protesting, though. Anyway, I knew the answer already. I just didn't like it.

Back.

Back down those awful stone stairs. Only legless now, dragged along by just the one weary arm, with a little gravity assist.

Back to the one place where I still might do some good. As if I had a snowball's chance in hell of making it.

Well, at least there'd be some illumination this time, trickling from the open window of this narrow room. The light of yet another day I never expected to see.

That's it.

Look at the bright side.

Now I suggest you move.

If only I could have strangled my badgering scold. But that would take two hands . . . plus a physical neck to wrap them around.

So I did the next best thing. I moved.

66

E Pluribus Pluribus

. . . all together now . . .

Less than four minutes had passed since Ritu and Beta and realAlbert entered the underground lab to stare down at a soulistic circus—complete with swinging trapeze act, frantic magician-impresario, and a pair of garish clowns pinned to targets at either end. And in between? A growing tangibility distortion made space seem to ripple and flow, like some caged power, pacing and preparing to burst free.

During those few minutes, a battle raged over which personality would imprint the new godwave.

Who would gain ultimate control over the vast, fallow soulscape? The genius who pioneered the way? Or one whose raw talent seemed made for the job?

The combatants never considered a third possibility—that the new frontier may not be as barren as they thought.

Somebody might already be there.

■   ■   ■

Like most of the audible meaning-squawks that are used by organic men, "already" comes laden with implications. Take past and present tense, for example—narrative deceits that help perpetuate a myth of linear time.

Not for *you,* though. You who were/was/am/are/will be Albert. Your story is complex, looped, and fractally nested. It calls for a style that's flexible, confident, *predictive.*

So here, let me tell you what I foresee.

Before doing anything else, you will relinquish fear.

■   ■   ■

There. Wasn't that easy?

Fear is marvelously useful to biological beings. You won't miss it.

■   ■   ■

Next, you will realize that your life—such as it was—has come to an end.

Surely you didn't expect to survive all these experiences unscathed? No anchored mind can gaze upon the soulscape and remain unchanged.

Forget those symptoms that you once thought to be caused by plague—by some war virus. Soon you'll realize there is nothing physically wrong with the clever animal that carried you around so faithfully, for so long. The sensations you mistook for illness will be recognized as natural separation pangs.

The body will live. Its embedded instincts won't even complain very hard when you move on.

■   ■   ■

Anyway, we have chores to do! Such as learning about the nature of time.

You'll notice that it seems frozen around us. Even Yosil's garish pendulum grinds to a halt, suspended in mid-slice, while the mad ditto's mouth gapes in an angry scream. This is the ortho-moment. The now of palpable reality. The narrow moving slit in which organic beings may move and act and perceive.

Great thinkers always knew that time must be a dimension, with inherent potential for travel, like any other. **But living organisms can't abide a paradox, Albert.** Incongruities of cause-and-effect turn out to be toxic.

How could the creative genius of evolution work its slow miracle—
gradually stirring raw chemicals into *soul-carrying beings*—without
enormous numbers of trials and outcomes? The "real" world needs consistency and countless failures in order for natural selection to do its job,
drawing complexity out of chaos.

It is the answer to the Riddle of Pain.

So we mustn't stretch time's fabric very much, Albert! Just a tweak,
here and there, as we spiral back and forth, helping to create ourselves.

■   ■   ■

Confused? You won't be when we take our first small step back . . .
almost a week . . . to last Monday evening.

No, don't try to navigate in normal terms. Follow affinities instead.

There! Pursue that trace of smugness, mixed with four parts stubbornness, plus some excess self-reliance and a dash of the romantic gambler. Track it and you'll find the *green ditto* that you were that night,
wounded and reckless as he crossed Odeon Square, harassed by bored
punks and chased by Beta's angry yellows, pelting you with stones.

Don't try to remember. Anticipate! It's much easier on this plane.

Soon you'll grasp necessity. *The green must survive,* but on its own.

Only the slightest interference will do. Enough to collapse the probabilities a bit. Something minor, easily dismissed.

Yes, go ahead. Experiment. Soon, at a crucial moment, you'll decide
to reach out and nudge the mind of that *waiter* over there, serving dinner
in a quayside restaurant, whose repeated clumsiness will offer distraction
at a crucial moment . . .

 . . . but carefully! For even a nudge spreads ripples, as you'll see.
Something about the way those dishes go flying—

Later it will bother one of your suspicious selves. He'll worry over
it, like a sore tooth. As I said, clever animals get jittery around a paradox.

Yosil Maharal, amid his brilliance and his flaws, imagined that the
raw material of the soulscape would be like simple clay for him to mold,
to meddle with however he liked. **But you will see—it's far more subtle
than poor Yosil ever imagined.**

■   ■   ■

You'll find our next stop even stranger, skipping forward one day to
a patch of desert road, far outside of town, as someone hefts a bulbous
weapon preparing to ambush the occupants of an approaching car. Yes,

the silvery ditto bears a soul-imprint of Aeneas Kaolin. Also note the biting stench of dread. Everything isn't going to his liking.

But don't probe too deeply! Never mind about such mundane mysteries as who or why or what or where. Forget motives and crimes. Leave the real-world detective work for your successor to solve.

That's no longer any of your concern.

Here's what I predict you'll choose to do. You'll watch as the ambush unfolds.

Notice and appreciate the feral-mammalian gracefulness of real Albert Morris as he swerves the automobile, trying to avoid collision . . . then guns the accelerator when he sees the platinum take aim . . . and fire! Ah, it all happened days ago in linear time, yet the urgency feels so fresh.

Can you anticipate remembering what to do next?

Soon, you'll find there's no one conscious down there, under the desert stars. Albert and Ritu, stunned inside the Volvo's cab, won't notice as you take over a small fragment of ditKaolin, hanging on the car's window. You'll *use* the remnant, reaching inside, taking the vehicle's tiller . . .

. . . and yes, guide it to a narrow ravine, hidden from all those civilized eyes out there that might feel pity or concern, bringing rescue much too soon.

▪   ▪   ▪

You're about to be distracted.

Some information still pours into you through realAlbert's organic eyes and brain, pinning your concern back in the frozen ortho-moment of Friday morning in the underground lab. You will wonder, for instance, what is happening to Yosil Maharal's great invention? Which personality is winning control? Will the glazier beam shoot forth as predicted, soaring above both the real and spiritual planes?

You'll ask about the missiles—did realAlbert succeed in stopping them with his final sabotage? Will the people of the city be saved? Or will backup systems kick in, sending death bullets flying after all?

There is satisfaction in realAlbert's feral heart, having swung that metal chair a final time, smashing the computer controller to sparking debris. Yet, through a corner of his eye, he sees both slender Ritu and a much larger Beta rushing toward him. For once, the two seem united in purpose. Isn't it amazing how siblings can overcome rivalry when faced with threats and opportunities to the family at large?

Time jutters forward a few notches before sticking again. Those quick seconds bring the pair closer. A few more such jumps and they will be upon poor Albert.

Only now, far across the room, Al's eye detects *another* figure entering. This golem wears a beige spiral dye job, garishly corkscrewing from the top of its head all the way down. Its expression, surveying the vast chamber filled with expensive equipment, is one of towering anger!

At first you will imagine that it's yet another version of Beta. Then you'll realize that **looks are deceiving.**

■ ■ ■

Why?

Why is all of this happening? What is the context for all of this meddling?

That will be your question soon. And I'll answer, to the extent possible, after a few more errands.

First we shall move to coordinates a little closer in spacetime. Make it about half a day ago . . .

There! Albert Morris is alone in the great underground defense armory, sifting through computer records of the military base, tracking the secret thefts and treacheries of Yosil Maharal. Not far away stand columns of blank-eyed soldiers—sealed-to-preserve-freshness—ready to bake at a moment's notice, whenever their country needs them. Or when someone clever enough comes along to hijack them.

Shall we help ourselves? You will need just one.

First, look around for Ritu. An earlier version of that wounded-confused soul. You'll detect her soon, filled with self-loathing as she surrenders to an inner craving beyond her control, laying her shaved head between the poles of a high-capacity tetragramatron while autokilns warm up nearby, preparing several dozen giant golems built for war.

Come, while she's still fighting the compulsion, still showing some spirited resistance to that inner pressure. Beta never had to overcome such active opposition before! That means the imprint he makes upon the very first copy will be weak. You'll slip between the cracks and *take over* that one, pushing Beta aside. Yes, the ditto may be damaged. But it will be good enough—yours to command—first out of the oven.

Ready? Have you done it? Then bring along your warrior and we'll go find Albert.

What's that? Are we going to *rescue him?*

No, I don't expect Albert will call this much of a rescue. Not when he still winds up herded into that awful tunnel. And yet, time loops can be surprising. Even after an infinite number of recursions, they are never exactly the same. Maybe this one will amaze us.

No matter.

I'm sure that when the critical moment comes you will know what to do.

67

... and Roll

... Gumby hears a pitter-patter ...

As journeys go, this one was even worse than that miserable slog along the river bottom, back on Monday night. I didn't so much crawl downstairs as tumble most of the way.

What else could I do, with just an arm, a battered head, and a torso that kept dropping off bits with each bump or hard landing? I had no sense of smell, of course. (I could barely even remember the concept.) But oily vapors oozing off this body were easy to see. One reason for haste was to stay ahead of those fumes, which tend to accelerate final decay—it's why dissolution usually happens all at once, swiftly and mercifully.

No such luck for me. Too obdurate to give up, I guess. How strange that frankie mutation made me more like Albert than even he was!

Finally, and rather to my surprise, I ran out of stairs, arriving at the same landing where I chose the least traveled of three forks in the road. Was that half an hour ago? I didn't regret the decision to climb those dark steps. Stopping the missile launcher, even temporarily, was the greatest achievement of my bargain-basement life. Only now I faced another trio of options.

Back to the cave entrance and the vacation cabin, where maybe a working telephone might be found amid the debris?

Forward, toward Maharal's inner sanctum? That's where the pilot of the Harley scooter went—though now I doubted that he was ever Beta, after all. No doubt big happenings were going on, down that way.

But those two alternatives were out. I'd never make it more than a few meters. My sole choice lay across the corridor, in a niche containing that all-in-one home copier machine, warm and ready with its hopper full of fresh blanks. What I was about to try went against custom. You can even get fined if you're caught, though everybody tries it once or twice. *In my state, I'll probably make a slobbering monster.*

Still, the poor thing won't have to remember much. Step out of the kiln, run upstairs, and smash the launcher beyond repair. Easy!

All of which was moot until I reached the padded spot where an original must lay his head. Staring up, I wondered—*How the hell do I do that?*

My enzyme clock was ticking out, the missile codes might be restored at any moment . . . and now I had another reason to hurry. Through my battered abdomen I picked up vibrations, rhythmic and growing more forceful by the second.

Motors and wheels, I thought, recognizing some.

Other thuddings reminded me of running feet.

6 8

Wherever You're Atman

. . . or learning what's already known . . .

Next you'll discover the soulscape is far larger than you imagined.

And yes, inhabited.

Did you arrogantly expect that the entire universe was waiting upon man to arrive?

■ ■ ■

Well, in a sense, that's true. Our cosmos is but one of trillions spun off by a single fertile singularity, whose daughter black holes spawned countless more baby universes, each of them exploding and inflating and cooling into billions of galaxies, which in turn made their own black holes and more singularity-spawned universes, and so on. . . . Among all those experiments, intelligence surely occurred, though far less commonly than you imagined.

Even scarcer still are creatures made of earthly flesh who look up at the stars and covet them across huge gulfs of empty space.

Most exceptional of all are those who find another way, bypassing cold vacuum, uncovering shortcuts to far richer fields. Exceptional almost to the point of uniqueness. Hence the vast emptiness of what Maharal dramatically called the "spiritual plane." A deeper continuum, made of stuff more basic than energy and matter. A frontier he meant to stride upon like a god, using all that raw material to cast paradise in his image.

Oh, you are rarities, you hot-souled humans. So flawed. Wondrously bright. It's a privilege to watch as you begin to waken. As you start to choose.

■   ■   ■

Have you begun to suspect who and what I am?

This voice that you mistook for a guide . . . you'll soon notice that "I" never give commands, or even suggest very much. For the most part I only foresee, comment, and predict.

No, I'm not your Virgil. No mentor or font of wisdom. I'm your *echo,* you-who-were-Albert-and-more. A way to remember things that you haven't yet learned. One of many conveniences you'll soon grow accustomed to, where paradox is a normal fact of life.

■   ■   ■

Back in the ortho-moment—still moving forward in jerks and sudden stops—events will soon be coming to a head. Just three more swings of Yosil's pendulum while the glazier stores energy, preparing to burst forth *whether or not* a human imprint gives it personality. Whether or not a city full of dying souls awaits to feed it, in an orgy of necrophagia.

What, you still care about that? Very well then, let me predict that you will go back again to nudge events a little more. Go ahead.

You will find the green Albert who calls himself a "frankie" . . . what's left of him . . . less than an hour before the ortho-moment. Yes, right over there. Moments after his arm was snapped off by the closing scooter-canopy, sending him plunging through the roof of Yosil's cabin into a debris-strewn living room.

He might use a little encouragement at that point. What approach will you use?

Will you scold him for lying there in the dust, watching the Harley fly away, feeling defeated and ready to expire?

Well, then, try imitating my vatic tone, then listen as the green reacts!

■   ■   ■

Except that Clara will never get to hear the whole story ... and now the bad guys will win.

Aw, man. Whatever nagging inner voice had to put in that last bit? What guilt-tripping nag? If I could, I'd tear it out! Just shut up and let me die.

You gonna just lie there and let 'em get away with it?

Crap. I didn't have to take this from some obsessive soul corner of a cheap-model golem who was misborn a frankie ... became a ghost ... and was about to graduate to melting corpse.

Who's a corpse? Speak for yourself.

Stunning wit, that triple irony. And though I tried hard to ignore the little voice ... my right hand and arm moved, lifting slowly till five trembling fingers came within sight. ... Then my left leg twitched. ... Reacting to imprinted habits a million years old, they started cooperating. ...

Oh well. Might as well help.

◼   ◼   ◼

The bedraggled greenie moves! And just to be sure, you'll nag him again during that long drag through the grotto, then climbing the dark stairs, and so on.

Just don't exaggerate the importance of your badgering—or the reification triggered by your presence as an observer. These things matter far less than physical action in the "real" world of cause-and-effect. The green might have made it entirely without your/my/our interference!

No matter. You will do this and it will aggravate him. It may help save a million lives, and divert the Standing Wave toward a different destiny. So by all means go ahead.

Now perhaps you will also go back a few hours, to a moment in Pal's apartment, whispering for the green to turn his head and listen at a crucial moment. Perhaps ... oh, of course you will.

You always meddle at the beginning. It is part of learning. Becoming.

◼   ◼   ◼

Back in the ortho-moment—another pendulum swing has passed, like the ticking of a titanic clock. Surprising resonances perturb the amplified Standing Wave, raising concern in the two stalemated combatants. Probability amplitudes are collapsing like quantum dominoes all around.

Their battle is over. It's out of their control now.

To Yosil, the news is calamitous. The germ missiles may not launch at all! No viral rain of death virus to mow down millions and feed the glazier beam when it arrives. Hovering above the city, it will harvest only a trickle. The few thousand who normally die each day will discover an afterlife unlike anything they were taught about in church! But Yosil despairs that such meager reinforcement will never give the glazier the boost it needs to become a spiritual behemoth, capable of bending the soulscape to its mighty will.

The other personality—once rooted in Albert Morris—had succumbed to Yosil's dream, adopting it as his own. Can he now accept it's over and choose a more modest goal?

■　■　■

Others plunge into this fray.

While the glazier builds toward ignition, the organic body of real-Albert sways along the axis of the beam, like an anchor dragged by a rising storm—

—as Ritu and Beta arrive with arms outstretched, united in purpose at last, bent on pushing him aside, or worse.

I know you're curious to probe Ritu's complex, tormented soul. By all means, use the new powers of perception. Soon you'll see the crime that set her tragic tale in motion . . .

. . . the reason why her syndrome so resembles and exaggerates the very same one suffered by Yosil.

Not genes alone, but also a *trauma* they both suffered long ago, when a doting father tried using clever new technology to encourage and spur his infant daughter's developing brain, by imprinting talents from one loving soul to another.

Like playing music for a fetus in the womb—that is how poor Yosil imagined it—a harmless gift from one generation to the next, alas, before anyone understood about subjective uniqueness and soul-orthogonality. Before the dreadful harm was widely known. Before such things were outlawed.

Tragedy can have its own triste beauty, evoking tears or laughter. This one rippled on with gorgeously transfixing horror worthy of Sophocles, across years wracked with silent remorse, obsession, and pain.

Yes, you'll pity them. From this new perspective, you will commiserate, dwell upon, and share their agony.

Later.

■　■　■

Others plunge into this fray.

A spiral-patterned golem charges through the opposite door, shouting about betrayal in terms that only a multibillionaire would use. And you have to hand it to Aeneas Kaolin. (You *will* hand it to him, I predict.) It took ingenuity that no one imagined him capable of, to penetrate the many-layered disguises and defenses erected by a family of brilliant paranoiacs. Yosil and Ritu and Beta underestimated him. So did Albert Morris.

With a little more time . . . or if he trusted Morris enough to confide and ally with him from the beginning . . . Kaolin might have made a difference. But now? Even as he raises a weapon, shouting threats and demands to desist, Aeneas clearly knows that it's too late.

Same with the *warriors* now arriving from the military base, bursting through that dark tunnel under Urraca Mesa. Armed, armored, and representing the wrath of abused taxpayers, it is the cavalry at last—pulverizing Beta's rear guard to reach the high parapet and gaze down on all of this. Among their weapons are cameras, beaming images around the world.

Light cleanses. The World Eye was supposed to prevent all big nasty conspiracies and mad scientist labs.

It very nearly did.

Maybe next time it will.

If there is a next time.

◼   ◼   ◼

Has anyone noticed the alignment yet?

Like a superheated, pressurized mix of air and explosive, the amplified Standing Wave has grown beyond containment or forbearance. Nor can you retard the advancing ortho-moment any longer. The time for meddling is about to end—

—as Kaolin charges toward the red mirror

—as Ritu and Beta plunge toward the gray

—as soldiers throw themselves courageously over the balcony on ropes made of living clay

—as realAlbert lifts his eyes . . . the only one who seems, quite suddenly, to know what's happening.

69

Joe Friday

. . . as Gumby tries to do what comes naturally . . .

A tester once told Albert he was "born for this era," with the right combination of ego, focus, and emotional distance to make perfect duplicates.
Well, except for me, his first and only frankie. Still, I was willing to
gamble on that talent—

—providing I could somehow reach the scanning plate of a simple
copier.

This time there was a chair nearby. Fumes wafted from my poor arm
as it dragged me over there, one slither at a time. Worming around to
grip a chair leg with my chin, I hauled it back, positioning the chair next
to the big white duplicating machine. Only about a kilo of my body mass
melted along the way.

It doesn't go high enough, I quickly realized. Glancing around for
something else, I spied a wire-mesh waste receptacle three meters away.
With a groan that escaped through several cracks other than my mouth,
I set out to fetch it—a journey that felt like crossing the North Pole while
being pelted by asteroids.

Half of my remaining ceramic teeth fell out while gripping the metal
basket on my way back. Then, the first time I tried tossing it on top of
the chair, I *missed* and had to repeat the whole damned thing.

This had better be enough, I thought, when the basket was finally in
place, upside down on the cushioned seat. Any minute, someone might
restore contact with that missile launcher upstairs and resume the countdown. And those vibrations of running feet grew closer by the second.
Whatever was going on, I wanted the power to act! Even as the shambling
replica of a frankie.

Well, here goes.

From the floor I reached up, grabbed the edge of the chair, and pulled
hard. My head and torso weighed much less now—and grew lighter with
each passing moment—still the strain was enormous. Fresh pock-fissures
erupted all along my quivering arm, each one venting noxious steam . . .
till at last my chin broached over the ledge, taking some of the pressure.
That made things a bit easier, though no less painful. Commanding my

elbow to twist up and around, I managed to push down now, dragging my attenuated body to perch at the edge of the seat.

So much for the simple part.

Halfway to the copier platform now, I could see a glowing green START button within easy reach, but useless till my head reached the perceptron tendrils. Still, I took a moment to smack the button, telling the machine to start readying a blank. If I did manage to make it, there'd be few seconds to spare. Machinery rumbled and rumbled.

Now things get tricky.

Fortunately, the chair had arms . . . twice as many as I did, actually. That helped as I leveraged myself alongside the upended wastebasket, flopping and wedging my body against the metal mesh while my sole decaying limb pushed. Then I had to reach higher, onto the copier itself, searching for fingerholds—and as I strained again, a couple of digits broke off, liquefying horribly as they fell past my good eye to splat on the floor.

This time, the fissures along my arm resembled chasms, sweating fluid the color of magma. It was a race to see whether dissolution would win, or hard baking from heat, like happened to that leg I threw at the missile launcher. Suppose I self-cooked in place! What a sculpture I'd make. Call it *A Study in Obstinacy*, reaching and grimacing while struggling to haul a useless body. . . .

That's it, I realized, grateful for any inspiration, *drop the deadweight!*

Barely thinking, I applied lessons that I learned upstairs, pulling my *self* inward and away from remote parts. The whole bottom half of my torso was useless to me now—so ditch it! Scavenge the remaining enzymes. Send them up for the arm's final tug.

I felt what was left of my abdomen crumble away. With the load suddenly lightened, my arm gave a hard *yank* . . . and snapped off at the shoulder.

I don't think I could ever describe what it felt like as a ragged head and upper chest, sailing high enough to look down at my goal, the white surface where a human original was supposed to lay in comfort, blithely commanding obedient machinery to make cheap doubles—a perfect serving class that can't rebel and always knows what to do.

How simple that used to seem!

During my flying arc, I wondered, *Assuming I land okay, will I be able to use my chin and shoulder to maneuver around? To guide my head between the tendrils?*

Would that automatically trigger imprinting, now that the START button had been pressed? If not, how was I to press it again? Problems, problems. And you know what? I would have found solutions, too. I know it. If that darn trajectory had just carried me where I wanted to go.

But like Moses, I could only watch the promised land from afar. Coming down, my head barely *missed* the platform, caroming off the copier's edge and then against the wastebasket, knocking it off the chair so it tumbled, landing upright on the floor.

As if that weren't enough, what happened next was the real capper.

I rolled across the seat and teetered for a fragile moment, then fell off to land (appropriately enough, at the end of one hell of a week) inside a receptacle labeled TRASH.

70

Soul's My Destination

Will it be all right, now that the glazier beam has fired?

What a sight that was.

The titanic Standing Wave blasted through both clay mirrors, hurling the pendulum—with ditYosil aboard—deep into a stony ceiling. Yet all the others who were standing around barely got singed. For the mighty wave distortion instantly *turned* on an axis that lay at right angles to every known direction, vanishing into a distance no living eye could follow.

Except for realAlbert, that is, who turned his head as if to track its departure, wearing a smile so enigmatic, so knowing, that Ritu and her twin brother simply stopped in their tracks. One moment they were rushing toward him with hands raised to strike. The next, they simply dropped their arms and backed away, staring at him.

Yes, the "anchor" is still attached, by a slender thread.

Shall we follow?

■　　■　　■

From the beginning, when brilliant, tormented Yosil Maharal still thought he could design and control everything, the beam's first goal had been the nearest city. Where else could so many spirit-flickers be found close together, clustered like a tidy field of crops growing alongside a fallow prairie? It must have seemed a good place to harvest nourishment for the next step.

Had he bent his egomania enough to involve peers and collaborators— even a whole civilization—Yosil might have discovered and corrected all the flaws in his splendid plan. Technical and conceptual flaws. Moral flaws. But "mad scientist" is almost defined by solipsism—a neurotic need to avoid criticism and do everything alone.

Without Maharal, it might have taken another generation for humanity to make this attempt. *Because* of him, humanity could have been destroyed.

As it turns out, there is no plague tearing through the metropolis when the glazier arrives overheard. No charnelhouse of rapid pestilence providing enough death manna to gorge upon at length. Just a few thousand souls per day, cast free of their organic moorings by accident or natural causes, rise gently to the hovering waveform, finding welcome room for their vibratory modes. After some initial surprise, they add breadth and subtlety to a superposition of states. . . .

But it's no feast.

This Standing Wave won't become a "god" by raw power alone.
Yosil's simple plan has failed.
Time to try something else.

■　■　■

Turning sideways again, the macrowave pursues a scent that few ever noticed before. Out to sea it flies, two thousand kilometers, where blue pelagic currents course above deep trenches—an abode for cephalopods, some nearly as long as a supertanker, with eyes like dinner plates and brains reeking of high intelligence. Aliens, right here on Earth.

Is this it?
Plunging deep where sunlight never goes, we join the world of giant squid, sampling what it's like to flow along by sphincter-driven water jet, touching and experiencing a liquid world with long suckers that dangle beyond the limits of vision. We feed. We chase, mate, and spawn. We compete and scheme by logic all our own, expressing concepts in warm flashes of intricate color along our flanks.

And, once in a great while, we also *tremble* and *worship* when Death comes plunging down at us from Hell, the hot world above. For that narrow instant, while fleeing desperately, we clasp and cherish something that glimmers like hope—

Then the devil is upon us, massive, black, devouring. His shrill voice strikes deep, paralyzing, turning guts to jelly! Then come jaws, small but powerful. White teeth reflect the protest pigmentations of our bioluminescent skin as they tear unto us, dragging us upward . . .

■ ■ ■

So, it wasn't the giant squid who attracted the glazier beam this way. They're so exotic, perhaps they'll find another soulscape of their own.

It was their hunters who drew the macrowave here.

Sperm whales, returning from the crushing depths, their hunger sated on fresh cephalopod, now gather at the pleasant wavetops to breathe and splash. Though occupied with natural concerns—the quest for food and reproductive success—now and then as many as a dozen creatures *congregate,* touching massive brows.

Contained within, far larger than any other organ, is a mound of waxy substance, malleable as wet clay, subtle at refracting and reshaping sound, enabling these stalkers of the deep to propel cunning beams that find—and stun—their prey in utter darkness. Sculpted sound is to them as the dynamic recoloring of flesh is to squid, or syntactical word chains to a human being. All are ways to gossip, cooperate, deceive, meditate, or—when all else fails—seek urgent meaning in prayer.

The sperm whales congregate, flared tails pointing outward like a petaled flower, or mandala, or rose window. Brows meeting, they exchange complex sonic shapes/images/ideograms with properties that long ago emerged from the background noise of mere survival. Meanings congeal in the wax, delicate as spiderwebs, unique as snowflakes, multifarious as an ecosystem.

They were doing this long before Bevvisov learned to imprint souls in clay.

■ ■ ■

Off again!

Using so much energy, shouldn't the glazier be growing hungry? There was beauty amid the squid and whales—but no great nourishment. Then why does the macrowave seem *un*disappointed as it rotates through an axis invented on the spot—twisting the very context out of which raw vacuum arose—then building speed on a course that it makes up as it goes?

We seem to have discovered outer space.

In flickering sequence we pass great sweeps of stars. Mammoth clusters of bright pinpoints roll by in leaps that devour emptiness as if it wasn't there. Metric itself becomes a component of the wave, its ally in travel, rather than an obstacle.

Searching . . . examining . . . every now and then, we pause briefly to scrutinize—

a red giant, tumid and swollen as it slowly expands, eating its children. Then—

an aged white dwarf, born during the galaxy's first generation. Having blown away much of its substance, it will (ironically) endure long ages more on a starvation diet, glittering faintly for no one—

unlike a gluttonous blue super-giant, whose mere million years tick by with blazing speed. Far too massive for any other goal, it must choose glory over life—

that is, until it's cleaved by a surprising force, slicing the colossus in two. A singularity! Not a black hole, this one is long and stringy—an exceptional relic of creation, a faceted flaw in spacetime, deadly, gorgeous only to those who know its language of pure math—

having already stirred turmoil when it passed through an immense molecular cloud, spinning vortices that self-gravitate, flattening to ionized skirts that whirl and merge into newborn systems—

then on again we speed, past spiral arms that gleam like diamond dust, until—

we find ourselves zooming down to a modest yellow sun . . . a star of pleasant middle age . . . a steady hearth, unpretentious, with a retinue of planet-specks—

one of which seems luckier than most . . . warm-not-hot, massive-not-ponderous, wet-not-drowned, and kneaded by just enough falling objects to keep things interesting.

■   ■   ■

We plunge to this world, gorgeous in its balance of ocean and sky, sea and shore, mountain and plain, lake and hill, pond and knoll, tree and shrub, prey and predator, fungus and rotifer, parasite and prion, clay and crystal, molecule and atom, electron and . . .

Diving ever smaller, we cry out to wait!
Go back!

What was that passing glimpse we just had of gleaming, multibranched spires built by fascinating hands? A brief impression of docked ships and shops and tree-perched homes where shaded figures spoke a demure language, like song?

Backtrack. It should be easy to find. Just return to a size and scale midway between a cosmos and a quark.

Another civilization. Another race of thinking, feeling beings! Wasn't that what you were looking for?

Apparently not.

71

Head Basket

. . . or how to become a real boy . . .

Little remained of the gleaming me that stepped out of a kiln Tuesday morning, resigned to cleaning the house and running the chores of Albert Morris. A body that wound up living—let's see—close to three extra days, thanks to Aeneas Kaolin, and a dash of mulish stubbornness. A self who wound up doing a whole lot more than scrub toilets! Who gathered so many interesting memories and thoughts—what a pity there'd be no chance to deposit them. To share them.

The things I've seen.

And hallucinated, reminding myself of all the fun echoes and trippy/bossy voices I made up along the way. Oh, realAl was going to miss out on a lot. Assuming that he escaped the burning of his home, Albert probably spent the whole week at a computer screen, or waving his arms under a chador, coordinating ebony researchers and gray investigators and dickering with insurance agents. Working hard, the poor dull fellow.

And yet, he can't be a complete bore. Not if Clara loves him.

I'd smile if I could. How nice if my last mental picture could be of her . . . a woman I never met in person, yet still adored.

I could see her now—a final, pleasant feat of imagination as the last of my torso dissolved, leaving only a pathetic head rolling at the bottom of a dustbin. Yes, it was she who came before me, all blurry in a Hollywood-romantic way that softens any image, even one wearing a duralloy helmet covered with spiky antennas.

Through that gauzy light, Clara seemed to peer down at me, her sweet voice beckoning like an angel.

"Well, I'll be cut to bits and served as tempura," said my illusory seraph, pushing aside a pair of holo goggles that gleamed like sunlit cobwebs. *"Chen! Does this dit look like an Albert to you?"*

"Hm. Maybe," said another figure, crowding in to have a look. While my conjured Clara seemed all soft and feminine (albeit wrapped in heavy armor), the newcomer was fanged and scaly.

A demon!

In its hand, a slim rod poked my brow.

"Damn, you're right! The pellet says . . . wait, this can't be."

A third voice, much higher, squeaked, *"Oh yes it can!"*

From around Clara's shoulder a thin face like an eager fox appeared, bending over to leer down, grinning at me with twin V-rows of shiny teeth. *"It's got to be the one who signaled,"* said the ferret-figure I had dreamed up, looking quite a bit like my old companion Palloid. *"Maybe this is old Gumby, after all."*

I would have shaken my head if I could, or closed my eyes if I had lids.

This was all too much, even for a dream.

Time to melt, before it got worse.

Only, I had to rouse a bit when Clara called.

"Albert? Is that you in there?"

Illusion or not, I couldn't refuse her anything. Though lacking a body—or any other means to make sound—I somehow gathered strength to mouth four words.

". . . just . . . a . . . . fax . . . ma'am . . ."

All right. I should have come up with something better. Everything was fading, though. Anyway, I felt happy enough. Before utter blackness, my final image would be of her smile, so reassuring that you just had to believe.

"Don't worry, sweetheart." Clara said, reaching into the wastebasket. *"I've got you. Everything will be just fine."*

PART IV

But this man that you wish to create for yourself is short of days and full of passion.

—the Book of Job

■

72

Rigmarole

. . . or in memory still green . . .

With a wide-open main gate, the estate seemed to lack security, an illusion the owner could afford. Cruising toward a great stone mansion, our limousine passed groundskeepers at work. They were ostentatiously real.

"This *is* kind of familiar," said Pal from his life-sustaining chair. "I remember thinking we'd be lucky to get out of this place alive." Somehow he had managed to absorb some bits of memory from the smashed mini-golem—my companion across a frantic Tuesday and Wednesday. It felt good knowing some of clever Palloid survived.

Sensors turned a narrow patch of the limo's body transparent wherever a passenger's eye happened to focus, creating an illusion of no roof or walls, though nosy outsiders would spy just a few dim circles, darting about madly. Still, in order to inhale the scent composition of Aeneas Kaolin's gardens, I had to roll down a window.

Smells kept surprising me, like memories of another life.

Someone else took a deep breath when I did. *Albert,* to my left, gave one of his distant smiles, clearly enjoying hints of autumn in the breeze. Except for a small bandage below an ear, and one around his thumb, he didn't look too bad. He could even dress and shave himself, if gently coaxed. But his attention lay elsewhere.

Are you a neshamah? I wondered. *A body without a soul?*

If so, what an ironic role reversal. For I, a golem, felt well equipped in that regard.

Is there no one home in there, Albert? Or are we just getting a "busy signal"?

I must have been staring again. A gentle squeeze from the other side drew me back as Clara's slim, strong hand took mine.

"Do you think we'll get to look over Kaolin's medieval armor collection?" she asked. "I'd love to try a few cuts with that big, two-handed Claymore."

This from a beautiful young woman wearing a sun hat and a light summer dress. Clara sometimes enjoyed downplaying her "formidable" side. It enhanced her feral attractiveness.

"He may be in no mood to play tour guide," I predicted, but she just smiled.

Closer to the house, Clara glanced pointedly at a sunken parking area holding two more automatic limos, just like this one. We had timed our arrival to closely follow that pair.

■   ■   ■

Red-striped guardits watched a forklift remove a tall shipping crate from a delivery truck by the chateau's main entrance. They turned warily as we pulled up . . . till some hidden signal made them back off.

"I always wanted a job like that," Pal murmured as the grunting forklift hoisted its cargo on sturdy legs, ascending wide steps to the house.

"No, you didn't," I replied, maneuvering his life-support chair onto the pavement. Hard work wasn't Pal's style.

Clara examined the chair's medical dials, then fussed over realAlbert, straightening his collar. "Will you two be okay out here?"

Pal took Albert's arm, getting another enigmatic smile. "Us? We'll just stroll the grounds, helping each other over bumps and looking for trouble."

Clara still worried, but I squeezed her hand. What place could be safer? And their presence would make a point to Kaolin.

"Go on in." Pal nodded toward the mansion. "If Mr. Zillionaire gives you any trouble, holler. We'll bust in, right, old buddy?"

Instead of responding, Albert turned, as if following something barely visible against the blue sky. He pointed with his bandaged thumb, like some kind of metaphysical hitchhiker.

"Dust," he said in tones of bemused interest. *"They left shapes in it. Deep ones. Everybody did."*

We all waited a few seconds, but there was no more.

"O-o-okay," Pal commented. "I hope that's *good* news. About dust. Hm."

Absent and unruffled, Albert put a hand to steady Pal's chair on the gravel path. Clara and I watched till they rounded a corner, toward the sound of cooing doves. On the roof, several stories above, a reflective dome was said to house the famed hermit himself—realAeneas Kaolin.

With a glance at each other for encouragement, Clara and I headed up broad granite steps.

■   ■   ■

After rolling along for a while, Pal gives the signal. At last!

I drop from the undercarriage of his chair onto sun-warmed pebbles. Wait for the wheels to pass and . . . now!

Skittering on-belly, dodging Albert's human feet, I dash into shade beneath a gardenia hedge. Oof, what stench! Too much of my small head was modeled on a critter who hunts by scent. Should have left more room for brains.

Ah well. Just do what my maker wants. And satisfy the built-in craving of curiosity—better than food or sex. Go!

But keep alert for sensors, trip-threads. My clever eyes tune to see IR beams. Also cockatrices, tripfalls, and regular old gopher traps.

A decorative brickwork niche runs all the way up. Get inside. Deploy claws tipped with diamond augments. Strong paws sink those shiny diamond-tipped claws into stone.

Lovely what you can do with clay, these days.

■   ■   ■

A platinum rox stood in the foyer, watching servants direct the grunting forklift toward a large study—the same place where Yosil Maharal's open coffin lay a couple of weeks ago. But Kaolin wouldn't expect me to know about that. Those memories were destroyed. Supposedly.

The shipping crate was his immediate concern, though he beckoned us to follow. Clara happily aimed her implant at the old spears, shields, maces, and other pointy things on display. Only when the forklift gently dropped its cargo by a southern wall did our host turn with an extended hand.

"Major Gonzales and ditto Morris. You're early. By several hours."

"Are we? My fault then," Clara said. "I'm operating on East Coast time these days."

A dubious excuse. Still, the convenience of a real guest outweighs annoyance to any ditto, even the ditto of a trillionaire.

"Not at all. You two are busy people these days! Thanks for accepting my invitation. Though I imagine you had your own reasons for coming."

"There are matters to discuss," I agreed.

"No doubt. But first, how are the bodies working out?"

I glanced down at the one I wore today. Its buff shade of beige-gray, plus realistic hair and skin texture, pushed the tolerant edges of legality. But no one complained amid all the buzz about my "heroics." I cared

more about other features, those letting me smell and see and touch Clara
with utter vividness.

"Impressive work. Must be expensive,"

"Very." He nodded. "But that doesn't matter if—"

The platinum golem flinched as one side of the shipping crate fell
with a sharp bang. Servants moved on to the other panels.

"Naturally," ditKaolin resumed, "you'll be supplied with these hyperquality blanks, gratis, till the problem with your original is sorted out.
Have there been any signs . . . ?"

"Plenty of signs. But none that say welcome."

After two weeks of expert study, it was evident that the mind/soul of
realAlbert Morris had "gone away" in some fashion no one understood.
Yosil Maharal might have explained. But he too was gone, even more
decisively.

"Well, you can count on Universal Kilns. Either until it becomes
possible to reload to your original, or else . . ."

"Or else till I pass my limit at performing ditto-to-ditto transfers."

He nodded. "We'll help with hyperquality blanks and the experimental golem-prolongation process. In part because we owe a debt—"

"You sure do," Clara muttered.

The shiny golem winced. "Though in exchange, my technicians naturally wish to monitor your remarkable endurance. No one else ever
achieved such fidelity, imprinting from one animated doll to another!"

I noticed Kaolin's right hand quiver slightly. If anything, he was
downplaying his eagerness.

"Hm, yes. *Monitoring.* That may present a problem if—" I stopped
as Kaolin's servants finally broke apart the shipping box, liberating a
heavy crystal display cabinet. Within stood the dun brown figure of a
small, well-built man—a soldier with Asiatic features, hand-molded and
kiln-fired roughly two thousand years ago. His confident half smile
seemed almost alive.

"Only ten of the Sian terracottas have left China," ditKaolin breathed
happily. "I'll keep this one here to honor my late friend Yosil. Till his
heir returns to claim it."

The tycoon clearly didn't expect that to happen any time soon, though
I saw a portrait of Ritu Maharal prominently displayed atop the grand
piano. Had it been deliberately moved there as a gesture?

My "memory" of this room came from a voice-recording Clara found
under Urraca Mesa, inside the shattered Albert gray who was kidnapped

from this very estate, subjected to cruel torments, then assigned to serve as a "mirror" in that bizarre experiment. Fortunately, the gray's diary spool survived the culminating explosion, offering a compulsive sotto voce recitation about the murderous activities of a mad ghost. Another recording spool, removed from realAlbert's neck, offered a sporadic, low-quality transcription of a few more puzzle-piece events—a roadside ambush, desert treks, and underground betrayals, shedding some light on how Yosil's daughter got involved.

How much more convenient if all three versions of us had been able to recombine memories at the end! As things stood, Clara and I had to rely on old-fashioned detective work.

"Have they made any progress treating Ritu's condition?"

"Just diagnostic work. Contact's been made with the Beta personality. Doctors are probing for any more siblings lying dormant within." Kaolin gave a melancholy sigh. "None of this would have happened before the age of golemtech. Surely not the original tragic blunder Yosil inflicted on Ritu as a child. And even if she did still get a divided-personality syndrome, it would never have manifested so powerfully in the outer world. Who would ever expect such a character as Beta to emerge and—"

"Oh, spare us," Clara interrupted.

We turned to see her examining the Sian soldier, one warrior to another. But her attention to our conversation never drifted.

"You knew about Beta for years," she added. "You found it convenient to maintain a relationship with one so uncannily skilled at deception. Someone able to consistently fool the World Eye! One of the last brilliant underworld figures, and you were in a position to blackmail him into doing all sorts of favors, because Beta was ultimately vulnerable at the source. Come on, admit it."

Platinum fists tightened, but anger was futile. As realAlbert's assigned guardian and my nominal owner, Clara had legal standing. I was *her* adviser, not the other way around.

"I . . . admit no such thing."

"Then let's investigate. Subpoena cam-records going back years, interview employees under the Henchman Law. Heck, it won't take much for me to interest the national security apparat, now that—"

"—of course speaking *hypothetically*," Kaolin rushed in. "For the sake of argument, suppose I did have prior dealings with the figure known as Beta. You'd scour forever without finding a single genuine criminal act on my part. Sure, I may have committed a few civil torts . . . all right, maybe a lot of those. Gineen Wammaker and some other perverts could sue for copyright damages.

"So? Would you jeopardize our beneficial relationship on her account?"

Implicit was a threat. The hyperquality bodies I got free, plus gear for high-fi imprinting and replenishment, were matters of survival to a stranded soul. My unique copying talent still needed plenty of help, until realAlbert finally chose to let me climb back into the only organic brain on Earth that could accommodate me.

Would it work even then? I couldn't help still regarding myself as Frankie—or Gumby—a rebellious green puppet who ran off one day, declaring independence while dreaming of becoming a real boy. Perhaps my Standing Wave and Albert's strangely mutated soul were too far diverged ever to rejoin again.

I might be a ghost.

Well, if so, I was a ghost with full sensoria, loved by an exciting woman, with important work to do. One can imagine worse afterlives.

"Let's talk about this triangle that you had going with the Maharals," Clara urged our host. "You and Yosil and Beta and . . . I guess it was a *square* if you include Ritu herself . . . each one using the others, scheming and exploiting each other's talents and resources, making and breaking deals—"

"No," I interrupted.

When she gave me a questioning look, I added, "Later, please, Clara."

ditKaolin seemed relieved. "Yes. Later. Anyway, I forget myself. Please come this way. I ordered refreshments."

■ ■ ■

A sure-enough paranoid bastard lives here. Good thing I'm one, too.

My chosen path upward is choked with prickly things—detectors and nanowires . . . toxin-mites and mini-caltrops. Ridiculous overkill!

I must switch routes. Try climbing the open wall instead, where the nasty stuff will all be weathered by sun and smog and rain. Anyway, who looks out for burglars climbing a flat wall in broad daylight?

Can't answer that. Brain's too small for memories. But I seem to know what's possible.

Pixelated skin on my back mimics the reflectance of each bit of wall I pass over. Got the idea from a cool trick of Beta's. Bought the tech-details off a UK techie for a Henchman Prize. Cheap! Other gimmicks are military—Clara has connections. But the cleverest come from hob-byists, unhappy with UK's long refusal to share source code.

Take the special eye in the middle of my right paw. Press it against an opaque window as I pass by. It hijacks the room's attention monitor and voilà! A narrow circle turns clear for a whole millisecond!

Long enough to verify, nobody's in that room. Ah well. The next one seemed likelier for architectural reasons that I can't remember now.

Just a little farther . . .

■　■　■

Following behind our host, Clara glanced back at the terracotta sol-dier of Sian, part of a legion modeled—some say imprinted—from real warriors who served the legendary First Emperor, duty-bound to come fiercely alive whenever called. Clara played much the same role in scores of replicas. Only now she had another job, helping investigate how things went so wrong in the Dodecahedron, where the halls were now resound-ing to a staccato thud of falling heads.

On a veranda we found food and drink—generous portions for Clara and nibble-bites that appeal to a high-class golem like me, with tastebuds but no stomach to speak of. Clara laughed, pointing at two figures across the tree-flecked meadow, one rolling in a wheelchair. The other broke pace to skip, like a small boy.

ditKaolin jotted on a clipboard held by an ebony assistant. "More lawsuits," he explained. "Now from Farshid Lum and those *ditto liber-ation* freaks! As if *I* dug their stupid tunnel into UK headquarters."

"Perhaps they want to learn who set them up for blame in a case of industrial sabotage. I'm curious, too."

Aeneas shrugged. "Beta, of course. No one was better at such ploys. He schemed with that Irene deviant, tricking an Albert into—"

"Into doing some quasilegal technology sniffing, they claimed. A prion bomb never featured, till someone else hijacked the plan."

ditKaolin groaned, sitting down to grab a glass of Golem-Cola. "Yes, I'm familiar with the popular theory. Beta and I were allies, but had a falling out. I took revenge by waging total war, furtively using the Albert Morris Detective Agency, among many weapons. Despite his brilliance, Beta had an Achilles heel when I found his secret point of origin. Soon I eliminated his copies and took over his operations. Right?"

"According to some popular theories."

"But it gets better! Next, I manipulated Irene and Wammaker and

Lum and everybody else . . . *to sabotage my own factory!"*

The words formed a lovely confession, ruined by Kaolin's dripping sarcasm. "Can't you see how foolish it all sounds? What motive could I have?"

I nodded in complete agreement.

"Yes. Motive is key."

ditKaolin stared at me, then went on, "True, I didn't just sit there when Yosil and Beta turned on me, stealing from both UK *and* the government." He nodded to Clara. "I won a few rounds. Still, I'm the victim!"

"It's hard to tell. All the maneuvers—"

"—disguises and double-crosses," Clara added, "even the belligerents needed a multidimensional diagram."

"So? The Maharals were geniuses! Father and daughter, in all their manifestations. And crazy! What could I do but act in self-defense?"

I answered silently, *You might have gone public. Called on the cleansing immune systems of an open society. That is, if you had no craziness of your own to hide.*

Clara bore in. "So you admit you waged clandestine war against your former allies."

"I'd be a fool to deny it after you arrested my ditto right there in Yosil's lab, wearing a Beta disguise!" Kaolin smiled then. "I was getting pretty good, actually. I sure had *you* fooled, both in dittotown and in the scooter, didn't I, Albert?"

Don't call me Albert, I almost said. But what's the point?

Then the mogul's expression darkened. "I never expected you to follow, grabbing the Harley when I took off . . . and it's a good thing. You thwarted a catastrophe—the whole city's in your debt.

"As for those damned germ missiles, I swear, I never had any idea Yosil planned to take things so far."

■   ■   ■

Third window on the second floor—it's just the right position for a waiting-meeting room.

Carefully check for motion detectors and pressure-sensitive coatings. Okay, now press the paw with its clever gel-lens into one corner and—

Ha! Our best guess was right.

Within—a comfy salon. Plush chairs. Plenty to drink. Just the place for Kaolin to stash folks at an awkward moment. Like when Clara and

Gumby drove up, hours earlier than expected, interrupting a secret meeting!

A convention of scoundrels.

■ ■ ■

That was crucial, as far as both the public and the law were concerned. Could Kaolin be pinned with crimes against real people?

Clear evidence blamed Yosil Maharal, driven by visions of transcendence, for trying to blow up Albert Morris in his home, then stealing war germs to aim at millions. Plenty of onus remained left over, to heap on the small group of Dodecs who chose to hide those bioweapons, instead of destroying them by treaty.

But what could Aeneas be accused of? Shooting at realRitu and realAlbert on a desert highway? The act was criminal—endangering organic citizens. But anyone would say Ritu and Al were just asking for trouble by traveling disguised as grays. Besides, they survived that attack. At most, Kaolin would pay triple golem-geld.

Likewise if it were proved that he participated in Beta's old ditnapping empire—lawyers and accountants might stay busy for years, but that's what they're for.

Oh, the tally could add up, starting with a new car for Albert. Repairs to the Teller Building and Pal's dittotown apartment. A free supply of high-sensitivity ivories for the maestra of Studio Neo. Settlements for Lum and Gadarene. So? Kaolin could buy his way out of all that with pocket change.

He knew that I thought him responsible. *Prove it,* he'd be thinking. *Offer a motive anyone would believe.*

What about the filmstrip Palloid and I found at the Rainbow Lounge? Why did Kaolin, disguised as spiral-Beta, want *me* to transmit it? To undermine my reputation as an honest investigator? Or to muddy the waters? Clara tried explaining once, but the interconvoluted logic fell right out of my floppy brain.

It's what I deserve for getting mixed up in a war among prodigies. All my "victories" were gained through sheer doggedness. That plus—

Across the meadow, I saw realAlbert pluck up something from the path to show Pal. A pebble maybe, or another miracle—

—plus some help I'll never understand.

No, the key to all of this wouldn't be found among the murky twists and turns. In an era when everyone has means, opportunity, and too-easy alibis, just one thing stays elemental.

Motive.

■　■　■

How strange to see through a clever eye in my paw. No stranger than having paws, I guess. Or a brain too small for speech.

Grabbing another stolen glimpse through this "opaque" window, I feel like a stealthy, leering predator. Inside, sitting or pacing the room nervously, I see a covey of conspirators.

Three are easy to recognize. The perversion queen, Gineen Wammaker. And James Gadarene, who preaches that folks should go back to living one life at a time. Those two are easy because they're real. And Farshid Lum, the fanatic "mancie" who claims that mayfly creatures like me should get the vote. His duplicate wears an honest copy of his own face.

Three others came today as nondescript dittos, but we already know their names—movers and shakers who want to help control the coming changes in dittotech.

Which of them is worth watching before I move on?

Easy! The maestra crosses her long legs, seductively vamping the puritan, Gadarene, who stomps away. But seconds later he can't help looking back again!

Blushing in shame, he's under her spell, poor Jimmy-boy.

Oh, she's the maestra all right. In every provocative remark and saucy move, queen of the city's seamy side, tantalizing with subtly implicit sadomasochistic thrills that her fans prize.

And me, drooling at the window? I'm relishing it, too!

■　■　■

"Those virus warheads changed everything around here," Kaolin said.

"No kidding," Clara replied. "Six current and retired Dodecs in prison. The whole defense establishment—"

"No, around *here*." The platinum ditto motioned toward the house, with an upward emphasis.

"Oh, you mean upstairs. Your real . . ."

"My lifestyle has been ridiculed by carping fools for over a decade. But since that close call with the germ rockets, thousands have sought my advice. I'm thinking of starting a new line of business."

"Helping people to cut themselves off from the world?" Clara asked.

"You could put it that way. No offense, Major, but your mission to restore public confidence is doomed. Our near escape from Yosil's mad effort to *liberate souls* revealed a key truth."

"What truth?"

"Humanity's vaunted technology now threatens us with annihilation."

"It always has. So?"

"We've been shaken from our complacency. Organic flesh is vulnerable, as you should know better than most!" Kaolin jabbed a finger at me. Where an organic might have flushed, his ditto cast an angry glow, revealing a fine pattern of speckles that I quickly recognized.

He's been replenished. Often.

The flush also highlighted a scar where ditKaolin's shoulder met his neck. Repair spackle, dyed to match his skin. *Dang,* I thought, remembering when that injury was made. Two weeks ago. Over a dozen lifetimes.

▪ ▪ ▪

I can't stop watching Wammaker through this tiny eye in my paw!

Odd. Albert always found her voodoo charm repulsive. But my tastes seem shifted by . . . this body Pal provided! Among all the high-energy built-ins, he must have slipped something kinky as a practical joke. Thanks loads, Pal.

Well, I know a remedy. Think of it as having something in common with Gadarene!

Okay, I'm cured. Mental note to self: Don't let anyone talk you into wearing the body of a weasel, ever again.

▪ ▪ ▪

Our host regained his composure, and sighed. "Sometimes I wish Yosil and Bevvisov never showed up at my studio, offering to give souls to my animated dolls."

"You're kidding." Clara glanced at our surroundings, paid for by the industry spawned that day.

"Am I? Since helping usher in a Golem Age, I've seen how new things get misused when they're shared with the masses. From printing to cybernetics to bioengineering, every new medium becomes a conduit for pornography and callousness toward the human form."

Didn't he say the same thing, last time I was here? Another of

Kaolin's characteristic memory lapses. "Each of those tech-revolutions also unleashed unparalleled criticism and creativity," Clara answered.

"Along with social upheaval, alienation—"

"And empathy. New ways to know different, races, genders, species—"

"Ditexperience junkies and rox-potatoes—"

"Inventors of new sports, new art forms and explorations." She laughed. "Every step in human progress challenges us, Vic. Some wallow in excess. Others fearfully reject change. And a surprising number combine the new with verve and common sense, rising beyond all expectations."

"Progress? Is that what you'd call events in Yosil's secret lab?"

I joined in. "You said the key word: 'secret.' Maharal tried to shortcut the way science uses criticism to avoid error, with near-catastrophic results. But the actual problems he was working on—long-range dittoing, non-homologous imprinting . . ."

"Mythologies! My friend was obsessed, guilt-ridden, demented from trying experimental processes on himself."

"Some top minds in soulistics think he was onto—"

"Ravings!"

"Well, *something* blasted those ditto 'mirrors' and left realAlbert in this state. Beta and Ritu believed in their father, enough to join forces at the end—"

"All right." ditKaolin waved a hand. "Assume it's true! Yosil discovered a vast plane of hyper-reality, running parallel to all we know. A *soulscape*. Then it means we're in trouble worse than all the bombs and bugs and eco-calamities of a generation ago. Because now our fate won't be in the hands of elites *or* the benighted masses.

"It will be decided by an angry God."

■   ■   ■

Being real, Wammaker and Gadarene arrived here in a black limo, believing no one could see inside. Another conspirator came disguised as a red-striped security guard. Two were shipped in canisters and thawed. All for a risky/urgent meeting with one goal, to get their stories straight!

Only then Clara and Gumby/Albert appeared, interrupting and dragging their host away. It's got them nervous. The awkward allies fidget, mostly avoiding each other.

What mix of bribery, blackmail, idealism, and self-interest binds them? Even a brief try to theorize hurts the brain inside this little skull.

Enough. Away!

Attaching a tiny transducer to the window, I go back to climbing the sun-drenched wall. Slither a bit. Dig in diamond claws. Hunker while my pixelated back resembles stone. Check the way ahead for traps and sensors.

Then slither up some more.

■　■　■

Across the meadow I glimpsed Pal and realAlbert unfolding a gold and red kite, laughing as the wind filled its gull wings. It leaped, a symbol of soaring innocence. Innocent in fact, since it carried no weapons or instruments. Nothing that a vigilant securityman could worry about. Just a kite. Alluring.

It even caught the eye of ditKaolin, who smiled slightly, then shook his head with an expression of poignant regret. "I should be the one flying kites. In fact, I'm planning to retire soon."

"You surprise me, sir," Clara said.

"Why? Don't I deserve a rest? Anyway, I've long felt uncomfortable with this world I helped create, where people blithely talk of 'copying souls.' Only now it's grown far worse than mere effrontery of jargon. Before, only a few kooks blathered about soul-amplification. Now, inspired by Yosil, enthusiasts and mystics and techno-hobbyists have all started experimenting on their own, by the thousands, millions, chattering about using science to become gods."

Clara mused. "Mormons have always believed that people have the potential to—" But she stopped when I shook my head. Our little spy-golem should be getting into position about now. We had spent enough time on chitchat.

"Vic Kaolin, please. We know your plans to retire have nothing to do with respect for religion. May I suggest another reason?"

The platinum golem blinked. "Go on."

"It's the world's oldest story. The same obsession drove the ruler of that ancient terracotta army you admire. You shared it with Yosil Maharal, differing only in details.

"You don't want to die, Vic Kaolin.

"You want to live forever."

■ ■ ■

From the laboratory-hospital in the basement all the way to a rooftop sanctuary that no living outsider has seen in years, the mansion is a nested puzzle. If money and power could defend secrets against a modern age, this is the place.

My climb reaches a slate attic where I must angle a bit and change my skin reflectance. Stopping by a dormer window, I peer in at rows of cooler units built for holding ditto blanks. Most now stand empty, their ready lights turned off. Only a dozen look active, with contents ready to bake and release.

Yup, I thought, turning to resume my climb. Damn that distraction, wasting time by staring at the maestra! I'm running late.

■ ■ ■

"Who does want to die?" asked the platinum copy of Aeneas Kaolin. "We all fight to live, at all costs."

"Not all costs."

"Okay. But what's your point? That I seal myself away as an organic hermit, interacting with the world by telepresence and ditto? Are you comparing a fastidious lifestyle—which hurts no one—to Yosil's willing-ness to sacrifice millions for some mystical transcendence?"

I shook my head. "No comparison. You're more pragmatic and subtle. Though your plans suffered recent setbacks, they aren't dashed. If your former allies proved erratic, you'll replace them with others, less brilliant but more easily controlled."

His expression was blank as a robot's. "Go on."

"Take that gray Albert who carried the bomb to Universal. He thought he was looking for hidden technologies. And there were! A whole series of breakthroughs from Project Zoroaster. First, golem-replenishment—"

"Which had worrying side effects, so I held back from announcing it. There's nothing sinister. In fact—"

"In fact, you use the process yourself."

"It's obvious? Well, maybe I'm just trying to get the most out of these expensive shiny dolls." ditKaolin chuckled dryly. "Aren't most rich hermits penny-pinchers?"

"You've been reboosting this one for weeks."

"It shows?" Kaolin feigned a vain look in a nearby mirror. "All right, my aim is to *test* the process." He raised a jittering hand. "No doubt you've noticed the shaking."

What I *noticed*—with growing respect—was his multilayered cover story. Peel one level back, and he slid easily to another.

"And memory lapses?"

"Another unpleasant side effect you should watch for, Morris. Call it one last sacrifice for my customers."

"Admirable. And the explanation might stand, if replenishment were the only new technology. But there's dit-to-dit imprinting—"

"You're the pioneer in that area, Albert."

"Am I? Your technicians hope to learn from my peculiar Standing Wave. But the machinery for high-fidelity transfer seems far advanced. Farshid Lum thinks we're entering an era when long-lived dittos will pass their memories on to fresh blanks without needing a rig, creating their own sense of personhood—"

"And millions, maybe a majority, will resist that weird future!" dit-Kaolin shook his head sadly. "We'll see a return to the social upheavals a generation ago."

"No doubt. Then, to make things worse, there's *remote dittoing*. Specialists like Gineen Wammaker see a golden chance to expand markets. Top experts in any field may dominate their professions worldwide, not just in the city where they live. Will that throw the rest of us on the purple wage?"

Clara sat on the edge of her chair, clearly wanting to poke holes in this argument, but she suppressed the impulse. *Good girl.*

ditKaolin raised his shoulders.

"All right, Morris. I admit it. I saw these trends, over a year ago, and didn't like where they're taking us. So I dragged my feet in bringing them to market."

"Frustrating the chief innovator—"

"—and thus maybe pushing toward mystical pursuits. Dammit. I should never have launched Project Zoroaster in the first place."

His sigh was so dolorous and reflective . . . I hated to spoil such an artful pose.

"You express ambivalence, Vic Kaolin. Yet the R&D workers at Universal got every support, almost to the very moment the technologies were ready. It was only then that you pulled back. And, coincidentally, someone hired an unsuspecting Albert gray to investigate rumors of squelched—"

"I see where you're taking this," he answered with a frown. "Beta and Wammaker and Irene all had reasons to *want* the new techniques. So did Lum's Emancipation zealots. None of them had a motive to wreck the Research Division, any more than I did."

"Less reason than you, sir."

The frown deepened.

"You imply that I acted on my fears about the coming new age. That I arranged for the bombing as an act of *conscience*, to safeguard society from destabilizing and possibly immoral technologies?" ditKaolin paused, looking down. "Have you any idea how much I'd sacrifice? The friendships, wealth, position, and power?"

Clara nodded. "Yes. Though even your enemies would credit you with the valor of strong convictions . . .

". . . if any of that were true."

■ ■ ■

Here comes the tricky part. A rat's nest of fibers entangles the roof, surrounding the reflective dome.

I must extend my claws, far longer than any natural beast, using them as stilts to step carefully over the detector filaments. My belly brushes them, gently as a local breeze.

The same breeze lofting Albert's kite, a gorgeous eye-lure, high above the meadow. . . .

Pay attention now! With my body arched high, the pixelated skin on my back can't pull off the invisibility trick. Not in all directions at once.

I'm running late. But hurry is out of the question. Mustn't overheat.

Pal couldn't do this. It's not a matter of brains (not many in this skull), or guts (Pal has more than anyone), or even soul. Patience is what I bring from Albert.

Steady now . . . then quickly, to the silvery dome!

■ ■ ■

Across a hilly field, Pal and realAlbert maneuvered their gold and red kite, playing the exquisite toy against rolling white clouds. A pretty distraction.

My real concern? The little spy-golem we sent climbing the mansion wall was late checking in! This could all turn into a big bluff.

■ ■ ■

"Why are there so few of you?" I asked our host. "There used to be dozens of these platinums running around. But now, UK employees see you mostly by telepresence, if at all. What happened to hands-on management?"

ditKaolin's tremor permeated to his voice, stammering angrily. "Enough! I've been forbearing with you t-two . . . but this impudent g-grilling has gone too—"

He sputtered to a halt as beams of light shot up from a nearby table. Rays swirled, resolving into the figure of an elegant gray-haired man in his hale seventies, wearing a loose white robe. The face, pinkish-brown, matched the platinum's, but details of crease and wattle were more finely etched. Perfectly imperfect, down to the pores.

"I owe you an apology, Major Gonzales and ditto Morris, for assigning this golem as your host. It's old and so often replenished, the poor thing isn't thinking clearly."

The shiny ditto started to protest—then shut its mouth and sagged. For all intents and purposes, it was no longer there.

"Of course I see where you're going with this line of questioning, detective. You've shown that I did have a motive to sabotage UK—my ethical and social concerns about new golemtechnology. Concerns borne out by recent events.

"Not that I'm admitting anything. But with a possible motive established, shareholders will act to safeguard their interests. My retirement won't be voluntary. You can see why I might have acted clandestinely—"

"Setting up others to take the blame!" Clara accused.

"Again without confessing, tell me who was harmed. The arch criminal Beta? He's a figment in the mind of a sick young lady. As for that strange person, Queen Irene, it's too bad what happened to her. But she chose her own path. One with no exit."

Moving closer to the holo image, I wondered—was it artificial? Among all the promises of the so-called Digital Age, one of the best-fulfilled was lifelike simulation in 3-D. High-level computers can fool you in a conversation, especially if a golem provides backup for the hard questions.

We had a plan to check on that.

I held up a finger, starting to enumerate. "First you devoted vast resources to Project Zoroaster, urging Yosil and his team forward. But when prototypes were built, you forbade mass production."

"I said, I changed my mind."

"After moving prototypes here, to your house! Then you tried to have the R&D Division destroyed—"

"I never admitted—"

"—snaring Wammaker, Gadarene, and Lum, to scatter blame on both those who favor and oppose the new methods!"

Kaolin's expression was cold. *"A clever plan. If it worked that way."*

"And it almost did! But for the Maharals. They surprised you, Vic. When you tried pushing Yosil aside, he stole truckloads of equipment and vanished. That could only happen with Beta's help, so you set out to destroy your ally . . . only to discover he was linked to Ritu, the assistant who knew your business inside out!

"The Maharals threw you into panic. You made hasty mistakes."

"Like underestimating you, Mr. Morris."

I waved that away. "Worse, events under Urraca Mesa drew unwelcome attention. The World Eye is alerted now. Your scientists are blabbing like songbirds. So there's no longer any hope of *suppressing* the new golemtechnologies. But you do have another option. Is it possible to *distract* everybody, enough to still have your way?"

"How would I manage that?"

"By provoking social war! Give Lum's emancipators enough new tricks to demand golem-citizenship. Help the maestra transmit 'hurt-me' succubus-ivories to every town. Neo-Luddites like Gadarene will denounce all this from pulpits, gaining scads of angry new followers. So long as they all keep their stories straight, everyone profits handsomely!"

"You make it sound so cynical."

"Hence the new role you've chosen!" Clara stood up. "Your days at the helm of Universal Kilns are over, but there's still time to affect style and spin. Cry out about pornography and God and declining morals. Convince half the public that your aims were pure, and they'll protect you from the other half! Your new businesses will thrive, and nobody will remember all the toys you stashed away in your basement."

The holo figure shook his head.

"I should never have replenished that green. But I was shorthanded and needed somebody to send over to Irene's." After a pause, Kaolin smiled. *"This is all very clever. But it assumes I had a reason—a goal— worth so much effort, cost, and risk. Why cause turmoil, just to monopolize a few new wrinkles in golemtech?"*

His questioning smile seemed confident. Without proof, all I could do was bluff. Where *was* our little spy-golem?

"You had plenty of reason," I said quite slowly. "Because those new wrinkles, put together just right, add up to a form of immortality. Something you want, Vic Kaolin. Because, in fact, you're actually—"

That very moment, my implant lit up.

Finally!

Letters began resolving in the focal plane of my left eye, forming a message from the tiny ferret-ditto we had sent scaling the mansion walls. The information I needed to complete my sentence.

"Because, Vic Kaolin, you are actually—"

—NOT DEAD.

■　■　■

Damn. I owe Pal fifty.

Well, Gumby owes it, in a bet over whether the head of UK was still alive.

It seemed obvious! What other reason could Kaolin have for all the schemes, tricks, and betrayals? He had *to be dead! Everything pointed. The hermit thing. Only being seen in ditto or holo form. And those shiny platinums getting scarcer every year . . .*

The memory problems made sense if his copies were stockpiled months or years ago. Each one must study briefings when it's thawed. Then each golem tries to last as long as possible to maintain the illusion. To keep away the coroner and probate. To prevent folks from crying "ghost!"

Why else would he pay a fortune to develop dit-replenishment and dit-to-dit, then keep them off the market? It all made sense.

Yet there he stands, inside the dome, glimpsed by the clever eye in my paw—a gaunt figure with mottled-pale skin that meets every spectral test my clever implant can apply, wearing a white robe while facing a holo display that shows Clara and Gumby . . . who look dumbfounded as I transmit the news.

NOT DEAD, *my message reads inside their glowing implants.*

■　■　■

From across the meadow float sounds of laughter, tinkling like bells, mocking how certain we were. Everyone but Pal, who made the bet, offering odds and saying—

"Naw. A trillionaire can afford to be more clever than just dead. There's got to be more to it than that."

■　■　■

"Because I'm actually not *dead?"*

The holo image of Kaolin raised an eyebrow. *"Did I hear you right, ditective? My motive in this grand scenario is that I'm still alive?"*

Internally, I tried to gird myself. A bluff is a bluff, after all. You must carry it through.

"That's right, Vic Kaolin. Because . . . because the dead-man scenario is too obvious! Someone would put it together and get a writ, demanding to see you in person."

"It's been tried."

"Yes, but people will persist, eventually finding cause to invade your privacy screen and demand proof of life." I shook my head. "No, the immortality we're talking about isn't yours. At least not now. Rather, it's—"

I paused, buying a few seconds by coughing behind my fist. The man in the holo tilted his head, prompting me.

"Yes? It's—"

"It's about business!" Clara blurted. "Because . . . you're a business-man. And an avowed elitist. You've watched your fellow zillionaires, many in their waning years, grow desperate for more time. Why not provide it and make a buck? With renewal and dit-to-dit, your peers can release their dying organic bodies, then continue in a daisy chain of dittos!"

Clara grinned, barely able to contain herself. "But that's only part of the plan. It has do be done in secret because—"

"Because the law says only organics are people!" I exclaimed. "To make it work, your customers have to become hermits, like you, allowing no one near enough to check flesh. And it could look awfully suspicious if more than a few turned recluse at the same time. That limits your market, except—"

Clara hurried in. "Except for the recent frenzy over those *plague missiles* that Maharal so nearly launched. All of a sudden, life seems perilous again. Any day, without warning, the air may be filled with nasty viruses. Justification enough for scores of wealthy old eccentrics to order shiny new reflective domes built atop their mansions, swearing to venture forth only in clay . . . blaming the dangerous world when, in fact, they're preparing for the pragmatists' version of life after death. Where you can actually take it with you."

The face in the holo display stared at Clara, then back at me.

"This is the most astonishing scenario I ever . . . What proof can you—"

I laughed.

"Why none at all. Yet. But the scheme counts on two fickle elements, money and secrecy. What about the heirs who stand to lose if Gramps never dies? Some will gladly pay for a *real* investigation and—"

Clara gasped, staring at nothing. "What is it?" I asked.

Her jaw hardened. She turned and glared at Aeneas Kaolin. "We had better not learn those missiles were your idea . . . sir. Cleverly arranged, in order to set up this very situation."

Her tone chilled my ersatz spine. And it rocked our host, who paled as he raised both hands.

"The . . . the missiles surprised me as much as anyone, I swear it! I— I'm just taking advantage . . . the mood of fear . . . to do a little business.

"Again, where's the harm?"

A great knot seemed to let go where my intestines would be, if I had them. Our new speculation, drawn impulsively from the ruined story we had been so sure of, was on target! In the end, it wasn't logic that pinned Kaolin—he could have called our bluff—but the raw power of Clara's personality.

"We'll see," she told the nervous hermit, keeping her momentum.

"I promise, you'll have every chance to prove your innocence."

73

Riding the Wheel
. . . or learning to steer . . .

The kite, fluttering and swooping against the sky, is beautiful. Isn't it? Like so much in the world. A big part of why you can't let go.

Yosil was right about the "anchor" effect. You'll never do all the ambitious things that he planned, or achieve his goals. Those vast new territories to conquer, to mold by will alone—you'll leave those for another generation, perhaps a wiser one.

■   ■   ■

Still, you understand something that he didn't.

Nature is necessary.

Without a gritty, paradox-free level of reality, bound by implacable physical laws, rich complexity could never emerge. Only fierce selection on an enormous scale could produce human beings—so competent at tooth-and-claw, yet rising to dream far beyond, to qualities like art, love, and soul.

But evolution clings! Your body yearns for the tingle of fair wind, the sting of rain, the luscious scent and taste of food, the fight-flight rush of adrenaline.

The rub-slap-tickle of a happy lover.

The music of laughter.

■   ■   ■

You who make the world by observing it—causing the probability amplitudes of stars to collapse and whole galaxies to reify, just by looking at them—you remain wedded to cause-effect because it offers hope! Hope that evolution will play fair. (Though it hasn't yet.) Hope that you may win, no matter how unlikely it seems. (Because you are descended from generations of winners!)

Hope to stay alive, though death always waits.

You know it better than others. For you've seen the barren soulscape, where just a few billion algae-colonists struggle at the shoreline, clinging till the very last moment. Then, leaping for a moment's glory like salmon plunging upstream, they try to achieve some goal beyond reckoning—something religions hint at, the way sketches on a cave wall once flickered by torchlight, almost coming alive.

Yes, every flicker that launched itself has failed, so far. But falling back, they left impressions. There, in dust.

And impressions last.

■   ■   ■

So, what will you do? Cut loose and try for higher ground? Without the stored energy that Yosil tried to gather, your chances will be slim. His calculations were good, even if his soul was warped.

Stay here, then? Half in one world and half elsewhere? Share a bed with Clara and the far-more-human version of your former self . . . the Albert variant who changes bodies, living from day to day?

It could work. But is it fair?

■   ■   ■

Or will you try something else? Something creative. Something never seen . . . at least in this cosmos.

The odds seem low. But then, it's all in the trying, right?

For creatures rising out of flesh or mud, that's all there's ever been.

74

Impressionism

. . . or learning the finer art . . .

Departing the veranda of Aeneas Kaolin's stone mansion, Clara and I wandered down the back steps, through a rose garden and past an elaborate dovecote, all the way to the grassy verge where Pal and realAlbert flew their kite.

As expected, they had drawn attention—not from the security staff, but people living in an enclave of small houses that lay tucked behind the hill, built for servants and their families. A crowd of children stared, or ran shouting excitedly.

Even today, there's something about a well-handled kite.

Pal was clearly having a ball, controlling it from his medchair. Though golems give him access to the world, I never saw any of them provide such simple joy. Causing the wing panels to warp just right, he sent it swooping, climbing, then diving in mock attacks that drew delighted shrieks from kids and their parents.

All except one pair of adults who seemed less happy. They kept chivvying at three boys, trying to herd them back toward the small faux neighborhood. I sensed a glaring meanness there. But for now, the kids were having none of it, screaming and running like the others.

Turning to the platinum ditKaolin, who still accompanied us after his original signed off, I asked, "Are those the heirs?"

Grim-faced, the ditto nodded. "Nephews. Sons of a half sister who died three years ago."

This truth had been part of the price Clara and I demanded.

"Do they know?"

ditKaolin shook his head. "Their mother left me . . . left Aeneas . . . with full legal authority. You cannot interfere."

Clara sighed. "Well, for now just remember that we know. We'll be watching."

"Of that I'm sure."

The golem's voice lacked any hint of resentment or resignation. I might have felt better if it had.

■　　■　　■

It took a while to collect Pal and realAlbert and the little spy-ferret, leaving the kite behind in the hands of some kids.

I thought about our "victory" during the limo ride back. Despite having cornered the great Kaolin and extracted the truth, I didn't feel especially elated. Maybe long ago, before the Big Deregulation, we might have nailed him for all sorts of criminal offenses—from fraud to black-mail to extortion. But those were all civil torts now and most of his victims were happily bought off.

The most we could do was make him pay some more. And put crimps in the worst parts of his plan.

For one thing, the scattered team from Project Zoroaster would be recombined, along with outside critics, under the auspices of a neutral foundation. The aim: to release those new technologies in the *least* un-settling sequence, not the most disruptive. Though in truth, much of Kaolin's social war seemed unavoidable. We were due for interesting times.

Another foundation, bankrolled by a generous Kaolin Grant, would look into the more "mystical" interests of Yosil Maharal. Not timidly, but with due attention to the raw feelings of millions, who still believe some lines aren't meant to cross. As if there would be any way—over the long run—to keep folks from crossing.

Poor Ritu would be cared for, and quite wealthy when she stepped out. Doctors even spoke of teaching her to collaborate with a "rehabilitated" Beta personality. An exceptionally interesting person might emerge . . . and the world would be well advised to keep a wary eye open.

As for Kaolin's new customers, he was welcome to try selling pack-age tours of tomorrow for those who had everything except time. But since the new dittoing techniques won't be secret anymore, everybody will have a fair idea what's going on. So then, let heirs and lawyers and advocacy groups and ad hoc juries all thrash it out. Maybe elites will throw their influence behind the emancipators and to get ditimmortality declared legal. Perhaps not.

So long as the whole thing happens in the open, it's really none of a ditective's concern. Is it?

■   ■   ■

Pal bid us drop him off at the Ephemerals Temple. He had a date with the volunteer healer there—Alexie—who repaired me twice when I was green. His old flame who, Pal freely admitted, he "didn't deserve."

Perhaps. But who could refuse Pal's company for very long? Half of him was more alive than most men I've known. Certainly more fun.

The little ferret-golem agreed. After reporting what he'd seen climbing the walls at Kaolin Manor, that small version of me figured he might as well find whatever excitement the world offered during life's second half—the next dozen hours. So he hopped onto Pal's shoulder and together they wheeled up the ramp, giving me that familiar old sensation of déjà vu.

Turning back to the car, Clara and I had a surprise. realAlbert sat inside, smiling as he waited. And we could see him clearly! Even though *we* stood on the pavement outside.

In fact, *all* of the limo walls and panels were completely transparent, not just one narrow, jittery dot per occupant. "Goodness," Clara murmured. "That means he's looking *everywhere,* in all directions at the same—"

"Yes, I know."

When you get right down to it, this was no surprise at all.

Taking her hand, I glanced back at Pal and the smallest Albert, entering the temple together under the rosette window, past all the injured, broken, and spurned roxes who gather there each day for comfort and hope, passing into a place that welcomed all souls.

■ ■ ■

"Where to now?" queried the limo's automatic driver.

I looked to my owner, the woman I loved.

She, in turn, glanced over at realAlbert. His attention might be everywhere at once—omni-awareness—but his smile seemed present right here with us.

"Home," he said, in a voice clear and commanding. "Time for everybody to go home."

■ ■ ■

For now, home meant Clara's houseboat, just a kilometer downstream from Odeon Square . . . though it felt like years since I schlepped that distance underwater, thinking that I'd be in heaven if only I could unmask the infamous ditnapper, Beta.

Ah well. Heaven is a state of mind. I knew that now.

One favor that Yosil Maharal had done for us was forcing Clara and me to finally live together. Sure, I missed my house and garden, but we were both surprised at each other's willingness to compromise in all the details of sharing a roof. Even one so cramped. Even with there being two of me.

It was an odd menage, even by modern standards. I mean, with hyperquality blanks and top equipment, I might last quite a while. So could realAlbert. Two halves of a complete husband for Clara. Able to father children. Able to help raise them. But in separate units.

"Kind of handy," she said, putting a positive spin on things. But I could see worry. There were careers to balance, her new duties with the Dodecahedron, several kinds of biological and ceramic clocks, and two half-men to love . . . with no room aboard the houseboat for all the grays and ebonies and such we were going to need.

Time to get a house. At least now we could afford one.

realAlbert was in the tiny forward cabin puttering with the imprinting equipment. I quashed an impulse to go stop him. Though childlike in his state of perpetual distraction, he was no simpleton. In fact, quite the opposite.

"Dinner is cooking," the houseboat computer announced to Clara. *"I have also prioritized four hundred and seventy-two messages for you and five hundred twenty for Mr. Morris. And the University called to inform you that you received incompletes on all of last semester's courses."*

Clara cursed colorfully. The life of a student and part-time warrior was one more thing due to change. Welcome to the life of a full-time professional, dear. C'est la vie.

Then humming sounds drew our attention toward the bow—equipment warming up. Clara glanced at me as if to say, *Make sure he doesn't hurt himself.*

I hurried forward on time to hear realAlbert mutter happily to himself. Something about how *"we're all bosons in this dust,"* or something like it. Arriving at the cabin, I saw him lie down on the platten with his head—our head—between the tetragramatron tendrils, waving gently on all sides. I noticed that the transfer switch was pulled to UNLOAD.

After staring for several seconds, I asked, "Are you sure?"

The last time we tried this, there had been a busy signal. The organic brain was full, or fully occupied, with something immensely large. No more room inside. No room for me at all.

For the first time since Urraca Mesa—or since our soul-paths separated the Tuesday before—I felt complete attention from those eyes, durable organic eyes, built to last for thirty thousand days, or more.

"She's all yours, Pinocchio," I heard my own voice say, and it had something else—a tone that said farewell.

There would be room, now, I realized. A clean slate. A home to reimprint with all that I was and all I had become. Everything necessary for this wayward puppet to be a real boy.

And boy, won't Clara be surprised.

Lying down on the other table, the one with a recycling bucket underneath, I took a moment to wish myself a nice trip.

Then I put my clay head down to begin life once again.

75

Soul Comfort

. . . or doing what folks always do . . .

**Are you frustrated with the typical
"dating service"?**

Find Your SoulMate!

Utilizing the very latest discoveries, we can take you
to the famous *"spiritual shoreline"*
that you've heard so much about this year

Observe the wonders of the Maharal Soulscape!
Gaze down at your friends and neighbors
bared to their inner essence!

Then use our patented SoulMate technology
to find that special
compatible someone
The one Standing Wave that's most harmonious
to your own private song

The one meant for you!

Yesterday's unsolvable mysteries—
resolved today at reasonable prices

Don't delay

Acknowledgments

Kiln People is one of the more challenging works I've taken on, expressing different points of view and time through seldom-used authorial tools like second-person, future tense. But that's just part of the tradition in a genre that thrives on the unusual and loves to take on clichés.

I'd like to thank those who provided assistance, especially with critical readings of early drafts, and with insights on the historical, literary, and philosophical implications of golems.

Special appreciation goes to Cheryl Brigham, Beth Meacham, Stefan Jones, Vernor Vinge, Tappan King, Wil McCarthy, Ralph Vicinanza, John Douglas, Lou Aronica, Mason Rourman, Steve Sloan, Mark Grygier, Steve Jackson, Joe Miller, Vince Gerardis, Beverly Price, Stephen Potts, Hodge Cabtree, Robin Hanson, Steven Koerber, Alberto Monteiro, Steinn Sigurdsonn, William Calvin, Trevor Sands, James Moore, Nick Arnett, Ruben Krasnopolsky, Robert Qualkinbush, Jim Kruggel, Tamara Boyd, Manoj Kasichainula, Pat Mannion, Amy Sterling Casil, Daniel Jensen, Rachel Heslin, Alex Spehr, Lisa Gay, Bret Marquis, Brian Sidlauskas, Stella Bloom, Rae Paarlberg, Joshua Knorr, Dr. Globiana, Daniel Rego and Matt Crawford, along with members of the CalTech and University of Chicago Science Fiction Clubs.